The Fugitive Prince

Lee Duigon

STOREHOUSE PRESS

VALLECITO, CALIFORNIA

Published by Storehouse Press
P.O. Box 158, Vallecito, CA 95251

Storehouse Press is the registered trademark of Chalcedon, Inc.

Copyright © 2013 by Lee Duigon

This book is a work of fiction. Names, characters, businesses, organizations, places, events, and incidents either are the product of the author's imagination or used fictitiously. Any resemblance to actual persons, living or dead, events, or locales is entirely coincidental.

All rights reserved, including the right of reproduction in whole or in part in any form.

Book design by Kirk DouPonce (www.DogEaredDesign.com)

Printed in the United States of America

First Edition

Library of Congress Catalog Card Number: 2013934850

ISBN-13: 978-1-891375-61-3

ISBN-10: 1-891375-61-X

CHAPTER 1

Ellayne Has a Visitor

If you have read the books that come before this, you have already met Ellayne. But on this particular summer night, you might not have recognized her.

More than a year had gone by since she and Jack had come home from their adventures. Her hair had grown long again, and she wore it with a thick braid down the back: no need, anymore, to disguise herself as a boy. Instead of her brothers' hand-me-downs, she had on a nice blue dress and new shoes. By the light of a lantern, she was softly reading aloud from an enormous book that lay on the grass before her.

"'And then Abombalbap, thinking he might yet save the damsel, leaped lightly from his horse and drew his sword. But the dwarf in the cart cried out as if he were a madman and immediately came galloping forth from the Castle Odious the Black Knight of the Dark Tower—' Wytt, you're not listening!" she said.

This she addressed to a little hairy manlike creature no bigger than a squirrel, with no tail and reddish-brown fur over every inch of him. Instead of paying any heed to the story, he kept jumping up and down, trying to catch fairy-flies that were attracted to the light. You or I would call them lacewings, but people in Obann called them fairy-flies because with their silvery wings and delicate way of flying, they looked like fairies. Wytt liked to eat them.

Ellayne's father, Roshay Bault—once the chief councilor of the town of Ninneburky, but since then created baron of the realm by His Grace the King—lived in the finest house in Ninneburky. He had a stable for his carriage and horses. Between the back of the stable and a dense, high hedge that ran around three sides of his property was a quiet grassy space where Ellayne and Jack liked to sit and talk. Ellayne came there often to play with Wytt. Her mother the baroness didn't like the sight of him; somehow he made her think of a large rat. But her father understood that the little Omah had more than once saved his daughter's life, and was glad to have him there. Wytt preferred not to be seen by too many Big People at once and seldom came into the house.

"We can't treat her like she was made of fine china, Vannett, not after where she's been. Let her play with the creature whenever she likes," the baron would say to his wife. And Ellayne's mother, who was much better about things like that than she used to be, would say, "Well, of course you're right."

You know already, if you have read the books, that it was Ellayne and Jack who climbed Bell Mountain and rang the bell—the bell that King Ozias hung there thousands of years ago, so that God would hear it when the time came for it to be rung. This was a great and noble feat; but the baron and the baroness agreed that the children ought to stay home from now on and not live like famous persons.

So they lived a quiet life, Jack having moved in to live as a member of the family. He was probably playing chess right now with the baron in the parlor, Ellayne thought.

(Obannese chess is just like ours, only the bishops are called presters and are allowed to make a special move to a different-colored square than the one they started on.) Ellayne's mother taught them their numbers and their letters, and every evening the baron read to them from the New Books. "Someday," he said, "we'll have the Scriptures themselves, the Old Books, in language we can understand. The queen has promised it."

That was one of those things they were working on, far away in the great city of Obann—King Ryons, Queen Gurun, and Obst, who used to be a hermit and had led Jack and Ellayne most of the way up Bell Mountain until his strength failed. They were all terribly busy in Obann. Queen Gurun—who was not truly a queen, but everybody called her one—wrote letters to Ellayne to keep her up to date.

But on this particular summer night Ellayne had no work to do, nothing to worry about. You might think reading to an Omah would be a waste of time, but Ellayne didn't think so. Wytt had no proper language, as you or I know language; but he certainly understood every word Ellayne or Jack spoke to him, and they understood most of what he answered. Whether he understood anything at all about the adventures of Abombalbap is not a question we can answer.

"You might at least stop bothering the fairies," Ellayne said to him.

He showed his teeth at her, an Omah smile. He wore a lock of her hair in a kind of torque around his neck. For reasons neither she nor Jack could ever fathom, which Wytt had no idea how to explain, Omah set great store by Ellayne's hair. She'd met Omah in many different places, and it was always the same: "Sunshine hair," they called it.

Suddenly the grin vanished from Wytt's face, and in the blink of an eye, he vanished into the hedge. He took just time enough to chirp, "Someone coming," before he disappeared. Ellayne wondered who it could be. Once upon a time she would have been alarmed; but what could happen right here at her father's house?

She heard a twig snap—

And then out from behind the corner of the stable stepped the very last person she expected to see in all the world.

"King Ryons!" she cried.

The last time she'd seen the king was a year ago at his palace in Obann. But the first time she'd seen him was in Lintum Forest, as a refugee. That's what he looked like now: scrawny, dirty, dressed in rags, his dark hair all over the place. You'd have thought he was a runaway slave.

"Your Majesty! What's happened?" It must be something bad, she thought.

"Ellayne?" he said. "You are Ellayne, aren't you?"

"Well, of course I am. You know me!" she answered. "But what are you doing here? Why aren't you in Obann, in the palace?"

Somewhere inside the hedge, Wytt started chattering. The king flinched, startled; but he stood his ground.

"Heaven help him," Ellayne thought, "he looks terrible! What's the matter with him?" Why, for instance, hadn't he grown? Ryons himself didn't know how old he was, having been born into slavery and never taught anything but how to avoid a beating. He was younger than Ellayne, but not by much. They'd been about the same size last year, but now Ellayne was sure she was a little bigger.

But Obann City was a long way from Ninneburky, and anything might have happened—anything.

Wytt fussed something awful. "Not him! Not him!" he chattered.

"Oh, Wytt, please—pipe down!" Ellayne cried. "Go get Jack, bring him here now." His noise stopped, so he must have obeyed. She turned back to the poor bedraggled king. "Your Majesty, won't you come into the house and have something to eat? You'll be safe here with my father."

He shook his head violently and backed up a step. She was afraid he might run away. What was wrong with him? Had he gone mad?

"Ryons, please, there's nothing to be afraid of," she said. "Here—why don't you sit down? Jack will be here in a minute. You want to see Jack, don't you?"

"Yes. I want to see him." The boy looked all around, like a hunted animal, and then cautiously sat down. "But no one else!" he added.

CHAPTER 2

Fnaa

Jack was playing chess with the baron, and winning, too.

He was a black-haired, blue-eyed boy who used to wear shoes only in the winter and he'd had to tie a piece of rope around his waist to keep his pants up. Now, thanks to the baron and the baroness, he had proper shoes, proper pants with a belt, and could read and write, add and subtract, and play chess.

He was about to make a decisive move when Wytt sent up a racket, somewhere close to the open window in the parlor, safely hidden in the night.

"That's Wytt," Jack said. "Ellayne wants me in a hurry, but he doesn't say why."

"Then you'd better go see what it is," Roshay said. "We don't want the baroness disturbed by that noise. I'll be right here if you need me."

"But the game—"

"I resign. Go, Jack. Make him stop screeching."

"All right, Baron." Jack couldn't call him "father," and certainly couldn't call him "Roshay Bault." But if the truth be known, the baron was quite fond of his new title; so that was how Jack addressed him.

He rushed out the back door and saw the light of Ellayne's lantern between the stable and the hedge. Wytt called to him from the dark. "Someone here—come and see!"

"Who's here, Wytt?"

Wytt didn't understand human names. To him Jack was "Boy" and Ellayne was "Girl," and he made up names of his own for other Big People.

"No name," he answered Jack: which meant a stranger.

He found Ellayne sitting near the hedge with someone, a boy. When Jack got close enough to see his face, he had a shock.

"What in the world!" he cried. "King Ryons!"

"Shh! Don't make so much noise!" Ellayne snapped at him. "Sit down and be quiet. The king wants to talk to us."

Having been on as many adventures as he already had in his short life, Jack knew something was afoot. This was how they started.

He stared hard at Ryons. He might not have recognized him if he'd passed him on the street. This, he thought, was how someone looked when he'd had an adventure that was too much for him.

"Your Majesty, are you all right?" he asked.

"Are you Jack?"

"You ought to know me when you see me!"

And Ryons made a rather ghastly smile and answered, "But I've never seen you before."

Jack had heard stories about people who'd lost their memories. These were not especially accurate stories, but he didn't know that. Something must have happened to the king to make him lose his memory—fell off his horse and hit his head, got struck by lightning, or just woke up one day and didn't know who he was anymore.

"What are you doing here, Your Majesty?" Jack said. "How come you don't know us when you see us?"

"You think I'm King Ryons," said the boy. "Well, I'm not! My name is Fnaa."

Jack and Ellayne exchanged a look. Bad enough he'd lost his memory, Jack thought; now he thinks he's somebody else. But he said, "Fnaa? That's a funny name."

"Funnier than Jack?" was the reply.

"Your Majesty—"

"I'm not the king."

"But you are!" Jack cried. "Something's happened to you to make you forget."

But Wytt, who understood everything Jack and Ellayne said, chattered and chirped. He even came out where Fnaa could see him. The king shrank from him. "But he knows Wytt!" Jack thought. "He shouldn't be afraid of him."

"Not him! No name!" Wytt would have said, if he could utter human speech.

"He's saying that you're not King Ryons," Ellayne said.

"Do you believe him?"

"Wytt has eyes as good as ours," Jack said, "and he has a nose, too. Just like a dog. You can't fool his nose."

"But you look exactly like King Ryons!" Ellayne said. "Anyone would think so."

Fnaa gave her a bitter little smile. "That's what my mother says," he said. "And that's why I'm here. To save the king's life, and my own, too."

"You'd better come into the house and talk to my father," Ellayne said. "He'll know what to do."

Fnaa—if that was really his name—shook his head. "No, no!" he said. "I came all the way from Obann just to talk to you—to the two of you, and no one else."

"But the baron can protect you," Jack said.

"No, he can't. No one can."

"Well, then, what do you expect Jack and I can do?" Ellayne said. "If my father can't protect you, how can we? We're just a couple of kids."

"You are famous," answered Fnaa. "You went up the mountain and rang the bell. Everybody knows that. God Himself watches over you. That's what my mother says. She heard it from a lot of people. She sent me to you."

"But who are you?" Ellayne said.

"And where are we going to put you?" Jack wondered.

"I'm just a slave," Fnaa said, "and so is my mother. She used to have crazy dreams about a bell ringing, when none of the bells in the city were moving. But then she finally found out about the bell on the mountain, and that was what she heard in her dream. We're slaves in a great house in the city of Obann."

"But what do you want us to do?" Jack said.

Fnaa sat up a little straighter. "You're the king's friends. You have to take me to the king so he can see me with his own eyes," he said, "and you must tell him that everything I say is true, so that he'll believe me and be safe. No one's to know about it but you, until we see the king."

"Oh! Is that all?" Jack said. "We take you all the way back to Obann without anyone knowing where we are or what we're doing, and then take you to see King Ryons. Is that it?"

"Yes."

Wytt stepped up to Fnaa and touched his hand. The boy winced, but didn't snatch his hand away.

"This is good boy," Wytt chirped.

"He likes you," Ellayne said. "He knows about people, what they're like inside, so that's a point in your favor."

"But we oughtn't to go all the way to Obann, just us!" Jack said. "We ought to take Martis with us. He should come, too."

"Except he's not here!" Ellayne said.

Martis swore an oath to protect Ellayne and Jack for as long as he lived, for which the king had given him the honorable title of Knight Protector. But with the children safe at home in Ninneburky, Martis got involved in other things as well: and for that reason he was out of town just now, somewhere up in the mountains on some kind of secret business. "Just when we really need him," Ellayne muttered.

"Listen, Fnaa—you'll have to tell us more," Jack said.

"My mother told me I was to be very careful, even with you," Fnaa answered.

"But what does Ryons have to be saved from?" Ellayne asked.

"Me," said Fnaa.

CHAPTER 3

How They Set Out for Obann

The story Fnaa told them, Ellayne thought, was like something out of the tales of Abombalbap. What would her father think, if he could hear it? But Fnaa refused to see the baron.

"No one who knows the king must see me, no one but the two of you," he said.

"Don't tell me you came here all the way from Obann with no one seeing you," Jack said. "All kinds of people must have seen you, who've seen the king."

"Well, I got past them all right."

"How?" asked Ellayne.

"I'll show you." Fnaa moved a little closer to the lantern, put his hands over his face for just a moment, then took them away.

"Wha—?" Jack sputtered; and Ellayne said, "Oh, my!"

Fnaa now looked like the most pitiful half-witted simpleton ever to stumble into a doorpost, blank-faced, goggle-eyed, daunted by the task of remembering his own name. When he stood up, he wobbled and almost tripped over his own feet.

"Wan' my mumma," he babbled, and then began to snivel.

You wouldn't have known him. And while Jack and Ellayne stared at him, he stood up straight, relaxed his features, and suddenly went back to being just Fnaa.

"How do you do that?" Ellayne cried.

"My mother taught me. She didn't want me to be taken away from her and sold, so she taught me how to act like a simpleton so that no one would ever want to buy me.

"My mother is the daughter of a chief among the Fazzan people, away out East. Some Wallekki stole her and sold her, and then she was sold again to some people in Obann. I was born there. The people who own us think I'm a half-wit. That's what gave them the idea to murder King Ryons."

Ellayne's mother came out on the back porch and rang the dinner bell. That didn't mean a late supper; it was her way of summoning Ellayne to bed without having to go look for her.

"We have to go now," Ellayne said." If we stay out, my father will want to know why, and he'll come out to see."

"But where's he going to stay tonight?" Jack said.

They decided the stable would be best. There was an empty hayloft above the stalls. Wytt could stay down below and warn him when the groom came in the morning with the horses' food. There was no reason for the groom to go up to the loft.

"We'll sneak out some breakfast for you in the morning," Ellayne said.

"I don't eat much," said Fnaa. "Just don't tell anyone I'm here. You have to promise."

"We promise," Jack said, and wondered, "What are we getting into?"

Of course they couldn't sleep that night. Jack lay awake wondering what Ellayne was thinking, and she lay in bed wondering what he was thinking. At just about exactly the same time, each got up and went to see if the other was asleep. They bumped into each other in the hall and tiptoed to the drawing room, where no slumbering adults were likely to hear them. To be on the safe side, they whispered. There was enough moonlight coming in through the windows to keep them from knocking over any chairs on their way to the settee.

"Well?" Jack said. "Do you believe him?"

"Of course I do—who would ever make up a crazy story like the one he tells? Besides," Ellayne said, "things like this used to happen sometimes, in the olden days."

Abombalbap be hanged, Jack thought. But he said, "Oh, it all sounds like such rot! A bunch of rich men doing away with the king and putting Fnaa in his place so they can tell everybody, 'Poor King Ryons, his wits are gone—he can't be king anymore.' Really!"

"But it's a clever plan, if they can get away with it," said Ellayne. "No one would ever suspect the real king had been replaced. And with some poor half-wit on the throne, sooner or later people would get tired of it, and then the schemers could bring back the Oligarchy. No more kingdom."

"But Fnaa isn't a half-wit."

"They didn't know that. That's what was wrong with their plan," Ellayne said. "They must have been mighty surprised when Fnaa gave them the slip."

"I'll bet they're hunting for him all over the country," Jack said.

"Probably—but I don't think they'll find him. "They'll be looking for some poor booby who doesn't know where he's going."

Jack had thought their adventuring days were over. For the first time in his life he was living in a nice house and sleeping in a real bed. He had real shoes. He played chess, and his reading and writing were coming along just fine. If he wanted to, when he was old enough, he could take part in the family's lumber business along with Ellayne's two brothers—the baron said so. Someday he would have a house of his own. All of those things made adventures seem less attractive to him.

"We've got to do it," Ellayne said. "King Ryons is our friend, and it was God who made him a king. Those men who are plotting to get rid of him—well, they have to be stopped."

"And all we have to do is get Fnaa into the king's palace without anybody knowing. It sounds easy enough!" Jack said. "Only I don't see why you and I have to do it all alone. Not when your father could order up a company of militia and take us to Obann in style."

"Fnaa won't trust anyone but us. If my father gets involved, Fnaa will run away."

Jack didn't like it. He especially didn't like not being able to have Martis' help. As a former assassin in the First Prester's secret service, Martis knew all about this sort of business.

"We should wait until Martis gets back and have him take charge of this," he said. "We'll just have to convince Fnaa to go along with that."

"Only we don't know when Martis is coming back.

Nobody knows," Ellayne said. "We can't wait all summer for him."

Jack had to give in. After all, you couldn't let people plot against the king. And it was only a trip to Obann in the summertime. They'd done many harder and more dangerous things than that. Compared to some of those, this hardly counted as an adventure at all.

The next day they spent getting ready. Ellayne would need boy's clothes and a pair of scissors so that Jack could cut her hair. Roshay Bault would be looking for a girl and a boy, but they would travel as three boys.

They had to find shoes and decent clothes for Fnaa—those came out of brother Dib's closet—and a pack for matches, rations, and money. The hardest part was to keep Fnaa up in the loft all day, where it was hot and stuffy.

When she was alone, Ellayne wrote a note to her father.

Dear Father—Please don't be angry, but Jack and I have to do something very important and we're not allowed to tell you what it is, or where we're going. But if you show this note to Martis, he may be able to pick up our trail without our breaking our promise not to tell. This thing was not our idea, but we have to do it and we have to keep it a secret, even from you. But at least it's not dangerous, like when we went to Bell Mountain, so please tell Mama not to worry. We will be back as soon as we can. Love, Ellayne

P.S., Don't blame Jack, I had to talk him into it.

"There!" she said to herself. "He'll understand. Really, it's God's business we're going on, so we can't say no."

Jack made sure he packed his slingshot, and a big knife that was almost as good as a sword. His worst thought was that the baron and the baroness would think he was ungrateful and would never trust him anymore.

"You can't tell anybody," Fnaa said again, when they brought him Dib's shoes. "I don't know how many people are in the plot. I don't know all their names, or who they talk to, or where they all come from. My mother told me not to trust anyone except the two of you and the king himself."

Jack and Ellayne had agreed not to argue with him until after they were on the road. Later on, maybe, they could talk some sense into him.

"It'll be nice to see the king again," Ellayne said. "When we first met him, you know, he was as raggedy and dirty as you. I don't know how anyone could tell the two of you apart."

"Have you ever seen the king, Fnaa?" Jack asked.

"No, but my mother has. She's seen him riding down the street with his Heathen horsemen all around him. She says I look just like him."

They decided to leave in the middle of the night, when the household was asleep. Getting out of Ninneburky wasn't as easy as it used to be, because now there was a stockade around most of the town and pilings laid aside where they could be put up quickly in case of trouble. But some of the wall had been taken down in the spring, at the request of herders and carters, and there were several streets leading out of town that no one bothered to guard in peacetime.

With regrets, they decided not to take Ham, their donkey, who'd gone most of the way up Bell Mountain with them. Children leading a donkey would be more conspicuous than children without a donkey. But Wytt would go with them: they couldn't have kept him from coming, anyhow. Fnaa had made friends with him during his night in the loft.

"You'll see," said Jack, "he's good at sniffing out danger before it catches up to us. I can't tell you how many times he's saved us."

Still, Jack didn't like it. Here and now, with the crickets chirping and the katydids tattling in the trees, the stars strewn like dust across the sky, and the three of them setting out with packs and blankets on their backs and Wytt racing ahead, scouting, Jack still didn't like it. Something felt wrong, and he was sure they were headed straight for trouble.

What was the point of having a father and a mother, he wondered, if you don't trust them with things that really mattered—didn't even tell them, when such things came up? Jack's own father, a militia man, died in a battle right after Jack was born; and his mother died a few years ago. He knew Roshay and Vannett Bault weren't truly his father and mother. But they'd taken him into their house and treated him like a son, and it made him feel mean and lowdown to be sneaking out on them. Nor was he at all happy about marching off without a word to Martis, although that couldn't be helped.

The only thing that eased him was when Ellayne said, after they had just taken up their packs but were still in the stable, "We ought to pray before we start out on this journey."

"What? Go to the chamber house at this time of night and wake the prester?" Fnaa was incredulous.

"No, no—of course not," Ellayne said. "I mean a quiet little prayer, just the three of us."

"We never went to the Temple, my mother and me," Fnaa said. "The master and his family always went, but my mother says the Obann God doesn't care about slaves and our people's gods are too far away to do us any good." He paused, then added, "But we heard that King Ryons has men from Fazzan in his army and they now worship Obann's God."

"We'll explain it to you later," Jack said. "Say us a prayer, Ellayne."

She and Jack closed their eyes, as Obst the hermit had taught them, and Ellayne spoke softly, knowing God would hear her even if she didn't speak aloud at all: "God, please keep us safe on this trip to Obann, and let us get there in time to help King Ryons. You made him king, but wicked men are out to get him." And she and Jack both whispered, "So be it."

"That was a prayer?" Fnaa asked. "But you were just talking."

"That's all you have to do," Jack said. "A holy man taught us. All you have to do is talk to God, and He hears you."

"Sounds funny to me," Fnaa said. "Can we get started now?"

Following Wytt, who made less noise than a rat, the three children crept out of the town of Ninneburky in the middle of the night. Jack felt a little better for the prayer, but still misliked sneaking off like a housebreaker.

For the first time, but not the last, he wondered if Fnaa

was really who he said he was, wondered if Fnaa's outlandish story was really true, and wondered how soon it would be, and how unpleasant, for them to find out otherwise.

"Lord God," he prayed silently, as they passed out of the town and saw the Imperial River in the near distance with starlight shimmering on glossy water, "if this is a trick or a trap, please watch out for us!"

CHAPTER 4

How Martis Sought for Tidings

Martis went up Bell Mountain to assassinate Jack and Ellayne and almost perished on the summit. When he came down, his beard had turned white and he had sworn an oath to protect the children with his life. His beard was still white, his hair still brown, and he still bore the same faintly sad, pensive expression on his face. He did not look like a killer, but he was.

He had not forgotten his oath, but with the children safe in Roshay Bault's care, they didn't seem to be much in need of protection. Martis soon went back to doing some of the same kind of work he used to do in the service of the Temple. Not the murdering—not that, ever again, but there was plenty of work these days for a man who knew the Heathen countries on the other side of the mountains. Martis knew those lands and peoples about as well as any Westerner, and so made himself useful to the kingdom.

The vast army that the Thunder King sent against the city of Obann was utterly destroyed, and the Thunder King himself buried in an avalanche. But everyone in Obann who was wise knew that that did not mean peace, but only a breathing spell. There was a new Thunder King, and he would raise new armies, and there would be war again.

Martis' work was to help Obann make ready for that war. That was why, instead of being in Ninneburky when Jack and Ellayne needed him, he was many miles to the east, in the foothills of the mountains. On the night the children set out for Obann, Martis was sitting by a campfire in the forest, conversing with barbarians.

"Yes, it's true—the last of the Thunder King's mardars in our country have been killed. Their scalps flap in the wind over the camps of the Turtle and the Beetle clans. Not one escaped alive."

The speaker was an Abnak: shirtless, tattooed all over, with his head shaved clean but for a thick lock of black hair dangling from his scalp. The Abnaks lived on the eastern slopes of the mountains, and for hundreds of years used to come raiding into Obann. But now there were many of them in King Ryons' army, and the good news was that the whole nation had revolted against the Thunder King.

"The Thunder King will want revenge for that," said the third man at the campfire, a young Abnak named Hlah. His father was Chief Spider, who had been the first Heathen to proclaim Ryons as his king. Hlah now lived on the west slope of the mountains, with an Obannese wife named May. Like the rest of the Abnaks in King Ryons' service, he now worshipped the true God.

"I've heard the same sort of tidings from the Wallekki," Martis said. "It seems all the peoples between the Great Lakes and the mountains have risen up against the Thunder King—except for the Zephites in the north and some of the Griffs."

Many survivors of the Thunder King's lost army had found their way back across the mountains, bringing word of their total defeat under the walls of Obann. This, more than anything else, had shaken the Thunder King's rule over those countries.

"He'll only conquer them all again," said Hlah. "Those nations will never be free until they know the true God and put their trust in Him. Obann must send men to be God's messengers."

The older Abnak—his name was Shoosh—gave him a sidelong glance.

"I knew your father, old Chief Spider," said Shoosh. "It's hard to imagine him having anything to do with Obann's God. He was no dreamer!"

"And our God is no dream," said Hlah. Shoosh grunted, but made no answer. After a time, Martis asked, "Do you hear anything about another army coming west?"

Shoosh spat into the fire. Somewhere nearby, an owl hooted.

"No, they haven't gotten another army ready yet," he said. "All I've heard is that they're getting something ready—something big, the like of which we've never seen before. No one knows what it could be. Mardar magic, say the Attakotts—but what would they know? Something being brewed up in the Thunder King's New Temple in Kara Karram, the Wallekki traders say. Something worse than any army. You know as much about it as I do, Westman."

"Maybe," Martis said; but in truth, he knew nothing. Kara Karram was very far away, and no spy for King Ryons had ever gone there and returned. The Chief Spy in Obann, Gallgoid, would just have to keep sending them until one came back with information.

The peoples between the mountains and the lakes—Abnaks, Attakotts, Wallekki, Griffs, Fazzan—were demoralized. The Thunder King had taken away their gods, and then marched their warriors into Obann to destruction. When the Thunder King was ready to move West again, would they be able to oppose him? Martis knew they would try, but doubted they could successfully defend themselves.

"Obst taught us that the Scriptures say that someday all the nations of mankind will come to God," Hlah said. "I wonder if we'll live to see that time."

"You're dreaming, lad," said Shoosh. "We had a very fine god in our neighborhood: lived at the bottom of a pond and never gave us any trouble. If you wanted a favor from him, all you had to do was pour a little beer into the pond. But the mardars came and turned him into an old rotten log, fished him out, and carried him off to Kara Karram as a prisoner. We've had poor hunting ever since. But if the mardars come again, at least we have no more gods for them to take away from us.

"Mark my words," he said, looking Hlah straight in the eye, and then Martis. "One of these days he'll take away the God of Obann. And then where will you be?"

Hampered by the rules of Abnak etiquette, Hlah was slow to answer. But Martis said, "My friend, if your eyes had seen the things our eyes have seen, you would never speak such words. Surely your own ears heard the great bell when it rang from the top of Mount Yul; and surely your own eyes saw there was no more cloak of clouds upon the mountain."

Yul was the old name for Bell Mountain. For as long

as there had been mountains, the peak of Mount Yul was wrapped in clouds. But when Jack and Ellayne rang the bell that holy King Ozias erected there an age ago, then the eternal clouds around Mount Yul were torn away, never to return.

"I heard, and I have seen," Shoosh said.

"It was a sign from God," said Martis, "a sign for all the world to see. You'd be wise to trust in it."

"When the Thunder King returns," said Shoosh, "the Abnaks will need more than signs."

CHAPTER 5

How Their Journey Began

Following the road along the river, the three children hiked all night and on into the morning. It had been a long time since Jack and Ellayne had done any walking like that, and they were tired before the sun came up. But the new day revived them, and they kept on going.

"Will your father send men on horses after us?" Fnaa asked.

"He might," said Ellayne, meaning that he surely would. But he didn't know which way they'd gone, and he'd lose time questioning the groom, the cook, and the neighbors.

"Well, then, hadn't we ought to get off this road?"

"In a little bit. Then we'll find a place to rest and have a bite to eat, too."

Jack said nothing. He was hoping the baron would catch them before the day was done. Roshay Bault would be good and mad at them at first, but after they explained it all to him, he would understand. At least Jack hoped so.

They met no other travelers during the night. Just a year ago there were Heathen armies in this land. Some of the towns and villages had been destroyed, and it would be some time before all the farms were back in business. Indeed, there was a chance they might run afoul of Heathen stragglers. Not all of those had surrendered to the king as yet.

Birds sang the sun over the horizon. As the grey dawn crept away, wildflowers in all the colors of the rainbow refreshed the hikers' eyes.

"I wonder how far we've gotten," Jack said. "We might be half the way to Caristun. I think we'd better find a stopping-place."

He whistled as loud as he could, and in a minute or two Wytt came scampering out of the tall grass beside the road. It was too early for bees or butterflies to be at work.

"Find us a nice, safe place to rest, Wytt," Ellayne said. "Someplace with water to drink and where nobody will see us."

He chattered back at her. "I know a place. Come with me," was what he meant. "He's found us a place already," Ellayne said.

"How did you learn to understand him?" Fnaa said. "He just makes a lot of noises, like a squirrel."

"It's hard to explain," Jack said. "In fact, it's so hard to explain, I won't even try. It's just something that happened, up on Bell Mountain. Anyway, he's smart enough to understand us. He always was."

Wytt led them perhaps a quarter-mile from the road to a low place in a meadow where a little spring bubbled up out of the ground and made a pool. Between it and the road grew a healthy stand of inkbushes. A bird would see them camping there, but no human traveler would be likely to stumble over the site.

Gratefully, the children slipped their packs off and drank from the spring.

"Before we eat and sleep," Ellayne said, "I've got a surprise for you, Fnaa." She reached into her pack and pulled out a little jar.

"What is it?" he asked.

"It's some stuff that'll turn your hair red if you rub it in," she said. "The cook uses it. Otherwise, her hair would be grey. Hold out your hands, both of them."

Fnaa grinned, liking the idea. Ellayne poured some of the stuff onto his palms. "Now rub it in good," she said. "Don't stop until I tell you to."

Jack watched in amazement as Fnaa's dark hair gradually turned red. He'd had no idea that Lanora the cook did this to her hair. Wytt didn't like the smell of the dye, and said so. Ellayne ignored his protest.

"Does the baroness dye her hair?" Jack wondered. Vannett had golden hair like her daughter's, only not so bright.

"What a question!" Ellayne said. "None of your business, of course."

By and by the color was off Fnaa's hands and into his hair. Ellayne made him do his eyebrows, too.

"How do I look?" he asked.

"Odd!" said Jack; but Ellayne said, "You look like a totally different person. And you'll need a new name to go with your new hair. I think we'll call you Bomble. That's short for Ambombalbap—he was a hero."

"Bomble?" both boys said.

"Bomble will do just fine," Ellayne said. "And now, Jack, if you'll take the scissors and cut my hair—do try not to make a mess of it."

Since becoming a baron, Roshay Bault didn't lose his temper like he used to. But when he read his daughter's note that morning, his face turned red and he shook his fists at the ceiling.

"Is she trying to put me in my grave?" he roared. "Great sakes alive, that girl will drive me mad!"

He bellowed at the groom and at the cook and scared them badly enough so that he couldn't get anything out of them but wild looks and cringes. He didn't stop bellowing until Vannett threatened to throw a potful of cold water in his face.

"Thank you!" he panted.

"It's no use yelling at the servants," Vannett said. "Ellayne wouldn't have told them she was going to sneak off. And remember, the last time she left home like this, it turned out to be on God's business."

"I'm sure the Lord can manage a few things without our daughter's assistance. How can you be so calm about it?"

"I only look calm!"

It took all morning to find out that no one in Ninneburky had seen the children leave town, and no one had heard them talking about it. The country was at peace and no watch was posted in the night. Noon rolled around, but no one in the Bault household felt like eating dinner.

"If only that man Martis were here," Vannett said.

"Martis be fried," her husband growled. After all these hours he was still in his nightshirt. "But I wonder—maybe we should send for him. Ellayne says to show him the note. Maybe he might know something about this."

"But Martis is out East somewhere. Nobody knows exactly where he is."

"I'll send a rider, anyhow. And I'll send out more riders,

just in case she's on the road somewhere." Roshay ground his fist against his palm. "Why couldn't she have told us anything? And Jack! After we took him in—"

"Don't be unjust," Vannett said. "Let's just try to find them."

CHAPTER 6

How King Ryons Met a Man of God

King Ryons lay sleeping in his bed on a summer night—the exact night, for reasons you will understand, has been kept a secret—when he woke up suddenly.

All the lamps in his room were out and curtains drawn across the windows, so it was quite dark. Nevertheless, when by some unaccountable impulse he sat up in his bed, he saw someone sitting at the foot of it—not a shadowy shape, but a person who was plainly visible in spite of the darkness.

Ryons slept with the door of his bedchamber locked on the inside and one of his Ghol bodyguards stationed outside in the hall. The Ghols called him "father," although he was a boy and they were all grown men, and each and every one of them would gladly die to protect him. Therefore it was not possible for any stranger to be in his room; and yet there he was.

"Sorry to wake you, King Ryons," he said.

You would think that anyone would be startled and unnerved by this. But Ryons felt perfectly calm, although he found it strange that he could see so well in the dark. Probably he was still asleep and this was just a dream, he thought.

The visitor was an old man with a shiny bald head and an unruly white beard rippling down his chest. He wore farmer's clothes and spoke to Ryons in Wallekki, the language he'd grown up with. (But he'd studied hard and learned fast, and now he was fluent in Obannese.) For some reason Ryons was sure he'd seen the man before.

"I told you we'd meet again someday," the old man said.

Now he remembered! "Yes—when Cavall and I were on our way to the city before the great beast came, and the battle—"

The man nodded. When Ryons trekked all the way from Lintum Forest to the city of Obann with only Cavall the hound for company, this man met them and encouraged him to finish his journey.

And again, that time the people in the city closed the gates against him, it was an old man very like this one who went on ahead, leading the way. Ryons saw him, but none of the Ghols could. Riding along beside him, Queen Gurun saw someone else entirely. How that could be, Ryons never understood.

"King Ryons," said the visitor, "the Lord is pleased with you, and now He wants you to do something. Will you do as He asks?"

Ryons nodded.

"It's necessary for you to leave Obann for a little while. You are to leave tonight, right now, and return to Lintum Forest, taking no one with you but your dog, Cavall. When you get there, seek out your friend Helki. He'll know what to do."

What was all this for? Why leave Obann? Ryons

couldn't imagine.

"Am I still king?" he asked. "Or does God want someone else?"

The man smiled at him. "There is no one else, Your Majesty," he said. "Someday, if you keep God's commandments, a son of yours shall be king in Obann after you, and his son after him."

"But who are you?" Ryons cried. "And how is it I can see you in the dark?"

"Shh—not so loud. I am a servant of God. And it's time we were going. Please put on your clothes."

Ryons was able to find the clothes he wanted without lighting a lamp. This more than anything else made him sure he was dreaming. When he was all dressed, the man of God opened the door without unlocking it and beckoned him into the hall.

There Ryons found lamps burning and Kutchuk, his bodyguard for the night, seated against the wall beside the door, head bowed down and snoring contentedly. The man of God shut the door and the lock went snick. That tiny bit of noise should have wakened Kutchuk, but it didn't. The old man put a finger to his lips and led Ryons down the hall.

The royal palace was part of a vast government building that used to be the Oligarchy's headquarters, with offices, conference chambers, meeting halls, kitchens, and everything else. Now that the Temple lay in ruins, it was much the largest building in the city, and it took Ryons and his guide quite some time to wend their way to an exit.

All of the halls were lit, with soldiers and servants stationed here and there as needed. But no matter which way the man of God led Ryons, they found the people either sound asleep or absent from their posts. Ryons thought this the most outlandish dream he'd ever had.

Yet when he finally stepped outdoors and felt the cool night air on his face, and found Cavall waiting for him on the curb, wagging his tail, and the men stationed at the exit asleep on their feet, Ryons was forced to acknowledge that it wasn't a dream after all.

"Follow," said the man of God; and Ryons and Cavall followed, the great hound prancing for pure pleasure.

Ryons knew there were always people on the streets of Obann at all hours of the day or night. As he and Cavall followed the man of God, he heard people's voices, footsteps, the occasional clip-clop of a horse's hooves or the creak and rattle of a cart; but the noise always seemed to come from some other street nearby.

Only once did they meet anyone: a burly, bearded man who looked like trouble, Ryons thought.

"Ho, there! What's this?" the burly man said. "Hold up there, you two!"

Cavall growled, but the man had a cudgel in one hand and didn't seem at all afraid of the dog. Before Cavall could spring at him, the man of God said something Ryons couldn't hear, and the burly man dropped the cudgel and reeled backward, bumping heavily into a brick wall. He slid down the wall and collapsed in a heap, and Ryons heard him snoring.

"What did you do to him?"

"Nothing. He fell asleep. He will wake up in the morning with a headache. Come, Your Majesty. You must be out of the gate and on your way before sunrise."

It being peacetime, Obann's gates weren't closed at night; but they were guarded. But the guards at the East Gate just stood staring into the night, and paid no attention at all as Ryons and Cavall followed their guide through the gate.

Now they were outside the city, and the old man led them on a dirt track down to the river. There he pushed aside some reeds and showed Ryons a little boat resting on the riverbank. He smiled again.

"The first time you crossed the river, little king, you were riding the great beast to the rescue of your city. This time a little rowboat will have to suffice," he said. "Get in and I'll shove you off. You'll find a sack of provisions and other necessities, a waterskin, and a blanket."

Ryons climbed awkwardly into the boat, and Cavall leaped in after him. All the things he would need for his journey were there in a little pile.

"Put the oars in the locks," said the man. "You can row a boat, can't you?"

"I think I can," Ryons said. "I've never done it before, though."

"You'll do all right this time, Your Majesty."

"Why does God want me to go to Lintum Forest? Won't it make a lot of trouble in the city, when they can't find me and nobody knows where I am?"

"The Father of All wishes to magnify His servants and them that love Him," said the man of God, "at the expense of their enemies, and to demonstrate His providence. Now go, and trust in God's protection."

With surprising strength the old man pushed the boat

into the water, and it kept going as Ryons fumbled with the oars. It wasn't easy to get them into just the right position. By the time he accomplished it and looked up again, the old man was gone. At least Ryons couldn't see him in the dark.

You or I would have found it hard to row across the Imperial River. There was a strong current. You'd get across eventually, but at a point far downstream from the spot that you were trying to reach.

Ryons found it easy going, and before another hour had gone by, he'd rowed all the way across the great river. "I thought it'd be a lot harder than that," he said to Cavall. Had he known more about rivers and boats, he would have considered the feat miraculous.

When he bumped the prow onto the opposite shore at a place where it sloped gently to the water, Ryons and Cavall got out and the boy dragged the boat onto the land. He shouldered the pack and the waterskin, and tucked the rolled-up blanket under the strap of the pack. His education had advanced, so he knew by now the general location of Lintum Forest relative to Obann City, and how to find his way there. Behind him like cliffs loomed the ruins of Old Obann on the south bank, destroyed by God in His wrath.

"I wonder what we're supposed to do in Lintum Forest," Ryons said. God had already put him through so many strange adventures, it hardly occurred to him to question the need for yet another. Had the Lord not found him, the lowliest of slaves, and made him king? "I guess we'll find out when we get there."

Cavall grinned and wagged his tail.

With no more than another hour or two to sunrise, King Ryons began his trek to Lintum Forest.

CHAPTER 7

How Gurun Received a Throne

Everyone in Obann was busy. There would have been more than enough work for everyone just in clearing away the ruins of the Temple; after a year's labor, plenty remained of that task. But there were also the city's defenses to reorganize, Heathen brigands to be suppressed throughout the land, militia raised and trained, and farms to be restored.

On top of all that, an army of scholars and students toiled to render the Old Books into modern script and language so that all the people of Obann could be instructed in the Scriptures. And there were King Ozias' scrolls to translate and copy out—the ones found by Jack and Ellayne in the ruins of Ozias' Temple in the Old City. Were these truly long-lost books of Scripture? Scholars argued endlessly about it.

Everyone had quite enough to do without having to deal with the sudden disappearance of their king.

All morning long the Ghols ran up and down the palace, searching for him everywhere. They all knew Kutchuk would never have slept through the opening or closing of the king's door—and yet the king was not found in his bed that morning. There were fifty Ghols and they searched everywhere, growing more and more frantic by the hour.

"What shall we do?" said Chagadai, their chief. It was now past noon, and no one had found any sign of the king.

"It's my fault," Kutchuk said. "I should be put to death."

"So should we all, if we cannot find our father!" said another warrior.

"Don't talk like a fool, Kutchuk. What are we going to do? It'll take more than the fifty of us to search the city," Chagadai said. "Go, summon all the chieftains."

The Heathen chiefs who first proclaimed Ryons as their king were still in Obann to advise him and protect him. They were Heathen no more, but the people of Obann naturally looked on them as foreigners.

"And fetch the queen, too!" Chagadai shouted after Kutchuk.

Gurun came from a tiny island in the distant North, blown in her little skiff to Obann's shores by a ferocious storm that should have drowned her. But her people knew the Scriptures; God had given her the gift of understanding diverse languages; and for some reason the citizens of Obann had taken to her. She was tall and fair and only seventeen years old. The Ghols in particular liked her.

She followed Kutchuk to the conference chamber where the chiefs were waiting.

"What is it, Kutchuk?" she said. "You Ghols have been acting like wild men all morning."

"It's very bad, honeysuckle." That was the Ghols' nickname for her. "King Ryons is gone. We can't find him anywhere, and no one knows where he went." No one in the palace but Gurun and old Obst understood the Ghols' language, so Kutchuk could speak freely and loudly in the halls, and his harsh words rang up and down the marbled corridor.

"Gone?"

"We can't find him in the building—not even in the cellars."

Once in the chamber, the chieftains closed the doors and stationed guards outside. All the chiefs were there by the time Gurun arrived—fierce men who'd survived desperate battles and were ready to survive another one. But the king's disappearance, she could tell by their faces, had badly shaken them.

"Obst should be here, too," she said, after a curt exchange of greetings.

"He's been sent for," answered Shaffur, chief of the Wallekki. He glared at all the others and spoke to them in Tribe-talk, the common language understood by most of them. "I suppose we are all agreed that no one outside of this room must know the king is missing." Nods answered him. Gurun translated for the two or three who didn't know Tribe-talk.

"He's given us the slip before," said Uduqu, speaking for the Abnaks. "You all know the king's a special friend of mine. He's like a son to me. I think he would've told me if he had a reason to run away. But he didn't." He shook his scarred, tattooed head. Gurun knew him well enough to realize he was hurt—this hard old warrior who'd won fame in Obann by cutting down two enemy warriors with one swing of a giant sword. "So, whatever happened to him, it must have happened suddenly."

Someone knocked on the door. A guard opened it, and Kutchuk came in and bowed to the chieftains.

"Excuse me!" he said. "We've just discovered that the big dog, Cavall, is missing, too. He is not in his kennel and doesn't seem to be inside the palace, either."

Gurun translated for the chiefs. "That means King Ryons wasn't kidnapped," she added. "He has taken Cavall with him." The Ghols would be relieved to know that, she thought.

"How could he have done it?" asked Tughrul Lomak, chief of the Dahai. "Could he have climbed out his bedroom window?"

"Not without a long rope," Chagadai said. "It's possible he had such a rope, but no one saw it."

No one could propose a convincing solution to the riddle. By and by Obst arrived, panting because he'd hurried. He was old, thought Gurun, and today he looked it. He loved the boy king and had taught him much. He didn't speak until the chiefs had told him all they knew.

"He must be somewhere in the city, my lords," Obst said. "But how can we search the city for him without the whole city knowing about it? And then what will the people do, when they find out their king is missing?"

No one knew. The first time King Ryons left the city on an expedition, when he came back with Gurun, the people closed the gates against him, and there was fighting inside the walls. The people relented when they saw their king's face again; but what would they do if they couldn't see him?

Some of the chieftains wished to keep the matter secret. Others said that couldn't be done and they'd be fools to try. They argued back and forth. Usually King Ryons went out every day so that his people could see him. Today they wouldn't.

Uduqu suddenly stood up, silencing the discussion.

"I'm too old for so much talk," he said. "We have to find the king, and that's all there is to it. The more people we have looking for him, the sooner we'll find him.

"I think we ought to summon General Hennen back to the city and let him tell the people that the king is missing. They'll take it better, coming from an Obannese. Let all the people in the city search for Ryons—if he's here, they'll find him. Meanwhile, let General Hennen sit in his place, with us advising him; and let Gurun sit on the throne to keep it for the king."

"It's not right for me to sit on Ryons' throne!" Gurun said.

"Someone has to," Uduqu answered. "It can't be one of us chieftains—the city would rise up in rebellion. The people like me well enough, but only as a kind of friendly monster. But they think of you, Gurun, as something special. You don't have to sit on the king's throne. You can sit next to it. The people will accept you."

"For a little while, at least," Chief Shaffur added.

Gurun looked to Obst, but Obst only shrugged. "I think Chief Uduqu is right," he said. "One thing I'm sure of, Gurun: God brought you to Obann for a reason. Maybe this is the reason."

"Then I will do my best," said Gurun. "But we have no kings or queens where I come from. We know about them only through what we read in the Scriptures."

Obst smiled unexpectedly. "That should be enough!" he said.

CHAPTER 8

A Sermon in Cardigal

The first day's trek was hard, but in another day or two Ellayne and Jack had their adventuring legs again and could hike all day without aching.

They had fine weather for the first three days. They passed by Caristun, which had not yet recovered from being looted by the Heathen last summer, and were on their way to Cardigal, where the Chariot River flowed into the Imperial, when rain held them up for a day—not that they minded taking a day of rest.

They'd eaten almost all the food they'd brought from home, and Jack hadn't bagged anything with his slingshot. Ordinarily they would stop at Cardigal and buy all the food they wanted; but last year the Heathen burned Cardigal to the ground. Someday the town would rise again, the baron predicted. But it hadn't risen yet.

The children camped under a little knot of trees and sat huddled in their blankets around their campfire. Fortunately it wasn't raining very hard. Wytt was off looking for birds' eggs.

"Tell me again about Bell Mountain," Fnaa said, after they'd spent a good chunk of the morning doing it. "I've never even seen a mountain," he said. "Not close up, I mean."

"We've seen a lot of things we never expected to see,"

Jack said. "There are giant birds out on these plains—better hope we don't see one of those close up! One of them killed Martis' horse and ate it."

They'd mentioned Martis often, stressing his many services to them, trying to get Fnaa to trust him if Martis ever caught up to them. But Fnaa wasn't interested in Martis. "I keep thinking of that bell on top of the mountain," he said. "Is God real, and did He really hear it when you rang it? You thought He would end the world, and He didn't. Maybe He isn't going to do anything."

"Don't be silly," Ellayne said. "God hasn't ended the world. But He has shaken it up, and all kinds of things are happening."

"Things are always happening," said Fnaa; and not being theologians, neither Ellayne nor Jack knew how to answer him. All Jack could come up with was this.

"Nobody believed there was a bell up there," he said, "and yet there was. We know God heard it, because everybody in the whole world heard it. And you wouldn't be out here with us right now, Fnaa, unless God sent you."

"I just wish it'd stop drizzling," Fnaa said.

"He doesn't believe us," Jack thought.

They decided to stop at Cardigal after all, if only to see how the people were getting on. Besides, it was the best place to cross the river; and there just might be food for sale.

"If there's nothing there," Ellayne said, "we'll just go on a little ways to Gilmy. That's a village where Jack and I stayed once. The Heathen never touched it."

"I passed by Cardigal on my way out," Fnaa said. "It's all tents."

"Then the people in the tents will have food," Jack said.

They found a ferry taking folk back and forth across the river. You could see the cluster of tents on the north bank. The ruins had all been cleared away, and a few new buildings rose above the tents. The children joined a group of people boarding the ferry raft.

"Is there food for sale anywhere?" Jack asked one of the ferrymen.

"Aye—to them as can afford it," the man said. "It's been a good summer hereabouts: plenty of corn and a fine run of fish in the river. You'll find 'em selling it in Tent Town."

Cardigal's stone walls once entitled its chief councilor to be an oligarch; but they hadn't kept the Heathen out. With catapults the Heathen had hurled fire into the town and swarmed over the walls as the defenders fled to fight the flames.

Now men toiled to build a better wall. Most of the tents were pitched outside it, and most of the building was happening inside. Ellayne wondered how much they could finish before the winter and what people would do who didn't have proper homes by then.

But in Tent Town on a summer day—a sweetly sunny day, after a whole day of rain—no one seemed worried about the winter. Added to the noise made naturally by people, horses, cattle, and asses were the cling and clang of open-air smithies and the shouts and songs and chants of men and women who had something to sell.

With Ellayne's money the children bought some meat

pasties to eat on the spot, and bread, cheese, and apples to stow in their packs. "These prices really are too steep!" Ellayne said. "My mother would have a fit if they charged prices like this in Ninneburky."

"The pasty's mighty good, though," Jack said. Fnaa had already gulped his down. "For someone who doesn't eat much—" Jack started to say to him; but he got no further.

Rat-a-tat-tat-tat! Some wild-eyed fool was making an infernal racket, banging on a flat tin pan. Close behind him followed a tall, solemn-looking man in prester's robes.

"Here we go again," said the woman who was selling pasties.

"Attention, attention, good people of Cardigal!" cried the man who banged the pan. Rat-tat-tat! Most of the people in the area stopped talking. "Give ear to Prester Lodivar—hear him, hear him! Prester Lodivar of the Temple that is no more!"

The prester held up his two hands, and out of long habit, the people gave him silence.

"People of Cardigal!" He had a good pulpit voice, which carried. "You go hurriedly about your business, gangs of workmen labor to rebuild your city—but who in all of Obann labors for the Lord?

"The Temple of the Lord is burned and broken. And woe! Woe! The Lord God has withdrawn from you! He has turned His face from you; He abhors your heresy and disobedience. He closes His ears to your prayers, which the apostates in Obann City mis-teach you to make without a prester to lead you.

"Lo, I see a vision! Hear what the Lord Himself has shown me!"

He paused to let his eyes lock with the eyes of the people all around him. You could have heard grass grow, it was so quiet.

"The Lord," he said, "has shown me a vision of His New Temple—the great, glorious New Temple built to Him not in Obann but far away, among a people who were once His enemies. In Kara Karram by the Great Lakes the Lord God has chosen the place where His spirit shall abide, in the New Temple at Kara Karram. For the Lord has withdrawn Himself from Obann."

These were terrible words, and terrible to hear. People went pale. One or two dozen of the crowd, it seemed to Ellayne, went pale with anger; but everyone else was sore afraid.

Ellayne was one of the angry ones. "What rot!" she said under her breath. She was one of only a very few persons who knew that the First Prester's treachery had destroyed the Temple in Obann and that the New Temple in the East was the creation of the Thunder King, who called himself a god. "He's saying nothing but filthy lies!" She was, indeed, all set to interrupt the prester; but Jack grabbed her elbow and shook her.

"None of that—not here!" he whispered into her ear. "We've got to get to Obann, safe and sound. That's the only reason we left home."

"But don't you hear this stinking pack of lies?"

"We'll tell Obst all about it," Jack said, "after we get to Obann. He'll know what to do."

Inside Ellayne's pack, Wytt jabbed her with something sharp. It startled her back to her senses.

"Your God is in the East, O people of Obann!" the prester continued. "Humble yourselves to the East, before His wrath descends on you!"

"I don't want to hear any more of this," Ellayne said.

"Neither do I—let's go," Jack said. He jogged Fnaa's arm. "Let's go, Cousin Bomble."

CHAPTER 9

How They Came to Obann

The chieftains wavered and couldn't bring themselves to announce the disappearance of the king. Instead, they sent for Gallgoid, the Chief Spy, and bade him to see if he could find the king without letting out the secret.

"I don't like bringing him into it," Chief Shaffur grumbled.

"I'll bet he's already brought himself into it," Uduqu said.

Gallgoid had been Lord Reesh's confederate when the First Prester let the Heathen into the Temple by a secret passage and betrayed the city. Gallgoid was to accompany him all the way out to Kara Karram, where Lord Reesh was to be installed as First Prester of the Thunder King's New Temple. Gallgoid was the only one to escape the avalanche that buried Lord Reesh and the Thunder King at the Golden Pass, Gallgoid having fled secretly after he'd learned that there was no immortal Thunder King, but only a succession of masked pretenders.

"My men are already searching for King Ryons throughout the city," he told the chiefs, provoking a knowing nod from Uduqu. "I presumed it was to be kept a secret, so my men are being very discreet. Have no fear on that account."

"Do we say or do anything that you don't know about

before we tell you?" Shaffur said, scowling.

"It's my business to know, my lords." Gallgoid rose from his seat and bowed. "I am entirely your servant. If the people of this city ever learned the truth about me, I wouldn't live another day."

"Please, gentlemen!" Obst said. "Remember what the Scriptures say. It's always been God's will that someday all nations of men will worship Him in a temple not made by human hands. It profits us nothing to bring up the destruction of the Temple in the city, nor Lord Reesh's treason. Let Gallgoid serve God now, as do we all. He has repented of his service to Lord Reesh."

To this the chiefs agreed. But Gurun took it upon herself, later, to go down to a corner of an inner courtyard and take the king's hawk, Angel, out of her cage. Angel rested contentedly on her forearm. Gurun's father, Bertig, owned a snow-white hunting eagle, and she knew how to handle birds.

"You are a wise hawk," Gurun said. "That is why I am going to bid you fly and seek your master, King Ryons. Wherever he is on the face of the earth, find him—and bring him back to me."

Can a hawk understand such a commandment, and do it? Gurun thought so. She raised her arm, and with a single shrill cry, Angel flew up from the courtyard, circled the palace once, and flew away.

The road from Cardigal to Obann was in good repair, with many people traveling on it—too many for any special notice to be taken of three boys hiking along like all the rest. Jack, Ellayne, and Fnaa made good time, and they never went far without seeing a farmer with a cart, usually with produce in it.

Between villages, travelers felt safe enough to camp beside the road for the night. This close to Obann City, Heathen raiders dared not come. The king's Attakotts patrolled the countryside—little men with wiry hair who could run all day and not get tired, and who were only seen when they let themselves be seen. Every now and then you would spot one of them, or two, squatting on a hill. They carried bows and arrows, and the arrows were poisoned, such as they used in their distant homeland to bring down large game. They didn't used poisoned arrows in their frequent skirmishes with the Abnaks back home, deeming poison an unsuitable weapon to use against warriors. But against brigands who disturbed the king's peace and preyed on his people, they used poison that would kill a man if the arrow only scratched him. Evildoers knew this, and kept their distance from the Obann road.

We ought to reach the city tomorrow, if we have good weather," Ellayne said. She knew her geography better than Jack had learned his, and Fnaa knew no geography at all. "This trip hasn't been too hard."

"Will we see the king tomorrow, then?" Fnaa asked.

"I don't see why not."

"We might have to see some other people first," Jack said, "before they let us in to see the king."

"You're his friends. Why wouldn't he want to see you right away?" Fnaa said.

"Try not to be so stubborn!" Ellayne said. "You trust us, or we wouldn't all be here together. Well, there are other people you can trust just as much. Obst, Queen Gurun, and the chiefs in Ryons' army—you'll have to learn to trust them, too."

"Not until after I've seen the king."

That was where Fnaa stood, and there was no budging him. He still hadn't told them the name of the family who owned him and his mother. Jack had tried often enough to get more information out of him, but to no avail.

"You want to get your mother out of that house, don't you?" he would say. "Then King Ryons can protect her. If those people are traitors, the king's men will have to arrest them."

"Telling you right now wouldn't do any good," Fnaa said.

They camped beside the road that night, not far from a family of farmers who were roasting sausages over a fire. They bought a few, and when it was dark enough, Ellayne let Wytt out of her sack. He chattered impatiently until she appeased him with a chunk of sausage.

"He doesn't much like riding in the bag all day," Jack said.

"Cheer up, Wytt—we're almost there," Ellayne said. "King Ryons will be happy to see you again."

Wytt chirped a brusque reply, then ran off to hunt for moths.

Just a little after noon the next day, they came before the East Gate of the city. It was open, and people and carts were flowing in and out of it. Soldiers stood on the walls, watching, but they were mostly for show because Obann was at peace. Jack, Ellayne, and Fnaa walked right in. "If we'd come with my father on horseback," Ellayne thought, "we might have had a greeting."

Fnaa kept darting glances left and right, as if he expected his former master to pounce on him at any moment. "Relax!" Ellayne told him. "No one will recognize you with red hair. Besides, they think you're a helpless fool."

"I'm not used to being around so many people," he said. "I wasn't allowed out of the house very often."

From the East Gate to the palace was a straight run along Parade Street. The children had to hold hands to avoid being separated by the crowds. You might think it would be hard for Ellayne and Jack to walk on any street in Obann without being recognized and mobbed as the heroes of Bell Mountain, but although many people knew their names, very few knew their faces. Ellayne's mother and father had insisted on their daughter (and Jack) not becoming famous.

"But we ought to have a parade!" Ellayne protested to her father, the first time they visited the city.

"It wouldn't be good for you," said Roshay Bault, and that was that.

It took them almost an hour to make their way to the royal palace. It had a dozen doors facing on the street. Jack and Ellayne went up to the biggest door, the one in the middle, and spoke to the two mail-clad soldiers on guard there.

"We wish to see King Ryons," said Ellayne. "We're friends of his."

"He knows us," Jack added.

The guards exchanged a look, and one of them couldn't repress a smile. "Friends of the king, eh?" he said. "Come to see if he can come out and play?"

"It's the truth!" Jack said. "Tell him Jack and Ellayne are here."

"That's two names for three kids," said the other guard.

"This is just a friend of ours, from Ninneburky—King Ryons doesn't know him," Ellayne answered. "But he does know us! We're the ones who rang the bell on Bell Mountain."

The guards thought that was funny, too; but Fnaa looked like he was about to jump out of his skin. Jack put a hand on his shoulder to steady him.

"Obst knows us, too," Jack said, "and so does Queen Gurun. We've walked all the way, and we're hot and tired."

"Well, then, come in and sit down, and we'll see what can be done," a guard said.

They were made to wait inside the entryway while one of the men went off to consult with an officer. Jack and Ellayne sat on either side of Fnaa, knee to knee and close enough to grab him if he tried to bolt.

"This is outrageous," Ellayne said. "Nobody here knows who we are."

"Obst will take care of us," Jack said. Ellayne was always going on about being famous. Jack wished she'd drop it; he didn't see the use of being famous.

The other guard was gone for quite some time. "Probably having his lunch!" Ellayne muttered. But Fnaa hadn't spoken a word since they'd been let inside. Jack watched him closely. It'd be terrible if he fainted.

Finally the guard returned. He was in a hurry, and not chuckling anymore.

"Your pardon!" he said. "Queen Gurun wants to see you right away." He looked at the other guard. "And you and I are in the pot for making these kids wait! Come, children, come with me. I'll take you to the queen."

"We did come here to see King Ryons," Ellayne said. "We have an important message for him."

The man shrugged. "My orders are to take you to the queen, and to be right quick about it. I daren't disobey. Please come!"

And so they found themselves in a private audience with Gurun, in a little room looking out on the jumbled ruins of the Temple. Gurun kissed Ellayne first, then Jack. "But why didn't you send word that you were coming?" she cried. "You should not have been kept waiting. And who is your friend?"

"Please, Gurun, we have to speak to you alone," Ellayne said. "And it's very important that we see King Ryons."

Gurun dismissed the one handmaid in attendance and made her shut the door after her.

"I'm afraid you cannot see the king today," she said. "He is not here."

"Where is he?" Jack asked.

"Before I can tell you that, you must tell me why you've come."

They never would have expected such an answer from her. Jack shook Fnaa a little. "This is Queen Gurun herself," he told him. "Ellayne and I trust her, and you should, too."

"I must speak only to the king," Fnaa said. You could barely hear him.

"There is matter in this!" said Gurun. "Very well—I will tell you something that you must never tell anybody else. Promise me."

"We promise," Ellayne said. The boys nodded. Something was wrong, and not just a little bit wrong: Jack knew it.

Gurun lowered her voice and said, "The king is not here. He went to his bedchamber two nights ago, and in the morning he could not be found. No one knows where he has gone; but he took Cavall with him. No one has been able to find a trace of either of them."

CHAPTER 10

Fnaa's Story

Gurun spoke plainly. The girls of Fogo Island are taught to keep their feelings under control and not reveal them—which is not the same thing as not having any feelings. She would have liked to return to her family, but Obann had neither ships nor sailors, so it was impossible for her to go home. For better or for worse, Obann would have to be her home from now on.

Gurun loved Ryons and feared for his safety. The boy king could not have meant more to her if he were her own flesh and blood. But it wouldn't do him or her any good to go tearing around the palace, wailing and weeping.

"So that is how things are," she finished. "We do not even know whether the king is still alive."

Ellayne was speechless. Fnaa sat as still as a statue. But Jack turned to him and said, "You have to tell your story now, Fnaa—the whole thing. If you can't trust the three of us here in this room, then you can't trust anyone in all Obann, and everything you've done will be for nothing. You can see that, can't you?"

Fnaa took a long look at Queen Gurun. His shoulders slumped a little. At last he said, "All right. I'll tell you everything."

"My mother and I are slaves," he said. "We belong to a man named Vallach Vair. He's rich. He's a merchant. He has a great big house on River Street.

"He has a lot of friends, and they're all against the king. So they made a plan. But I don't know the names of any of those friends of his. My mother might know.

"I look like the king. Just like him! Ask Ellayne what I looked like before she colored my hair red. But my master thinks I'm a fool, because my mother taught me how to act like one. So their plan was to get rid of King Ryons and put me in his place. After a time, when all the people saw their king was feeble-minded, they'd get tired of having a fool for a king, and then the Oligarchy would come back. I'm not sure what an oligarchy is, but I think it'd mean my master and his friends would take over the city and everything else. So my mother told me about Jack and Ellayne and sent me to find them, so we could tell the king and stop all this from happening." He paused to look at Ellayne, and then at Jack. "I guess we're too late."

For some moments Gurun didn't say anything—just sat still, thinking.

"You believe me, don't you?" Fnaa cried.

"Oh, yes—yes, I do," she said. "But I am just trying to imagine you with dark hair like the king's."

"The dye washes out in warm water," Ellayne said.

Gurun stood up. "Wait here," she said. She went out of the room for a minute and came right back.

"I do believe you," she said. "I am thinking of what we might be able to do."

"To find the king?" Jack asked.

"No. Not that. Something else."

In a little while, someone knocked at the door, a maid with a big basin of water. Gurun took it and dismissed her. She set the basin on a table. "Wash your hair, Fnaa," she said. "I want to see your natural color."

He looked doubtful. "Go ahead," said Ellayne.

"I might as well," he said.

Fnaa bent over the basin and wet his head. He didn't know quite how to manage, so Ellayne helped him. By and by the water turned red, and Fnaa's hair went back to black. Gurun handed him a towel. He disappeared under it, drying. The last of the color came off on the towel.

Gurun's mouth dropped open when she saw him as he really was.

"It's true!" she said. "If I didn't know otherwise, I would swear you were King Ryons."

"That's exactly what I thought, when I first saw him," Ellayne said. "Me, too," Jack added.

"But what's the use," Fnaa said, "if they've already got the king?"

"I don't think they have," said Gurun. "Whatever might have happened, no enemy could have gotten past his Ghols. They guard him with their lives. And he has Cavall to protect him."

"But I don't see what we can do!" Jack said.

"Oh, but maybe there is something," said Gurun, "if our friend Fnaa is brave enough to do it."

Fnaa shrugged. "Tell me what it is," he said. "I can't think of anything!"

"Then listen," Gurun said. "Your master's plan was for you to take King Ryons' place. You spoiled that by running away. Now—how would it be if you did take the king's place? Only for a little while, I hope: only until we have him here with us again, or find out for sure what has become of him.

"I will tell the chiefs that you are King Ryons and that I found you hiding in my closet in my room. That's one place they haven't searched! I shall tell them that you've had a fever and have lost your memory—but otherwise there is nothing wrong with you.

"We can pretend; and while we pretend, there are servants of the king who can quickly act against your master, taking him by surprise. They can bring your mother to the palace, here with us, so she can be protected."

"But how can I pretend to be the king?" Fnaa cried. "I wouldn't know how to act! Until I ran away to Ninneburky, I was hardly ever outside my master's house."

"That is why I'll say you've lost your memory," Gurun said. "I'll help you. There will not be much you'll have to say or do. Ryons is just a boy like you. His chieftains and his advisers have always acted in his name."

Ellayne spoke up. "Fnaa, you've got to do it. We'll be here to help you. After all, if you could trick your master and his whole family into thinking you were a simpleton, when you weren't, it shouldn't be any harder to make people think you're the king. You fooled your master for years! But this would only be for a little while."

"Can you really bring my mother here?" Fnaa asked.

"I promise you it shall be done—and very soon, too," Gurun said.

Fnaa let out a long sigh. "Funny, isn't it?" he said. "I ran away so they couldn't put me in the king's place—and now I'm going to be put there anyway! But all right. I'll do it. It's not like I can just go back home again, is it?"

"No," said Gurun, mostly to herself. "Neither can I."

CHAPTER 11

How Wytt Inquired for the King

Wytt understood everything that Jack and Ellayne said to him; but he also understood most of what other big people said to them.

He knew Ryons. There was no "Ryons" in his mind—the Omah don't grasp the human idea of personal names—but rather an image of Ryons and a realization that Ryons was a friend. Curled up in Ellayne's pack, listening to Gurun and the children, he learned that Ryons had gone away, no one knew where, and he perceived that this was very upsetting to everyone concerned. Wytt also knew the king's dog, Cavall, and understood that Cavall had gone away, too.

If the Omah's mind were more like a human's, he might have wondered why big people had so little feel for their surroundings. Being so high off the ground, they didn't see things that Wytt saw easily. They didn't seem to hear very well at all. The constant stream of interweaving scents and odors that fed Wytt a feast of information had nothing to say to Jack or Ellayne. They were, in their way, more helpless than the pinkest little newborn Omah suckling at his mother's breast. They needed a great deal of looking after.

While Ellayne slept that night—Gurun had provided the children each with a nice bedchamber in the palace—Wytt hopped onto the windowsill and climbed down the stone walls as easily and silently as a lizard. Once on the grass, he began to follow wherever his assortment of keen senses led him.

He wished to find out about Ryons and the dog, because the humans couldn't do it. He was in an inner courtyard faced by stables, kennels, cages for hawks, and coops for chickens: a place where an inquisitive Omah could learn much.

He went first to the stables, then to the kennels. Animals cannot talk; neither could Wytt—at least, not as we know talking. But God has given to animals and Omah senses and perceptions of which human beings know nothing. So when one of the hounds caught Wytt's scent, and got up and growled, Wytt chirped at him and the dog stopped growling. Wytt crept close to the cage so that he and the dog could sniff each other. That's what it would have looked like to a human, but there was much more to it than just sniffing.

Wytt came away from the encounter with the knowledge—or rather, with the picture in his mind—that Cavall had gone away with a man who'd let him out of his kennel. This was not just any man, not one of the men of the palace. This was a Man who shone in the dark and had a sweet and soothing scent that the dogs liked. It gave the hound pleasure to recall it.

The dogs had neither seen nor smelled Ryons that night, so he must not have visited the courtyard. Wytt understood that Ryons slept in a particular room, just as

Jack and Ellayne were doing. The dogs knew nothing about that, so he went on to the mews where the hawks were sleeping. Ordinarily no Omah would dare approach a hawk. Along with snakes, badgers, and wildcats, hawks preyed on the little people. But these hawks were safely confined in stout mesh cages, so Wytt didn't hesitate to rattle one of the cages with a stick.

The two hawks in the cage woke with harsh protests, beating their wings at Wytt and wishing they could sink their beaks and talons into him. But they were tame hawks, captive-bred, who had never fed on Omah, and eventually Wytt was able to calm them and communicate with them.

The hawks, too, had seen the softly shining Man come for Cavall. He didn't disturb them or alarm them, but they saw him—and they would have liked to have seen more. More to Wytt's purpose, they knew the window in which King Ryons' face most often appeared; and the Man, that night, had appeared in that window, too. All the birds had been awake that night and seen the Man's light seeping through the crack between the curtains. They had hoped he would come back down and visit them, but he didn't.

Wytt climbed up the palace wall, the rough stone offering him an easy climb. There was no light in Ryons' room tonight, but Omahs see much better at night than humans, and even before he reached the window ledge, he smelled Ryons' scent, which he knew as well as he knew the boy's face.

Parting the curtains, he hopped into the royal bedchamber. Ryons' scent was all over the room, along with odors left by servants and bodyguards; but the strange shining man had left no scent at all. There was no trace of him that even an Omah might detect.

Wytt sniffed the floor and baseboards for rats, but there weren't any. Rats might have told him something, if they didn't attack him at first sight. He went to the door and heard people in the hall outside.

Had an enemy come into that room, had there been a struggle there, had Ryons been provoked to intense fear, Wytt would have known it. Those things left traces in the air, on the floor, in the bedclothes, traces undetectable by human beings but plain to animals and Omah. Their absence told Wytt that Ryons had left the room peaceably and unafraid.

With a satisfied chirp, he climbed up the curtain and back outside. No one saw him scramble down the wall. A dog barked—just a friendly greeting—as he scurried across the yard and then back up another wall. In another minute he was back in Ellayne's bedroom and snuggling up against her.

Gurun kept Fnaa with her all day in her room, letting no one see him, sharing her supper with him, and teaching him what to say tomorrow to the chiefs. He looked so much like Ryons that sometimes she forgot for a moment that he wasn't Ryons. He even sounded like the king.

"You'll do well," she told him. "Just remember that you can't remember anything! The people on the streets, when they see you, will never guess there's anything amiss."

"The servants in the palace will," said Fnaa.

"Maybe—but not right away."

The boy was intelligent, she thought. He would be able to do everything she told him.

"They'll all be mad when they find out they've been fooled," he said.

"But they won't find out tomorrow," Gurun said.

She let him sleep in her bed that night—it was big enough for her whole family, after all—and woke early to hide him in her closet. When a maid brought breakfast, Gurun shooed her away quickly, feigning a bad temper.

She had to solve the problem of Fnaa's clothes. He ought to be wearing some of the king's clothes. There was only one way to take care of that.

"Eat," she said, "and if you hear anyone at the door, hide under the bed. I have to get some clothes for you. I won't be long."

The king's bedchamber was a ways down the hall from hers. He wasn't in it, so there was no need for anyone to guard the door.

She met a servant hurrying along on some early-morning errand.

"Wait!" she said. "I want you to find Chagadai the Ghol for me and bring him to my room within the hour—if you please." The man nodded and said, "Yes, ma'am," and went off in the opposite direction. Gurun waited until he was out of sight and she could hear his footsteps no more.

Ryons' door was not locked: there was no reason to lock it. Gurun dashed in and snatched some clothes out of his closet, taking a moment to make sure they were some things he'd been wearing recently. She stuffed them under her dress and hurried back to her own room, meeting no one on the way. Half an hour later, she thought, and this hall would have been far too busy for her to do this.

Fnaa was hiding when she entered the room and locked

the door behind her. "You can come out," she said. "I have some clothes for you. Put them on."

He changed clothes behind a screen. They fit, of course. It wasn't the custom to dress Ryons in royal robes, but the clothes Fnaa had were much humbler than anything in the king's wardrobe. In other words, thought Gurun, they were sensible clothes.

"Chagadai will be here soon," she said, when Fnaa was dressed. "Don't be afraid of him. He and all the Ghols belong particularly to King Ryons, and protect him. They call him their father."

"They won't like it when they find out I'm not him," said Fnaa.

"Be brave," Gurun answered, "and leave everything to me."

"A tall order for a girl from Fogo Island!" she thought. But what else could be done? She prayed a silent prayer: "All-Father, be with me now to guide me."

In his short life, Fnaa hadn't had many opportunities to be brave or cowardly. He was so used to playing the fool in his master's house that it was second nature to him. But playing the king terrified him.

The chieftains—barbarians all, and one more fearsome-looking than the next, with all their scars and strange attire—made his blood run cold. Chagadai the Ghol, who called him "father," had slanted eyes and a livid white scar across his face. If Gurun hadn't been holding his hand, Fnaa would have run away. As it was, this formidable man seized his free hand and kissed it.

Gurun and Chagadai took him to a room where all the chiefs were seated around a glossy table, and there Gurun told them the story she'd invented. They listened with unsmiling faces; and when it was time for him to speak to them, Fnaa's mouth went dry and Gurun had to squeeze his hand to get him started. "If only she'd told them the king has lost his wits, not just his memory!" he thought.

"My lords," he said, very slowly, "it's just like she says. I don't know what happened to me. I woke up in a closet and didn't know how I got there. I didn't know anything at all! I didn't even know who I was, until she told me. I don't remember you, and I don't remember how I got to be a king. I'm sorry."

The hard faces softened. A tall old man with a grey beard got up and laid a big, knobbly hand on Fnaa's shoulder.

"You have nothing to be sorry for, Your Majesty," he said. "You were ill; it's not your fault. The men in this room, and Queen Gurun, will take care of everything. God made you king, and God will heal you. Then you'll remember."

One of the chiefs, a swarthy man who wore a wolf's head for a headdress, jabbered excitedly in a foreign language. And yet to Fnaa it seemed a familiar language, somehow.

"Chief Zekelesh, of the Fazzan," Gurun translated, "is afraid that some witch has put a spell on you." So that chief, Fnaa thought, was of his mother's people. Fnaa's mother sometimes sang Fazzan songs.

The old man shook his head and said, "Not so, my lord! What power could such heathen mummery have over God's anointed king? I tell you this is an illness that'll pass. You'll see."

"Well, we've got him back, at least," said the chief of the Wallekki. "If he had a fever in his brain, we're lucky he didn't die on us."

"Not lucky, Chief Shaffur. It was God's blessing," said the old man.

"I think the king ought to rest now, in his own bed," Gurun said. "It should help him to spend time in his own room and enjoy some healthy sleep. The people can be told that he was sick, but is now getting better, and they will see him soon."

"I'll see that the word is put out," said Obst; for that was the old man's name.

And so Fnaa went off to bed in King Ryons' bedchamber, in one of the king's nightshirts, and Gurun sat beside the bed and told him he'd done just fine with the chiefs. He might have enjoyed it if he weren't worried that they'd kill him, by and by.

"That is foolish," Gurun said. "None of those men will ever hurt you."

"What about my mother? When will she be here?" Fnaa asked.

"As soon as I can arrange it. Tell me her name and what she looks like."

"Her name is Dakl and she looks like me, with black hair and brown eyes, and she's the only grown-up woman who's a slave in that house." Fnaa paused. "She was born Fazzan, like that man with the wolf's head. She never told me that the men wore wolf's heads."

"I'll see to it that she's kept safe," said Gurun. "And you may as well try to take a nap."

CHAPTER 12

A Wanderer and His Baby

It was a frustrating day. Jack and Ellayne urgently wanted to see Gurun, but she and Fnaa were busy all day long behind closed doors. But at long last they got to see Obst, who came to them where they were waiting by the stables.

Their old friend rejoiced to see them and hugged them close.

"But what are you doing here?" he cried. "I never heard that you were coming, and no one told me you were here—otherwise I would have seen you right away!"

This was awkward. Fnaa would not have wanted them to tell Obst anything about him. Only Gurun was supposed to know.

"You want to tell me something; I can see it in your faces," Obst said. "Well, here I am."

Jack blurted out, "Is it a sin to tell a secret, when you promised not to tell—but you know you should?" Ellayne glared at him. "Blabbermouth!" she thought.

But this was Obst, who'd led them up Bell Mountain and almost died doing it. They would never have gotten there without him. Besides, he was a holy man.

"Jack, I can't answer that," he said. "I don't know what you're talking about."

"If you'd seen us when we came to the door of this

palace yesterday, you'd know," Ellayne thought. But she said, "What do you think of Ryons? Do you believe he's really lost his memory and doesn't know who he is anymore?"

Obst shrugged. "He says he has. Why should he say so, unless it's true? But it's good to have him back, in any case. We feared for him."

Wytt darted out from the stables and chattered excitedly at Obst. He knew Obst and trusted him. He was telling him what he'd learned during the night; but of course Obst couldn't understand him. He could understand every human language spoken in his presence, but only Jack and Ellayne could understand Wytt.

"What's he saying, children? It sounds important!"

"It is," Ellayne said. "But if we tell you, you have to promise not to tell anyone else. Not unless we say you can."

"Then let's move over by the chicken houses," Obst said, "where no one will be able to overhear us."

When they stood among the clucking fowl, Jack began: "First, the king is not the king. He's a boy who looks like Ryons. And we know, because we brought him here."

They told him everything they knew. He was most interested in Wytt's discoveries.

"A shining man!" he mused, absentmindedly twisting his beard into knots. "A man who didn't make the dogs bark, and who entered Ryons' room by night, in spite of the bodyguard at the door—and yet the boy was not afraid of him. How does Wytt know these things?"

"He knows!" Ellayne said. "He has ways of knowing things that people don't know. But he doesn't know how to make things up."

Obst began to pace, annoying the chickens. "Ryons left

here of his own free will," he muttered. "Cavall let a stranger take him out of his kennel and lead him somewhere. And just in time, you arrive with Ryons' look-alike!" He stopped pacing. "There can be no doubt of it: these things have been ordained by God for some purpose of His own, of which we as yet know nothing." He shook his head and let out a deep sigh. "And what are we to do? Where has Ryons gone? Is the shining man still with him, or is he on his own, but for Cavall? But I do think the man was heaven-sent—although for what reason I can't imagine!" He looked down at Wytt, who was fascinated by the chickens. "If the man were evil, I think Wytt would have known it. So we may with reason presume that he was good."

"But do things like that happen?" Jack said.

Obst smiled at him. "You of all people shouldn't have to ask! But yes, those things happen. God has not changed since the creation of the world. Did He not hear Ozias' bell when you rang it? Is He not shaking the earth in our time, even as we stand on it? I hardly think He's finished with us. Do you?"

"I guess not," said Ellayne.

Ryons and Cavall were crossing the great plain that stretched between Lintum Forest and the city of Obann. They'd crossed it once before, the other way. Then as now, it was an empty country. Closer to the river there were towns and farms, but this far south, there was nothing. A thousand years after the Day of Fire, the plains of South Obann were unpopulated.

Here and there rose hills that were not hills, but all that

remained of the great buildings of the Empire; and the bigger hills had once been cities. From Jack and Ellayne, Ryons knew that most of these ruins were inhabited by Omah; but he was not afraid to camp there. With Cavall present, the little hairy men chose not to show themselves.

"It'll be good to be back in Lintum Forest," he said to Cavall, several times a day. But why did God want him back in Lintum Forest? His ancestor, King Ozias, was born there. His friend Helki was there, hunting down outlaws. And he himself had been happy there, for the little while he'd stayed there.

Once upon a hilltop, just as he and Cavall were about to go down and resume their trek, Ryons spotted a cloud of dust, and then the horsemen who were raising it. By their headdress and their mode of riding he knew them for Wallekki; but he very much doubted they were any of his Wallekki, so he crouched behind a bush and didn't get up until they were out of sight. It was a reminder that the land was still full of deadly enemies, remnants of the vast host that the Thunder King sent into Obann last year.

"Close call!" he whispered to Cavall. He didn't want to think about what such men would do if they captured him and realized who he was. "Off to Kara Karram to get my eyes burned out!"

The country was unpopulated, but not barren. Wild blackberries grew everywhere, and Cavall caught unwary ground-squirrels and rabbits. Springs bubbled up from the ground. Wildflowers painted the landscape with glorious color. Ryons' favorites were the pale purple maidens-kisses, which attracted pale purple butterflies, and the brilliant vermilion huzzahs, which didn't grow east of the mountains.

So, on the whole, it was a pleasant journey, as long as one could avoid the Heathen stragglers by day and the gigantic hunting birds that came out at night.

Three days into his journey, in the middle of the day, Ryons saw black smoke rising ahead of him; but whatever was burning was hidden behind a stand of gnarled, twisted waxbushes. The sun glinted off their shiny leaves, and above them fluttered a multitude of sparrows, feeding on the various insects attracted to the waxbushes' scent. The presence of the birds suggested there was nothing to fear. Ryons advanced—cautiously, with a hand on the nape of Cavall's neck. Cavall would warn him if there was any danger.

The boy and the dog crept up close to the waxbushes. Ryons dropped to his hands and knees and crawled in among the stunted tress, Cavall behind him. The sparrows didn't like it, and chirped a protest. It was shadowy under all that foilage, with a lot of tiny bugs that persistently flew into your face. Ryons felt the hairs standing up on Cavall's neck; but the great hound had too much sense to give away their position by growling.

They reached a point where they could see what lay on the other side of the trees, and there they froze.

It was a wagon that was burning. Its wheels were broken, and there was no sign of any horses, mules, or oxen that might have pulled it. Black smoke billowed up from it.

Sitting beside it, roasting something on a stick, was a tall man in dusty buckskin clothes, with a shapeless cloth cap on his head. Standing beside him—towering over him, in fact—was a gigantic bird with long, strong legs, tiny wings, plumage more like filthy hair than feathers, a long, powerful neck, a head as big as a horse's head, bright yellow eyes like wicked jewels, and a massive beak with a cruel hook at the end of it.

Ryons had seen such birds before, but at a healthy distance. Up close, it was a sight to take your breath away. But this killer stood peacefully beside the man, and the man seemed to take no notice of it.

"Whoever you are in there," the man sang out, without bothering to look in Ryons' direction, "you can come on out. We won't hurt you."

Come out—with that murdering great bird standing there? But was it still possible to escape? Ryons didn't think so.

"Don't make us come in after you," the man said. "It's too nice a day for that."

Ryons crawled out from under the waxbushes and stood up, with one hand holding on to Cavall's fur. The great bird swiveled its head to look at them, but made no other movement. The man looked at them and smiled.

"Well, well—a boy and a dog," he said. "And what might you be doing out here, all alone in bandit country? You could wind up like the folks who owned this wagon."

"You're not a bandit?" Ryons couldn't help asking.

"No, not me. I just wander, seeing what's what. My name is Perkin." He jerked his head at the bird. "And this is Baby—my baby, actually."

Ryons didn't know how to answer that, and the man laughed at him.

"It's true," he said. "I raised him from a little chick no bigger than my hand. Boy, howdy, did he grow fast! But he's attached to me, and he won't go anywhere without me. Don't be afraid of him. He won't hurt you unless you try to hurt me. Come and sit down, and have a bite to eat."

Cavall didn't seem to be too much put off by the bird or the man, so Ryons decided to sit down.

"What's your name, boy?"

"Ryons."

"Just like the king, eh? Ever seen him?"

"No." Ryons shook his head. Maybe he should have lied about his name, but it was too late now.

"Never been in Obann City, myself," Perkin said. "I don't think they'd let me in with Baby, and I won't go without him." He looked up at the bird. "Sit down, Baby." And the killer sat down next to him. "Where are you headed, Ryons—if you don't mind my asking?"

Ryons shrugged. "Lintum Forest," he answered.

"That's a long way off. And the country's full of bandits. It's dangerous. Maybe I'd better go with you for a ways."

"Why would you want to do that?"

"I can do anything I please," Perkin said. "I want to protect you from the bandits. You see this wagon? There were people in it. The bandits took them to sell them into slavery, or else just kill them for the fun of it. They took the animals, too, and everything that was in the wagon. They didn't want the wagon, so they broke it up and burned it. I saw the whole business from a hilltop. But there were an even dozen of them, all on horseback, so Baby and I didn't interfere. When the bandits left, I came down to cook my dinner on the fire."

He withdrew the stick from the flames, sniffed it, and took a little taste. He tore off a piece and tossed it into the air. Baby caught it and swallowed it.

"Roast rabbit," he said. "Have some."

It was delicious, and finished all too soon. Cavall got a share, too. Perkin yawned and stood up.

"Let's move on," he said. "It's a nice day for a walk, and it's a long way to Lintum Forest." Ryons noticed, then, that he wore a short sword in a leather sheath and had a sling tucked into his belt.

Why would the stranger want to protect him? Maybe it was a trick. Maybe he and Cavall could quietly leave him during the night, Ryons thought. But he said, "It's good of you to travel with me, sir. Thank you."

Perkin had a lean, tired, weather-beaten face; but when he grinned at Ryons, he looked full of life and ready for anything.

"It's my pleasure to do it," he said. "Anyhow, I wouldn't like to trip over your skeleton someday and think it was my fault you were killed. Besides, you'll be someone to talk to for a few days."

Ryons walked off with the wanderer, with the enormous killer bird stalking ahead of them and Cavall sticking close to Ryons' side. He hadn't entirely made up his mind about these strangers. But Ryons reminded himself that he was under God's protection, and silently prayed it would continue to be so.

CHAPTER 13

How Dakl Came to the Palace

Gurun was not really queen of anything, although everybody called her one and she'd given up trying to make them stop. The people of the city cheered her whenever they saw her (which she didn't understand), and the chiefs accepted her because she, like Obst, had the gift of understanding tongues.

But now or never, she supposed, she would have to play the queen. If the chiefs decided to cast her out of the city, so be it.

She went to see the Chief Spy in his office, and she went alone, telling no one of her errand. It used to be a little-used storeroom in a remote corner of the sprawling government edifice that was now the royal palace. For all most people in the palace knew, it still was.

"How may I serve you?" Gallgoid asked. He didn't say "Your Majesty." But he did go to his door, peer up and down the hall before shutting it, and move a chair into position for her. Nor did he go back behind his desk until she was seated.

"I want to ask you to do something," she said. "It's for

the good of the kingdom; but for the time being, no one else must know about it."

"I try always to act for the good of the kingdom," Gallgoid said. Gurun knew he'd once committed treason, but that was in the past and it couldn't concern her now.

"I want you to arrest a man named Vallach Vair and all his household," Gurun said. "He has been plotting against the king."

Gallgoid nodded. "I've heard this," he said.

"There is a slave woman in his house named Dakl. She must not be harmed in any way, but brought to me instead—secretly, if possible."

"I think it would be best if she were taken with the rest of the household and separated later," Gallgoid said. "Also, Vallach Vair has a wife, a son who is a young man but still lives in his father's house, and a daughter who is still a child. There are eight slaves in the household, including Dakl."

"You do know something about this!" said Gurun.

"It's my business to know. You know something, too; but I won't ask you how you came to know it. I'll arrest them all this evening, when they're home for supper."

"I don't like the idea of arresting the man's children."

"I won't hurt them," Gallgoid said.

"The chiefs complain that you know everything before they know it," Gurun said.

"That's my penance," Gallgoid said.

Vallach Vair was having jellied eels for supper. He liked rich foods, and it showed. But this was a supper that was never finished.

With no forewarning from his doorkeeper, eight men armed with short swords burst into his dining room. He very nearly choked.

"What's this!" he growled. The intruders wore no uniforms, no badges, and he took them right away for strong-arm robbers. "You're making a big mistake, whoever you are!" But he fell silent when he found a sword's point at his throat.

"Come with us, Vallach Vair. All of you, come. Don't struggle or try to escape, or you'll get hurt."

They forced him up from his seat. He had only time to see them doing the same to his wife and children before someone pulled a felt hood down over his head and tightened it around his neck; and then he could see nothing at all.

Gallgoid only entered the room after all the family had hoods over their faces and their wrists fettered.

"Those two in the first coach," he said, "the son and daughter in the second. Don't question them until I say so."

Outside on the street, a cart was already pulling away with Vallach's slaves huddled in it, cowed by two unsmiling men with swords. Fnaa's mother, Dakl, was in that cart.

Gallgoid had the family taken off in closed coaches, then made his own way back to the palace. His agents had heard things about Vallach Vair, but he wondered how Gurun could have heard them. He deemed it best, for the time being, to pretend he'd acted on his own initiative. He would keep Gurun out of it, if he could. It would be safer for her. Having served as an assassin for Lord Reesh, and his confederate in treason, Gallgoid understood the subtleties of such a situation.

When he got back to the palace, a surprise was waiting for him.

"They're dead, sir—both of them, man and wife," one of his agents told him. "They were dead when we opened the coach to take them out. They must have had poison hidden on their persons."

"I didn't expect that." Gallgoid shook his head, blaming himself. "Don't tell the son and daughter, or the slaves. Find a maid to keep the little girl company. I'll question the son myself.

"I want the slaves separated for now. They'll be questioned later. Don't hurt them or scare them any worse than they're scared already. But the woman named Dakl, bring her to my office and privately inform Queen Gurun—and no one else."

———

Gurun was in Gallgoid's office when one of his men brought Dakl there. Gallgoid dismissed him.

"You are Dakl, the slave?" he said. She nodded. He gestured to Gurun. "Do you know who this is?"

"My lady, the queen," said Dakl, and curtseyed. Fnaa looked like her, Gurun thought.

"Queen Gurun has asked for you to be her personal attendant," Gallgoid said. "I have not asked her why. But I will ask you something.

"We believe your master, Vallach Vair, planned treason against the king. We are sure he had partners in his scheme. Can you tell me their names and anything else about them? Take your time, and don't be afraid. The queen is your protector here, and no harm will come to you."

Dakl took a moment to think. Gurun admired her coolness. If she was afraid, it didn't show.

"My lord," she said at last, "there were men who came to my master's house to see him, and they talked about how they might remove the king and bring back the Oligarchy. I never heard how they meant to do it. They were careful not to be overheard, even by us slaves. But there were two men who once were oligarchs, named Lord Blamor and Lord Gower, and also Prester Gweyr, and a rich man, a merchant, Folo Oych. They were the ones who came most often. There were others who came once or twice, whose names I never knew. That's all I know, my lord."

Gallgoid took some notes, then looked up and nodded at her.

"You're free to go now, Dakl—with Queen Gurun. You'd be wise to serve her faithfully."

"I will, my lord."

When they were gone, Gallgoid sat and reviewed a longer list he'd already made. The names Dakl had given him were on it.

She hadn't told him everything she knew: he was sure of that. Gurun was hiding something, too, and had a reason for protecting her. What that reason might be, Gallgoid didn't know; nor did he want to know. Safer for Gurun if he didn't know, he thought. He could always find it out later, if he had to.

Meanwhile, he mused, Obann City was rotten with treason. It was only to be expected. The former oligarchs wanted to be oligarchs again. Many presters and lesser clergy wanted to rebuild the Temple.

All of this lay just below the surface of life in the city.

Deeper down, Gallgoid knew, was worse—much worse. Lord Reesh was dead, and there was no new First Prester; but the evil that he'd hatched lived on after him, and grew. No one knew that better than Gallgoid, who'd served Reesh almost to the end. Vallach Vair and his confederates were insects to be stepped on. Gallgoid would take care of them. But the deeper treason, Lord Reesh's legacy, now being fed and fostered by the new Thunder King far away in Kara Karram—

Gallgoid shook his head.

Gurun took Dakl first to her room, and when they were alone, told her, "Your son, Fnaa, is alive and well, and he has done what he set out to do."

Dakl had a firm mastery over herself. Even so, Gurun thought she saw every muscle in Dakl's body relax when she heard that news.

"My lady, I'm glad we've been of service!" she said.

"Don't be too glad, yet. More service has been asked of you." And Gurun told her that her son was even now living in the palace, impersonating the king—because the king had disappeared and no one knew what to do. "You will pretend to be his new handmaid; that way you can be with him. And you will both be safe, here in the palace."

Dakl dropped suddenly to one knee, seized Gurun's hand, and kissed it.

"Please don't!" Gurun said. "They call me a queen, but I'm not one. Not unless King Ryons marries me when he grows up—if we ever see him again. You are a slave no more, Dakl, and I am not your mistress. I'm a plain girl from Fogo

Island, which is so far from Obann, it might as well be an island in a dream. So you and I must help one another."

"We shall!" said Dakl. Her face lit up when she was happy, and it stopped being a slave face. "But noble is as noble does, as people say in Obann—my lady!"

"Come now and see your son. He has missed you."

Gurun didn't like to stand there, intruding, as mother and son rejoiced in one another in the king's bedchamber. She let herself out and did duty as a guard outside the door, sending the Ghol bodyguard away on some unnecessary errand.

"Well, that's that," she thought. "Gallgoid will catch all the villains, and the throne is saved—and no king to sit on it! All-Father," she prayed silently, "protect King Ryons and restore him to us, who love him. But for as long as it must be, let Fnaa be a convincing substitute."

CHAPTER 14

How Jack Showed Bold Again

With Gurun spending every possible minute with Fnaa, teaching him how to imitate King Ryons and keeping him away from the chiefs, who knew their king so well, Ellayne and Jack found themselves neglected.

"We might as well go home—not that anyone would notice if we did," Ellayne said. It was the morning after they'd told Obst all of Fnaa's secret. Obst hadn't been back to see them since; they had no idea of what he might be doing. "Anyone would think we were just ordinary stupid kids," she grumbled.

Jack pretended that that didn't bother him. It didn't irk him as much as it irked Ellayne, but it did get under his skin; and it troubled him more than it had irked him yesterday.

"I have a better idea than going home," he said. "As long as no one's paying any attention to us, why don't we go out and find the king? Wytt might be able to follow his trail."

That was about the boldest thing Ellayne had heard Jack say in quite some time, and she hardly knew how to answer him. She'd been afraid he was getting stodgy. Normally he would object that if God hadn't called them to do something—in a dream, say, or by the word of a prophet—then they were better off not doing it.

"Are you sure?" she said.

"Well, someone has to find him, and nobody here seems to be trying to do it," Jack answered. "Anyhow, we've done what we came here to do. I think you ought to write a letter to your father. Ask him to send Martis after us as soon as he can. We might need him."

That last remark clinched it. Jack was serious.

"I'll do it right away," Ellayne said. "Don't you think, maybe, we ought to get one of the Ghols to go with us? Or two of them?"

"We can't. We'd have to tell them all about Fnaa, and it'd ruin everything."

"I'll get that letter written now," said Ellayne.

Obst had not forgotten them. In fact, he was acting on something that they'd told him. As Jack and Ellayne made ready to leave Obann, Obst was conferring with Preceptor Constan, the scholar in charge of making true copies of the long-lost Ozias Scrolls from the cellar of Ozias' Temple. Constan had been slow to believe in the scrolls; but by now, after careful study, he did believe.

"Prester Lodivar, eh?" Constan had a stern but fleshy face, and he took his time about thinking things through. Obst waited patiently. "No," he said at last, "I've never heard of him."

"Are there any like him here in the city?" Obst asked.

"No. Not yet. But there will be." Constan sat like an ox chewing his cud; but he was chewing ideas. "There are men who want the Temple more than they want God," he said. "If they can't have the Temple in Obann, maybe they'll turn to this New Temple in the East. You know the Scriptures, Obst. Prophet Ika, 40th fascicle: 'Oh, my people! Unstable as water, as dead leaves blowing in the wind!' They haven't changed since then."

"But what shall we do?" Obst said. "I'd hoped to have the preaching of the Scriptures well under way in all the chamber houses by now. The people need instruction—not by us, but by the Word of God. Everything is taking so much more time than I thought it would."

"It always does," said Constan. "And now false preachers are rising up among us." He paused for at least a minute, maybe more. "I can't hurry the translation of the scrolls. True copies of the Old Books are being made as fast as humanly possible. Maybe the king should summon all the presters to the city for a conclave. They might be encouraged to get on with the preaching."

Obst's plan was to get a faithful copy of the Old Books into every chamber house in the land and have the presters preach and teach from these every time the people gathered for assembly. And the work of making copies would go on and on, until someday many people could have them in their homes.

But now, of course, the king was missing. An imposter held his place for him, and the people weren't any the wiser.

Obst sighed. "This is a matter requiring prayer," he said, "and plenty of it."

"I'll join you," Preceptor Constan said; and the two men bowed their heads together.

Jack and Ellayne knew nothing of Obst's labors. Wytt said he could follow Ryons and probably find him, and that was good enough.

Ellayne insisted on seeing Gurun first, and finally she had her way, although they had to wait all day—which made Jack fume about lost time. An hour after supper, a servant conducted them to the king's bedchamber and the Ghol outside let them in. Gurun made sure the door was firmly shut before she would allow anyone to say anything. Supposedly none of the Ghols spoke Obannese, but Gurun preferred to take no chances.

Fnaa sat up in bed and grinned at them. On the edge of the bed, close to him, sat a pretty, dark-haired woman.

"My mother!" he explained. "Queen Gurun rescued her, just like she said she would." Fnaa's mother got up and curtseyed to them. "Thank you for bringing my son into the palace," she said. "Although I never thought it would turn out like this!"

"I'm sorry you've been left so much alone, these two days," Gurun said. "It could not be helped. The chiefs have been told the king was sick, and they believe I'm taking care of him."

"Well, we just came to say good-bye," Ellayne said. "And I have a letter for my father, which I hope you'll send to him by special messenger so that it'll get to him before we do."

"Are you going home?" Fnaa asked. "I thought you were going to stay."

Here they would have been wise to confide in Gurun, who would have seen to it that they had horses, equipment, and maybe a Ghol archer or a Blay slinger to protect them. But they'd decided for secrecy. After all, the search might not amount to anything. Ryons' trail might peter out. But of course the real reason was that they hadn't liked being ignored: that was no way to treat the two chosen ones who'd climbed Bell Mountain. Obst would have warned them that such pride was ungodly and liable to be a snare to them and dangerous; but they hadn't confided in him, either.

"We might as well go home," Jack said. "There's not much we can do here."

"Fnaa will have to get out of bed soon and take up some of the duties of the king," Gurun said. "We were hoping you would help him."

"Maybe we'll be back soon," Ellayne said.

That night Wytt busied himself in sniffing out Ryons' trail, beginning at the door of the bedchamber. He darted from shadow to shadow like a rat, hiding from servants and bodyguards. It was late, and most of the people in the palace were in bed.

Very little remained of Ryons' scent. But there was another scent that went along with it, starting a few steps from the bedroom door, that the Omah followed eagerly. He could not have told you what kind of scent it was—just something mysterious, that elated him and made him want to know more. He thought it might be the scent of the shining man that the dogs and birds had seen; yet he hadn't been able to detect it inside the bedchamber. The anomaly sharpened his interest.

He followed it all through the palace. Outside, he picked up Cavall's scent and followed it out the city gate and down to the river. That was as far as he could go: it seemed the dog and Ryons had gone into the river. He scurried back to the palace, woke Ellayne in her bed, and told her all about it.

In the morning Gurun saw them off, making sure their packs were loaded with provisions and their pockets with money.

"I have already sent your letter on ahead of you, Ellayne," she said, "and I sent a letter of my own with it, telling your father that you have performed an important service to the king, but begging him not to ask you what it was. I don't want him to be very angry with you—as my father will be with me, if I ever see him again.

"The fewer who know our secret, the better. I wish you would let me send you home in a carriage, with a soldier for an escort."

"Thanks, but we won't need it," Ellayne said. "It's very peaceful all along the river, and the weather has been so fine. Besides, we like hiking."

Gurun let them go. Had they been older, they might have guessed they hadn't entirely deceived her. But the ferry service took them to the south bank of the river, and instead of following the road, they plunged into the reeds and pools beside the river and let Wytt out of Ellayne's pack. He whistled impatiently.

"Yes, yes—you won't be stuck in the pack for a while now," Ellayne answered him. "Now we're on the other side of the river. See if you can pick up Ryons' trail."

He gave her a big piece of his mind, but soon set out through the tall grass, sniffing it and peering at the roots. The children got their feet wet and muddy, and more than a few bug bites, following him.

By and by they came to a place where the reeds thinned out and the river had piled up a smooth, pebbly beach. A rowboat lay baking in the sun. Wytt hopped inside it and chirped triumphantly.

"Boy and dog were here!" he reported.

"So they crossed the river in this boat," Jack said. "Can you follow them from here, Wytt?"

"Dog makes strong smell—easy to follow," Wytt answered.

"We just might do it!" Jack said, as Wytt led them away from the boat—and away from the road, too, in a southeasterly direction. "As long as it doesn't rain and wash out the trail, and as long as we aren't caught by bandits, we just might catch the king."

"I hope it's not bad luck to say a thing like that," Ellayne said. "But at least," she thought, "we're doing something."

CHAPTER 15

How Ryons Escaped the Bandits

Angel, the hawk, found her master the king and recognized Cavall when she saw him. But they were traveling with a man, a stranger, and a gigantic bird that didn't fly. Angel stayed high up in the sky where she was safe, content to follow Ryons. She didn't care how much time passed. She wouldn't come down while that man was with him.

"There's a hawk up there, been following us all day," Perkin said, as he and Ryons trekked across the plain. It was their second day together. Cavall and Baby were at peace with one another, although neither got too close to the other.

Ryons looked up and just barely made out a little black dot circling overhead. He almost blurted out, "I have a hawk," but didn't. "Why should a hawk want to follow us?" he asked.

"It's not something a hawk would normally do," Perkin said. "You don't see many of them out here on the plains. Buzzards are more likely: looking to feed on something that's died. But hawks prefer wooded country."

"How far are we from Lintum Forest?"

"Still four or five days, if the good weather holds."

Ryons liked Perkin, partly because the man asked so few questions, sparing him the work of inventing lies. Had he been a little older, the man's lack of curiosity would have struck him as strange.

Perkin was deadly with his sling. He killed a plump rabbit for their supper, dropped it with a single stone when it was a good fifty paces from them and scampering around. He bagged another rabbit for Cavall and some strange kind of animal that he gave to Baby. It looked like an overgrown woodchuck or an undergrown bear.

"I've seen a lot of strange animals, the last two years or so," he said. "They all seem to be coming up from the South. I wonder what made them move."

Obst said it was God who'd brought the strange animals into the country as a sign of the times, a sign of change. "He will not let the world remain the way it is," Obst said. "He brought down the Temple and He made you a king. And it's only the beginning."

Around the middle of the afternoon, Baby grew restive. He pranced around with his head held high, yellow eyes glaring, tiny wings fidgeting.

"He smells something that he doesn't like," Perkin said. "Bandits on horseback, probably."

"But Cavall hasn't scented anything," Ryons said.

"These big birds have better sniffers than any dog. Besides, they're higher off the ground and get a better taste of the wind."

But then Cavall barked; he'd caught a scent, too. Perkin

surprised Ryons by lying down on his belly and pressing an ear to the ground.

"Horsemen, all right," he said, "and plenty of 'em, too." He pushed himself up onto his knees. "Too many for the four of us."

"What'll we do?" Ryons cried: for the Thunder King had sworn to burn his eyes out and throw him into a dungeon forever. He couldn't help remembering that more often than he liked.

"We can hurry to a place I know and go underground. Come on."

Ryons couldn't possibly keep up with the long-legged wanderer, so Perkin scooped him up and made him ride piggyback. Cavall stopped barking, but all the hair along his back was standing up, which meant the brigands were getting closer.

Perkin ran toward a low, grassy hill, not really high enough to be a hill at all. Inkbushes grew all around it.

At the base of the hill, the man forced his way through the bushes. Ryons saw a black hole in front of them. Perkin put him down and said, "Crawl in—the dog, too. I'll be right behind you."

"What about Baby?"

"He won't fit. His speed will save him." He turned to the bird and made a harsh sound. Baby squawked once and ran away; and Ryons crawled into the hole.

After the bright sunlight on the plain, he couldn't see a thing. Instead of dirt, his hands made contact with something as hard as stone and as smooth as glass. Jack and Ellayne had told him about places like this; they'd been in some of them. They were places left over from ancient times.

In one such place they'd met Wytt; but Ryons didn't like the thought of running into wild Omah in the dark, underground. All he could do was to keep crawling and hope for the best. He heard Cavall behind him, panting, his claws clicking against the slick surface.

"Just in time," Perkin said, somewhere behind him. "I can't see them all, but there must be at least twenty riders out there. Be quiet now and keep on crawling—and don't let the dog bark."

Cavall wasn't the kind of dog who barked at the wrong time. Ryons wished he could turn around and see. Before he could try, his hands shot out from under him and he slid down an incline. Somehow he managed not to cry out.

He didn't slide far. It was over before he realized what had happened. He slid hands-first into a wall, and only just missed a nasty knock in the head. And then he discovered that it wasn't dark around him anymore.

He was in some kind of chamber. Overhead, a round hole let in the light. It also let in the sound of horses' hooves and men's voices. He heard someone call out in Wallekki, "It's no use, they must have gone another way—we've lost them."

Ryons lay perfectly still. If he could hear the bandits, they would hear him if he made enough noise. He saw Cavall's head and shoulders emerge from a narrow tunnel. Slipping and skidding, the dog slid into the chamber and sat down next to Ryons. There they stayed until they heard no more sound of men or horses.

"Stay there," Perkin called. "I'll make sure they're gone."

Ryons let out a sigh. His muscles were in knots without

him knowing it, and now they relaxed. Now, too, he took some note of his surroundings.

There was just enough space for him to stand. He could touch the ceiling, but the hole was at the end of a circular shaft. A chimney? But no—this was too small for any kind of living space. It was empty, too. Ryons looked for writing on the walls, or pictures, but there wasn't any.

Perkin came sliding down the tunnel and landed feet first. He was too tall to stand up in here.

"They're gone," he said.

"What is this place?" asked Ryons. "We would've been trapped if they'd seen us go in. They could have smoked us out like bees."

"Good thinking, Ryons—you've got a head on your shoulders." Perkin patted his arm. "But I know something about this place that nobody else knows. Stand aside."

He crawled to the opposite wall, felt around until he found something, and suddenly slid it down like the lid of a jewel box. This revealed a dark shaft, and on the far wall of the shaft, the rungs of a ladder.

"See?" he said. "If we'd had to, we would have climbed down that ladder. The rungs are bolted to the shaft. I'd have pushed up this panel again, and they never would've found us."

"But how did you ever find the secret passage?"

"I've spent a few nights here in bad weather. I get curious about things. I looked around, and felt around, until I found the sliding panel. I knew there had to be more to this place than what I saw."

"What's down there?" Ryons asked. He couldn't take his eyes off the shaft.

"If you want to climb down with me, I'll show you."

"Won't it be too dark to see anything?"

"You'll see."

Perkin maneuvered himself into the shaft, which took some doing, and began to climb down the ladder. "We'll be back," Ryons told Cavall, and followed Perkin down the shaft.

The rungs were made of iron or steel, and so firmly attached to the wall that they didn't move at all. It was dark in the shaft, but not quite as dark as the darkest moonless night in the middle of a forest. Ryons climbed carefully, and with each step of his descent, it seemed just a little bit less dark. He climbed for what seemed a very long time before his feet touched a floor; and by then he could just make out Perkin waiting for him.

"Where does the light come from?" he wondered.

Perkin pointed upward. Ryons looked and saw a high ceiling studded with what looked like an uncountable host of little stars; but they weren't by any means as bright as stars.

"I don't know what those are," Perkin said. "I haven't found a way to climb up and get a closer look at them. All I know is, they give just enough light to see by.

"This is one of those places left over from old times, before the Day of Fire. It's big—almost like an underground city. I don't know how big it is. I've only explored a tiny bit of it. I've found some dead men's bones, here and there. I've heard rats, although I've never seen them. There may be treasure down here, or there may be nothing. I think it would take a long time to explore this place."

Ryons slowly turned, trying to see everything he could.

Tall, rectangular columns supported the ceiling. The vast floor, what he could see of it, was bare. Except for their voices, silence reigned here. A Wallekki would have called this place the palace of a djinn, and died of fright. But in the wordless awe that filled the boy's heart, fright had to stand aside, powerless to move him.

And then Perkin astonished him by dropping to one knee, taking one of his hands, and kissing it.

"King Ryons," he said, "accept my homage!"

"How did you know?" Ryons asked. He'd tried to deny it, but those denials hadn't fazed Perkin, who remained kneeling.

"An old man told me you'd be coming and how to know you when I saw you," Perkin said. "He was a servant of God, and he knew everything that was in my heart. I never met anyone like him before."

"I know him, too," Ryons said, nodding. It didn't occur to him to doubt a word of it. "He told me God wanted me to go to Lintum Forest. He helped me get out of the palace without anybody seeing me. And then he was gone—just like that. But why didn't you tell me you knew who I was when we first met?"

"I didn't want to scare you. I thought it best to give you some time to get used to me. And I wanted to be sure of you. A king should have courage—which you have."

"I don't know about that!" Ryons said. "So many crazy things have happened to me. I wish I knew why I'm supposed to go to Lintum Forest."

"God knows why," Perkin said, "and you'll know, too,

when God thinks the time is right. But we'd better be on our way again. Come, let's see if we can find Baby. I'd hate to lose him."

CHAPTER 16

A Night on the Plain

Martis returned to Ninneburky the day after Roshay Bault received the letters from his daughter and Gurun.

"Don't get comfortable," the baron said. "You've got to go straight to Obann—but first read these!"

Martis read Gurun's letter first, and the last paragraph twice: "I am not entirely sure the children mean to go straight back to Ninneburky, so I have sent two trackers after them, two of my Blays, who will protect them. I cannot think where they might go, if not to Ninneburky. Maybe I worry for nothing. I pray that you will see them soon."

"I'd give gold to know what was the important service that those kids performed in Obann that had to be kept a secret from me, her father," Roshay said.

"Ellayne has a valiant spirit," Martis said; but there was already, he sensed, something in this to be dreaded.

"I'll give her a valiant spirit!" Roshay grumbled. "I'm responsible for the defense and good order of this entire district. I can't go chasing my daughter all around the country. But here, read her letter." And Martis read:

"Dear Father, Jack and I can't come home yet. Please don't be angry. If you can, please send Martis after us. Maybe he can pick up our trail. He should go to Obann and see Queen Gurun first. Maybe she will tell him something that we're not allowed to tell." There was more, but that was the important part.

"I should have been here," Martis said. "I should have kept my oath."

"It's her fault, man, not yours. Just find her, if you can."

"I would have had to go to Obann in any event," Martis said, almost to himself. "There's devilish trouble brewing in the East."

"I know," said Roshay. "That's why I have to stay here to raise and train militia. I suppose another Heathen army will be coming this way soon."

Martis shook his head. "They aren't ready to send another army yet. But what they couldn't win by force of arms, they hope to win by treachery. Be on the lookout for any man who preaches the New Temple.

"The Thunder King's armies are busy now, trying to stamp out revolts throughout the East. Before he sends them our way again, he hopes to divide and weaken us somehow. I've heard all sorts of rumors, but I couldn't stay to find out how much truth there was to them. Hlah will have to do that, if he can. For me, the only thing now is to find those children—which I will do, Baron, or die."

Roshay sighed. "If only I'd known they'd gone to Obann! My riders could have caught them. What in the world are those cuss't kids up to!"

What they were up to at the moment was trying to sleep in the daytime, in a shady little hollow under a clump of wild pecan trees.

Wytt insisted on it. During the day, he said, there were men on horseback riding up and down the country. "See! Look! They make tracks; they make a smell." He made his point by showing Ellayne a pile of dung she'd almost stepped on without noticing.

"We're far from the road," Jack said. "The Attakotts won't be patrolling around here. No more towns, no farms—I don't think anybody lives out here. We don't want to meet any of those men on horseback."

Ellayne knew geography a lot better than Jack did. Wytt had been following Cavall's tracks and scent all the way from Obann, and by now Ellayne thought she knew where they were going.

"If we keep on this way," she said, "we'll wind up in Lintum Forest. And I'll bet that's where Ryons and Cavall are going."

"Why should they go there?"

"We'll have to ask him when we see him."

Wytt went hunting and came back with a grasshopper impaled on his sharp stick, and news. He ate the grasshopper; Ellayne looked away and tried to ignore the crunching noise. Then he delivered his news.

"Two men on foot," he said, "all dead now. Horsemen killed them. They made a fight first, killed one of the horsemen."

"Where?" Ellayne cried. Her pulse raced, and all hope of sleeping fled.

"Not far." But it had all happened some hours ago, and the horsemen had ridden off in another direction. There was no danger, for the moment.

"What did the men on foot look like, Wytt?" Jack asked. But to Wytt all big people, except the ones he knew personally, looked alike. "They had a drink with a funny smell," he reported. The children would have recognized it as the smell of tea, but not Wytt. And of course they couldn't know that those were the two Blays whom Gurun had sent to watch over them.

"Well, we knew it might be dangerous," Jack said.

"I wonder if we could get back to the road," Ellayne said. Jack shot a look at her. A remark like that wasn't like her, not a bit.

"If you want to go back, we will," he said.

She sighed. "No—I guess not. Ryons is out here, too, with just Cavall for company. We can't give up on him."

"We'll be safer, traveling by night," Jack said.

Ryons and Perkin camped that night on a hilltop, under a lofty, lonely oak tree. They had a cheery fire. Perkin said the Heathen wouldn't come any closer to these hills than they had to. "They have their own stories about the Day of Fire," he said. "They know these aren't natural hills. There's a curse on all such places, they believe."

But the presence of the oak tree was a good sign, he said. It meant they were getting closer to the forest. "Oaks don't normally grow out here. A bird must have dropped an acorn on this spot, once upon a time. That acorn came from Lintum Forest."

Baby took some time settling down. He stalked the hilltop, looking for nobody knew what. The smell of roasting rabbit finally lured him back to the fire. He rattled his feathers and settled down beside Perkin, probably tired because he'd had to climb the hill. And after supper, Perkin told the story of his life—some of it, at least.

"I wasn't always a wanderer," he said. "I was born and raised in Caryllick. Ever been there? It's a nice town. We have a lovely chamber house and our own little seminary. I was a student there. My father was a reciter in the chamber house and wanted me to be a prester someday."

They studied the Commentaries, the New Books. It awakened in Perkin a desire for the Old Books, the holy Scriptures themselves.

"But they wouldn't teach us from the Scriptures," he said. "I never understood why. It seemed the preceptors couldn't be bothered with God's word. They said we wouldn't understand it. We'd have to go to the great seminary in Obann, they said, if we wanted to learn about the Scriptures.

"And I got to wondering why, for all my studying, I wasn't getting to know God any better. In fact, I got to wondering if there even was a God. He certainly wasn't in our seminary.

"So I left. I didn't know, anymore, what I wanted out of life. I went out onto the plains to be by myself. Don't know why I did that; it just seemed the only thing to do. That's how I became a wanderer."

Ryons thought of Obst, who left his seminary studies in Obann and went to Lintum Forest to become a hermit. But Obst had brought a Book of Scriptures with him and spent years and years studying it.

"Out here," Perkin said, "the thought crept up on me that there really is a God and that we never hear Him because we don't know how to listen. We never see Him because we don't know where to look. And I remembered a verse from Prophet Ika, a famous verse that's cited in many of the Commentaries: 'Because they will not honor me, I have drawn a veil of folly over their eyes so that they cannot see, and put a buzzing in their ears so that they cannot hear, and clouded their minds with self-love so that they cannot understand. But one day they shall see with their eyes and hear with their ears, and understand their faults; and all shall be astonished, and some shall repent; and I shall save them.'"

He talked like Obst, Ryons thought; and in his own heart, now, he hungered for the Scriptures. But he hadn't yet learned how to read them. Everyone was so busy in Obann, and there was never time for anyone to teach him.

Perkin went on. "I don't know how it happened. Walking all around, seeing what there is to see, trying to count the stars by night, listening to the birds by day, being out in all kinds of weather—well, it was sort of like I just woke up one morning and knew that God was here, and that He'd been here all the time, and always would be. And for God, 'here' means everywhere."

He sighed, leaned back, and rested against Baby. Pleased, the great bird shut its eyes.

"I still haven't read the Scriptures, though," said Perkin. "Never had a book, you see. Ain't likely I'll ever see one, either."

I know where we can get one," Ryons said. "I mean, in Lintum Forest." Obst had a cabin in the forest. He meant to take Ryons there and teach him the Scriptures, but never had the opportunity to do it. Maybe the book was still there.

Helki would know. "Could you read it, if we had it?"

Perkin grinned. "I'd make it my business to read it, Your Majesty!" There was something about the way he said "Your Majesty" that made Ryons laugh out loud, and the way Ryons laughed made Perkin laugh. Cavall raised up his head and wagged his tail.

Down below on the plain, in the dark, some creature howled: something much bigger than a wolf. Cavall stood up and went stiff all over. Baby opened one eye.

"What was that?" Ryons said.

"Don't know. But it won't come up here while we have a fire, so don't be afraid. The Lord will get us to Lintum Forest, sure enough."

Ryons believed, and his fear subsided.

Hiking by night, Ellayne and Jack heard something very similar and froze in their tracks. Wytt stood on tiptoe, sniffing the air.

"Big animal," he chirped, "with bad smell."

"What kind of animal?" Jack whispered.

"Don't know." That he didn't know troubled Wytt deeply. "I go see." And before Ellayne could stop him, he scampered off through the tall grass.

"Fry him!" she said. "What does he think he's doing?"

He's doing the same kind of thing we did in coming out here in the first place, Jack thought, but didn't say so. "He'll be all right," he said. "We'd better wait for him."

They sat down, hoping the grass would hide them from any hunting beast. Ellayne wanted to say more, but Jack convinced her not to: "We'd better be as quiet as we can."

They listened hard, but the howl was not repeated. Jack looked up and saw a shooting star. After an inordinately long time, Wytt startled them by jumping out of the grass right in front of them.

"Do you have to do that!" Ellayne hissed.

"No fear, animal's gone," was his answer.

"What was it? Did you see it?" Jack asked.

"I saw." According to Wytt, the creature was something like a bear only much bigger, with forelegs much longer than its hind legs and massive, wicked jaws like a badger's. It smelled like a badger, too, Wytt thought. Jack didn't like the sound of that.

"I wonder why it howled," he said.

"Oh, who cares! Let's get going," Ellayne said. "We have to find a place where it'll be safe for us to sleep tomorrow—if we can. I wish we had some weapons!" They had knives and Jack's slingshot, but they didn't count, Ellayne thought. She would have preferred something like Abombalbap's great sword, along with an armored knight to wield it.

CHAPTER 17

The King's Procession

"I don't know how to ride a horse," Fnaa said.

"Just keep your feet in the stirrups and your legs clamped tightly against its body," Gurun told him. "And wave at the people and look happy."

The king had been sick long enough, and it was time his people saw him; so today Fnaa was to make the king's regular ride around the city. Gurun would be right beside him, and several of his Ghols close by to keep him safe. How they would keep him safe from falling off the horse, Fnaa didn't know.

Dakl had seen King Ryons on several such occasions. "Don't worry," she told her son. "The king himself never looked at ease on horseback. And everyone knows you've been sick, so they won't expect too much."

At the appointed time in the morning, Gurun took Fnaa down to the royal stables, and old Chagadai practically lifted him onto the horse. Happily for Fnaa, she was a wise old mare who had learned to be patient with the boy king's clumsiness. Her name was Dandelion, for her yellow mane and tail.

It was a small procession that rode out of the palace. A servant in gorgeous red and silver livery led the way on foot. His job was to call out again and again, "Make way for King

Ryons, King of Obann by the grace of God!" Then came one of General Hennen's men in shining mail, mounted on a great black charger and carrying the royal banner, and after him a pair of knights with gleaming swords.

Fnaa and Gurun followed, side by side, with Chagadai and half a dozen Ghols bringing up the rear. No shining mail for them: they went in worn-out leather leggings and tunics, with their bows in their hands. The people of Obann didn't like them, but there was no leaving them behind. The boy king was their "father," and they went with him wherever he went.

"Smile!" Gurun said.

They paraded down the middle of the city's broadest streets. People stopped to watch and cheer and wave. "Queen Gurun! Long live the queen!" was what Fnaa heard most often. Still, there were more than a few glad cries of "Ryons! Ryons!" And several men and women cried out, "Feeling better, Majesty?" It wasn't long before Fnaa didn't have to force his smiles anymore. He almost forgot to worry about falling off the horse.

"They like us—they really do," he thought. True, it was Ryons that they liked, not him. But they thought he was Ryons. No one seemed to have the slightest doubt of it. The people waved at him and Fnaa waved back. With Gurun and the servants and the chieftains to do all the real work, he thought, being king wasn't such a bad arrangement. It was better than having to play the fool all day in Vallach Vair's house.

The little procession had just turned onto Market Street when someone, somewhere, sounded a harshly blaring horn. The people along the street looked up, for the sound seemed to come from above. Fnaa looked up, too—just in time to see a human body flung from the roof of a warehouse.

It never hit the ground. There was a rope around the neck, tied to something on the roof, and the body jerked to a stop and bounced against the wall. Bystanders screamed. Fnaa stared. The procession halted.

"A man has hanged himself!" said Gurun. And the Ghols crowded around Fnaa to shield him with their bodies and nocked arrows to their bowstrings. The two knights with the swords made their horses rear up, which kept the people at a safe distance.

The last glimpse Fnaa got of the limp body dangling from the rope was of some white things floating away from it, fluttering down to the street, where people ran to pick them up. Then Chagadai laid a hand on his shoulder and spoke something Gholish into his ear, which Fnaa didn't understand. But Gurun did.

"He says it's not a real body," she translated. "He urges you to show no fear at all."

"I'm not afraid," Fnaa said. He was confused, not frightened. "But let's not stay here."

Gurun signaled to the knights, the banner-bearer, and the crier. They cleared the way and got the procession moving again. Fnaa waved to the people, but knew better than to smile. No one had to tell him that the strange incident at the warehouse had upset the people's mood.

"What's it all about?" he wondered.

"We'll find out later," Gurun said. "Someone has already hauled the dummy back onto the roof. But don't let the people see you gawking at it."

By mid-afternoon Gallgoid's men had collected some of the white things that had fluttered down from the warehouse roof. They were pieces of white cloth with messages written on them. These he displayed to the chiefs and Gurun at the end of the day. For the benefit of the chiefs who could not read Obannese (most of them), Gallgoid read the messages aloud.

"They are short, my lords, but to the point," he said. "For instance: 'No Temple, no God in Obann!' And 'The Lord's New Temple has risen in the East.' And 'Your prayers are not heard, Obann.'

"I myself knew of this," said Gallgoid, "when I was in Lord Reesh's service. Lord Reesh was to be First Prester at the New Temple, built by the Thunder King at Kara Karram. This was to replace the Temple in Obann. This Temple was to be subservient to the Thunder King. But someday, Lord Reesh said, the Thunder King would die, and then the New Temple would come into its own. It would become the Temple for the whole world, on both sides of the mountains."

Shaffur, the Wallekki chieftain, scowled. "What do we care for the words of a traitor?" he said.

"My lord, I admit I was a traitor," Gallgoid answered. "I helped Lord Reesh betray our Temple to the Heathen. Prester Orth was also his confederate. It's because I was a traitor that I know things that will serve you now.

"Lord Reesh and the Thunder King were killed in the avalanche at the Golden Pass. There is a new Thunder King now, claiming to be the same King Thunder that we knew before, the man at the Golden Pass being but a servant. To the people of Obann he offers his New Temple in the place of the one that was destroyed. You'll hear much more of this, as time goes by. What effect it will have on the people of this city, no one knows."

Chief Zekelesh spoke up. "Where is the king? He should be here, if only just to listen and to learn."

"He is having his supper," said Gurun.

Uduqu, chief of the Abnaks, rose from his chair. "I'll go see him," he said. "It did my heart good to see him go riding today. Anyhow, I don't know what we can do about those messages. Who can understand city people?"

"My lord, I'll try to find out who wrote them," Gallgoid said. "Whatever you decide to do about it then, it would best be done quietly."

"Call me when the fighting starts," said Uduqu.

One thing Fnaa liked about being king was that they fed you well. This evening he dined on fresh-caught catfish from the river and honey-cakes and watered wine. He had his meal on a table in his bedchamber with his mother supposedly waiting on him, but, once the door was shut, dining with him to keep him company. He told her about his ride through the city. He knew the matter troubled her, but for his sake she put on a good face. "Just some fool playing a stupid prank," she said.

They were just about finished with their supper when Gurun came in with Uduqu.

Of all the king's councilors, Uduqu was the one Fnaa feared the most. They sang a song about him in the city, of how he'd cut two men in half with one sweep of a sword. There were those who swore they saw him do it. Long ago, some enemy warrior had tried to break out Uduqu's brains with an axe; the wound healed in a way that made the tattooed face even more fearsome to behold. Fnaa's supper shifted in his stomach when he saw him. But Uduqu sat down on the king's bed as if it were his own.

"I don't know about Your Majesty," he said, "but sometimes I miss my old deer-hide tent, and sitting around the fire with the other chiefs, smoking tree-beans like we did when we were boys. Those were good days, weren't they?"

Fnaa wished the old Abnak would leave. What was he doing here? But Uduqu didn't leave.

"I remember how you used to sass us—and you were still a slave!" he said. "Poor Obst, he would just about faint every time you did it. But it always made us laugh, and we all agreed that you were talking like an Abnak. Don't you remember?"

He had to say something; so Fnaa said, "I'm sorry, I don't remember anything."

"Of course you don't," said Uduqu. "How could you remember those things? You're not Ryons."

Those words made for a perfect stillness in the room. Fnaa could not have answered if his life depended on it. The corners of his mother's mouth went tight.

"My lord—" Gurun started to say; but when Uduqu looked her in the eye, she couldn't finish.

"I want to know where King Ryons is," he said. "I'm mighty fond of that boy, and he's our king—God gave him to us. This boy here—" he jerked his head at Fnaa—"fooled me for a while. But you couldn't keep it up forever. He looks like Ryons as one pea looks like another, but looks aren't everything."

Fnaa saw Gurun's face go pale. He hadn't thought she could be afraid of anything, but she was afraid now.

Dakl got up from the little table and bowed her head to Uduqu.

"My lord," she said, "you mustn't blame the queen for anything. True, this is not King Ryons, but my own son. Let your anger fall on us, and not Queen Gurun."

"Ha! Who said I was angry?" Uduqu answered. He grinned at Gurun. "You ought to know I'd never think you'd do anything against the king. I know you wouldn't harm a hair on his head, no more than I would. But tell me why this boy is here, and not the king! At my age, I know how to keep a secret; and I'll lift the scalp of any man who twitches a finger against you. And will you two women please sit down!"

Fnaa and Dakl let Gurun tell the tale, all of it. Uduqu listened without interrupting.

"So, as you can see," she finished, "the city is full of treason. I was afraid of what might happen if it became known the king was missing. Where he has gone, no one knows. Obst said he went willingly and took his dog, Cavall, with him."

Uduqu rubbed the knotted scar on his forehead. "So Obst knew about this, and he didn't tell me," he said. "But what about Gallgoid? Does he know, too?"

"If he does, I have not told him," Gurun said.

"You were wise, girl. This city is a hornets' nest, and easily stirred up. But someone has to find the king, and I don't see anyone trying to do it."

"No one knows where to look. And Obst says we must wait for God to give us guidance."

Uduqu spent some moments pondering. "Chagadai ought to be told," he said. "Otherwise he'll figure it out for himself, sooner or later. But if we can't trust the Ghols, we can't trust anyone."

"It seems to me," said Gurun, "that God took Ryons out of this city to protect him, that he was in danger here."

"Which means that I'm in danger now!" Fnaa blurted out.

"I think," said Uduqu, "that probably we all are."

CHAPTER 18

"By Commandment of the First Prester"

Now that he had an Obannese wife and a baby son on the west side of the mountains, Hlah the son of Spider found himself on the eastern slopes, scouting in the service of King Ryons.

Hlah was one of that Heathen army that converted to belief in God and fought against the Thunder King. Until he fell sick, got well again, married, and had a child, it had been his dream to return to the Abnaks' country and proclaim God there. He was there now, but for a different purpose: to try to find out the enemy's plans. For no one believed the Great Man in the East would ever leave Obann at peace.

Every rumor led him on and on toward Silvertown. When he crossed back over to the west side of the mountains, he would be there. A Heathen army occupied the place, having captured the city and gutted it with fire.

"You'll have to go to Silvertown," a Wallekki trader told him, days ago. "Then you'll see why the northern clans don't rise against King Thunder—much as they would like to!"

The Abnaks had risen. There were no more mardars in the foothills to compel obedience to the Thunder King. Up and down the valley of the Green Snake River, the Fazzan tribes had thrown off the yoke. King Thunder's invasion of Obann, and the disaster of it, had shaken his power over many nations.

But not here. On the mountain paths that led to Silvertown, Hlah saw bodies hanged from trees; and on some of the trees were nailed placards. Upon them, in Obannese, were written messages, most of them concluding with the words, "By Commandment of the First Prester."

Now Hlah knew that First Prester was the title of the highest official of the Temple in Obann. There was no more Temple in Obann, and no First Prester. But the dead bodies warned him to proceed cautiously. As an Abnak and a hunter, Hlah stayed off the paths and melted into the underbrush, becoming invisible and silent whenever he heard a cart or a squad of warriors coming.

At the top of the pass he came upon a woman weeping by a tree. Above her dangled the body of a man. The woman waved a leafy branch, trying to keep the ravens off the man. Because she was all alone and he was curious, Hlah stepped out of the woods. He picked up a stick, threw it, and clouted a raven. He roared at them and they flew away. They'd be back, but not immediately.

"May God uphold you," he said to the woman. Hlah spoke perfect Obannese, with a mountain accent.

"Thank you." She wiped tears from her eyes. Her face was dirty. She waved at the body. "This was my husband," she said. She wanted to say more, but couldn't.

Hlah read the placard on the tree. "Behold: This one rebelled against the Temple. Hanged by Commandment of the First Prester."

"There is no First Prester anymore," Hlah said. "How can this thing be?"

The woman shook her head. "There's a New Temple somewhere in the East. That's what they say. There's a man in Silvertown who calls himself First Prester—a monster who delights in the Heathen and drinks the blood of his own people." She took a closer look at Hlah. "But who are you, that you look like an accursed Abnak and yet show kindness to me?"

"I serve God," Hlah said. "The Temple in the East is not a temple to the Lord, and any man who pretends to be First Prester is worse than a Heathen. God will punish them, who do such things."

"God has forgotten us," the woman said.

She couldn't tell him any more; she wouldn't leave the tree; and there was nothing he could do for her, so Hlah went on his way to Silvertown. He would have to go some distance down the mountain. This he accomplished in two more days, taking care that no one should see him.

Finally he looked down on Silvertown. He'd seen it once before, a prosperous city with a stout stone wall, the center of Obann's mining operations in the mountains.

Now it was a sprawling jumble of huts and tents and the frames of burned-out buildings. Some half-baked effort had been made to restore the wall, resulting in a haphazard pile of stones. Most of them were raised around a log fort of some kind, which looked new and clumsily constructed.

Above all else it was an army camp, and a big one. Hlah recognized the standards of half a dozen Wallekki clans flapping from poles. He smelled their stabled horses and their cooking fires.

He saw Zephites in their horned helmets that made them look like bulls, and black men from the distant South with their short spears and cowhide shields, and warriors from assorted nations around the Great Lakes—many thousands of men, all told. It was fear of this army, he thought, that held the Wallekki in submission. It could just as easily march east as west.

One thing he didn't see was any sign of Abnaks. But there were gangs of Obannese men toiling on the tracks that led west, laboring to improve them into roads fit for the great machines of war. The whole scene reminded him of a very busy ant hill.

Where, he wondered, was the new First Prester? How had he become First Prester? He would have to talk to people, to find out. But with the Abnaks in revolt against the Thunder King, it wouldn't do for him to get too close to the city. Some of the warriors down there were Zamzu, eaters of men. Hlah had seen them do it.

He spent many more minutes studying the place, fixing everything in his memory. Then, staying away from the paths, he began his trek down the mountain.

At the same time, Martis was in the tent city at Cardigal, buying provisions for the rest of his journey to Obann. He would have to talk to Gurun before he could begin searching for Jack and Ellayne. She might know something that could help him find them. She would at least know why they'd gone to Obann in the first place.

As he turned from a stall where he'd just bought oats for Dulayl, his horse, a little girl accosted him. She was younger than Ellayne and carried an earthen cup in her hand.

"Give to the New Temple, mister?" she said.

"What new temple is that?" he asked; but apparently she didn't know, because she only shrugged.

"Here, you!" said the man who sold the oats. "Don't you go bothering people with that nonsense!" And the little girl turned and ran away.

"What was she talking about?" Martis asked.

"Oh, that's one of Prester Lodivar's little beggars," the man said. "They say there's a New Temple being built, way out in Heathen lands—as if anyone could have a proper temple there! Wicked foolishness, I call it."

"Cardigal's prester is doing this?" Martis wondered.

The man spat on the ground. "He may be some folks' prester, but he's none of mine," he said. "We had our own prester—and a fat lot of good he was to us—ran away from town when the Heathen came, and hasn't been seen or heard from since. This fellow Lodivar, I don't know where he comes from. But the Temple's burned down and there's no First Prester, so I don't know who could've sent him here. Sent himself, I guess. And now he's raking in money from travelers and such who don't know any better. If you ask me, he's just a common cheat who ought to be horsewhipped out of town."

Martis would have liked to learn more, but he'd already stayed too long in Cardigal. He fed a ration of oats to Dulayl and continued his ride to Obann.

The fine weather held; Perkin was excellent company; and Ryons was enjoying himself. Perkin was teaching him how to use a sling, and Ryons, in dribs and drabs, told Perkin of all the adventures he'd had since that day Obst was first brought to the Heathen camp where Ryons was a slave. From time to time he worried about the friends he'd left behind in Obann, but there was nothing he could do about that. Besides, he'd gotten to the point where he could touch Baby without cringing. Cavall didn't seem to think much of that, but he was too wise to start a jealous confrontation with a giant bird.

"There's just one thing that troubles me," said Perkin. "That hawk up there—it's been following us for three days. Every time I look up, there it is. It's not natural for a hawk to do that."

It would have elated Ryons to know it was his own hawk, Angel, watching over him at Queen Gurun's command. But of course she was too high up in the sky for him to recognize her.

"It can't hurt us, can it?" he said.

"Not unless you believe those old stories about witches being able to spy on people by looking through the eyes of birds! No, it can't hurt us. But I don't like it when I don't understand a thing. The plain looks peaceful," Perkin said, "but it's not. You have to be careful out here."

"I know." Ryons remembered a beast he called a death-dog. He and Cavall had met it on their way to Obann. It would have killed them both, had it not been scared away by the bellow of the great beast that God had sent to guard him—the great beast that he rode to the rescue of Obann. He wondered where the great beast was now.

At midday they climbed a high hill that looked eastward, and Perkin pointed to a smudge on the horizon.

"Lintum Forest," he said. "Another three days' march will get us there."

"Then we'll look for Helki," Ryons said.

"The man who killed the giant, I heard about that. Wish I'd seen it."

Perkin wanted to camp atop the hill, the safest place for miles around, he said. Baby had had a very hard time climbing up with them—he wasn't built for it—and needed rest.

"You're quite a strider for your age, Majesty," he added, "but you look like you could use a rest, too. And up here is the best place for it."

Ryons found a patch of blackberries, which made a pleasing addition to their supper. Knowing this was no natural hill, it seemed odd to him that anything so nice and natural as blackberries should grow on it. And as they ate, and as the sun went down, Perkin told him a few stories from the New Books—how all the Empire was destroyed in a day, yet God preserved a remnant of all the nations so that the human race might live. Maybe it was the stories that inspired the dream Ryons had that night, or maybe not.

He lay awake on his back, looking up at all the stars, and didn't realize he'd fallen asleep because he slid so easily into the dream, and it picked up where reality left off.

It began with him admiring the stars, and then all around him grew up tall, dark shapes like the trunks of impossibly gigantic trees. All was silent. Then lights began to appear within the shapes, lights as many as the stars, and even brighter: red and blue and green lights, too.

Ryons watched, amazed, as other lights appeared, lights that traveled silently, sedately, back and forth across the night sky. He looked harder and saw that some of those were lighted windows, like the windows of rich men's carriages on the streets of Obann. But these carriages traversed the sky and needed no horses to pull them. He watched intently, and then he saw there were people inside the carriages, people calmly sitting as they were being carried through the sky. It was a wonderful thing to see.

The sky turned grey with the coming dawn, and Ryons could see the carriages themselves. They were as big as houses! Houses that flew like arrows …

And then, for no reason, it was suddenly on his lips to cry out a warning, to spring to his feet and wave his arms, and yell "Stop! Stop!"

But he was too late. In a single flash, as if the very sun had burst and gushed out all its light at once, it was all gone, lost, destroyed—

He was sitting bolt upright with a scream dying in his throat, and it was still the dark of night around him.

"Ryons! Wake up!" Perkin shook him by the shoulder.

"I am awake," Ryons muttered. The campfire had gone out, but there was enough light from moon and stars to show Cavall on his feet with his head cocked, and Perkin, and Baby with a glint of starlight in his eye.

"You've had a bad dream," Perkin said.

"It was awful!" Ryons answered and went on to tell him all about the dream. "It was so real," he said. "It was like I really saw it. I never would have guessed that I was dreaming."

"Maybe you did see something," said Perkin. "They say you're the descendant of King Ozias. He was a prophet. He composed the Sacred Songs. If you are what they say you are, then maybe the spirit of prophecy is in you, as it was in him. But I think you've had a vision of the Day of Fire."

"But that was ages and ages ago!" Ryons cried.

"A prophet sees what God shows him. But don't be afraid." Perkin patted him on the knee. "It might've been a dream, and nothing more."

But Ryons knew it wasn't.

CHAPTER 19

An Appearance of Magic

In the woods around what was left of Silvertown, several miles from the city, Hlah found outlaws. At least the authorities in Silvertown said they were outlaws.

"Oh, we're criminals, all right!" said a man named Uwain, who had been a reciter in the chamber house in Silvertown. Now he led a half-starved band of four men, five women, and three children. "That's why there's a price on our heads, waiting for some lucky traitor to collect it. We're guilty of the crime of not bowing down to the thrice-accursed dog who calls himself First Prester." He paused to spit on the ground. "And we're guilty of the crime of not going peacefully into slavery. As you can see, we're hardened criminals indeed."

Dirty faces, ragged clothes, and hollow cheeks—that's what Hlah saw. One of the women glared back at him.

"You're an Abnak, or else I've gone blind," she said. "Are you going to try to hand in our scalps?"

"Elva—" Uwain started to say; but Hlah forestalled him.

"You've nothing to fear from me," he said. "Yes, I'm an Abnak. But I believe in God and I serve King Ryons, and my wife is Obannese. We live on the west slope of the mountains, north of here. There are many of us now, with hunters and warriors, too. I can bring you with me when I go back. You'll be safe there. It's not a very hard journey."

"It might be, for the children," Uwain said.

"But it might be better than just staying here and waiting for the Devil's Prester to get his hands on us," said another woman.

"Tell me about him," Hlah said. "I've come here to scout this country for the king."

"What king!" barked a man.

"The king that God has chosen," said Hlah. "Tell me about this Devil's Prester, and I'll tell you all about the king. King Ryons is his name."

They agreed to that. Their camp was no more than a few wobbly lean-tos in a clearing, with a circle of stones to hold the fire. They all sat down together, but Uwain's people had no food to give their guest. Hlah gave the children the little bit of jerky he had in his pack. That made some eyes go wide, to see an Abnak do a thing like that. He thought of his father, Chief Spider: it would have popped his eyes, too. But Spider lived long enough to become a servant of God, so he wouldn't have said it was a waste of food.

"First thing," Uwain began, "the man is not a prester. Our prester was a saintly old man, Prester Yevlach. The Heathen killed him when they took the city.

"And then in the spring they built that fort inside the city, and the Heathens' mardars went up and down the land proclaiming that there was a New Temple of the Lord out East somewhere—and a new First Prester here in Silvertown. And that we had all better obey the new First Prester because God was angry with Obann for burning down the Temple in the city, and that God had chosen the Thunder

King to rule over us." Uwain paused to make a face. "It pains me to repeat such filth," he said.

"And filth it is," said Elva, "and they killed a lot of people around here and forced most of the men into their road-building gangs. There weren't many of us who escaped into the forest."

"We'd rather die, and our children with us, than live as slaves to any heretic," said one of the men.

"But who is he?" Hlah asked.

"He's nobody," said Uwain, "just a dirty traitor. His name is Goryk Gillow. I knew him slightly, when he was a captain in the city garrison. He spied for the Heathen, told them how they could get past our defenses. He's been in their service ever since. He's no more any kind of prester than you are. As to how the Heathen picked him for the job, who knows? I suppose they had to have somebody, and he was handiest to their purpose."

Hlah thought he might have heard the name of Goryk Gillow once before, but he hadn't. He wasn't in Obann the two times Goryk went there as the herald of the Thunder King. But he would remember the name when he made his report to Baron Roshay Bault; and then King Ryons' advisers would know what devilry was brewing in Silvertown, and who was brewing it.

"I think I'd better go back right away," he said, "so that news of all these matters might be taken to the king as soon as can be." But first he had to tell Uwain's people all about King Ryons. Silvertown was a long way from Obann, and communications had been shattered by the war. Most of the people had not yet heard that Obann had a king.

When he told of the boy king riding to the city on the

back of a great and awful beast whose like had never been seen by any living human being, or even imagined; and how the beast drove off the Heathen host even as it forced the city's gates and set fire to the Temple; and how that mighty host was destroyed and scattered in a single hour—when he told the tale, one of the women cried out:

"Why, my old aunt had a dream about all that! She told us all about it, and she said it was all true and really happened; and we just thought she was crazy. She died a week later, poor thing. But what you told us was exactly how she dreamed it!"

Hlah nodded. He knew God had loosed the spirit of prophecy in these present days.

He told the refugees how God had miraculously restored, in the person of a slave boy, the ancient line of kings, of the blood of blessed King Ozias. Uwain nodded and wiped a tear from his eye.

"It's all according to the Scriptures," he said. "I think we can believe this good news—the best news that ever was in all my life."

"But can we believe him, Reciter?" said one of the men.

"I do!" said Uwain. And so Hlah wound up with twelve hungry people to take back with him to safety in the north.

Wytt followed the dog's scent across the plains; it was stronger than the boy's. Sometimes he lost the trail, but he always picked it up again. One night, though, he lost it for longer than usual; and before he found it again, he found something else—a lot of big people standing around a fire, making loud and happy noises.

"What did they look like?" Ellayne asked. It was always hard to remember that Wytt didn't pay much attention to what human beings looked like. If he knew how to shrug, he would have. But then Jack said, "Listen! I hear people singing."

"It's a hymn!" Ellayne said, marveling. Then Jack recognized the melody, too. They'd both helped sing it in the chamber house in Ninneburky, often enough.

"Who would be holding an assembly at night, out in the middle of nowhere?" Ellayne wondered.

"Let's go see," Jack said. There was nothing to fear: Heathen bandits wouldn't be singing hymns.

Wytt did not want to go see; the noise of the singing disturbed him. And he disappeared into the tall grass rather than climb into Ellayne's pack. The children didn't stop to look for him. They knew he'd never stray very far away from them.

They found several dozen people, quite a large crowd under the circumstances, gathered around a roaring bonfire that lit up a good portion of the night. Waxbushes, Jack thought: they burn the brightest. The people sang in Obannese and looked Obannese. Nearby were parked several wagons with mules or oxen in harness.

It was bad manners to interrupt the singing of a hymn. But there was a woman on the edge of the throng, sitting on the ground: not singing, but trying to shake a pebble out of one of her boots, which she'd removed. Ellayne went right up to her and touched her shoulder.

"Pardon me, ma'am—but what's happening?" she asked.

"Don't you know a worship service when you see one?" was the answer.

"But out here, at night, and no chamber house?"

"We don't have a prester for our chamber house," said the woman. "Heathen killed him on his way home from Obann. Where are you from, girl, that you don't know that? You can't be from Caryllick."

Ellayne shrugged. She hadn't known that.

"I never heard of holding services at night, outdoors," Jack said.

"It's a special occasion," the woman said; and then the hymn was finished, and she shushed them. Hastily she tugged her boot back on and stood up to watch and listen. Jack and Ellayne weren't tall enough to see anything, but there were other children watching from atop the wagons, so they climbed up to join them.

"Good people of Caryllick, and the country round about—thank you for showing your faith by attending this assembly."

The booming voice that spoke those words belonged to a little fat man who stood on a tree stump by the fire. His voice was several sizes too big for him, but he made good use of it.

"As you came here in peace," he said, "be assured that you will go in peace, too, and soon be safe again inside the stone wall of Caryllick. But walls are no protection from the wrath of God; and it is God's wrath that you have to fear.

"O wicked and ungodly nation, that burned the Temple of the Lord! That left it for the king of all the Heathen to build it up again! How can your prayers be heard, without the Temple and its presters? Who can intercede for you?"

He went on and on about the Temple, which he said King Ryons' army and the people inside Obann City had destroyed. Jack and Ellayne knew that was a lie, but it seemed these people didn't. Jack was afraid Ellayne would start yelling about it in that shrill, piercing voice she had when she was fighting mad, and that the congregation would beat them into powder for it. He grabbed her hand and squeezed it, hard.

"He's preaching a lie!" Ellayne said, but didn't raise her voice.

"And these folks are worked up, good and proper!" Jack whispered into her ear. "Don't make it worse."

"I'm not stupid!" she protested.

"Turn to the New Temple!" boomed the little man. "Already the Lord has chosen a new First Prester, and raised him up in Silvertown. There's no more enmity between the Lord God and the Thunder King. But there is destruction and disaster for those who will not return to their allegiance to the Temple.

"So that you may know I speak the truth, and believe in the New Temple and in the Thunder King, I show you this sign. See it and believe!"

And he raised his right hand over his head, and rays of light shot out of his palm.

The people gasped, and jostled each other as they shrank away from him. You could hear their bodies thumping against each other.

"Magic! Magic! Dear Lord, it's magic!"

That's what they thought, all of them—everyone but Jack. Startled and amazed he was, like everybody else. But Jack did not believe.

"A trick!" he said through clenched teeth.

But it sure as sunshine didn't look like a trick, thought Ellayne. You couldn't make light shoot out of someone's hand! Not unless that someone were a witch, like Raddamallicom, whom Abombalbap slew, cutting off her head before she could cast a spell that would have burned him to cinders on the spot—and certainly, she thought, there used to be witches. Maybe the Thunder King had brought them back.

"For two pennies," Jack said, "I'd march right back to the city and tell Obst all about this."

"But didn't you see—?"

"Foo! It's like when that juggler came to town and pulled potatoes out of everybody's ears."

Ellayne tugged on his arm. "We're much closer to Lintum Forest now than we are to Obann," she said, "and we're the only ones who are following the king. If we don't stay on his trail, no one will ever know what happened to him. We can't quit now!"

"You're right about that," he conceded. "But it makes me mad to see them get away with tricks and lies, and make people think it's magic!"

"I don't know what else you'd call it!" Ellayne thought, but didn't say so. All she wanted was to be away from there, quick as could be. If Jack thought this was like a juggler's trick, he was crazy. Maybe he'd listen to reason, by and by. "Let's just get out of here!" she hissed into his ear. The man had light pouring out of his empty hand, and she didn't want to see any more.

Still grumbling, Jack climbed down from the wagon. Ellayne jumped down after him. And the people were still carrying on and making a great to-do as Jack and Ellayne marched off into the night.

CHAPTER 20

Sunfish Has a Dream

You may remember, as Gallgoid remembered, that Prester Orth was Lord Reesh's partner in treason and his choice to succeed him as First Prester. On their way to the mountains, Orth lost his nerve and ran away, and Gallgoid never saw him again and didn't know what became of him: starved to death somewhere in the wilderness, he thought most likely.

And so Orth would have, had Hlah not found him—a dirty, bedraggled, mindless madman who couldn't remember his own name.

He had a new name now—Sunfish. And he ministered to the growing community of refugees, Obannese and Abnak, living in the forest on the western slopes.

He remembered nothing of his life in Obann. His career, his power, his wealth, and all his luxuries: it was as if none of these had ever existed. God had also blotted out the memory of all his treasons, leaving him with nothing but this: a word-perfect recall of every verse of the Holy Scriptures, and the power to preach it and teach it to people who had long been ignorant of God's word. Everything else was lost to him; and he was content that it should be so.

He lived in a little cabin that the people built for him. Hlah's wife, May, and some of the other women, took care of him. In many ways he was like a child. He didn't know how to cook for himself or mend his clothing. No one minded doing these things for him. Sunfish recited to them the Old Books, fascicle by fascicle, a little bit every night, around a cozy fire. And he answered all their questions.

As Hlah hiked homeward, leading Uwain's little band from Silvertown, Sunfish one morning had something unusual to tell May when she brought his porridge.

"I've had a dream," he said, "and I don't know what it means. But maybe you can tell me."

He was a big man, with a great black beard shot full of silver. May, young enough to be his daughter, thought of him as a little boy who would never get any older. Her baby son, Wulf, babbled delightedly whenever Sunfish held him in his arms: something that he loved to do. That would have astounded anyone in Obann who'd known Prester Orth.

"Now, how can I tell you anything about your dream, you silly man?" May said.

"All men dream, but the interpretation is of God," he quoted from the Book of Beginnings. "I dreamed I stood inside a great dark space, jam-packed full of people, all looking up at me; and I was preaching to them. I don't know who they were, or where I was. I've never seen so many people."

"Nor have I," May said. "But I suppose you could preach to a great crowd of people in the city of Obann in the Temple. Only, the Temple was destroyed." She shook her head. "I've never been to Obann. Hlah says you never saw so many people in one place or such great buildings—with walls like cliffs, he says. I'd love to see it, someday."

"I didn't know there were so many people in the whole world," Sunfish said. Prester Orth had preached in the great

Temple many times, to overflowing crowds, but Sunfish had no memory of that. "I wish I knew the meaning of that dream. It may be that the Lord was trying to tell me something."

"Oh, well—eat your porridge," May said. "Sometimes a dream is just a dream."

But in this case she was wrong.

In Obann, Martis had an audience with Gurun and Obst together. "We can trust the Knight Protector," Obst said; and they told him how Jack and Ellayne brought Fnaa to be a substitute for the king. But of the king himself they had no news.

"I sent his hawk, Angel, to seek him," said Gurun, "but she has not returned. I sent two of my Blays to watch over Jack and Ellayne, but they have not returned, either."

Before he left the city, Martis received a message from the Chief Spy to come and see him. He knew Gallgoid from when they were both in Lord Reesh's service. He tried to forget the things he knew about him. "He was no worse than I was," Martis said to himself. But he couldn't warm to the man.

"You can be here for no other reason than to seek the two children from Ninneburky," Gallgoid said, when they were alone in his office. "I believe they went to Lintum Forest in search of King Ryons. They were seen to cross the river on the ferry. Shortly afterward two Blays took the ferry, too, sent by the queen, of course."

"Do you think the king has gone to Lintum Forest?" Martis asked. "Why?"

"South of the river, there's nowhere else to go. But I don't know why he went. He went of his own free will, taking his dog with him, and no one saw them go. The queen doesn't know that I know the boy in the palace is a double. Where he came from, I don't know! Jack and Ellayne brought him, and that's all I know. It's a perplexing situation."

Lintum Forest, Martis thought: Ryons had come to Obann from there. He might have been happy to go back.

"The king is better off, out of the city," Gallgoid said. "Obann is full of treason. To what depth, I haven't yet discovered."

Martis nodded. "There is a sham prester in Cardigal," he said, "preaching the Thunder King's New Temple."

"Of which Lord Reesh was meant to be First Prester."

"This is a treason with deep roots," Martis said.

"The people want the Temple," Gallgoid said. "That was what they knew. They're afraid to carry on without it—never mind what Obst says about a temple to the Lord made without human hands, inside the human heart. The people want a building they can see."

"And the Thunder King has built them one," said Martis, "which he will give them, if only they submit to him. Very clever. Nasty."

"The city might have risen against the king by now," Gallgoid said, "only the people are restrained by their love for Gurun. She prays for them. She's young. She stands for the new temple in the heart—when they see her and hear her, then they're more willing to believe in it. She's the great obstacle between the plotters and their ambition."

"Then guard her well, Gallgoid."

The spy smiled coldly. "With my life and the lives of all

my agents, Martis! She is guarded better than she knows."

It struck Martis as ironic that the queen's safety should depend on such a man as Gallgoid—once upon a time, the slimiest of Lord Reesh's servants. "But was I any better?" he asked himself. He had to admit he wasn't.

Late that morning, with Lintum Forest plainly in sight in all its green vastness, Angel the hawk decided to come down. The man and the giant bird were no threat to her master. The dog's acceptance of them proved it, and Angel trusted the dog.

She flew a little ways ahead of them and then circled down, crying out to tell Ryons she was coming. She landed on an inkbush and called to him. The dog barked, but only once; he recognized her right away.

"There's that hawk—" Perkin started to say. But Ryons cried, "Angel!" And just like Gurun and Chagadai—keen hawkers from opposite ends of the world—taught him, he held up his forearm and whistled. Angel came to him and settled on his arm.

"This is my hawk!" he beamed at Perkin. "Angel, have you followed me all this way from Obann? How did you know where to find me?"

In the language of hawks she tried to tell him that Gurun had sent her, but of course Ryons couldn't understand that language. Nor did Perkin.

"That's a wise bird you've got there, Majesty," said Perkin. "She probably recognized you days ago, but didn't come down because of me and Baby. Well, it's fitting that a king should have a hawk, along with his hound. But you should also have a noble steed."

"I'm not much of a rider," Ryons said. He stroked Angel's breast with a finger, which she liked. "But I'm so glad Angel's here! I missed her, Perkin. I always fed her by hand, every day." Indeed, he missed all the true friends he'd left behind in Obann, and only just now realized how much.

"Another day, and we'll enter Lintum Forest," Perkin said. "King Ozias was born and raised there. It ought to be a friendly place to you."

As a slave of the Wallekki, who liked to stay on the move, Ryons had never been in any one place for long. He'd been in Obann for a year, which was the longest he'd been anywhere, but the city didn't feel like home to him. He'd stayed in the forest for just a matter of weeks, and he'd been happy there. He expected to be happy there again.

"Let's get going," he said. "I can hardly wait to see Helki!"

CHAPTER 21

A Change in Plan

As they rested during the heat of the day, in a dry gully that Wytt had found for them, Jack and Ellayne were having a theological argument. It was hard for them because neither had ever studied theology. Nor were they aware that prophets and wise men had had the same argument centuries ago.

"We saw what we saw," Ellayne said, and not for the first time. "And all those people saw it, too. You have to believe your own eyes."

"Just because we saw it doesn't mean it's magic," Jack said. "There's no such thing as magic." She was getting tired of him saying that.

"Then why was it against God's law to be a witch?" she demanded. She'd heard Obst say this once or twice, but she had no idea where to find it in the Scriptures.

"That doesn't mean that witches really can do magic," Jack answered. "It's against God's law to worship idols, too, but that doesn't mean that idols can really do anything. But it's the same kind of law."

Wytt crouched beside them, watching with a twinkle in his eye. His head went back and forth from one to the other: you might have thought he understood what they were saying. But who can say he didn't?

"All right—how did that man make light shoot out of his hand last night, if it wasn't magic?" Ellayne said. It was like talking to a tree stump, she thought.

"Just because I don't know how he did it doesn't mean beans," Jack said. "I don't know how they make matches, either, and matches aren't magic. If I knew how, I could make light come out of my hand, too. Don't you remember what that man Gallgoid said? The Thunder King's servants tricked and cheated people and made them think it was magic! That business last night was just more of the same. Once a cheater, always a cheater!"

"Oh, now that's really smart!" Ellayne said. But it was true, what Gallgoid had said. The only thing Ellayne could say was that she'd seen this magic; but if she said that again, they'd wind up fighting about it.

"Those were only barbarians who got fooled," she said.

"They're not cuss't stupid!" Jack answered. "Anyway, those were our own people who got fooled last night."

Suddenly the argument lost all interest for Ellayne. A new thought struck her—hit her so hard, it almost took her breath away.

"Look here," she said. "Does it even matter whether it was real or not, if people think it's real? Don't you think someone ought to grab that little fat man and make him tell the truth?"

Jack saw, right away, what she was getting at, and he abandoned their argument, too. "It's too bad we're so far from the city," he said. "You're right—somebody ought to stop that cluck before he's got the whole nation fooled. I'll bet Uduqu could get that man to tell how he does his trick."

Ellayne saw the next step. "It means we ought to go back, doesn't it? All the way back to Obann! They've got to be told what's going on out here, and we're the only ones who can tell them. It has to be us."

"I thought we came out here to find the king," Jack said.

"Well, we can't be in two places at once!" Ellayne shook her head. "He's headed for Lintum Forest, anyhow. We can tell them that. He'll be safe in Lintum Forest. He won't be there long, before Helki finds him."

"They ought to send out all those Ghols on horseback and all the Attakotts on foot and catch that fake magician before he gets a chance to do his stuff again," Jack said.

"They'll catch him, all right," Ellayne said, "once we tell them."

After that, they really couldn't sleep. They couldn't bear to sit in the gully all day, waiting for the night, so they decided to risk some daytime travel and just keep going until they were so tired that they had to sleep. Ellayne said they could find their way back to Obann by the position of the sun. It didn't occur to Jack to doubt her.

Wytt didn't comment on their change of plan. He would have, had he been a human being. He just went on ahead, scouting out the way. The children soon lost sight of him.

Toward the end of the afternoon, they saw smoke ahead. "Someone has a campfire," Jack said. It was right in front of them somewhere, so they halted.

"If it's Heathen with horses ..." Ellayne started to say; but there was no need to finish.

Wytt popped up from the grass. "One man, with a fire," he reported. The man had a cart, too, with a single ox to pull it. There was no one else around for miles, Wytt said.

"Want to sneak up and take a look?" Jack said.

"As long as we don't get too close." She didn't have to remind him of Hesket the Tinker, who'd drugged them and would have sold them into slavery. Wytt killed him while he slept.

Wytt led them to the campfire, keeping upwind of the ox in case the beast should catch their scent and give a warning. Soon they could smell the fire. They dropped to their hands and knees and crept cautiously through the tall grass.

Fire, cart, ox, and man were in a low depression with a spring-fed pool. Jack and Ellayne peered through the grass.

Ellayne almost cried out. "It's him!" she hissed through her teeth.

It was the little fat man who'd done the magic, peaceably boiling tea in a tin cup over the fire. He wore buckskin pants and a much-stained linen tunic that had once been white. His hat lay beside him, full of blackberries. He had sandy hair as short as stubble, a reddish beard, and whistled a cheery little tune.

"If we spy on him," Ellayne whispered, "we might find out how he does the magic. Maybe Wytt can go through his things while he's asleep. It's a golden opportunity."

"A golden opportunity to get caught!" Jack thought. He pinched Ellayne's elbow and signed to her that they'd better back off a ways, so they could talk. She understood, and they crawled back some fifty yards the way they'd come, stopping behind a screen of bushes.

"We'll never get a better chance to find out what he's up to," Ellayne said. "Heroes take those chances when they come."

A grown man with good sense would have taken Ellayne by the hand and walked away, fast. But Jack was not a grown man; and compared to some of the things that the two of them had had to do over the past year or so, spying on a fake magician didn't seem like much. Still, he thought, they ought to do it right.

"We won't see anything, just sneaking around. And we can't keep up with a wagon, either," he said. "The only way to do this is to travel with him. Let him get used to us. If we can just stick with him for a few days, that's how we can find out something."

"We can tell him we're lost," Ellayne said. "We'll say we came from Lintum Forest, trying to go to Obann."

Together they cooked up a story. Wytt, of course, would remain in the background, unknown to the magician. If they got in trouble, Wytt could rescue them. Wytt took this in without saying what he thought of it.

They stood up, and hand in hand like lost and weary children, walked back to the campsite.

That was how they became fellow travelers with the man who called himself Noma: who said he came from a little village a few miles south of Caryllick and was northbound for the river. Jack and Ellayne could travel under his protection, in return for helping him set up camp and tend to his ox and wagon. Wytt would be going, too, but Noma wouldn't know that.

"I like to do a little peddling in the towns along the river," Noma said, "and a little preaching, too, when the spirit moves me."

"Are you a reciter?" Jack asked. Noma's camp was already made; he wouldn't be moving on again until the morrow.

"No, not me. I'm just a man who loves the Lord, and loves the Temple, and I preach for the love of preaching."

Ellayne bit back her question, "What temple?" She and Jack weren't supposed to know much about anything. They'd introduced themselves as "Jack and Layne," two boys from Lintum Forest. "Let him think we're kind of stupid," Jack had said. "Just a couple of hicks from the forest."

After the sun went down, Noma fetched a concertina out of his cart and played some songs. He didn't do any magic. Before long, and with a smile on his face, he laid his head on his bedroll and went to sleep. After a little while, Wytt came out of hiding and stood over him, listening to him snore.

"Is he sound asleep?" Ellayne whispered.

"He sleeps," Wytt said, and hopped over to cuddle with her.

"I wonder if we ought to search his cart."

"Not yet!" Jack answered. "Let's just keep watching him closely for a day or two, like we agreed. We know he's up to no good, and that means he'll be cautious. He might have mousetraps in there, to catch anyone going through his things."

Ellayne was impressed. "I never thought of that!" she said.

"Because you're too busy thinking about magic," Jack

said. She didn't know Van once put a mousetrap in the breadbox, and Jack got his fingers caught when he reached into it. "Noma's a trickster, and we'll have to be careful."

Noma didn't look dangerous, Ellayne thought. But anyone who could cast light out of his bare hand was not to be treated carelessly.

Jack's last thought before falling asleep was: "Well, at least he thinks we're stupid! We never asked him what he's doing out here all alone, with bandits all over the country." And a little voice in the background of his mind added, "You'll see how stupid you've been, when we run into some of those bandits."

CHAPTER 22

How Fnaa Received a Prophecy

Zekelesh, chief of the Fazzan, took half a dozen of his men to visit Nanny Witkom's monument and lay a wreath of flowers on it. Nanny was honored as a prophetess. Her monument stood in Lord Gwyll's garden because she'd lived most of her life in his house and died there. There was also a monument to Lord Gwyll himself because he died in defense of the city.

Zekelesh had trouble expressing himself in Tribe-Talk, and usually needed an interpreter. But he had a secret, which it seemed good to him to keep strictly to himself: he'd learned to understand Obannese. Because no one knew he understood it, he heard things that otherwise would not have been said in his presence.

Today he heard more, as he and his fellows marched down the street.

"Look at them! You'd think they conquered us."

"Cusset Heathen—the king's their prisoner."

"King? They said he was a king!"

"Well, he came here on that great beast, didn't he? And smashed that Heathen army. Only all these other Heathen came in with him. I never understood that!"

Zekelesh heard such things every time he ventured from the palace. He was hearing more and more of it, a little more each day.

Not that the council of chiefs was unaware of the temper of the city. They knew. Shaffur wanted to move the king and his government back to Lintum Forest. General Hennen wanted them to move to Durmurot, many miles to the west.

"We must stay here," was Obst's advice. "The Old Books must be copied and sent out to the chamber houses everywhere. The Lost Scrolls must be studied and copied and taught to the people. The Lord's real work for us is here."

"And the day after we depart," Uduqu would add, "they'll throw off their allegiance to the king and turn the whole country against us."

Lord Gwyll's family had not returned from the west; maybe they never would. Two of Hennen's spearmen guarded the house, out of respect. They saluted Zekelesh, and he went into the garden. He laid the wreath on the gleaming white stone of Nanny's monument. Zekelesh had loved her, and he missed her.

"Boss, why do we do this?" asked one of the men. "Does God want us to? Does it make the old woman's spirit happy?"

"I want to do it," Zekelesh answered. "Nanny was a great woman, and a prophet."

"I wish we could go home," said another man; but they all knew, of course, that the Thunder King would kill them the moment they set foot in the valley of the Green Snake River.

"Trust God," said Zekelesh. "He will know when to bring us home again."

"Yes," said the converted pagans, who had not had the benefit of a formal education in a chamber house, "we trust in Him."

In his office in the palace, Gallgoid was finishing a confidential letter to Gurun. He'd questioned all the servants from Vallach Vair's house, and arrested and questioned a number of persons mentioned by those servants.

He preferred Gurun to the council of the chieftains: not because some of them viewed him as a traitor and would never trust him, but because Gurun was young and intelligent and courageous. The chiefs had courage and were wise, but Gallgoid's instincts turned to Gurun. It was the same inner voice that had commanded him to escape from the Golden Palace of the Thunder King, just before the whole place was buried in the avalanche. A more devout man would have said it was the prompting of God's spirit, but Gallgoid was afraid to venture an opinion on that.

"Gallgoid to Gurun," he wrote:

"It would be easier to name those who are loyal to the king in this city, than those who are not. One plot against him I've squelched; but there are, and will be, others—how many, I have not yet been able to find out.

"Every former oligarch in the country is against the king, and they all have agents in this city. They seduce the people with promises to rebuild the Temple. The younger clergy, who looked to the Temple for promotion, are with them. The elders, who listen to Prester Jod of Durmurot and to Preceptor Constan at the great seminary in this city, are for us. But the young men are more energetic.

"There is much murmuring against the king's army, which he brought into the city with him. Hennen has the Obannese troops well in hand; but in other cities, the soldiers are being seduced by the oligarchs. If for any reason more troops must be brought into the city, it is likely they will turn violently against King Ryons' men.

"But the greatest danger is this—that the former leaders of Obann will make an alliance with the new Thunder King. His emissaries are at work along the river, throughout the countryside. To the oligarchs they offer restoration of their seats of power, under the Thunder King. To the discontented clergy they offer a New Temple in the East. I have heard of a new First Prester, appointed by the Thunder King, in Silvertown."

Gallgoid paused, thinking there ought to be more to his letter. He hadn't said anything about what ought to be done. That was because he didn't know. Besides, he didn't give advice; he provided information. At last he decided to let the letter stand as written, and reread the closing paragraph before signing it:

"As far as I can determine, the people honor King Ryons for his rescue of the city, but few truly believe him to be the descendant of King Ozias. They mistrust the chieftains and their warriors, although Chief Uduqu is a hero in their eyes. They believe Obst is mad, but they also accept him as a prophet. Finally, Lady Gurun, they revere you personally, as having been sent to them by God. You are King Ryons' greatest asset in this city. Your servant, Gallgoid."

He sealed the letter shut and summoned a trusted man

to deliver it to Gurun.

Children and servants hear things they are not supposed to hear. So it was with Fnaa and his mother.

Servants gossiped back and forth, in the kitchens, in the halls, mostly whispering but sometimes getting excited and forgetting that they might be overheard. Dakl heard her share of it. Things like this:

"Lord So-and-so gave his wife a golden necklace and said to her, 'By this time next year, my lass, you'll be wearing this to the Oligarchs' Ball.'"

"My nephew will be a captain soon, and his captain a commander, and his commander a lord; and then we'll have our own house in the city."

"My sister wants me to come and live with her at Prester Ronwy's house and be a servant there. She says it won't be safe in the palace."

Dakl knew better than to give the name of any servant who said such things, but she did let Gurun know what kinds of things were being said. Gurun didn't ask who said them. "Gallgoid probably knows already," she said.

As king, Fnaa wasn't privy to servants' gossip. What he heard was of a different order altogether.

One or more of the Ghols watched over him discreetly wherever he went, whatever he did. By now Chagadai had been told his secret. Fnaa was surprised by how gently the old Ghol treated him.

"It's nothing," said Chagadai, in his labored Obannese. "I have been blessed in that God has let me hold my children's children in my lap. The oldest of them would be about your age now. Besides, we both serve King Ryons. I pray we'll see him again!"

So Fnaa went about his business as King Ryons would have, sitting for his lessons in this or that, practicing his horsemanship and archery, attending sessions of his chiefs, and letting his people in the city see him every few days. And there was one more thing that Ryons did, that Fnaa now had to do.

There was a little girl named Jandra, from Lintum Forest, who lived in the palace and had a great reputation as a prophet. The chiefs all venerated her. She was fond of Ryons, and it was his custom to spend time with her. He would take her to the stables so she could pet the horses and play with the cats, or watch over her as she fed the chickens.

This wasn't easy for Fnaa. Jandra had a bird—maybe you could call it a snake with wings and legs and feathers—that never left her side. Jandra was a nice little girl who prattled and skipped and sang silly little songs; but the wretched bird was always there, glaring at you with red eyes and rattling its dirty purple feathers, and hissing if you got too close. Fnaa was sure the cusset creature knew he was a fake and only waited for a good excuse to bite him.

Everyone swore that Jandra was a prophet, but Fnaa had never seen any sign of it. She liked to hold his hand and swing it back and forth as she sang, "Helki kilt the giant," or some such rigmarole. She was just an ordinary little girl; but Chagadai said her prophecies had made Ryons a king and guided the destiny of the army—and this when she was just a toddler. The whole business seemed to Fnaa just about the oddest aspect of an altogether very odd situation.

And then, of course, one day she did speak prophecy again.

They were among the chickens, with Jandra scattering corn and a Ghol leaning against a chicken coop, half-asleep, and the snake-bird perched on a crate, intently watching everything that moved. And Jandra stopped feeding the chickens, her arms went slack, and the corn dribbled from her hand; and she looked up at Fnaa in a way that made his skin prickle from the scalp down.

When she spoke, it was in a deep voice that was not a little girl's voice—not possible for so young a child to speak with such a voice. And she said:

"Hear the word of the Lord, Fnaa, son of Dakl.

"You have not known me, but I have known you from the time I shaped you in your mother's womb and breathed the spirit of life into you. And now you shall know me.

"For I am pleased with you, my child; and I have chosen you to provoke folly in the heart of those men who will not hear my voice. Fear not, for there is nothing they can do to you; for I shall protect you, and you shall be a snare to them. Only be courageous: and what comes into your mind to do, so do; for I am with you."

Fnaa's knees shook, but he was not aware of it. At the moment he was more afraid than he had ever been in all his life: as if Jandra were a slavering bear that stood before him to break his bones and eat him. And yet it was a fear, too, that blew through his heart like a fierce cold wind: and whatever that wind left standing was strong and good, and glorious. His senses reeled.

But then Jandra's blue eyes rolled up and her lids came down, and she crumpled to the earth, scattering the chickens. Fnaa thought she'd fainted, but she was sleeping peacefully. There were many in the king's army who'd seen this, several times before, and could have told him that she always fell asleep after she spoke God's words, and remembered nothing about it when she woke. The woman named Abgayl, who took care of her, swore the child didn't know she was a prophet. But here was only the Ghol, who woke with a start and came rushing over, clucking at Fnaa in his barbaric language, not a word of which the boy could understand. He scooped up Jandra in his arms. Her monstrous bird hopped down from the crate and hissed at him, showing its sharp teeth, but he ignored it.

"What happened? What happened?" Fnaa cried. The Ghol tried to tell him, but they couldn't communicate. So he barked some orders at a groom who came out of the stables, who had enough sense to go looking for someone who would understand. In a few minutes—she must have been nearby—Abgayl came and took the sleeping Jandra from the Ghol. By then Fnaa had succeeded in calming himself—at least in looking calm. Inside, he was still quaking.

Abgayl smiled at him. "It's been a while since the Lord God spoke to you, hasn't it?" she said. Fnaa had never spoken with Abgayl before, but fortunately Gurun had told him all about her. "What did the Lord say?"

What a question! Vallach Vair and his family used to go to assembly at the Temple, but Fnaa had never heard much talk about God until he came to the palace. It could not be said that Fnaa believed in God. But he knew that it couldn't have been Jandra who'd said those things to him; nor did he know what those things meant. So he could only shrug.

"Your Majesty, what's the matter with you? You can't

shrug off God's word!" Abgayl said. "What did He say?"

"That He was with me." Somehow Fnaa kept the quaver out of his voice: he was supposed to have had this experience before. "That I ought to do whatever's in my heart to do."

"And what is in your heart?"

"Just now? I don't know! I mean, we were just feeding the chickens."

"You should ask Obst about this," Abgayl said. "He can guide you. And now, if you'll excuse me, I'll put Jandra to bed."

She walked off, and the Ghol came up and laid a kindly hand on his shoulder, which made him flinch. But the warrior only grinned at him. "Good thing she speak—yes, father?" he said in broken Obannese.

Fnaa just nodded, and went to sit down on a bale of hay before his legs gave out on him.

CHAPTER 23

Back to Lintum Forest

Martis allowed himself to take a little pleasure in the swiftness of his Wallekki horse, Dulayl, in a flat-out gallop on the plain. But after a few minutes he reined in: it wouldn't do to let Dulayl get winded, only to stumble into some emergency that would demand another burst of speed. At his best (and his best was very good) Dulayl could just outrun the giant birds. Martis hadn't seen any of them yet, but he was wary.

So far he'd picked up no trace of Jack and Ellayne, although he had good tracking skills. In the vastness of this empty land, the children might be anywhere. It would be easy to miss them. The best he could do was to zig-zag in the direction of Lintum Forest and question the few people he met along the way.

He encountered a band of Wallekki marauders, but he knew the words of friendship that would keep him safe from them. Besides, their chief concern was finding food.

"There were twelve of us," they told him, "but seven of us starved in that accursed winter." There were only five left.

"Why do you stay?" Martis asked. "Why haven't you gone back East?"

"Better a robber, than a slave of the Thunder King," said their leader.

"You could submit to King Ryons and receive a pardon."

"We have heard he hangs bandits."

"He grants peace to those who seek peace," Martis said. "There are many Wallekki in his service now, who once were stragglers like you. You should consider this."

"We shall," said the robber.

During his service to Lord Reesh, Martis had sojourned many days among the Wallekki, and he knew their ways. He knew that these, having exchanged the words of friendship with him, would be true to him and that they would grant him any favor that he asked of them. A man who didn't know those words would have been robbed and killed by now.

"My brother," he said, "I seek two children who are crossing this country alone, probably making for Lintum Forest. If you meet them, tell them you are Martis' friends and protect them. The king will reward you for it." These men's natural impulse would be to sell the children into slavery, but Martis knew that now they wouldn't.

"Shall we escort them to the forest, Martis? We know the way."

"If that is where they wish to go, my brother Kwana," Martis said. "And if you are wise, you will seek King Ryons' pardon, in my name—and eat like honest men this winter."

Kwana laughed. "As the old song says, my brother Martis, 'The life of a robber is a man's life.' But I suppose we'll think better of it when we see the winter coming."

They parted and Martis rode on. Whenever he encountered a hill, he climbed to the top and surveyed the land in all directions. But it would take a soaring eagle with an eagle's eyes, he mused, to find the children in this country.

Long ago, Lord Reesh used to tell him, these lands were heavily populated. In the Day of Fire, God emptied them: or so said the Commentaries. The First Prester hadn't believed in God.

But Martis had learned to believe, on the summit of Bell Mountain. Now he said his daily prayer for the children's safety; and when night fell, he built a roaring fire for his own.

Hlah led his little troop of refugees from Silvertown over the lowest foothills of Bell Mountain. They couldn't see the mountain for the trees; but at rare places the forest thinned, and there you could look up and see the peak.

Like Jack and Ellayne, Hlah had grown up in sight of Bell Mountain and seen it every day of his life. He knew, as everybody knew, that the cloud that cloaked the mountain's peak had been there forever, and would be there for all time—until the day the bell tolled and the cloud was blown away, never to return. Abnaks didn't know the strange, exciting noise was from King Ozias' bell, placed there ages ago against the day when someone would climb the shrouded peak and sound the bell, and God would hear. Abnaks knew nothing of God, and even less of Scripture. But Hlah now knew.

"The cloud will never return," said Uwain the reciter. They'd all paused to look up at the mountain. Like everyone else in all the world, when the bell tolled, they'd heard it. Uwain turned to his fellows. "See the sign that God has given you. Have hope!" he said.

"We'll need it," answered one of the men. "Why God

let the Heathen come and burn our city, and take my farm and everything I owned, is more than I can see. I heard King Ozias' bell, but it rang no good for me." And some of the others nodded. Uwain frowned.

Hlah said, "You should have seen the Heathen host that laid siege to Obann. They were as many as the leaves in this forest. And you should have seen the great beast that God sent to scatter them! If you'd seen that, you'd have hope."

"We've seen another miracle," a woman said, "an Abnak leading us to safety! Who would have ever thought a thing like that could happen?"

At last Ryons and Perkin came to the edge of Lintum Forest. Ryons didn't know it, but he'd returned to the exact spot from which he'd first come out of the forest a year ago on his way to Obann. Cavall knew and barked for joy; but he didn't know how to make Ryons understand. It was very hard to make humans understand anything.

Baby, a creature of the plains, didn't like the forest and his neck feathers stood up uneasily. Angel was invisible in the foliage aloft, but she came down whenever Ryons called her. There was good hunting here, she tried to tell them. Cavall and Baby understood, but not the humans.

"Now we have to find Helki, and he'll tell me why the Lord wanted me to come back to the forest," Ryons said. "I do love it here! I missed it, in the city."

"Your ancestor, King Ozias, was born and raised here," Perkin said. "It's natural for you to be happy here. But how do we find Helki? Or will he find us? I have to admit, Your Majesty, that I don't know my way around a forest."

"It's all right. Cavall does!"

It had been more than a year since Ryons left the forest. In all that time, he'd had no news. Everyone in Obann City took it for granted that Helki was putting down the outlaws and making the country safe for honest folk. And so he had, to a degree. The settlement he'd founded at the ancient castle had survived the winter, and now the people there had cleared the land and planted crops. Helki's rangers patrolled the woods in bands of six. They were expert archers, all of them, and lawless men had learned to fear them. Helki was called the Flail of the Lord, and many of his enemies had surrendered to him. But there were always more to take their place.

Ryons would have been surprised to know that, as he and Perkin spoke, many miles away at the opposite end of the forest, Helki crouched in the middle of a blowdown while two dozen men hunted for him all around it, eager to take his scalp.

Helki had a secret path into the heart of the blowdown, and another secret path out. It was one of his hiding places, three or four acres of dead wood all jumbled together years ago by the freakish tantrum of a mighty storm. All but the smallest animals would go around it, no matter how far out of their way they had to go. A few bare, white trunks still stood, here and there; all the rest was a vast tangle.

The men who hunted Helki were no ordinary Lintum Forest outlaws. Someone had sent them down from Silvertown, several hundred of them. They were real woodsmen, trappers, who'd grown up in the forests on the skirts of the mountains. They were Obannese, but now they served the Thunder King. They'd come to Lintum Forest for no reason but to murder Helki; this he knew from one he'd captured alive.

Helki smiled to himself as he heard them calling to one another. They were beginning to consider setting fire to the blowdown. He had to applaud their skill in following him here. Things would get interesting if they resorted to fire. They wouldn't be able to control it, once it started. "That man in Silvertown must want me pretty badly," he thought.

By the calls of blue jays and purple peeps, he knew pretty much where all the men were. They were spread out thin, trying to surround the blowdown. "Reckon it's time I stirred up some excitement," Helki said to himself. "Only two hours of good sunlight left."

As silently as the little red-backed salamanders that crept around the leaf mold under all the dead wood, Helki began to creep toward the edge of the blowdown. In his garment of sewn-together patches of every color you could salvage from other people's worn-out clothes, he was almost invisible. He didn't want his enemies setting fire to the blowdown: it was one of his favorite places in the forest. But they were spread out too thin for their own good, and they would pay for it. He allowed himself an hour to get to the edge of the blowdown without making a sound. The birds considered him a creature of the forest like themselves and didn't comment on his movements. Possibly they couldn't see or hear him.

As he neared his exit from the blowdown, Helki sniffed the air. He was in luck: only two men were anywhere near him.

When he emerged from the blowdown, they weren't ready for him, and he gave them no time to get ready. "Helki the Rod!" he roared; and they had just enough time to hear his voice before his staff descended on their heads and ended their hunting days forever.

"Two for me and none for you, my boys!" he bellowed. "Better get back to the mountains while you can!"

That ought to bring the rest of them running, but he wouldn't be there when they came. He fled into the greenwood. They'd never catch up to him by nightfall. And tomorrow would see another day's sport.

CHAPTER 24

How Jack Stole Noma's Magic

The second day after Jack and Ellayne joined him, Noma encountered bandits, half a dozen Wallekki on horseback who galloped up and made him halt his wagon. Ellayne noticed he didn't seem the least bit afraid of them. She was, though. The men looked tired and hungry, and ready for anything.

"Wa na-malaki," Noma said, or something like that. Whatever it meant, the men lowered the points of their swords and spears, and the one with the most feathers in his headdress replied at length. The children didn't speak Wallekki and had no idea what was being said. Noma wasn't being given many chances to answer.

But then he held up his hand and said, "Mardar shu!" And the riders all stared wide-eyed at him. They fell silent. He spoke to them calmly, without raising his voice. They kept on staring at him. When he lowered his hand, they put their fingertips to their lips and bowed their heads. Muttering, they backed their horses off, then suddenly turned and galloped away as fast as they could go. Noma watched them, apparently without surprise.

"What did you say to them?" Ellayne wondered. "Those men looked like killers!"

She and Jack had been riding in the back of the cart. The bandits couldn't have missed seeing them, for the canvas cover had been rolled up on its frame. And yet the Wallekki, many of whom were habitual slave traders, had paid no attention to the children. That was very strange indeed.

"Well, they haven't killed us, have they?" Noma said. "I just told them we had nothing worth stealing—as they could see for themselves—and that I am an adopted son of a chief in their clan."

"Are you really?" Jack asked.

Noma laughed. "Why, of course! I used to do a lot of trading in Wallekki lands." Slaves, probably! Jack thought. "You can tell a Wallekki's tribe and clan by his headdress. Those men were of the Mount Immr clan. They would know Chief Jahi, my adopted father. And truly, they apologized most sincerely for disturbing me."

"What if they'd been from another clan?" asked Ellayne.

"Then I'm afraid I might have had to tell them a lie," Noma said. She looked for a twinkle in his eye, but didn't see one. "I really don't like to tell lies, and I hope you children don't, either. It's a very bad habit, and the Temple has always taught that lying is a sin."

"You snake in the grass!" thought Jack. He didn't say it: just fumed, and kept on fuming until they stopped for tea, and he and Ellayne went off to gather firewood. As soon as they were out of earshot of Noma, he grabbed Ellayne by the elbow.

"Ow!"

"Shh!" He lowered his voice. "I saw something that Noma doesn't know I saw—that sneaking skunk!"

"Saw what?"

"He had something in his pocket! Something that he took out and hid in his hand as soon as he spotted the bandits coming. I saw him."

"Well, it must've been something awfully tiny," Ellayne started to say. But something of Jack's thought was already hatching in her mind. "Something he could hide in the palm of his hand, where we wouldn't see it … but those Wallekki saw it."

"You bet they did!" Jack said. "Did you see their faces? They were scared! And maybe what they saw was light coming out of his hand—which we couldn't see because his hand was facing away from us. But when the Wallekki saw it, they skedaddled. And I'd like to know what he really said to them!"

"Yes—they did act like they were good and scared," Ellayne said. Her thought raced ahead of her words; she had to pause a moment. "That stuff about him being the adopted son of a chief—that wasn't what he really said. He told us a lie. Those men were afraid of him—and we probably should be, too."

"I'd like to know what he had in his pocket."

Ellayne couldn't imagine how anything you might have in your pocket could make light stream out of your hand. But there were magical implements in stories—things like wands and swords and cauldrons—so she supposed Noma might have something like that, only smaller. Something that would make six armed men afraid of one little fat man;

and she didn't like the thought of that.

Wytt traveled under Noma's wagon, catching and eating some of the many insects stirred up by the ox's hooves and the wheels. Sometimes he rode, but only for the novelty of it. To him it was no hardship to scamper all day in the shade beneath the wagon.

Wytt knew Noma was a bad man and a liar. He couldn't speak Wallekki any more than the children could, but he understood the sense of things that people said, regardless of what language they spoke. When Noma spoke to the bandits, he told them he was a big man, bigger than the six of them, and he could kill them if he liked; and fear seeped out of their pores so Wytt could smell it. Wytt understood the questions asked by Jack and Ellayne and knew that Noma's answers were lies. Why the two of them wished to travel with such a man was more than Wytt could fathom.

That night after Noma was finally sound asleep, Wytt woke the children. At his urging they stole away some distance from the dying campfire.

"What is it, Wytt?" asked Ellayne.

He made fierce jabbing motions with his sharpened stick and chattered furiously, struggling with himself not to make too much noise. "The man sleeps—now we kill him!" was his message. "We don't, then sometime he kill you. Big men on horses ran away from him, but you stay. Not safe." That was what he said, without the use of speech as we know it.

"We don't want to kill him!" Ellayne answered—almost too loud. "We don't want to kill anybody!"

"No, we don't," Jack agreed. "But we do want to find out what he has in his pockets! Maybe now's as good a time as any to conk him on the head and search his things."

"What do you mean, conk him on the head? What if you conk him just a little bit too hard—or not hard enough? What are you thinking?"

"Well, how else are we going to get into his pockets?"

"Jack, we can't just rob the man!" Ellayne felt like shaking him.

Wytt interrupted. "Too much talk!" he growled.

"Wytt's right," Jack said. "And so are you, but I can't help it. What else can we do? Noma is a servant of the Thunder King. He preaches lies. He's either a magician or he pretends to be, to fool people and to stir them up against King Ryons. You can wait here if you don't want any part of this. But I'm going back to do what has to be done."

Jack's pulse raced, and something in his stomach curdled. He'd never done a thing like this before: never even thought of it. He remembered stories in which one glance from a wizard's eye turned someone into stone, or worse. What if Noma suddenly opened his eyes and put a spell on him? Jack didn't believe in magic, but at the moment, he had his doubts.

Noma lay sleeping by the campfire, on his back, with his head pillowed on his bedroll. "Martis or Helki or Baron Bault could do this," Jack thought. "And so can I!"

He had a rounded stone in his hand. If it were any bigger, he'd need two hands to hold it. He was concentrating so hard on what he had to do that he didn't know Ellayne had followed him back to the campsite and was standing close by, watching him.

"Lord," he prayed silently, as Obst had taught him to, "if what I do is wrong, forgive me! I'm trying to do right."

He sank slowly to his knees, raised the stone, and with both hands drove it into Noma's forehead.

The "thunk!" it made when it hit almost made him faint. Noma jerked up and fell back down, gurgling deep in his throat. Blood flowed from his broken skin. Jack's hands lost their grip on the stone and dropped it. He found it hard to breathe.

"Did you kill him?"

Ellayne's voice startled him back to his senses, but Wytt answered first: "No, not dead. Listen—he breathes. I hear his heart still beating."

"Search his pockets, and let's get out of here!" said Ellayne.

"Climb into the wagon and empty out his bags," Jack answered. "See what you can find."

Noma had two pockets in his britches, one on either side. They were deep pockets. Fighting off a pang of nausea, Jack reached into one. The body was warm. Noma made a horrible snoring noise. Jack found some matches and a broken comb in one pocket; but in the other his fingers made contact with something round and hard and flat. He pulled it out.

What was it? About the size of a gold coin—the coin called a "spear" because it was stamped with the image of a spearman—it was much lighter. It weighed almost nothing. Jack had never seen anything like it; and the fire was all but out, and the moon wasn't much help, so he couldn't get a good look at it. But it felt very strange to the touch: too light for any kind of metal, perfectly stiff, and perfectly smooth all over except for some tiny round projection in the middle. It fit easily into the palm of one's hand, and Jack was sure this was the object he'd been looking for.

"I think I've got it!" he called to Ellayne. She climbed out of the wagon.

"Nothing in his bags but spare clothes and things," she said. "What have you got?"

"I don't know. It's too dark to see," Jack said. "Maybe there's writing on it, or a sign. Wish I had some light."

He was feeling the object all over with his thumbs and fingers; and just as he finished speaking, light burst from it.

Ellayne squealed and jumped a step back. Jack dropped the item. It lay on the ground and a white beam of light poured out of it.

Jack felt as if he'd accidently grabbed a rattlesnake. He didn't dare touch the thing again. But Wytt wasn't afraid. He stood over it and sniffed it—then, before Ellayne could stop him, picked it up.

"Don't touch it, Wytt!" she cried.

"Not afraid. Nothing to hurt," he answered. To him the light-giving talisman was fascinating, nothing more: a very nice thing, he thought. "Very pretty light," he said.

Seeing Wytt take no hurt from it, Jack finally reached out and cautiously took it from him. The light was too strong to be allowed to shine right into one's eyes for more than a moment or two, but the object hadn't gotten very hot. How could all that light be coming out of such a little thing, and why wasn't it burning hot?

"Be careful!" Ellayne said.

"I don't think it can hurt us," Jack said. And then, without meaning to do anything in particular, he pressed the tiny projection in the center of the object—and instantly the light vanished. Without a sound, without a puff of smoke, it just went out.

"What happened? Why did it go dark?"

"I don't know!"

Noma groaned, and tried to roll onto his side. He didn't succeed, but that was enough to remind the children of their danger.

"We can't stay here," Ellayne said.

"So who wants to?" Jack turned to Wytt. "Lead us away from here, Wytt—to someplace where he can't find it."

Wytt peered closely at the prone body. "He will hunt you sometime. Not dead yet."

"We aren't going to kill him, Wytt," Ellayne said. "Just find us someplace safe."

The Omah whistled loudly. "Come—this way!"

As they followed him into the night, Jack carefully put the light-giver into his own side pocket and wadded his handkerchief on top of it so that it couldn't fall out.

"Aren't you afraid it'll burn a hole in your leg?" Ellayne asked. "Trust me, Jack—there's no telling what a magical thing like that might do."

"There's no such thing as magic," Jack said, and tried very, very hard to keep believing it.

CHAPTER 25

An Ancient Vision, and a New One

Back in Obann, in his private chamber within the seminary library, Preceptor Constan sat as still as stone. Occasionally one of his eyelids flickered. He hardly seemed to breathe.

On his desk before him, half-unrolled, lay one of the Lost Scrolls discovered by those children from Ninneburky in the ruins of the First Temple, in Old Obann across the river. Constan and his scholars were copying these: first an exact copy, in the original paleography and language, and then another copy in the script in use today. After that, the seminary planned to translate the text into modern Obannese. The language had changed much since King Ozias' time, ages ago.

According to what was written in the scrolls, Ozias returned to Obann as an old man, made his dwelling in the ruins, and there received the Word of God, which he wrote down in his own hand. Many of the scholars didn't believe that. Many were their theories as to who else might have written them and why. But Constan believed. He hadn't, at first.

A student came into the room and spoke to him. Constan didn't answer. Used to his master's ways, the young man gently but firmly jogged his shoulder.

"Preceptor, it's almost dinnertime."

Constan looked up.

"Go to the palace," he said, "and find Obst. Tell him to come here at once. I need him."

"But your dinner—"

"At once," Constan said. The young man shrugged and went to do his bidding.

How long he waited for Obst, Constan didn't know. It might have been some minutes, or it might have been hours. The preceptor had his mind on more important things, and however long he waited, he never stirred from his chair. Nor did he hear Obst when he came in and spoke his name.

"You sent for me, Preceptor. What is it?" Obst said. He found a stool and sat down. The noise it made scraping the floor caused Constan to look up at him.

"I have read something in this scroll," said Constan, "and I want you to hear it. Listen:

"'On the fourth day of the fifth month the word of the Lord came to me. And He said, Ozias; and I said, Here I am. And the Lord said, Behold, I have ordained destructions for this people of Obann, the Tribes of the Law, which law they break and treat as nothing; but the time will come when they will have learned all they can from chastisement and destruction. And the wise will keep this wisdom in their hearts, but my people will not hear them, nor cease from their iniquities. Nevertheless, when I have satisfied my wrath, I will save them.

"'In those days I shall raise up my righteous servant,

and he shall grow up as a branch from the root of Ozias the king; and he shall bear the iniquities of all the sons and daughters of men, and all the nations. For their sake he shall be broken like a reed and poured out like water, so that the law might be fulfilled; but I shall raise him again, and he shall reign over all my people forever. By him shall the children of men be reconciled to me, and I will be their God in the midst of them forever.

"'And I said, When, O Lord? And the Lord said, I have determined the time from the beginning of the world, before I made the heavens and the earth; but it is not for any man to know the time. And I swooned in my bed, and was as a dead man for three nights and three days: for the spirit of the Lord exhausted my flesh.'"

Constan looked up from the scroll. "Well?" he said. "What do you think?"

Obst spread his hands. "It's prophecy," he said. "There are echoes of it elsewhere in the Scriptures."

"It sheds light on what the Old Prophets told the Children of Geb, when God brought them to this land from the sinking of Caha."

Obst nodded. He knew the verse Constan was thinking of, from the Book of Beginnings. It was a saying by the Lord Himself, when the elders of the tribes received the law by the shore of the Great Sea, where the people rested from their crossing.

"Sin shall continue," he recited, "but not forever. For my righteousness shall prevail upon the earth, and it shall move among you in the flesh."

"No one has ever known what that verse means," said Constan. "But there have been destructions. Shall there not be salvation, too? And what will the people do, when this prophecy is read to them in every chamber house in Obann?"

Obst didn't know what they would do. He sighed. "Once upon a time in my life," he said, "I thought I understood the Scriptures. I believed that when Ozias' bell on Bell Mountain rang, God would end the world: that He would unmake the work of His hands and wipe it out. I was sure of it—and look how wrong I was! So it may not be useful to ask me what I think of anything in Scripture."

"My question is," said Constan, "whether we are living in the time when the seed of King Ozias will fulfill this prophecy, or is that time yet to come?"

It jolted Obst when he suddenly saw what the preceptor was getting at.

"Do you mean Ryons—our King Ryons?" he cried. "Could he be the righteous servant in the prophecy, of the root of King Ozias? For Ozias is his ancestor." Obst reeled inwardly as memories flooded his mind—of Ryons as a slave boy, undernourished and unwashed, without even a name to call his own; of a boy sassing the chiefs of the Abnaks because he knew they liked it; of the child who was his only friend when first he came among the Heathen. "But he's just a boy! A good boy, but hardly God's own righteous servant."

Constan shook his head. "I'm not thinking about him," he said. "I'm thinking that these verses, if let loose on the people of Obann at this time, will be like a torch thrown into a loft full of dry hay." He rubbed his face wearily. "But I will not suppress these Scriptures."

He was right, Obst thought: there was no telling how

the people would react. But then, of course, there was no telling what would happen when Ozias' bell was rung. God commanded it, and Jack and Ellayne obeyed. Would he have done the same? He wondered.

"I agree, Preceptor," he said. "We must proclaim God's word as it is given to us. The consequences will be up to Him."

"As they always are," said Constan. "But it comforts me to know that it'll be some time yet before we can do it."

Without much difficulty, Hlah led the refugees from Silvertown to his own home settlement. There were several like it now in this part of the hills: Obannese who'd escaped from slavery and Abnaks who'd revolted from the Thunder King and couldn't get back to their homeland. They all lived like Abnaks now, hunting and gathering. Abnaks raise no crops, but neither do they starve. There was plenty of food for new arrivals, and soon they had their own cabins, too.

Uwain, the reciter, was a help to Hlah: he could write. Together they composed an urgent letter to Baron Roshay Bault, who would send it on to the king and his advisers:

"Know, my masters, that the Thunder King has built a New Temple at Kara Karram by the Great Lakes, and that in Silvertown he has raised up a base and treacherous person, one Goryk Gillow, as his own First Prester. This Goryk oppresses and spoils the people for many miles around, for he has a strong Heathen army in Silvertown to enforce his will. But those of our people who accept him as First Prester, he rewards richly and with flattery.

"The chamber house in Silvertown having been

destroyed when the Heathen took the city, this Goryk has appointed some of his vilest creatures to be presters and reciters, and he is building a new chamber house, of timber, not stone. For the time being he has ordained assemblies out of doors, in which he preaches his abominable lies and blasphemies, all in the service of the Thunder King: which false and wicked king he declares to be God's vicar on the earth and threatens the people with God's wrath unless they submit to the Thunder King. Such outrageous things should not be spoken in Obann.

"The people resist as best they can; but unless the king can send an army to drive out the Heathen and recapture Silvertown, we fear this province of Obann will be lost."

Hlah dispatched his two best runners to carry the message to Ninneburky. And by then Uwain had something else to discuss with him.

"This man Sunfish, who ministers to your people, has the most wonderful command of Scripture that I ever heard of," the reciter said. "He must have studied it for many years; and yet in some ways he seems as simple as a child. Who is he? How did he come to be here?"

"I don't know who he is. I found him starving in the wilderness." Hlah told Uwain how he brought the wreck of a man to safety and gave him the name of Sunfish because he couldn't remember his own name. "He's our teacher, and the people love him."

"I see how much they love him," said Uwain. "Strangely, though, I can't stop thinking that I know him from somewhere else."

"There's only one like Sunfish," Hlah said. "Who can he possibly remind you of?"

"I don't know! No one I can think of."

But some years ago Uwain once traveled to Obann City as an assistant to Prester Yevlach, in a great conclave of presters. It was the only time he'd ever visited the great city: not an experience he was likely to forget.

He was in the great nave under the vast dome of the Presters' Palace, in the Temple, when Prester Orth preached to the assembled clergy of all the land of Obann. The beauty of Orth's speaking voice, the force and clarity of his message, his powerful presence and handsomeness of person—these remained bright in Uwain's memory.

Sunfish wore rags and skins, not the gorgeous robes that Orth wore; and his hair had grown into a shaggy mane, and his beard into an unruly cascade reaching halfway down his chest, as opposed to Orth's impeccable and expensive grooming. So it was hardly strange that Uwain didn't recognize him. But there was something about Sunfish that haunted the reciter.

Sunfish treated him with great respect, as if Uwain were the chief prester of a major city; and Uwain was present when Sunfish told Hlah about the dream that troubled him.

"May told me that there is no Temple anymore, that the Temple was destroyed," Sunfish said. "So how am I to preach to all those people in the Temple, if there is no Temple? I was going to ask you, Hlah, to take me there!"

Of course Hlah couldn't do that, and Sunfish walked away shaking his head as if some fear were growing in his heart. They overheard him muttering, "God wills it! God wills it!"

"What do you think of that?" Hlah asked Uwain.

"I hope he hasn't had a vision of the Thunder King's temple of blasphemy," Uwain said. "But he's never heard of that place, has he?"

"Not from me," said Hlah.

CHAPTER 26

A Message for Martis

Goryk Gillow was no fool. He took the lands, the goods, and the persons of those who resisted him, but not for himself. He gave them to those who acknowledged him as First Prester and obeyed him as such.

His supporters and their slaves were building a new chamber house in Silvertown. It would be finished well before the winter. Goryk lived in a modest house that had once belonged to someone else. Every morning he conferred there with the mardar who commanded the Thunder King's army in Silvertown. This was a man named Wusu who came from the land of the Dahai, south of the Great Lakes. Wusu used to distinguish himself by painting the lower half of his face bright blue; but for the sake of his campaign to win over the populace for the Thunder King and the New Temple, Goryk had convinced him not to do it anymore. Wusu still performed human sacrifices, but not in public. Goryk had told the people that the army of King Thunder had discontinued that custom. That they didn't entirely believe it didn't trouble him.

Today Wusu was in a bad mood because some of Goryk's rangers had returned from Lintum Forest with the news that Helki the Rod still lived.

"I have a big enough army to go into that forest and

drive him out," the mardar grumbled. "Were you not so high in favor with my master the Thunder King, I'd do it. Sending men after Helki by the handful is foolishness."

The complaint was long-standing. When one of King Thunder's armies invaded the forest last year, Helki made the survivors carry back the head of their mardar. Nothing would suit Wusu but Helki's head on a pole in the middle of Silvertown.

"Mardar, we may yet agree to send the whole army," Goryk answered. "But the people here are not yet broken to the bridle, and we need your strength to keep them under."

"You'll never tame them, as long as they have Helki's name to invoke."

Still, both men knew what had happened to the first army that went into Lintum Forest. Ten thousand men went in, and only half of them came out again. Why Wusu's ten thousand should fare any better was not clear to Goryk. One more defeat in Lintum Forest, he thought, and the whole country would rise against them.

"We're doing good work here, Mardar, in the service of our master," he said. "Every day more people surrender to us. They want the Temple, and Obann can't give them the Temple anymore. Our master can.

"We shall teach them that to obey our master is to obey their God. You must understand that the God of Obann is not like other people's gods. You can't uproot Him from His place and carry him to Kara Karram as our master's slave and prisoner. But if we act in this God's name, as our master has commanded us to do, we will in time become the masters of this people. And then our lord King Thunder will rule all the nations from the sea in the West to the sea in the

East, for which he will reward us richly."

Wusu frowned. "I sacrificed a slave last night and read the future in his entrails. There is danger for us here, First Prester." There was a hint of disrespect in his pronunciation of the title. "Danger that will come to us from Lintum Forest."

"Don't let the people know you're still performing sacrifices," Goryk said.

Wusu bowed his head. "So I can't see the look on his face!" Goryk thought.

"I obey our master's commandments," said the mardar.

"So do I," said Goryk. "Always!"

In spite of the deep fascination provided by the light-giving item for which they had no name, Jack found himself a bit gloomy the day after their escape from Noma; and Ellayne noticed it.

"What's the matter, Jack?"

"I don't know. I just don't feel so good." He shrugged.

"Are you upset because you hit Noma with that rock?"

"Well … yes! I mean, what if I'd killed him?"

"You didn't," Ellayne said.

"If I hurt him bad enough, he still could die."

Ellayne didn't like to see him like this. Besides, his sense of guilt was contagious. She hadn't stopped him, after all. She patted his back.

"What's done is done," she said. "And what about soldiers? They kill people all the time."

"They don't sneak up on them while they're sleeping and bash 'em with a rock!"

"Well, then, if it's eating you up so badly, you ought to pray about it." A snatch of remembered Scripture came to her. "King Ozias said you can confess your sins to God, and He'll forgive you. Why don't you do that?"

"I'm not even sure I sinned," Jack said. "I don't know if I did right or wrong."

"No—but God knows," said Ellayne. "Leave it up to Him. That's what Obst would say."

They were camping in a gully for the day. Jack climbed out and went to sit by himself behind some bushes for a while. Wytt was going to follow him, but Ellayne asked him to stay. The Omah found a little spot of moist ground and probed it with his stick, looking for worms. Ellayne looked the other way.

"We're not soldiers," she told herself, "but there is a war going on, and we're in it. Noma was on the other side. Jack did right to take the magic from him. It was the only thing to do!" And before she knew it, she was praying, too.

By and by Jack came back to the gully. He seemed to be in better spirits. He sat down beside Ellayne and took the light-giver out of his pocket.

"Don't play with that!" Ellayne said.

"I don't think it's dangerous."

"You don't know anything about it!"

Jack held it up in his fingertips. You could see through it, like glass; but it wasn't glass. "There really isn't much to it," he said. "It weighs hardly anything. It doesn't get very hot when it makes light. Doesn't make any noise, either."

Ellayne had never touched the cusset thing, and didn't plan to. There was a spell on it; she was sure of that. She flinched when Jack made the light go on and off. For all he knew, fire would suddenly shoot out of it and burn them up.

She startled when Wytt sprang to his feet and squealed. "Horses coming—fast!"

That could only mean one thing. Jack thrust the lightgiver deep into his pocket. They flattened themselves to the floor of the gully. Wytt disappeared into the grass. Maybe the riders would pass without seeing them.

But then Jack noticed that their little camp-fire was still sending up a wisp of smoke. They hadn't even needed one! Frantically he stamped on it, even as they heard the pounding of the horses' hooves, which suddenly stopped.

"Marabba kay or!"

A man spoke to them. He and a few others peered down at them from horseback—unwashed, bearded faces.

"You know Martis?" said the rider. "He ask us to look for you."

These were Wallekki. The man's Obannese was hard to understand.

"Martis?" Jack repeated.

"Yes, yes—Martis. You know him? He seeks two children, cannot find them. I am Kwana." The rider touched his heart and dipped his head. "Martis is our friend."

Ellayne scrambled to her feet. "He's our friend, too!" she cried. "Where is he? Can you take us to him?"

Kwana shrugged. "Where he is, we know not. Two days since we see him. But maybe we can find him. We try."

Martis knew how to make friends of the Wallekki. The children had seen him do it more than once. He'd taught them that these Heathen's friendship, once given, could be trusted. Jack stood up beside Ellayne and said, "Yes, please try! We want to see Martis."

Kwana turned to the others and rattled off something in their language. They dismounted and began to pluck up bushes.

"We make big smoke, and maybe Martis see," he said. He grinned at Jack. "We see your little-bit smoke! If Martis see mine, he will read."

It took them a little while to get their fire going. They were using waxbushes with green leaves. Those would produce a terrific amount of smoke, once they got burning properly. When at last the smoke was rising in a thick, grey column, Kwana and another man took a blanket and used it to make the smoke go up in disconnected puffs.

"If Martis sees that, he'll be able to understand the message?" Ellayne said.

"He will."

She nudged Jack. "Isn't that something!" It was one of the cleverest things she'd ever seen. "How far away can Martis be," she asked Kwana, "and still be able to see that?"

Kwana glanced up at the sky. "This weather, maybe two days' ride."

Jack whispered to Ellayne. "Can we trust these fellows?"

"They're Martis' friends," she whispered back. "But if they turn bad on us, flash the light on them at night and scare their eyeballs out!"

Her suggestion left Jack flabbergasted.

CHAPTER 27

A Terror for Jack

Fnaa was getting odd and dangerous ideas—dangerous to himself, probably, he thought. But how dangerous? Hadn't the little girl, Jandra, told him to do whatever came into his heart to do, and God would protect him? And didn't everybody say she was a prophet? Fnaa didn't know much about religion, but he supposed it was best to listen to a prophet.

And so one day, at supper with his chiefs and some of the more important citizens of Obann, he started giggling with a mouthful of soup so that it dribbled out all over, and rolled his eyes every which way, and finally laughed out loud; and everybody at the table stared at him.

"Your Majesty, what's the matter?" cried Gurun, sitting next to him. "You've spilled soup all over your nice clean shirt."

"I can't help it!" Fnaa said. "It's so funny, that man's beard." He pointed across the table to Obann's richest lumber merchant. "It's got all those bread crumbs in it!" He broke into a peal of high-pitched, quavering laughter that echoed up and down the banquet hall like the wailing of a ghost. He couldn't see his mother, who was standing somewhere behind him to wait on the banqueters, but he could imagine the look on her face. Meanwhile the wealthy merchant hurriedly applied a napkin to his beard; but he couldn't dab out the blush of embarrassment that reddened his cheeks.

"I think perhaps we've kept His Majesty too long at the table," said a man whose work crews were repairing the damage to the city's walls. Fnaa grinned at him and tried to make his eyes roll in opposite directions, and the man looked the other way.

"Yes—I'm sure you must be tired, Sire," said Gurun.

One by one the prominent citizens rose from the table—they were losing out on a good supper—bowed politely to the king, excused themselves with flowery words, and left. The chiefs remained at the table, still staring at Fnaa.

"I think I ought to put His Majesty to bed," Gurun said. "Come along, King Ryons."

"I will go with you," said Chagadai. Uduqu got up, too. "I think I'll tell the king a bedtime story," he said.

"Do you think that wise, Chief Uduqu?"

"Very wise, O Queen."

So four of them went off to the royal bedchamber, with Dakl hurrying after. "Oh, I'm going to catch it now!" Fnaa thought.

Chagadai commanded Dakl to stay outside and not let anyone stop by the door to listen. She wrung her apron in her hands, and he patted her shoulder. "Don't be afraid," he said. "We won't hurt him."

With the door shut and bolted, Fnaa had to deal with three pairs of grown-up eyes all trying to bore holes in him at once. For courage he turned to God's promise to protect him.

"Are you well, Fnaa?" Gurun asked. "Please tell the truth! Your mother has told me that you always used to play the fool in your old master's house, so that they wouldn't sell you. But why play the fool with us?"

"If he's playing!" Uduqu added.

Fnaa shrugged. "It's the thing I do best," he said. He told them what Jandra had said to him. Chagadai nodded: Abgayl had already told him of the incident. But this was the first time Fnaa told anyone what Jandra had actually said.

"Everybody says God speaks through her," he went on. "So I thought it was God telling me what to do."

The adults exchanged puzzled looks. They'd all had experience of Jandra's prophecies: there could be no doubting her. She was far too young to invent the messages that came out of her mouth. Besides, her prophecies came true.

"Why should God want the people of this city to think their king has lost his wits?" Gurun wondered.

"She said I should do anything that came into my heart to do," Fnaa said. He paused for a moment to concentrate. "She said God wants me to provoke folly in the minds of men who will not hear His voice. That's just want she said. 'Folly' means really stupid foolishness—doesn't it?"

Uduqu chuckled. "That it does!" he said. "But it might get ticklish for us, when all the people get to thinking we chiefs have unloaded a simpleton on them for a king. They might get nasty about it."

"You don't have to worry about that," Fnaa said. "The next thing I'm going to do is to send the army away—to Lintum Forest, I mean. Maybe that's where King Ryons is. Maybe you'll be able to find him there."

Chagadai's jaw dropped open. "What will people think of us," he said, "if we Ghols desert our father? My men will think I'm crazy! Except for the three of us in this room, and

Obst, all the chieftains believe this boy is King Ryons. And all the warriors believe it, too."

"Well, God said He would protect me," said Fnaa. "He didn't promise to protect anybody else, so all of you had better go. Then you'll be safe. I wouldn't want the real King Ryons to blame me for getting his army killed."

"There is wisdom in this," Gurun said. "The city is rotten with treason. If the people rise against us, better the king's army have no Obannese blood on its hands. But I do not think they will rise, if the chiefs and their warriors leave the city. I will stay here with Fnaa: I am told the people are very far from hating me."

"You are brave, honeysuckle," said Chagadai. "And you, too, Fnaa, are a very brave boy—just like King Ryons himself. I don't like to leave you! Even so, we have never gone wrong by obeying God. He has saved us out of worse troubles than this."

"Lintum Forest is almost like home, to Abnaks," Uduqu said. "But I'm getting too old to march so far, and I don't care to bounce all those miles on a horse's back. I think I'll stay, too. My men can choose a younger man to be their chief."

"It's dangerous to stay," said Fnaa.

"That's all right," Uduqu said. "I'm dangerous, myself. Anyone who wants my scalp will have a hard time earning it."

The five Wallekki made camp by the gully. All afternoon they sent up smoke signals. Ellayne was curious, and watched them closely. "Can you really send messages by puffs of smoke?" she asked.

"Oh, yes—not difficult," Kwana said. He was the only one who could speak any Obannese. "This smoke means, 'Two—friends—found—come.' If Martis sees, he will know what it means."

With five armed men around them the children felt safe, although Wytt kept himself out of the men's sight. Supper was short rations, for the Wallekkis' hunting hadn't prospered lately. Kwana said they would do better tomorrow.

By and by everyone was sound asleep but Jack. Some restless impulse led him to take the light-giver from his pocket and hold it in his hands. He rolled onto his side, facing away from the others, and wondered if he dared coax any light out of the object without the Wallekki seeing it and demanding an explanation—or maybe even hopping onto their horses in a panic and deserting. He supposed it would do no harm if he kept the object cupped tightly in his hands and held it close. After all, it made no noise.

He squeezed the bump in the middle of the disc and light leaped out. He held it close to the ground, close to his body, so it wouldn't wake the sleepers. He fondled the smooth, round rim of it—

And then something happened that made him yelp aloud, very loud indeed; and he almost threw the disc away; and men woke up with grunts and mutterings. He heard them fumble for their weapons. Ellayne sat up next to him and said, "Jack? Jack?" But he had the presence of mind to pinch the nubbin and snuff out the light, and jam the disc back into his pocket before anyone saw anything.

"It's all right!" he answered Ellayne. That was a lie: it was not all right, but he had to say something. "I just had a bad dream, that's all. Sorry!"

Kwana overheard, translated for his men, and they lay back down, grumbling. Kwana crawled closer to Jack and asked, "What did you dream?"

"Just a silly dream," Jack said. "I was climbing a tree and I fell."

"Stay out of trees," said Kwana, and crept back to his blanket.

After a few minutes Ellayne moved closer and whispered harshly, "Liar! You were playing with that cusset thing, weren't you? What happened?"

"I'll tell you in the morning."

"You let out a yell like someone burned you."

"I didn't get hurt!" Jack said. "Everything's all right. Now be quiet so the men can sleep!"

So Ellayne had to lie there and fume in silence until she fell back to sleep. But for Jack there was no chance of sleep that night. He wondered if he would ever sleep again. He couldn't say whether he'd been scared half to death or just astonished more than he could bear. It was quite a few minutes before his heart stopped fluttering like a moth in a jar. Belatedly he noticed he was drenched in sweat. Sleep was out of the question.

It wasn't until later in the morning, when the Wallekki had gone out foraging for food prior to sending up more smoke signals, that Jack had a chance to tell Ellayne what had happened. Kwana had decided to remain at this camp for a few days and give Martis a chance to find them. There was a spring at the far end of the gully, and near it a wild plum tree was in fruit—for hungry men, it was better than nothing. The children undertook to fill all the waterskins while the men hunted for food, and so they found themselves alone at last.

"Well?" said Ellayne. "What was all that yelling about last night? What did you do?"

"I only yelled once," Jack said, "and I didn't do anything—not on purpose, I mean. I wanted to make the light, just to see it, because I couldn't get to sleep. And—"

"And what?"

He hardly knew how to continue. There were some things that just didn't make sense no matter how you tried to say them.

"Come on, Jack!"

"It's this thing here." He patted his pocket, careful not to pat too hard and not daring to take the item out again. He didn't want to touch it. He might not ever touch it again.

"What about it?" Ellayne stamped her foot.

Jack groped for words, couldn't find any that would serve, and finally just blurted out: "This thing. There's someone in it!"

"What?" Ellayne shook her head. What in the world would make him say a thing like that? She couldn't have heard him right. "What are you talking about?"

"I saw her!" Jack said. "A woman. She's inside this thing. She looked at me!"

Ellayne took his arms in her hands and squeezed. "Talk sense, Jack—if you can," she said. "Don't talk nonsense! Are you all right?"

"Oh, sure, I'm all right—except for being scared out of my skin." He took a deep breath. "I saw a woman's face. She was inside the cuss't thing. She was smiling. She had red lips. Great big eyes: too big. And then she blinked. I know what I saw!"

"But Jack—it's just a little tiny thing that fits in your hand. There can't be anybody inside it. They wouldn't fit! It must have been a picture that you saw. Some kind of picture."

"A picture doesn't blink at you," Jack said.

He felt sick. For two spits he'd crush the filthy thing with a rock, if he dared lay hands on it again. He wished it weren't in his pocket. All he had to do was close his eyes, and he could see that face again. The woman had eyes twice as big as any normal person's and lips as red as blood.

Ellayne saw by the lack of color in his face that he really was scared and wasn't joking. A dread crept over her, starting at her scalp and prickling its way down. "This is what comes of messing around with magic!" she thought.

"You'd better let me see it," she said.

"I don't want to see it again. I don't want to touch it. If you want to reach into my pocket and take it, you can have it."

"I don't want it! I just want to see."

At that moment Wytt joined them, jumping out of cover with a piercing chirp; and Jack jumped an inch off the ground.

"Fry your eyes, Wytt, don't do that!" he cried.

Wytt glared at him and chattered like a scolding squirrel. The meaning he conveyed was, "Why are you so scared? There's nothing bad here. Not now. Men will be back soon. What has scared you, Jack?"

Jack tried to explain. "It's that thing I took from Noma, the thing that makes light. There's a woman inside it."

He almost screamed when Wytt leaped up on his leg, took a hold on his belt, and stuck his face in the pocket. Wytt sniffed deeply.

He chirped and twittered, "No one there! Nothing living, nothing breathing." He gave Jack what looked like a reproving glance and hopped back to the ground. Ellayne believed his report and felt deeply relieved.

"It's not a real person, Jack," she said. "It's something magical, and you'd better not fiddle with it anymore." And she couldn't help adding, "Do you believe in magic now?"

He was so mad at her for saying that, he forgot to be afraid.

CHAPTER 28

How Ryons Was Captured

Lintum Forest is a very great forest. Ryons soon realized that you don't just walk in and "find Helki." Indeed, unless you know it well—even Helki didn't know all of it—you are liable not to be able to find anything, and lose yourself while you're looking for it.

That was what happened to Ryons and Perkin. After two days of pushing into the forest, they found themselves in the middle of an unknown and uninhabited country, with nothing to see but trees and no idea of how to get back to the edge of the forest. There were paths aplenty, but those had been made by animals without a thought for the convenience of humans. Ryons and Perkin had taken many of them to get to where they were now. A woodsman would have blazed his trail so he could pick it up again, but Ryons and Perkin weren't woodsmen. Perkin had tried to set a straight course east, but too many of the paths led into bogs and briar patches to allow anything at all like a direct route anywhere.

"In short," said Perkin, "we're lost."

Cavall looked up at him expectantly, wagging his tail. He wasn't lost. Angel perched up in a tree somewhere; she wasn't lost either. Baby stood beside Perkin, eyes half-closed. He was lost, but he didn't care. This morning he'd caught and devoured an opossum, and he was beginning to like the forest.

"I guess we ought to find a nice place and make camp," Ryons said. "Someplace where there's water and berries, and where we can set traps or make bows and arrows. Helki always said there's no reason to go hungry in the forest, but I'm getting pretty hungry."

"A good idea, Your Majesty. My sling doesn't seem to be of much use in all these trees." They hadn't had any fresh meat since entering the forest.

When he was here last, Ryons held court at a ruined castle where Helki had resettled people who'd been driven off their homesteads by outlaws. It was probably a regular village by now, Ryons thought. He'd love to go back there, but didn't know how to find us. "Someone in Lintum Forest must know where it is and how to get there," he thought. But there didn't seem to be anyone at all in this region of the forest.

By the end of the day they found a place where a spring bubbled up into a pool and a little rill went running off deeper into the woods. Around the pool was well-churned mud: many animals came here to drink. "So the hunting ought to be good, if we can manage it," Perkin said. There was enough of a clearing for a lean-to and a fire. A blackberry patch grew nearby.

Ryons went to pick some berries. There was nothing else for supper. Cavall followed him, and in a moment or two, began to growl.

"What is it?" Ryons said. Cavall stood stiff-legged, with his nose pointed at skewed and flattened canes with tufts of black hair clinging to the brambles. Ryons called Perkin to come and see.

"I think a bear was here," the king said. He was sure he'd heard, somewhere, that bears ate berries.

"Whatever has been here, Cavall doesn't like it," Perkin said.

"Maybe it isn't safe for us to camp here?"

The man shrugged. "We'll have a fire," he said, "and most animals won't want to come near it. And I don't think even a bear would want to tangle with Cavall and Baby together."

That was true. But there were other predators in this part of the forest, and they were watching.

Not all of the outlaws had been tamed by Helki. Quite a few simply moved beyond his reach. This meant slim pickings for them, having to keep to regions where there were no settlers to be their prey. Like spiders, they preyed on one another.

One of these was Hwyddo, who with his brother and two friends escaped Helki's rod and fled to the west end of the forest. The spring and the berry patch, where Ryons and Perkin now camped, Hwyddo considered to be his property, in the middle of his territory.

"We can take them now," whispered Culluch, his brother.

"We can take them whenever we please, as long as the dog hasn't caught our scent," Hwyddo whispered back. "I prefer to watch them for a while. The big bird will make a fine feast for us."

Culluch nodded; he was an expert archer. All four had

bows and arrows, but only Culluch could be relied on to hit anything.

The wind was blowing the wrong way, so Cavall couldn't smell the men in hiding. But Angel saw them. She whistled an alarm. Cavall barked, and Baby crashed through the berry patch and disappeared among the trees.

The outlaws could have shot down Ryons and Perkin in their tracks, but there was no money in corpses. Captured alive, people could always be sold to the Heathen. One of the lads let fly an arrow at Cavall, but missed. It thunked into a tree. Cavall knew all about arrows and made himself scarce, now barking frantically. Hwyddo would have clouted the man who loosed the arrow, but he was out of reach.

"Down!" Perkin said, and pushed the king face-first to the ground. He dove right after him.

No more arrows followed. Disgusted, Hwyddo gave a signal and he and his men stepped into the open. Culluch had an arrow on the string, ready to shoot the dog if it attacked. But Cavall didn't show himself.

"Stay down, you two, and give up quietly," Hwyddo said. "We won't hurt you if you don't resist."

"We won't!" said Perkin. "But we haven't anything worth stealing."

One of the outlaws laughed. "Then we'll just steal you!" he said.

Ryons thought fast. "Sell us to Helki the Rod," he said. "He's a friend of ours. He'll give you a good price! Better than anyone else would give." Perkin stared at him but didn't speak.

The one who'd laughed started to say something, but Hwyddo silenced him with a wave of a hand.

"Helki's sworn to string us up, if he can catch us," Hwyddo said. "Who might you be, that he'd ransom you and let us go free?"

"They're a couple of his spies," said the other man. "I say we ought to hang them from a tree—teach Helki a lesson!"

"Shut up, Hass. You talk too much." Hwyddo nodded at Ryons. "Stand up, both of you, and tell me exactly who you are."

In his days as a slave Ryons had learned to lie as naturally as the grass grows. It saved him many a beating. This skill came back to him now.

"I used to live with Helki," he said. "He was like a father to me. He sent me to Obann City because he thought it'd be a better place for me to grow up, but I didn't like it so I decided to come back.

"This is Perkin. He helped me to travel safely across the plain country. He wanted to see me safely to Helki and claim a reward, but we got lost."

"What about the hound," asked Culluch, "and the giant bird?"

"The hound is mine," Ryons said, "and Perkin raised the bird from a chick. They won't give you any trouble. All we want is to get to Helki. I promise he'll pay you for us and not hang you."

"You haven't told me your name, boy," Hwyddo said.

"It's Ryons—same as the king."

"What king?"

Perkin spoke up. "Sir, there is a king in Obann now. Don't ask me how that came to be, because I don't know. I suppose it's because of the war; that's thrown everything out of kilter. Last summer the Heathen almost took the city.

They burned down the Temple. There's no First Prester now, and the oligarchs have all been killed or run away."

"We've heard nothing of any of this," Hwyddo said. Looking at the bearded, dirty faces and the ragged, unwashed clothes, Ryons could easily believe that.

"Nevertheless, it's true," Perkin said.

The fourth bandit spoke. "So what are we going to do, Hwyddo? Are we going to sell these birds to Helki and take our chances with him? I don't like it!"

Hwyddo didn't answer right away. He rubbed his fingers through his beard.

"It's late in the day," he said. "Let's sleep on it and decide tomorrow morning."

Martis' zig-zag course across the plain took him toward the forest only slowly. Because of this, he was able to see Kwana's smoke signals.

"Two—friends—found—come." He read the message accurately. "Is that for me?" he wondered. There was only one way to find out. He turned Dulayl and rode back in the direction of the signals. He would lose ground by this, but it couldn't be helped.

Martis urged his horse to greater speed.

CHAPTER 29

A Demon in His Pocket

Helki had eleven Griffs who had attached themselves to him after he led them in a desperate battle against a band of Abnaks, and they had all by a miracle survived. At their own insistence they bound themselves to him by complicated oaths, as was the custom of their nation. Tiliqua was the name of their chief man, a tall fellow who managed, in all circumstances, to keep his black hair piled up in a truly impressive coiffure. Under Helki's direction they were becoming expert woodsmen.

The Griffs came looking for Helki while he was still being hunted by the men from Silvertown. The hunters weren't expecting anyone to come for Helki, and before they knew it, the Griffs killed half a dozen of them. The survivors lost heart and fled the forest altogether.

"Who were they?" Tiliqua asked when they found Helki.

"All I know is that they were Obannese," Helki said, "and that they came here just to kill me. Too bad we didn't take one alive. We might've learned something interesting. But what are you men doing here? You're supposed to be scouting in the south."

"Your pardon, Chief!" said Tiliqua. "But when you were late for our rendezvous, we feared for you."

"Anything going on in the south?"

"There is no enemy within a whole day's journey of Carbonek." Carbonek was the name given to the village growing up around the ruined castle, after an enchanted place in an ancient story.

Helki nodded. His men patrolled aggressively all around the village. After the first few hangings, outlaws learned to give the place a wide berth. Many of Helki's men had once been outlaws themselves: they were the most zealous fighters he had.

"Those bushwhackers you chased out of here," he said, "came into the forest from the east. Either the Thunder King has put a price on my head and they wanted to collect it, or else somebody sent them. They were too many to share any kind of reward that might be put up for me, so I reckon they were carrying out someone's orders."

"Let them try!" Tiliqua said, grinning. "They would need a very big army to flush us out of Lintum Forest."

"That's what worries me," said Helki.

In the morning Hwyddo decided to sell his two prisoners to Helki. His brother Culluch agreed, and the man named Hass just shrugged. But the fourth man, Maelghin, strongly disagreed.

"I say cut their throats and bury 'em right here," he said. "And if they're really friends of Helki's, that goes double! What about all our friends that Helki killed?"

"Use your head, Maelghin," Hwyddo said. "If we kill them and keep it a secret, what kind of revenge is that? But if Helki finds out, he'll make sure to finish us."

Ryons saw Perkin turn pale. He'd judged Perkin a brave man: he must not be used to this kind of talk. As a slave among the Wallekki, Ryons had heard worse.

Hass said, "I don't trust Helki. There's many a good lad who ain't alive anymore on account of him. We don't want to end up the same way, do we?"

Culluch nodded. "He's got a point there, brother," he said.

Then Perkin began to whistle—and very loudly, too. Everybody stared at him. He and Ryons had their ankles and wrists tied, so they couldn't try to get away or to defend themselves. Maybe Perkin's nerve had cracked, Ryons thought. That whistling sounded crazy.

"Stop that!" Hwyddo said. But Perkin wouldn't stop, not even when Hwyddo kicked him in the thigh. It wasn't even a proper tune he whistled, Ryons thought.

And then Baby burst out from the trees, and the great heavy beak snapped shut on Hass, killing him instantly; and Baby lashed out with a heavy taloned foot and felled Culluch. And with a great howl Cavall burst out of the woods right behind the giant bird. Hwyddo and Maelghin took to their heels, but Cavall pulled Maelghin down from behind and savaged him. It was all over in the blink of an eye.

"Your hands, Ryons—hold out your hands!" Ryons obeyed automatically, and Perkin untied his wrists for him, with movements swift and sure. "Now untie mine—if you please, Your Majesty."

Ryons labored on the knots. Baby had begun to eat a bit of Hass: not something you wanted to look at. Culluch lay whimpering and groaning; he wouldn't be doing much for a while. Cavall stood over Maelghin, growling, but the man lay perfectly still and silent. Ryons fumbled with the knots and finally loosened them. In a moment Perkin's hands were free, and then he untied their ankles. He took some time, but not too much, to recover their belongings.

"We don't dare stay here," he said. "Hwyddo might come back with more men, and this time they'll shoot us before we know they're there."

But there was something Ryons wanted to know. "How did you teach him to do that?" he cried, pointing to Baby. "He came when you called!"

"Oh, he comes when I whistle to him. But I didn't know he'd attack those people, although I certainly hoped he would! I know he wouldn't like anyone to hurt me. Your Majesty, we've got to go!"

Ryons called Cavall to his side, praised him and patted him. It wasn't the first time the great hound had saved him. He held up his arm and whistled for Angel, who swooped down from a tree with a glad shrill cry.

"We're all here. Now we can go," said Perkin. He patted Baby, whose head shot up from the remains of Hass, and for a moment his feathers stood up on his neck. He didn't like being interrupted in his feeding, but when Perkin insisted, he came along.

"What about them?" Ryons asked, looking back to the fallen men. Culluch was still alive, and Maelghin might be.

"They'll have to manage without us, Sire."

Not knowing where they were going, they hurried down a path other than the one Hwyddo had chosen. Perkin led the way, but Baby overtook him and stalked on ahead, his great head bobbing back and forth. Cavall stayed close to Ryons' side, and Angel flitted from tree to tree. Where in the forest they would be, at the end of the day, they had no inkling.

Kwana pointed to a few tiny puffs of smoke sailing in the sky, some indeterminable distance in the east.

"Martis is coming," he says. "He says we must wait for him. This is a good place for camp, so we stay here."

The Wallekki were happy because they'd been able to bag an animal something like a deer, and that meant fresh meat for all. It was another one of those strange animals you sometimes saw these days. Instead of hooves like a deer's, it had three stout, thickly padded toes. None of the men had ever seen anything like it before, but they were hungry enough to expect a good meal out of any creature.

"That's really Martis sending that message—and you can really read it?" Ellayne marveled.

Kwana nodded. "It says, 'Coming. Wait,'" he explained. "I think it must be Martis, but soon we know."

Jack said nothing. He was trying not to think of the face in the disc, that appeared the last time he held it in his hand, but it kept swimming up to the surface of his mind. The cusset thing had blinked at him; and only living things can blink. Somewhere inside that little piece of whatever-it-was existed a living thing. And he had it in his pocket.

Ellayne told him there was a magician in one of the Abombalbap stories who confined a demon to a magic jar and made it his slave. When he spoke a certain word, the demon had to come out and do his bidding. Jack wondered if he had a demon in his pocket, and whether he could get rid of it.

He stole a hard look at Ellayne. She was the one who'd wanted to go to Obann. He would have been just as happy to stay home and play chess with the baron. "All her fault!"

he thought. But what would have happened if they hadn't delivered Fnaa to the city in time to take King Ryons' place? And it certainly hadn't been Ellayne's idea to take the magic-thing from Noma.

What would he do if the demon came out of it and spoke to him? It looked like a woman, but Jack had only seen its face. It might be a serpent from the neck down, or a giant beetle. Once you got involved with magic, anything could happen.

"Which is why there's no such thing as magic!" whispered an urgent little voice in the back of his mind. "God doesn't let just anything happen!" But then if magic wasn't real, why did it say in the Scriptures that it was forbidden to practice magic?

"Watch, Jack!" Ellayne jogged his elbow, snapping him out of his reverie. "Isn't it interesting?" How she could be so interested in smoke signals at a time like this was unfathomable.

"Sure," Jack muttered. "Interesting."

"Well, Martis is coming and I can't wait to see him," Ellayne said. "He always knows what to do."

"He won't know what to do this time," Jack answered. "I wonder if you can get rid of magical things by throwing them into the river. Or do they just come back to you?"

She yanked him close and whispered right into his ear, "Shh! Don't talk about it in front of the men! Haven't you got any sense at all?"

Sometimes I wonder if I do, Jack thought. But he said, "All right, all right! No need to pinch my arm."

CHAPTER 30

How the Army Left the City

Once again King Ryons' army rode forth, this time to leave the city that they'd come so far, and dared so much, to save. It was a bigger army now, its numbers swelled by some thousand Heathen warriors salvaged from the Thunder King's vast host that was driven from the city in a panic a year ago. General Hennen's Obannese spearmen stayed behind as a royal guard, seven hundred of them. But four thousand men, all told, departed from the city.

Once again they raised their voices, singing the anthem of the army in a dozen different languages at once:

"For His mercy endureth forever!"

For these had all converted to belief in God.

Once again, but this time with grief in his heart, Obst rode among the chieftains on a donkey. He'd wanted very badly to remain and supervise the work on the Lost Scrolls; but the chieftains wouldn't let him.

"You're our teacher. Your place is with us," said Shaffur. "Besides, you understand all languages. Our councils would be in ruins without you."

Nor would Preceptor Constan let him stay.

"The work's proceeding very smoothly," Constan said. "Prester Jod has sent us his best scholars from the seminary in Durmurot. But the king may need his Heathen army someday, and you're the only man who can hold it together for him."

As the army paraded down Grand Avenue, the people of the city thronged the street, many of them waving and cheering; but not all. Chief Zekelesh, marching beside his men of Fazzan, heard things that made his ears tingle.

"There they go, the murdering Heathen!"

"And good riddance to them, too."

"I'd rather they stayed. When they come back, they'll be fighting for the Thunder King."

They were Heathen no more, they'd murdered no one, and each and every one of them had renounced the Thunder King forever. They'd shed their blood fighting for Obann, and this was the thanks they got. Zekelesh was glad there were but few men among them who could understand Obannese.

He himself couldn't understand why they were leaving King Ryons among these ungrateful people. But it was the king's command that they guard the lands between Lintum Forest and the great river. Queen Gurun had explained it to the chieftains.

"There is danger in the East," she said. "The Thunder King has a great army at Silvertown, and there are traitors at work up and down the river. It will take time to raise and train militia in the provinces. Your swords are of more use there than here."

That was only good sense, and no one could deny it. And so they paraded out of Obann City: Wallekki on horseback, in all their feathered finery; the Fazzan in their wolf's-head caps; grim, tattooed Abnaks; long-legged Griffs showing off their elaborate hair-dos; the wiry Ghols of the king's own bodyguard on their wiry little horses, with their bows of horn; Hawk and his four brothers from the faraway Hosa country, black-skinned, armed with long shields and short spears, like no man had ever before seen in Obann; the Dahai in their checkered kilts; men from countries east of the Great Lakes, whose kind had never crossed over the mountains before; and on the flanks, fleet-footed, half-naked Attakotts with poisoned arrows in their quivers.

They sang as their spirits moved them, creating a babble that echoed up and down the streets of great Obann, praising God, and with a roar that the people of the city would long remember, the chorus: "His mercy endureth forever!"

Gurun kept her bodyguard of eighteen Blays, all that was left of a contingent of the Thunder King's host—short, barrel-chested men, expert slingers, who had attached themselves to her before she came to the city and would never leave her. They feared the Thunder King because he took away their gods, and then his army was destroyed and they were hopelessly far from home with nowhere to go. They fell into awe of Gurun because she taught them God would save them and taught them how to pray. Nothing would part them from her.

She stood on the roof of the palace, watching the parade with Fnaa, Uduqu, Hennen, Constan, and other city notables. She wondered where Gallgoid was, and knew he would be watching more closely than anyone.

His last words to her, two days ago, were these: "My agents will be busy, but don't expect to see them. Don't mention my name to anyone but Hennen or Uduqu. As far as anyone else knows, I am nobody. It won't be safe for us to see each other face to face. If you need to communicate with me, wear this necklace and leave the rest up to me." And he gave her a thin gold chain with a green stone, of a type common enough in the city that any well-to-do lady might be expected to own.

Already, she mused, the servants and the functionaries in the palace had noticed a change in their supposed king. Fnaa was doing things that caught their eyes—and made them gossip, too, Gurun supposed. "It must be all over the city by now," she thought.

It was a marvel to watch him staring fixedly at a spider in its web, with his mouth open, and sometimes drooling. Or walking with his eyes apparently unfocused and bumping into someone. Or making a rude noise at the supper table and laughing about it. He had more tricks than a traveling puppet show, and you'd swear they weren't tricks at all and that he truly was going diddly. "No wonder his old master couldn't sell him!" Gurun thought.

The chieftains had wanted Jandra to go with them, too; they would bring her back to Lintum Forest. But Gurun pleaded with them. "Please don't take both Obst and Jandra! Or else wait for God to speak again through her and show us His will in this matter." The chiefs seemed puzzled when Uduqu and Chagadai strongly supported her.

"We'll do as you ask," Chief Shaffur said, "but for no one else would we do it."

"All will be made plain to you before long, my lords,"

Obst promised.

Hennen, standing next to Gurun while the parade went by, had to speak twice before he got her attention.

"I said, my lady, that I hope we see these men again," he said. "There's never been another army like it, has there? Not since the days of King Ozias himself! They have no general, and yet they've never lost a battle. They came to Obann to sack the city and wound up saving it. They've never been inside a chamber house in all their lives, and yet they love God and would die for Him. My lads and I will miss them. It's been an honor to serve with them. And who would have thought it? A leaderless mass of Heathen has become the army of the Lord. I wish I were marching with them!"

"Oh, they'll be back, all right," Uduqu said. "This song is a long way from being sung to its finish." Fnaa climbed onto the rail for a better look at the parade, the kind of thing a very foolish child would do, and Uduqu snatched him back to safety before he could fall. "Here, Your Majesty! You sit up here on my shoulders, and you'll see everything." He set the boy on his shoulders and held on to his ankles. Fnaa waved delightedly to a passing bird. Gurun saw people down below looking up at him, and a few of them pointing.

"We're all going to wish we'd marched out with the army, by and by," she thought.

In the evening the army camped on the plain beside the great river, and the chieftains pitched their great black tent that had once belonged to a mardar of the Thunder King. Obst said he had to speak to them; they gathered in the tent at sundown. Shaffur made a point of setting King Ryon's ivory stool in the midst of them, conspicuously empty.

Obst stood to address them. He spoke in Obannese, but each of the chiefs heard his words in his own native tongue.

"My lords," he said, "the time has come to tell you something that you did not know, because it was kept a secret from you. Please hear me out before you get angry!

"A month ago and more, King Ryons disappeared. You couldn't find him anywhere inside the palace, nor could he be found outside. His hound, Cavall, was missing, too—as you were told at the time."

He told them how, when the matter seemed most hopeless, Ellayne and Jack brought to the city a boy who was the image of King Ryons; and how, lest disorder should break out in the city, Gurun installed that boy in Ryons' place and presented him to everyone as the king himself, recovering from a sudden illness that had blotted out his memory.

"Chieftains, the boy we left behind today is not the king, but a brave boy who has agreed to hold Ryons' place for him until he returns. Chief Uduqu knew of the substitution, and Chief Chagadai. But we dared not tell the rest of you. If somehow the matter became known in the city, we feared there would be an uprising against us. There is a great deal of treason fermenting in that city."

Shaffur smote his thighs and roared a profanity.

"I knew it!" he said. "There was a stink in all these dealings, Teacher! And meanwhile, where is our king?" All the chieftains grumbled loudly, and it took some time to settle them.

"My lords, we don't know where King Ryons is," Obst said. "Somehow, one night, he got out of the palace and out of the city without anyone seeing him. There is nothing to suggest he's been abducted. After all, his hound is with him! We don't know how he got away, or where he went, but we think he may have gone to Lintum Forest—of his own free will, for some unknown reason. But whatever the case, he hasn't been in Obann for some time. And meanwhile the Thunder King sows treason everywhere. It was judged best for this army not to be penned up in the city."

"Well, that's good sense, at least!" said Tughrul Lomak, chief of the Dahai. "Had we stayed there much longer, we might have forgotten what our swords and spears are for."

"But how are we to find King Ryons?" wondered the new chief of the Abnaks—Buzzard, one of the many sons-in-law of the late Chief Spider. "If only we'd been told as soon as he was gone! We would have tracked him down—we, or our friends the Attakotts."

"Attakotts would have found him," said their chieftain, Looth.

"My lords, my lords!" said Obst. "Be sure that all of this has come to pass by the will of God and that He will protect Ryons better than we ever could. Has He not promised him the kingdom?

"Besides which, I must tell you now that God has spoken to the boy Fnaa through Jandra, whom you know as a true prophet. Fnaa has the Lord's protection now. It remains for us to wait for the Lord and learn what is His will for us."

It took most of the night for Obst, with help from Chagadai, to reconcile the chiefs to all the deceptions that had been practiced on them. Shaffur questioned Gallgoid's role in it, but Chagadai convinced him that there was no way King Ryons could have eluded the Ghols' guardianship, except by God's providence. But the tall Wallekki couldn't quite stop fuming.

"It seems to me, sometimes," he said, "that God asks too much of us. The old Wallekki gods wouldn't dream of trying us so."

"My lord!" Obst protested, but Shaffur held up a hand to quiet him.

"Peace, old man!" he said. "I'm as much God's man as you are. If He knows everything, as you say He does, then He knows that, too."

CHAPTER 31

What Sunfish Saw

Ryons and Perkin were thoroughly lost. The forest had swallowed them up. Fleeing from the outlaws, they followed whatever path seemed easiest. Once they had to splash through a bog. Finally they found a place to stop—they really couldn't go any farther without rest—where there was a little creek nearby, but nothing to eat.

"I wonder if I ought to build a fire," Perkin said. "But we have nothing to cook, and the smoke might help Hwyddo find us."

"Oh, let's have a campfire!" Ryons said. "It'll be dark soon, and I don't want to sit around in the dark for hours and hours."

"I doubt either of us will stay awake for many hours," Perkin said. Before the night closed in, he made a little campfire. Cavall lay down beside Ryons, and Baby settled down by Perkin. "We're safe from wild animals, at least," thought Ryons.

But Cavall never stretched out and shut his eyes. He kept his head up and his eyes open. From time to time his ears twitched, but Ryons couldn't hear anything but the normal nighttime noise of birds and frogs and insects, and the night breeze creeping through the treetops.

"I'm hungry," he muttered.

"So am I, Your Majesty," said Perkin. "Maybe tomorrow we'll find something we can eat."

Ryons would have fallen asleep much sooner if he hadn't been so hungry. They'd been on the run all day with nothing to eat. His stomach rumbled. An owl hooted in reply. Perkin began to snore. Their fire died down to a feeble glow, and Ryons couldn't see anything but the solid black wall of benighted forest all around him, and high above, directly overhead, a patch of sky strewn with stars. He saw a shooting star streak past, and fell asleep waiting for another one.

In the grey morning Ryons woke. Cavall lay sleeping beside him, and Baby was up, drinking from the creek. Perkin still slept. Ryons sat up, yawned and stretched—

And then froze: because there at his feet, lying on the ground, he saw the carcass of a large, plump hare.

He grabbed Perkin's sleeve and shook. "Perkin—wake up! Look!"

Something in his tone woke Perkin in a hurry. When he saw the hare, the last vestige of sleep fell from him.

"Now how did that get there?" he said. "Cavall must have caught it during the night."

"Did you?" Ryons asked the dog. Cavall looked at him and wagged his tail. "But I don't think he left my side all night."

"We ought to get this cleaned and cooked right away," Perkin said. He picked it up, studied it, shook his head. "Sire, Cavall never touched this hare. See—these punctures in its side. No dog's teeth did that."

"Then what did?"

Perkin frowned. "I don't know. It wasn't Angel. She wouldn't fly by night. Nor was it any weapon I'm familiar with."

"Let's eat it anyway!" Ryons said. "Then we can wonder about how it got here."

"At least we can be sure it wasn't put here by an enemy," Perkin said.

Expertly he cleaned the hare and skinned it, tossed the innards to Angel, while Ryons gathered firewood. Soon the hare was cooking on a spit; not so soon and it was ready to eat.

"Let's remember to give thanks before we eat," said Perkin; but Ryons had already bowed his head in prayer.

Far away, in the hills below the mountains, at about the same time as Perkin was cooking the hare, Sunfish came out of his little cabin and rubbed his eyes. The village was already astir, and May was just coming to wake him.

"Oh," she said, "you're up already."

"I've seen something, May. It scared me."

"What was it?"

"A man, I think. A man with a face of shining gold," he said.

"That must have been a dream, Sunfish."

"I don't think so. I think I was awake!"

She couldn't calm him herself, so she took him to Hlah; and after Hlah heard what Sunfish had to say, he asked his wife to wake Uwain. May came back with the reciter, and Sunfish told his tale again. He took a deep breath and launched into it.

"This is what I saw, Mr. Uwain. I was lying on my bed, and then I was in some place with a crowd of people. They couldn't see me or hear me, and I couldn't speak to them.

I wanted to, but no words would come out of my mouth. But they were listening to someone who stood above them, on a rock, I think, and preached to them. Only it was bad preaching.

"When I turned to see who it was, it was a man with a bright and shining golden face and a robe of many colors that kept changing so you couldn't tell what color it really was. And he had a sword in his hand, a big sword, but very old and rusty. And I think somehow the people believed he was a god, because he told them that he was. And he said, 'All of you who will not worship at my Temple, which I have built for my brother, the God of Obann, this God will cast them into a devouring darkness.'"

Sunfish paused. His face shone with sweat.

"Surely this was a dream," said Hlah.

"I don't know," Sunfish said, and shook his head so hard that beads of sweat flew off. "When the sun first peeked over the mountains, I found myself back inside my cottage. And then I was sick all over the floor." He lowered his eyes. "What was it, Mr. Uwain?"

"I thought it best to ask you," Hlah said, "because you're a learned man."

Uwain shrugged. "There is, I think, something like it in the Scriptures—"

Sunfish interrupted him, reciting: "Then I, Ryshah, was sick upon my bed three days, and I could eat no food, although my jailer brought it every day. And when the thing was told to the king, he commanded that I should be let out of prison."

"Yes," Uwain said, "yes, that's one of the verses I was thinking of."

"That's why I think it was no dream," said Sunfish. "But why should God's spirit speak to me or show me anything? Where was that place, and who was that man with the sword?"

"But that's no mystery," Hlah said. He put an arm around Sunfish's shoulders to comfort him. "That was the Thunder King. He bears the sword of the War God—well, some Heathen nation's war god. They say he wears a mask of gold, and everybody knows he's built a New Temple at Kara Karram, east of the Great Lakes."

"But the Thunder King was killed in the avalanche at the Golden Pass!" Uwain said. "His people pretend he didn't die, but the Thunder King they follow now is just an imposter in a mask."

"But you know what the mardars are telling the people in Silvertown," Hlah said. "They say the Thunder King can't die."

Sunfish shuddered. "It's unspeakably wicked!" he said.

Uwain patted his arm. "Sir, you know the Scriptures better than anyone I've ever known," he said. "You know that God chooses prophets. They don't choose themselves. I believe you've been given a vision of the Thunder King—or, rather, the man who now calls himself the Thunder King, and hides behind a golden mask. I believe the Lord showed you this to remind us of our danger. It's peaceful, here in the hills; but war could break out again any day."

In his old life, when he was Prester Orth, Sunfish counterfeited what was meant to be taken for a long-lost prophecy of Batha the Seer, exhorting God's people to cross the mountains and slaughter the nations of the Heathen. He did this at the bidding of the First Prester, Lord Reesh, and most of the College of Presters believed the prophecy was genuine; but many of them didn't. As Sunfish, he had no memory of doing this. Orth's false prophecy had since fallen into some disrepute. But all the presters and reciters in Obann would have been astonished to learn that the author of a counterfeit prophecy had, much against his will, become a true prophet.

"I would rather this new Thunder King came West," Hlah said, "and that God would bless some lucky Abnak with a chance to take that golden mask and the scalp that goes with it."

"That may yet come to pass," said Uwain.

CHAPTER 32

A Token from the Past

Kwana and his men had decided to spend only one more day at their campsite, sending smoke signals; but by dint of hard riding, Martis found them while they still lingered over their breakfast. They spotted the dust raised by Dulayl's hooves and reached for their weapons. When they saw it was only one rider, they relaxed.

"Martis comes!" Kwana said, grinning at Ellayne. The men waved a greeting, and the rider waved back.

Ellayne had never been gladder to see anyone in all her life. Martis' feet were hardly on the ground when she threw herself into his arms.

"I knew you'd come!" she cried. "I knew you'd find us!"

"Oof! You almost knocked me over," Martis said. Jack was just as happy to see him—maybe even happier—but he couldn't bring himself to carry on about it like Ellayne. Martis looked at him over Ellayne's shoulder, reached out, and pulled him into his embrace; and Jack was glad he did.

"You two never make it easy for me, do you?" he said. Once upon a time Lord Reesh sent him forth to kill these children. Now he loved them—he who had never loved anyone before. His heart was full.

"These be the children you look for, Martis?" Kwana said. The joke raised smiles all around. Martis released the children and grabbed the Wallekki's hand.

"My thanks, my brother!" he said, in the courtliest Wallekki. "My debt to you is the debt between friends, which has no price." Here followed an exchange of complicated speeches of the kind much prized by the Wallekki. It took some minutes to conclude.

"Where shall we go now, my brother?" said Kwana. "Shall we ride together, or part?"

"I can't decide until I talk to the children and find out what they were doing out here in the first place," Martis said. Kwana nodded, and soon led his men out to hunt for food while Martis rested. He had to have a drink of tea, he said, before he could deal with questions and answers.

"You'd better have a good story for the baron," he said, after his first few sips of tea. "He was in quite a temper when I left him."

"We can deal with that," said Ellayne.

"But there's something else first!" Jack interrupted. "We've found something—"

"Found it?"

"All right!" Jack glared at Ellayne. "A man had it, and we took it from him."

"It's a magical item!" said Ellayne.

It took time to get out the story in a way that made any sense to Martis. Jack and Ellayne bickered, but neither could have told the story without the other. Wytt came out of hiding and chattered a greeting to Martis, and more.

"What's he saying?" Martis asked.

"He thinks we've been very silly, lately," said Ellayne.

"Are you going to show me this magical item? Where is it?"

"It's in Jack's pocket."

"Take it out, Jack," Martis said.

Jack hadn't touched it for days, not since he saw the face in it.

"Come on—let me see it," Martis said, as gently as he could. He knew Jack didn't scare easily, so he respected the boy's fear.

With great caution Jack reached into his pocket. The cusset thing was still there; he hadn't been lucky enough to lose it. He used to like the feel of it, the smooth, hard texture. He didn't like it anymore.

"Here," he said, offering it to Martis. "Be careful how you handle it. Don't let the magic out."

"I thought you didn't believe in magic, Jack."

"I don't! But this thing's not natural."

Martis took the object from Jack's hand. The moment he touched it, and got a good look at it, he knew.

"This isn't magic!" he said. "Do you know what this is? It's a thing—a thing left over from the ancient times. I've seen hundreds of things like it. Lord Reesh collected them; he had a whole roomful of them. How do you get it to make light?"

Jack told him. Martis pressed the bump and startled a little when he saw the light.

"Ah! Lord Reesh would have paid his weight in gold for this little bauble!" he said. "He would have killed both men and women to possess it. How he would have loved to clap his eyes on it!"

"You've seen something like this before?" Ellayne marveled.

"Not exactly like this one—but many things similar to

it. They're so old, of course, and almost always damaged in some way, so I've never seen one that can really do anything, as this one does." Martis caressed it with his thumb. "Lord Reesh had a thing that made a kind of a clicking noise, if you shook it, and another one that buzzed. That was all they did. But that they did anything at all made them the gems of his collection."

"So they're just things?" Jack said. "What were they for?"

"Nobody knows," Martis said. "But tell me—how do you get it to show you that image of a woman?"

"I'm not sure. I didn't do it on purpose. Just fooling around with it. I didn't know what was going to happen!" Jack said. Martis so obviously had no fear of it that Jack was quickly losing his. It wasn't magic, after all! The thought made him feel like dancing a jig. "I think I was sort of rubbing it around the edge."

"Are you sure it can't hurt us?" Ellayne asked.

"That it can do anything at all, after passing through the Day of Fire, is a miracle," said Martis. "It's a thousand years old, at least. No, I very much doubt it can hurt us. But let me see …"

His fingers massaged the item, rubbing the rim; and suddenly the woman's face emerged in the midst of it, with the light shining through.

"There it is!" he said. "Someone's face, who lived during the Age of Empire. I wonder who she was."

"You mean it's just a picture? Really?" Jack said.

"But she looks so strange!" Ellayne said. "Her eyes are so enormous, and her mouth's so small. Did people look like that in ancient times?"

"Yes, it's just a picture. No, they didn't really look like this," Martis said. "Sometimes that's how they drew faces. No one knows why. You can see faces like this one on some of the other things, or even painted on a wall. Not many of those paintings have survived. Lord Reesh used to study them. He always said that if we studied these remnants long enough, we might learn how to do some of the wonderful things the ancients used to do."

"The kinds of things that got them wiped out in the Day of Fire?" Ellayne said. "No thanks!"

Martis experimented with rubbing the object in the opposite direction. The woman's picture disappeared. He pressed the knob in the middle and the light went out.

"The ancients were like gods, Lord Reesh said." Martis seemed to be talking to himself. "They could do things that men can't do anymore. Talk to each other while they were miles apart. Travel through the sky like birds and in the sea like fish. Kill their enemies across great distances. Lord Reesh dreamed of being able to do such things again." He paused. The children waited for more. He continued: "But in their power they were proud and sinful, wicked beyond anything ever seen in the world since then. That's why God destroyed them, and all their great works with them." He bounced the little item in the palm of his hand. "Unimportant little things like this are all that's left. I suppose God left them so that we would know that the writings preserved in the Commentaries are true."

Jack and Ellayne both nodded. Obst had told them about the Commentaries, which most people called the New Books. They weren't Scripture, but the presters used them to teach people to honor the Temple, and how to pray in unison and under direction. But there were also Commentaries that were rarely read and poorly understood, even by scholars, because they spoke of events and things whose like could no longer be found in the world, Obst said. The glory of the Empire, and its instant destruction in the Day of Fire, was one of those things.

"Now," said Martis, "tell me exactly how you came by this treasure."

Jack felt ashamed of himself when he told of hitting Noma with the stone while the man slept, but Martis had no reaction to it. Well, he'd done a lot worse things than that, Jack reflected, many times over. The children knew those actions troubled Martis sometimes. He'd told them so.

"We were going to steal it all along," Ellayne said, "as soon as we got the chance. We were going to take it back to Obann and tell Obst all about it. We thought he'd better know."

"You should have seen how all those people looked at Noma when he shone the light at them. They thought it was magic," Jack said. He turned to Ellayne. "So did she."

"And so did you, Mr. Bucket!" She knew Jack didn't like that nickname. "Well, who wouldn't think so?"

Martis turned the light on and off a few more times and sat there looking at it, and thinking.

"They're trying to awe the people into submitting to the Thunder King. That's obvious," he said. Then he fell silent for so long that it made Ellayne fidget.

"What are you thinking, Martis?" she said. "Have you decided what we ought to do?"

"Oh, we have to take this back to Obann," he said. "The people have to be taught not to be afraid of something like this, not to think it's magic. They have to understand that things like this are nothing, really—just odds and ends left over from the past. There must be other agents of the Thunder King traveling the countryside, with other pretty baubles in their keeping. His army couldn't conquer Obann, but maybe he can use lies to overthrow it."

He didn't tell the children everything that was in his heart. He didn't reveal the extent of his fear.

If the Thunder King had found little things left over from the Age of Empire, might he not also have found big things? Maybe more had survived in the East than in the West: Lord Reesh used to think that might be so. What if the Thunder King had found something that could slaughter people at a distance? What if the sinful pride of those ancient days had found a new servant in the Thunder King?

"I hate to leave King Ryons wandering around alone," he said at last. "But we might search all our lives and never find him; and meanwhile the king's counselors and chieftains must be warned, and we're the only ones who can warn them. We can make good time, straight back to Obann, and we'll be reasonably safe if Kwana and his men ride with us. Do you agree?"

"We hoped to find King Ryons," Ellayne said. "Wytt kept picking up his trail. But this business with Noma changed everything."

"We always wind up sorry for it, if we don't listen to you," Jack said. "I guess I've learned that lesson."

But of course they didn't know that Obst and all the chieftains had just left Obann, and there would be no one in the city to advise them.

Wytt listened quietly to the humans' talk, understanding it in his own fashion. Besides which, he'd already made his own plan.

He would find King Ryons.

CHAPTER 33

For the Welfare of the City

In the city of Obann, with the chieftains and their warriors gone, there were only Hennen's spearmen to guard the palace and the city gates, and eighteen Blays (two were lost) to guard the queen. There were two thousand militia now in Obann, but these were new recruits who'd not yet been tested in battle. All in all, there were nowhere near enough troops to defend so great a city; but no one expected there would be a need to defend it—not from any enemy on the outside.

On the evening of the same day that the chiefs departed, a group of prominent citizens invited themselves to the palace and politely demanded an audience with the queen and General Hennen.

"We are concerned for the welfare of our city and for the welfare of our good King Ryons, too," said their spokesman, a rich wool merchant named Merffin Mord. "Every king, especially a king of such tender years as Ryons, must have a council to advise him and show him what ought to be done. Not a council of Heathen warlords—some of them never saw a city before they came here!—but a true council of Obann's loyal citizens. I have been chosen by the people of Obann—"

Here he was interrupted by a series of rude noises coming from just outside the doorway of the audience chamber. They were the kind of noises that important people least expect to hear when they are talking business.

"Your Majesty, please!" cried Gurun; for she guessed at once who was making the noises. And into the hall strutted Fnaa, with his mother trailing after him like the poor helpless servant of a distracted king. Fnaa let his eyes rest for a moment on Merffin Mord, then turned to Gurun.

"What does this fat man want? What's he doing here?" Fnaa said—quite loudly, too. "I didn't ask him to come!"

Merffin bowed to the supposed king, and his fellow delegates bowed, too.

"Sire," Gurun said, "these are very important men in the city. They want to be your councilors."

"I don't need any councilors. Tell them to go away."

Gurun shrugged. "Good sirs, I think we should talk of this some other time. I have no right to make decisions that belong properly to King Ryons, and he is not in a mood for it. Please come back another day."

With more bowing, and some inadequately suppressed grumbling, the prominent citizens began to leave. But none had reached the door when Fnaa cried out, "Wait! Don't go!" And they halted.

"Do these men," Fnaa asked, "want to come here and do dull work? All that foolery about taxes and roads and fixing up this or that building? You know I hate sitting around and listening to all that rot! If Mr. Fatty-fat wants to bother with it, why shouldn't he?"

Merffin, whose reddening face showed what he thought of the nickname Fnaa had given him, said, "Sire, we know the city, and we will give you good advice. You don't want the city's business to miscarry, after all. But it can indeed be dull business, as you so rightly say. There's no need for you to be troubled with it."

Gurun wanted to answer, but Fnaa didn't let her.

"Very well, then, that's settled!" he said. "These men will come to the palace every day, and if there's anything to do that's dull and costs money, let them do it. I, the king, command it!" Fnaa had gotten rather fond of that phrase lately.

When at last they got a chance to talk to him alone, just before bedtime, Gurun and Dakl wanted to know what Fnaa thought he was doing.

"Anything that comes into my heart to do—just like the prophetess said," he answered.

"Those men who were here this evening did not mean well," said Gurun. "They think you have become a simpleton."

"The whole city thinks that," Dakl said.

"They will steal the city out from under us," Gurun said. "They wouldn't have dared to try, while the chieftains were here."

"Uduqu's still here," Fnaa said. But Dakl said, "Pish! He's a fierce old man who is as helpless as a babe, in a place like this. Men like Merffin Mord will have no fear of him."

"Well, the prophetess said I was to lead them into folly," Fnaa said. "That's what God wants, and she says He'll protect me."

Dakl looked at Gurun. "There's wisdom in it, my lady," she said. "As long as they think the king's a fool, to be blown this way and that as it suits them, and will never turn on them as long as they give him a hobbyhorse to ride, they'll be happy to have him on the throne. They won't murder him."

"Please don't call me 'my lady,'" Gurun said. "I will tell you what worries me. In the Scriptures, in the Book of Thrones, it tells of King Emver, who became king when he was just a boy. His nobles ruled the kingdom, and in his name did all kinds of wicked deeds. So the elders made a conspiracy and killed the king."

"I don't know those Obann Scriptures!" Dakl said, wide-eyed. Gurun hadn't meant to frighten her, but it was too late to take back what she'd said.

"It's all right, Mother," said Fnaa. "God's protecting me."

———

In his office in the palace, which no one but Gurun and Dakl knew he had—but they did not know that he'd moved it to another room, even more out-of-the-way than the first—Gallgoid listened to the report of one of his agents. The man was in the palace as a humble servant who mopped floors, and had also served refreshments to Merffin and the others when they came to see Gurun. Gallgoid thanked him and dismissed him, after writing down the names of all the delegates. From now on they would all be watched.

"They've lost no time, have they?" he asked himself. "They have their hearts set on becoming oligarchs. The king's foolishness invites it."

Gallgoid knew about the boy king's capers. His agents kept him very well informed. He didn't know why the king was behaving so oddly, but he suspected Gurum knew. But he resisted the temptation to question her about it.

"They won't find it as easy as they think, to become oligarchs," he mused. He liked the idea of letting them do the mundane work of governing the city until, in their false security, they judged the moment right to declare themselves its rulers. He would try to upset their plan just a moment before that moment arrived.

Someone, he thought, should have reminded them of that ancient proverb: "Traitors, beware of treachery."

Far away in Lintum Forest, Hwyddo and Maelghin toiled eastward. Hwyddo knew the way, having lived in the forest all his life. Maelghin nursed a forearm badly savaged by Cavall's teeth.

The attack by the giant bird had panicked Hwyddo. But after fleeing for some miles, he remembered that he's left his brother behind, and headed back for him. So he chanced upon Maelghin, who'd gotten up and come looking for him.

"It's no use," Maelghin said, when Hwyddo mentioned it. "That monster kicked poor Culluch right in the belly. He's done for." Hwyddo thought it over, and decided Maelghin was right.

"This forest isn't big enough for us and Helki," he said.

"Maybe we could go to Silvertown," Maelghin said. "The Thunder King has an army there."

"And maybe the commander of that army would like

to do something about Helki, eh?" Hwyddo was thinking clearly now. "They have a score to settle with him. Maybe they'd like to see Lintum Forest go back to the way it was, before Helki made himself so big."

"The Thunder King's general might like that very much," said Maelghin. "Do you think there really is a king in Obann now?"

"The important thing is that there shouldn't be a king in Lintum Forest," Hwyddo said.

CHAPTER 34

Concerning Prophets

Angel saw everything that happened on the forest floor. She would have provided her master with wood pigeons and other edible birds: he had only to command her, and she would do it. That Chagadai had not gotten around to teaching Ryons how to hunt with a hawk, Angel didn't know. She would never think of hunting for her master unless he commanded it. She hadn't been trained to do so. But she did know where the freshly killed hare came from, and she didn't approve.

Cavall knew, too, but he approved. He tried to make the hawk understand, but there was no getting through to her. In all other respects he considered her a worthy comrade and quite intelligent, for a hawk.

As for Baby, he didn't like going deeper and deeper into the forest where there was no room to run; but he would follow Perkin anywhere. He'd learned to tolerate the dog, who was excitable, to ignore the hawk, and not to look upon the boy as a potential meal. Baby heard things in the forest that made him edgy, and it annoyed him to have his line of sight continually hemmed in by trees. Nevertheless, he stayed with Perkin. Nothing could make him desert the man who'd raised him.

Three days in a row, Ryons and Perkin woke in the

morning to find fresh-killed food provided for them. This gave them something to talk about all day as they wandered in the woods, searching for Helki.

"The prophet, Sychas the Mighty One, was given his meals when he wandered in the wilderness," Perkin said. "Crows brought food to him every day. But that was God's doing, and I'm hesitant to believe that we're the beneficiaries of a miracle."

"Is that a story from the Scripture?" Ryons asked.

"Yes, Your Majesty—from the Book of Royal Prophets."

"Tell me!"

Perkin obliged. "There were wicked kings in Obann, long ago. Sychas defied them, in God's name, so they sent soldiers to kill him. Sychas would have defied the soldiers, too, but the Lord commanded him to hide in the wilderness, and he obeyed. While he was there, God made a famine in the land; but the prophet had his food from heaven, and water that sprang up from beneath a rock. And the famine prevailed until the people cried out to God and begged him to bring Sychas back to them. And when Sychas returned and stood before the people atop the Holy Hill, where the Lord's altar used to be until the wicked kings took it down, it rained at last; and the crops grew in the farmers' fields—grew up almost overnight. And every day, Sychas preached upon the hilltop, teaching the commandments of the Lord, and the people came to him to learn.

"Then the most wicked of the kings, who was also the greatest and most powerful of them all, came with an army to scatter the people and to kill the prophet. When the people saw the chariots, they wanted to run away; but

Sychas wouldn't let them. So mighty was his voice that it seemed to root them to the ground.

"'Now,' said Sychas, 'see the judgment of the Lord!' And he took off his bearskin cloak and shook it at the king and his army; and they all clapped their hands to their eyes and fell out of their chariots, groaning: for the hand of the Lord had struck them all blind. And Sychas with his own hand slew the king. So all the other kings repented and left off their wicked ways."

Ryons whistled, a habit he'd learned from his Ghols. "That's a story!" he said. "Did it really happen? The Wallekki tell marvelous stories, but I think they're mostly lies. And the Abnaks are even bigger liars."

"There are no lies in the Holy Scriptures, Sire," Perkin said.

"So do you think God has made some bird or animal bring us our meat these last three mornings?"

Perkin shrugged. "I don't think any forest animal would dare to come so close to Cavall and Baby," he said. "My great bird sleeps soundly, but what could possibly sneak past Cavall?"

"Nothing," Ryons said. "That's what makes it such a puzzle."

They talked it over and over, and they might have wandered in the forest until Doomsday before they found Carbonek, for all their ignorance of woodcraft. But before the day was done, it turned out otherwise.

They had just disentangled themselves from a patch of sticker bushes when a harsh voice called out to them, "Halloo! Who be you, down there?"

Cavall barked. Perkin and Ryons stopped in their tracks,

while Baby looked all around for someone to attack.

"I say, who you?"

"If you want our answer, let us see you!" Perkin said.

"Ha-ha! So you big dog can bite me? Or you big bird? No, no—you say first."

"He's up in a tree," Ryons whispered.

"If we're already surrounded by outlaws, we won't be any the worse off for answering this one's question," Perkin said. He raised his voice. "We're looking for a place called Carbonek. This boy has friends there. The dog is well-trained; he won't attack you. The bird belongs to me, and he won't hurt you, either. Now please come out where we can see you." He draped an arm around Baby to make sure the bird stayed put.

"No tricks!" said the voice. "I come from Carbonek."

Right in front of them, a man jumped down from the lowest branches of a very leafy tree, landing lightly, without losing his balance at all. Baby would have lunged for him, but Perkin held him back. Ryons made Cavall sit, but couldn't keep him from barking one more time.

The man was short and squat, with his head shaved bald but for a thick black topknot. He sported purplish tattoos around his eyes and on his bare shoulders; he wore buckskin leggings, but no shirt. He clutched a stone tomahawk in his right hand and grinned fiercely at the newcomers.

"You're an Abnak!" said Ryons.

"Too right," the man agreed. "Bandy my name, son of Dinga. We Crow clan. Why you want Carbonek? Tell you names." His Obannese was bad, but not too bad. "Very funny, you bring great-big bird!"

They gave their names. Perkin had never seen an

Abnak before, but had heard many bloodcurdling tales about them. But Ryons felt almost as if he'd been reunited with his army.

"Tell me, warrior," he said, "what are you doing here in Lintum Forest? This isn't Abnak country."

"Oh, I come with Helki. I scout for him."

"May you never run out of tree-beans!" Ryons said. "Helki's my friend, and the very man we're looking for. Can you take us to him?"

"Sure. I reckon I can do all things you want." Bandy dipped his head politely. "I do all things whatever you like—for King Ryons."

"You know this boy is the king?" Perkin cried.

"Righty, sure thing! Helki make us all take oath to serve King Ryons. He say King Ryons someday will come, and here you be. He tell us many stories of brave King Ryons, the boy king. King Ryons' man, me—all of us with Helki, king's men, too. Obann God save king!"

Ryons could have turned cartwheels, he was so happy. He could see Perkin had his doubts. "Cheer up!" he said, and slapped the man's arm. "An Abnak would rather die than pretend to be your friend. It's true they like to tell stories, but they have honest hearts."

"In that case, then, I'm pleased to meet you, Bandy," Perkin said. "But tell me—for how long have you known we were in the woods?"

"I hear you from far-away, this morning. I been watching you two-three hour. You make a lot of noise!"

"You haven't been following us for three days?"

"No. Just today, like I say. Why you ask me three days?"

"Because someone has been bringing us meat for three days," Perkin said. He explained the situation. "If it wasn't you, then it's still a mystery."

"Dog don't catch him?" Bandy said.

"Cavall is a great watchdog," Ryons said, "but we haven't heard a peep out of him."

"Funny thing, that." Bandy thought it over for a few moments. "Sounds like brownies, I say. Brownies sing magic; dog won't bother 'em. Only brownies don't give you things. They take."

But at least, he said, Carbonek was only an easy two days' march away, and he would take them there. He was still talking when Angel called from the top of a tree. Ryons held out his arm and whistled for her, and down she came.

"Nice hawk," Bandy said. "Good hawk for a great chief. Looks like hawk that Helki used to have."

"Helki gave her to me," Ryons said, "so maybe she's the same hawk."

"Maybe. So—when you like to go to Carbonek? Now, maybe?"

"Right now, indeed," said Perkin, "and the sooner we get there, the happier we'll be."

"Don't worry, Perkin," Ryons said. "Everything's going to be all right from here on in."

Things were not all right for Sunfish. It was getting so he feared to sleep at night. Ever since he'd had what Uwain told him was a vision of the Thunder King, he'd been having dreams that sorely troubled him.

"They're bad dreams," he told Hlah and May, one

morning. "They scare me, and now I have them every night. Three nights in a row! What does it mean?"

He described them. "I'm always in some great big place that's strange to me, and almost always there's a big crowd of people in it with me. Sometimes not. Sometimes it's dark in there, but other times it's like broad daylight. Sometimes I'm up in front of all those people, preaching to them. Other times, I'm sitting or standing in the midst of them and someone else is preaching. But when I wake up, I can't remember what the preaching was about. Never! And sometimes there's a man with me—not a good man, someone I'm afraid of. But I don't know his name; I don't know who he is. He just scares me, and I don't know why."

He paused to lick his lips, for his mouth had gone dry. Then he continued.

"Just at the end of my sleep, just now, I dreamed I was alone with this man and he was telling me something. I can't remember what it is—only that it was a secret. But I thought it was a devil whispering to me, and I didn't want to know the secret. And all of a sudden I woke and was all in a sweat, and my teeth were chattering!"

"What did the man look like?" May asked.

Sunfish shook his head. "When I wake up, I can't see his face anymore. But I think he's old, very old. And I think it must be evil secrets that he tells me, that I must be afraid to remember."

It was a beautiful summer morning in the hills, with the green leaves shimmering and birds singing, and all the people of the little settlement up and going about their business. They had no crops to tend, but there was plenty of hunting and fishing to be done and gathering of berries, wild nuts, and other edibles. Some of the women had babies to take care of and quiet little songs to sing.

Sunfish was happy there. To him it was like Heaven. He loved instructing the people in the Scriptures and leading them in prayer.

"You would have made a great prester," Uwain said to him the other day: and he was a reciter, so he should know. "A lot better than some of the ones we have nowadays, more's the pity." But for some unknown reason that compliment made Sunfish quite uneasy. Sunfish was sure he would never want to be a prester, although he couldn't have told you why.

"We Abnaks have shamans who are great dreamers," Hlah said. "Their dreams carry them up into the world of gods and spirits, and they see many visions. But I know now that those little Abnak gods are nothing, really; and so I know those shamans must be crazy, or else great liars. But what does the Holy Scripture say about dreams, Sunfish? If anyone knows, you do."

"That's a fair question," Sunfish said. "God spoke to many of the prophets in their dreams. In a dream the prophet Ika saw the throne of the Lord with angels attending it, and in that same dream the angels commissioned him to be a prophet of the Lord. And sometimes great kings, and even pagan kings, had dreams sent to them from God, in which the Lord showed them things He meant to do. Indeed, King Ozias had many such dreams, which he recorded in the Sacred Songs.

"But I'm no prophet! And I'm not a king. If I knew a prophet, he could tell me the interpretation of my dreams. But there are no prophets anymore."

"That's not what I've heard," Hlah said. "When I was in the army and we were marching to Obann, people said the city was full of prophets. And other cities, too. So there must still be prophets in Obann."

"Oh!" Suddenly Sunfish grabbed Hlah's shoulders. "Could you take me to Obann, Hlah? So that I might speak to a prophet and be told the interpretation of my dreams? Then I would know whether God was speaking to me or it was just some fever in my soul."

Hlah patted Sunfish's hand. "If I ever go to Obann, my friend, surely I will take you with me."

Greatly reassured, Sunfish left them. But May asked her husband, "Why would you ever go to Obann?"

Hlah shrugged. "I'd like to see the king again," he said. "And maybe I said something because I knew it would comfort Sunfish. Everybody loves him, but we all know he's a little mad. And maybe he's more of a prophet than he knows! But if I do go to Obann, I'll take you and our baby with me, too. That is, if you'd like to go."

May grinned at him. "Me, see Obann? Yes, I think I'd like that very much!"

CHAPTER 35

Fools Can Be Dangerous

In Obann, the king commanded that Merffin Mord and his fellows be allowed the use of the great hall in the palace, there to meet whenever they pleased, as the new High Council of Oligarchs.

The first thing the council did was to proclaim that the Temple should be reestablished, and someday rebuilt, as "the spiritual center and heart of Obann," complete with a new First Prester to be elected as soon as all the presters in the land could be summoned to the city for a conclave. At the same time, the Oligarchy was to be restored, to manage the affairs of Obann.

Alone in his office, Gallgoid read the proclamation, copies of which had been posted all along the streets:

"Be it known that although the great edifice was destroyed in the late war, the Temple of the Lord remains the spiritual center and heart of Obann and shall continue, so that the people of Obann might be guided in the practice of religion; and that the presters of Obann shall assemble in this city to elect a new First Prester; and that the Temple edifice shall be rebuilt, by the grace of God, in all its former glory.

"And be it known that the governance of Obann shall be, as it has always been, invested in an Oligarchy, to govern in King Ryons' name; and that said King Ryons shall continue in his office, by the grace of God; and that Merffin Mord, in the king's name, shall serve as governor-general of the Council at His Majesty's pleasure. Amen."

Gallgoid suppressed a laugh.

"How long will it take them," he wondered, "to decide they can save themselves a great deal of money by making peace with the Thunder King and recognizing his New Temple as the Temple of the Lord? And how long before the peace they make with him is transformed into submission?"

They gave themselves such airs! The last governor-general, Lord Ruffin, who perished in the defense of the city, would have thrown Merffin into prison—once he'd finished laughing at the man's pretensions. Ruffin had been a wise man. He would have recognized a dangerous folly when he saw it.

As did Gallgoid. "I can't jail this fool, as Ruffin would have done," he thought; "but I'll find a way to clip his wings."

Preceptor Constan read the proclamation and then had a private audience with Gurun.

"This is, pure and simple, a treason against the king," he said. "Do they think the Lord decreed the destruction of the Temple for nothing? We're blessed that God let us off as easily as that! Do these fools not know God's mercy when they see it?" For Constan, that was an impassioned speech, and by now Gurun knew him well enough to recognize it as such.

"What do you think the presters will say?" she asked.

"Godly men will do God's will. The others will choose a new First Prester and try to have everything back the way it was.

"You are young, Gurun, but you have understanding. You'll remember that I, at first, didn't believe in the Lost Book. I was sure it was a fraud. But as I read the scrolls and studied them, God opened my eyes and I understood what He was telling us. I understand why Ozias' last writings were kept hidden until now."

Gurun nodded, out of respect. She was a Fogo Islander: they'd never had the Temple there, so it was easy for her to imagine life without it. But for a man like Constan, it must be very hard, she thought.

"God will not have His spirit confined in the Temple anymore," he said, "with presters and scholars hoarding His word like misers, keeping it to themselves and never making any use of it. The Temple's time is over. God is making a much greater temple for Himself, one made without human hands, inside the human heart. And all nations, in the end, will come to worship Him there." He paused. "But in the meantime, in our own time, we must protect King Ryons."

Gurun suppressed a wince. The preceptor didn't know that the boy cutting capers in the palace wasn't Ryons, and it was not her place to tell him. He would understand the need for keeping it a secret. The day the likes of Merffin Mord found out the truth would be the end of Ryons' reign in Obann. In secrecy lay the only hope of safety.

"What can we do," she said, "but to continue with our work? King Ozias' words, and all of God's word, must be preached to all the people. Even my poor pagan Blays hunger for it! And in this they are wiser than the people of Obann, who never seemed to care that the Scriptures were being kept from them for all those years."

"My copyists are working as hard as they can," said Constan, "and I've recruited seminary students to go out and preach as soon as we have books for them. Maybe by the winter we'll be ready."

"God will help us," Gurun said.

While they talked, Fnaa ran up and down the longest corridor in the palace, kicking a leather ball. Dyllyd, his tutor, ran after him.

"Please, Your Majesty!" he cried. "It's time for your lessons!"

"Bogs on lessons!" Fnaa answered. "I'm the king; I don't need lessons!"

Dyllyd was a young man who took his duties seriously. Like everyone else in the palace, he understood that the king had had a sickness that had robbed him of his memory. Why it should have also robbed him of his good sense, and of all his understanding of what a king should be, Dyllyd was at a loss to understand. The boy was very deeply changed, and all the tutor's pleading was in vain. The boy king whooped and rejoiced as the ball caromed off a famous suit of armor on a stand, making it rattle noisily, and Dyllyd cringed at the sound.

Uduqu entered the corridor and caught the ball just as the king's next kick sent it flying right at his face.

"Oh, fine catch!" Fnaa cried.

"Chieftain, forgive it!" Dyllyd said. "His Majesty didn't

see you coming. I've been trying to get him to sit down for his reading lesson. Please don't be angry!"

"I don't need a lesson! Give me the ball, Uduqu!"

Uduqu noticed two or three servants watching discreetly from farther down the hall. Before the midday meal was served, he thought, the whole serving staff would know about the king's behavior, and the whole city by nightfall. "One more story about what a simpleton the poor king turned out to be," he thought. "As if they hadn't heard enough already."

"Run along, Dyllyd," he said. "I'll be coming to you for my own lesson, by and by. But first I want to have a word with our king."

Dyllyd bowed deeply and fled to his classroom. The other servants ducked out of sight when Uduqu made a point of looking at them.

"Dyllyd's afraid of you," Fnaa said. "They all are. And yet when you go out on the street, children follow you around."

"Shows they've got no sense!" Uduqu said. He took Fnaa by the shoulder and steered him into a less frequented corridor. "Anyone would think you didn't have much sense, either."

"My mother taught me that if I played the fool, I'd be safe."

"Let's not talk too loud." Uduqu lowered his voice. "Have you heard about the proclamation by that fine new council of yours?"

"I read it. Don't stare at me like that! I do know how to read—learned it before I ever came here."

"Did your mother teach you?"

"No—she can't read. I just picked it up on my own."

"Smart boy—and you let poor Dyllyd think he's teaching you." Uduqu grinned. "I had him read the thing to me this morning. I can't say I understand what those bellyscratchers are getting at, but it doesn't sound good. Sounds to me like I'd better keep my knife nice and sharp. They're up to something."

"I only pretend to be a fool," Fnaa said, "but Merffin is the real thing."

"Fools can be dangerous, boy. Don't you forget it."

"I won't. But my ma said you're the one who'd better watch himself. She says you're like a baby, here in the palace."

Uduqu chuckled. "That's what I want everyone to think," he said.

Jandra sat in the stable-yard, humming to herself and playing. Abgayle watched over her and daydreamed of Lintum Forest. She was homesick for it.

Jandra played with her bird, if you want to call it a bird. It had feathers and wings, but it also had a beak full of sharp teeth. The creature never left her side, and all the servants were afraid of it. Jandra made little heaps of pebbles, which the bird squawked at and kicked over, and that made her laugh.

In the middle of one of those games she suddenly looked up at Abgayle and said, "I shall set Ozias' throne in Lintum Forest." And having spoken her prophetic utterance, her eyes rolled and she fell asleep sitting up.

Abgayle gathered her up in her arms and hustled to

put her to bed, the bird chasing after them. Then she rushed to find Queen Gurun, because someone had to be told that Jandra had prophesied again. With Obst and all the chieftains gone out of the city, Abgayle didn't know who else to tell. "They should have taken us with them!" she thought.

"What can it mean?" Gurun wondered.

"Who knows?" said Abgayle. "Obst would know, but he's not here. I've told you because prophecies mustn't be ignored."

"I won't ignore this one," Gurun promised. And before sundown four of General Hennen's men were riding after the departed army as fast as they could go, to deliver the prophecy to Obst.

CHAPTER 36

Wytt Takes Command

Wytt could not explain why he insisted on chasing after Ryons. Omah don't explain things. He simply broke into the conversation between Martis and the children and declared that they must follow him to Lintum Forest. He stood among them as they sat on the ground, chattering at them like an angry squirrel.

"Wytt, you don't understand," Ellayne said. "We have to go back to Obann."

"No, no—first we catch Skinny." That was his name for Ryons. He didn't have a word for "city," or "Obann," but he understood what Ellayne was telling him and struck his sharpened stick against the ground. "You come, not go back."

Martis couldn't understand any of the Omah's vocalizations, but he knew the children could. "Ask him why, Ellayne," he said.

"He doesn't understand the idea of 'why,'" Jack said. "He wouldn't be able to answer that."

"What will you do, Wytt, if we go back to the city?" Ellayne asked. Wytt slept in her arms every night, when possible. Sometimes he sat on Jack's shoulder. He'd been with them practically from the beginning of their journeys, every step of the way, and saved their lives more than once.

He wore a lock of Ellayne's hair around her neck. He'd never tried to leave them, and they were sure he would die for them.

Wytt simply ignored the possibility of their going back. "I go find Skinny," was his answer. Wytt didn't even know what a king was, Jack thought. To him Ryons was just another human boy. How could he know it was so important to find him? Jack shook his head, completely puzzled.

"You won't come with us, if we go back to Obann?" Ellayne said.

He planted the butt of his stick in the ground and let it be known that they were to come with him to the forest.

"We ought to go to Obann—but we can't leave Wytt behind!" Ellayne looked up at Martis. She's going to cry, Jack thought. "I won't do it, Martis!"

"No—we couldn't do that," Jack said. "Besides, if Wytt says he can find King Ryons, it means he really can. He doesn't know how to tell lies."

Martis let out a deep breath. It's ridiculous, he thought.

"Wytt doesn't give reasons for things," Jack added, "but you can be sure he has some good ones."

"I believe you," Martis said. "Now all I have to do is find a way to go in two opposite directions at once." He shook his head. "But my oath binds me to go wherever you go. And it's very funny—the three of us taking our orders from a little Omah. Anyone would think we'd lost our minds."

"But what'll we do with that thing from ancient times?" Ellayne said. "Can we trust the Wallekki to take it back to Obann?"

Martis thought for a moment. "It would solve our

problem," he said. "But the Wallekki are the most superstitious people in the world and easily frightened. I'll need a delicate touch."

Kwana and his men came back to camp jubilant because they'd brought down a couple of pheasants. Martis waited until their bellies were filled. Then, "Kwana, my brother," he said, "the children and I have decided to go on to Lintum Forest, but I think you should go to Obann—to claim a reward for your kindness to us and to take service with the king."

"We have decided to do that," said Kwana. "The king at least will feed us."

"I do have one more favor to ask of you, my friend."

"It shall be done, if we can do it."

Martis took a complicated, roundabout approach of the kind so dear to the Wallekki, which eventually led to the proposition that something might look like witchcraft, but not be witchcraft: "Such as when people who have never seen or heard of horses first see a horse and rider. They might think that was witchcraft."

"By the star that shone on my birth!" said Kwana. "We are by no means as ignorant as that! What is this thing that you want to show us, Martis? We have traveled far and seen many strange things."

"I will show it to you now," Martis said, "and I swear by my own head that it is not witchery." He reached into his pocket. Jack, watching intently, was glad the item wasn't in his own pocket anymore. He and Ellayne couldn't understand the Wallekki language, but it was plain from the amount of time it took to get this far that Martis had done his best to prepare them for a shock.

"This is a thing that was made in ancient times," he said, holding out the relic so they could see it. "No one living now can make such things as this, but it is nevertheless the work of ordinary men. I would like to you take it to Obann and give it to Queen Gurun."

Kwana looked disappointed. "Why, O my friend, did you think we'd be afraid of a little thing like that?" he said.

"Because of what it does," said Martis. "It has the property of giving off light, and it can also show a picture—I know not how. These children took it from one of the Thunder King's slaves, who was using it to scare people."

One of the men laughed out loud, but Kwana didn't laugh.

"Show me, Martis."

The sun was high in the sky: folly to do this after it began to set, Martis thought. He pressed the knob, and there was light.

Kwana's men jumped back, fumbled for their weapons.

"Ai! Accursed!"

"There is a jinn inside it!"

"Put it away, my brother. Let us see it no more," Kwana said. He turned and snarled at his men. "Serves you right for laughing!" Martis stopped the light and returned the object to his pocket. He hadn't even shown them the picture.

"I believe you, that it is not witchcraft," Kwana said. "Nevertheless, none of us will consent to touch it, nor have anything to do with it. Upon all the things of ancient times there lies a curse."

"No one would deny that," Martis said.

"I think we had a close call," Ellayne whispered to Jack.

When Martis and the children set out again for Lintum Forest, Ryons and Perkin followed Bandy to the village of Carbonek, which was growing up nicely around a ruined castle in the middle of the forest. Ryons hadn't seen it in a year.

"Look at that, Perkin! They've built all those cabins and laid out all those fields. I think that's corn they're growing. I wonder how many people live here now."

Perkin was too busy restraining Baby to answer.

Bandy waved his arms and yelled, "The king is here, the king is here! Come and see King Ryons!"

They soon had a crowd around them. It included a few people who'd been there from the beginning and recognized Ryons. Perkin wrapped his arms around Baby's neck and clung with all his strength, praying the nervous creature wouldn't kick anyone—not that anyone dared to get that close. Whether the king of Obann or the captive bird were the bigger curiosity, who could say? But to Ryons' disappointment, Helki wasn't there.

"He went out to hunt some spies from Silvertown," said a headman among the villagers, "and he hasn't come back yet. The woods are full of them, he says."

"Is this really King Ryons?" someone cried.

"Of course it is!" someone else answered. "He's been here before, you know."

"What are we to do about that giant bird?" asked someone else. "Those things are killers! What were you thinking, Bandy, bringing it here?"

"My bird and I will camp some little distance from your dwellings," Perkin said, panting. Baby was testing him, but didn't exert his full strength for fear of hurting him. "I raised him from a chick, you see, and he's perfectly tame. But he's never been around so many people before, and he'll need some time to get used to it."

"We'll need more time to get used to him!" a man said.

The villagers had the rest of the day to get things sorted out, and they did. Ryons, as befit a king, had a place made up for him inside the castle, with a roost for Angel. Men built a corral for Baby, and made sure to build it high and strong, with a shelter for Perkin right next to it. Baby calmed down a bit, once he was fenced in. And in the evening there was a feast for everybody.

"Good old Lintum Forest!" Ryons said, as he dug into a fresh, orange melon. "If only my Ghols and my chiefs were here, too, and Obst and Gurun, and Helki! I do miss them! I hope they don't think I've forgotten them."

"I don't think you're the kind who forgets his friends," said Perkin.

CHAPTER 37

A Message to the Oligarchs

It's a very long way from Obann City to Silvertown, but a team of relay riders can do it in less time than you'd think possible.

Goryk Gillow had such riders, so he knew there were new oligarchs in Obann who wished to rebuild the Temple. This posed a serious problem for him. After some hours' deep thought, he composed a letter.

To the High Council of Obann,
And to the Governor-General, Lord Merffin Mord,
Greetings in the name of the Thunder King.

We congratulate Your Excellencies on your wise decision to assume the government of Obann & most confidently look forward to the day when there will be lasting peace between us.

We wish Your Excellencies to know that His Worship the Thunder King has built a New Temple to the God of Obann in his city of Kara Karram. As we wish to spare Your Excellencies the crushing expense of rebuilding the Temple in Obann; & as we are now at peace with the God of Obann; &

since it has pleased Him to dwell in our New Temple; therefore, we wish our two countries to be as one, in all matters of religion.

We request Your Excellencies to send us presters & reciters & preceptors to serve in the New Temple, at our expense, to the end that there should be one Temple for all nations on either side of the mountains.

Why should there be war between us, when there might be peace, & prosperous trade flowing back and forth between our countries, & new chamber houses being built all throughout the eastern lands? Why should you not proclaim this peace throughout Obann & be hailed as saviors by your people?

We eagerly await your response, knowing that such a peace would indeed benefit us all.

By Goryk Gillow, First Prester

He read it to Mardar Wusu before sending it on to Obann.

"You made no mention of that king they have in Obann," said the mardar. "Are they such fools, these men, as not to know that the only peace they'll ever have is submission to us?"

"The problem of the king will take care of itself," Goryk said, "seeing as how the oligarchs don't want a king."

"Why should they serve our master, then?"

"Because our master has the power to reward them for their service. Really, Mardar—what's the good of our New Temple, if they're only going to rebuild the old one?"

Wusu frowned. "It sounds to me like we'll be back to where we started, when our master first invaded Obann."

"Not at all," said Goryk. "At least, not as long as they have no temple in their city. Mardar, it will take time to replace the armies that our master has lost in Obann. Time is the one thing we can't afford to give our enemies. It's not necessary for them to accept our peace proposal out of hand. If all we manage to do is sow dissension and debate, we'll have done enough. Sooner or later they must surrender to our master. But why chase the bird, if you can get it to fly into the cage?"

"They won't do it," Wusu said; "and I would be a great deal happier if our army held Lintum Forest."

Goryk smiled. "Oh! I think we can insist that they help us clear the outlaws out of Lintum Forest," he said.

The target of Mardar Wusu's malice, Helki the Rod, was still busy hunting down assassins in the eastern regions of the forest. There were more of them than he'd thought; and there were still homegrown bands of lawless men that he hadn't subdued. These, in a spirit of self-preservation, were joining together to resist him. So Helki and his handful of rangers remained in the field; but most of the time he preferred to hunt alone. His Griffs still had much to learn about woodcraft.

He didn't know King Ryons was at Carbonek, or he would have hurried back to see him. As always, most of his rangers were patrolling all around the settlement to protect it from surprise attack. He had nowhere near enough men to make all of Lintum Forest safe for peaceful settlers. But he hoped the dread inspired by his name, and by his deeds, would serve in lieu of men.

This morning he surprised five outlaws sitting around their campfire with a joint of venison. His rod laid two of them on the ground, and the other three surrendered. He'd approached their camp so stealthily that not even the blue jays gave a warning.

"I don't know why you attack us, Helki," said one of the survivors. "We never did you any harm."

"No, but you burnt out a farm last week and sold the wife and children into slavery," Helki answered. "You're part of Nummick Fishbelly's band, and I'm at war with him. Where is Nummick, by the way?"

"We don't know! Unless there's a job to be done, we split up and go our own ways. It's safer, Nummick says. He knows you're after him."

"And I'm going to get him, too," Helki said. "Meanwhile, tell the truth and I'll let you keep your heads on your shoulders. Has Nummick had any talks with anyone from Silvertown?"

"Why, of course he has! And more than once, too. The woods are full of men from Silvertown, trying to get all the free men together to take you down. You knew that, didn't you?"

Helki nodded. Nummick had some three dozen followers. Naturally, Silvertown would want to make use of him. If all the bandit chiefs in the eastern forest joined forces, they could send two or three hundred men against Carbonek, plus whatever assistance Silvertown might give them. "And if they can wipe out Carbonek while it's under my protection," Helki thought, "everyone in the whole cuss't forest will be after my scalp, and no honest man or woman will listen to me ever again." He didn't even want to think about what would happen to the settlers at Carbonek if the likes of Nummick Fishbelly conquered them. Helki shook his head, not knowing what to do.

"My problem now," he said, "is what to do with you three birds so that I won't have to fight you again. If I let you go, you'll just go back to Nummick."

"You promised not to kill us!" cried one of the three.

"Would Nummick keep that promise?" Helki said. Of course he wouldn't, and none of the outlaws dared to answer that. "I reckon you'd better come with me for now. If you show yourselves trustworthy, I might let you join up with my bunch, by and by. Otherwise, your futures don't look bright."

"We'd be happy to join up with you," said the wisest of the three.

Up in the foothills, Sunfish came to a decision.

He really had no choice. The dreams tormented him every night, and every now and then a fragment of one would darken his day—only for a fleeting moment, but he didn't like it.

"I've got to go to Obann, Hlah," he said.

"To ask a prophet about your dreams?" Hlah said. "You may be able to find one nearer than Obann."

"No—it's got to be Obann," Sunfish said. "Oh, I wish I knew how to tell you! Sometimes I feel like there's another person inside me—someone who wants to get rid of me, so that he can be! And it all has to do with Obann. I don't know how, but it does."

It wasn't a bad time of year to journey to Obann, Hlah

thought. The settlement could get along without them. May loved the thought of going to see towns and cities, and Hlah welcomed the opportunity to stop at Ninneburky and confer with Baron Roshay Bault. Besides, he was very curious indeed to see what a prophet would say about Sunfish's dreams and visions. There might be much more to them than anyone suspected.

"I'll take you to Obann, old friend," Hlah said. "But I hope you'll want to come back to this place, afterward."

And Sunfish answered, "More than anything else in all the world!"

CHAPTER 38

How Fnaa Spent the King's Money

Obst called the chieftains together to hear Jandra's prophecy: "I shall set Ozias' throne in Lintum Forest."

"What does that mean?" Shaffur grumbled. "What good is the throne without the king to sit on it? We should have brought the little girl with us."

"She couldn't explain it to you, Chieftain," Obst said.

"Well, I wish somebody would!"

The army hadn't marched as fast or as hard as it could have, and had yet to reach Cardigal, where the Chariot River flows into the Imperial. Along the river, trade flourished, farmers raised and sold their crops, and the militia kept away the broken bands of stragglers left over from the Thunder King's vast host. People rebuilt their burnt-out villages. Not a few of them fell into a fright at the army's approach; but when heralds assured them it was King Ryons' army, they praised the king whom they had never seen and sold provisions. The chieftains were surprised by how famous they'd become; and if some of the heroic deeds ascribed to them were fictional, they didn't mind. As Chagadai reminded them, fame was one of the things they'd crossed the mountains to win.

"I think I understand the prophecy," he said. "I think God means for the king to rule the country from Lintum Forest and not from that wicked city anymore. I wonder if King Ryons has gone back to the forest ahead of us. Surely we should seek him there."

"If he's there, we'll find him," Chief Buzzard said. And so they all agreed to march to Lintum Forest, and the warriors applauded the decision. They longed to be reunited with their king, and didn't much care if they never returned to Obann.

But Obst cared. What would happen to the work of copying and sending out the Scriptures, if the king were not to rule from Obann?

"Do you suppose God hasn't thought of that?" said Zekelesh, when Obst had voiced his misgivings. "He knows what to do, and how to do it."

Obst grinned at the swarthy little chief with his wolf's-head helmet. "You've become wise, Chieftain!" he said. "I surrender to your counsel."

"It's only common sense," said Zekelesh.

In Obann the new oligarchs—they liked to call themselves "the king's servants and advisers"—were already collecting taxes, having first increased them, hiring men to police the streets and discourage criticism, posting edicts and proclamations everywhere, and giving speeches about the war with the Thunder King being over. Those who didn't think so found themselves drafted onto work crews, repairing the city's walls and gates, clearing away the rubble of the Temple—labor for which they received little or no pay. At

Merffin Mord's insistence, he and his colleagues did everything in the king's name.

Fnaa learned to ride Dandelion, showing more of a flair for it than Ryons ever did; but no one noticed. For nowadays he liked to ride in the streets of the city every day with bags of coins tied to his saddle; and he exasperated his councilors by coming back each day with empty bags, having flung all the money to the people. Boisterous cheering followed him everywhere he went. Uduqu always marched beside him to keep him from being mobbed.

"Why, why, Your Majesty, do you do this thing?" Merffin cried.

"Because the people like it," said Fnaa, "and I like to watch them scramble for the money. I'm the king, and I'll do as I please!"

"I think they hate you, boy," Uduqu said, when they were alone with Gurun after supper, ostensibly to put the king to bed. Uduqu now slept in a chair outside the door to the king's bedchamber.

"Oh, I know they do!" Fnaa said. "But now the people love me."

"On Fogo Island, where I come from, we have no kings, nor councilors, nor cities," Gurun said. "I know but little of such things. But I think we are placing ourselves in greater and greater danger."

None of the three knew that Gallgoid had already placed an agent in the royal kitchen, a brave woman who made sure to taste everything that was meant for the king's table. In Lord Reesh's service Gallgoid had arranged for the poisoning of several individuals. Lord Reesh considered him an expert. "Martis for the knife between the ribs on a dark night," he used to say, "but always you, Gallgoid, for a fatal dish that never tastes of poison." Gallgoid's agent had vials containing some of the most common antidotes sewn into her dress. He expected she would need them.

Gallgoid also knew about the message that the oligarchs had received from the Thunder King's First Prester. They were keeping it a secret. But one member of their council, a great trader in wheat and corn, kept Gallgoid well-informed of all the council's doings and discussions. He did this, he said, for love of Obann and in obedience to God. None but Gallgoid himself knew what this man did.

Gallgoid relished the irony of a man like himself being the instrument used by God to protect God's chosen king. He would have relished it even more, had he known that the boy he was protecting was not King Ryons.

"It makes them furious when you throw money to the people," Gurun said. "Your mother is afraid."

"I'm sorry for that," said Fnaa, "but I have to do whatever's in my heart to do. That's what the prophet said."

"It's a good thing they don't know that Dakl is your mother," Uduqu said. "Don't ever let them find that out!" He didn't want to say more. Abnaks had a reputation for cruelty. "But I suppose some of these city men could give us lessons," he thought.

"If only we knew where King Ryons is!" Gurun said. "Then we could all go to him—although I don't like the thought of leaving Preceptor Constan alone with all these scheming men. The Scriptures must go out among the people."

Uduqu sighed. "A young maid from a country no one's heard of, a silly boy whose gift is to play the fool, and an old scalp-lifter with more scars than brains—the three guardians of God's word! The Lord don't like to do anything the easy way, does He? And He made quite a few Abnaks like that."

Meanwhile, Constan had the project running smoothly. The scholars sent to him by Prester Jod from Durmurot were a great help. Jod had resigned, rather than accept what he was sure was counterfeit Scripture foisted on the country by Lord Reesh; but since the destruction of the Temple, and at the insistence of the people of Durmurot, he'd resumed his prestership. His best men supervised the copying of the Lost Scrolls and their translation into modern language, while Constan's students at the seminary worked day and night to get it into books. The Old Books, too, had to be copied and bound. By winter, Constan hoped, he would be able to start delivering the Scriptures to the many chamber houses, with exhortations to the local presters and reciters to study them and preach from them at every assembly of their congregations. He now believed that this was the work that he was born to do, and he was doing it with all his might.

"Preceptor," a student said, as he bent to inspect a page of copy, "there's talk of a New Temple in the East, built by the Thunder King." The enemy's agents in Obann had started such talk. "Could that be the fulfillment of Prophet Ika's words? 'All the nations shall know me, from east to west, from north to south; and all peoples shall sit down at my table.'"

Expressionless, Constan looked back at the youth for a full minute before saying, "No. The New Temple is a snare laid for us by the enemy." He pointed to the manuscript page on the boy's desk. "There is the foundation of the Lord's new temple—His word itself, to be raised up in the human heart; not by hands, but by God's spirit. We must do our work well, or He will pass us by and find someone else to do it."

CHAPTER 39

The Mad Preacher

It was like old times—Jack and Ellayne riding Dulayl, with Martis leading him, and Wytt scampering far ahead, trying to pick up Ryons' trail. Martis doubted Wytt could find it again: the children had been almost to Caryllick when they turned aside to follow Noma.

But Wytt knew Ryons was bound for Lintum Forest. It wasn't in him to communicate to humans all the things he knew, or how he knew them. They would have been surprised! Ryons was traveling with a grown man and a giant bird. A fox saw them and remembered it, and Wytt learned about it from the fox. Soon he found tracks to confirm it—tracks that were much too old and worn-away for Martis to read. Once they were in Lintum Forest, Wytt knew there were many birds and animals that would remember seeing such a strange group of travelers. The Forest Omah would help, too.

"I wish we could have sent a letter to my father," Ellayne said. "He'd be mighty glad to know you're with us now."

"He'd also want to know why I haven't brought you straight home!" Martis said. "I don't look forward to answering that question."

Baron Roshay Bault hadn't forgotten about the children, but there was nothing he could do about getting them back home, just now. The king had made him responsible for the defense of all the towns along the river from Caristun up into the foothills, and he had militia to raise and train, palisades to build around the towns that didn't have them, inspection tours to make, and a communications network to organize. Messages came to him from all directions. And there was a powerful Heathen army in Silvertown to be kept track of.

"They'll be all right," his wife comforted him. "They made it to Obann safely, and Martis will look after them, once he catches up to them."

Roshay smiled at her. Once upon a time Vannett would have been in a perpetual panic over this, and he not far behind her. But since the morning the bell rang on Bell Mountain, fearfulness and Vannett were strangers.

"I have to go to the chamber house," he said, "and see the wandering prester that the patrol brought in last night. Ashrof says the man's a fraud."

"Try to be home in time for supper."

Ninneburky had changed since Jack and Ellayne first left it. For one thing, there were more people in it, many of them refugees from other towns. Having survived an attack last spring by the army of the Zeph, much had been done to make the town's defenses even stronger. New militia marched in and out for drills, and work crews toiled to reinforce the wooden palisade with stone. They dug the moat deeper. They built new wharfs on the river, and barges came and went with cargoes of lumber, stone, and provisions.

Jack's mother's great-uncle, Ashrof, now a prester, waited for the baron at the chamber house, meeting him at the door. It was Ashrof who'd prayed for deliverance from the Zeph, and God provided it—an unseasonable storm of snow and freezing rain.

"Thank you for coming, Baron," he said.

"What don't you like about this wandering prester, Ashrof?"

The old man frowned. "I know the names of almost all the presters," he said, "but I never heard of any Prester Lodevar from a town called Wyllyk in the Southern Wilds. Maybe there's no such place. But what I've heard is that this man preaches the Thunder King's New Temple, and that the people must turn to it or God will turn away from them. Also I think he might be quite mad. I had to put a guard on him."

"Well, let's question him," said Roshay.

They had him locked inside the prester's meditation closet, with a militiaman on guard at the door.

"Glad to see you, Baron!" the guard said. "This cluck's been talking my ear off with his nonsense, all day long, and he won't shut up. He finally gave it a rest just a few minutes ago."

"Let's have a look at him."

The man who called himself Prester Lodevar sat on the stool that was the only piece of furniture in the room, red-eyed, with his chin propped on his hands and his elbows on his knees. Roshay expected a frothing-at-the-mouth, doing-handstands lunatic, but this man looked sane enough. He looked weary, too.

"Why have you confined me as a prisoner?" he said.

"I take it that you, sir, are a man of authority. What have I done, to be treated so?"

Very reasonable questions, Roshay thought. Not knowing the answers, he responded, "They tell me you're mad. Madmen are confined for their own good."

"Please don't get him started up again!" muttered the guard.

"Mad, am I?" said the prisoner. "If I'm mad, what shall we call people who incur God's wrath and won't repent? Who can't see the sign of His wrath in the destruction of the Temple in Obann? Who, when their enemy makes peace with God and builds a New Temple for Him, refuse to worship there? What would you call that, if not madness? And is it sane to punish anyone who tries to call these people to their senses?"

Ashrof interrupted. "But you call yourself a prester, and you are not!"

"And yet you are?" Lodevar said. "Are any of the presters left in Obann truly presters? Who ordained them? In what Temple do they serve? Their Temple lies in ruin, by God's decree, and their First Prester died in its destruction."

"Did he?" Roshay said. He was one of the few who knew that Lord Reesh betrayed the Temple, escaped, and died with the first Thunder King in the avalanche at the Golden Pass. But Obst had cautioned him not to speak of that.

"The First Prester died!" Lodevar said, raising his voice. "But there is a new First Prester now, and he ordained me. So I'm more a prester than this man here."

"A new First Prester?" Roshay said. "And who ordained him?"

Lodevar laughed. "The Thunder King himself, by the

grace of God—that's who ordained him!"

"This is blasphemy and foolishness," Ashrof said. "The First Prester is elected by the College of Presters, and the Thunder King is a wicked Heathen."

"You're the one who's spouting foolishness, old man. There's no more Temple in Obann! Your College of Presters is extinct—no Temple, no college!"

"If you shout at us again, I'll have you bound and gagged and shipped to Obann facedown in a flatboat," Roshay said.

Lodevar made an effort to restrain himself and answered the baron's questions as calmly as he could. Roshay already knew something about this Goryk Gillow and his activities in Silvertown, thanks to reports from Hlah. But he learned more now: most importantly, that Goryk had ordained many false presters and sent them into Obann to preach the New Temple.

This prisoner would have to be sent on to Obann soon, he decided. This was a matter for the king's advisers. He left Lodevar under guard and had a last word with Ashrof before going home for supper.

"I don't like this at all," he said. "This traitor Goryk has enslaved the people in Silvertown, and he has a Heathen army there."

"Do you think they will invade Obann?" Ashrof asked.

"I do—but not until Goryk's preachers do their work. I think they all ought to be rounded up and put away. Otherwise they'll confuse the people."

"I'm confused!" Ashrof said. "How could anyone accept these base persons as presters? 'Ordained' by a traitor to Obann, no less! Everything's gone all topsy-turvy since the Bell rang."

Roshay shrugged. "See if you can get him to tell you the names of any more of these Silvertown presters," he said. "Keep him talking, and have someone handy to write down everything he says."

Obst's Book of Scripture was held for safekeeping at Carbonek, all of the Old Books in a single volume. Ryons could hardly lift it, but he was delighted to have it at last. He was a little less delighted when Perkin put it on a table for him and opened it, and he got his first glimpse of a page.

"I can't read this!" he said. "The letters Dyllyd taught me never looked like these."

The man peered over Ryons' shoulder. "It's the ancient language, Majesty," he said. "The letters are different because some scribe took great pains to make them fancy, and tried to make them look like ancient letters."

"What does it say?"

"I'm rusty at this," Perkin said, "and I never did complete my studies. Still, I'll try to read it." He bent a little closer to the book and read aloud. "Ayn micklen rukh os myner Godd, Ih sal niht fyle hem hallen-var." He smiled down at Ryons. "'A mighty tower is my God, I shall not fail to praise Him.' It's from one of King Ozias' Sacred Songs. I remember that verse."

Ryons thought for a moment, then asked, "Why does God need to be praised?" And Perkin laughed.

"He doesn't!" he said. "But it is His due, and a good and wholesome thing for us to do. We need to praise God because it nourishes our souls."

Ryons wasn't sure what a soul was, or how it got nourished. But he did understand that King Ozias had just spoken to him, out of this book. And Obst and Jandra said that King Ozias, the servant of God, was his own ancestor.

"Teach me that language, Perkin! I want to hear more. I want to know what it means!"

"I'll try, Your Majesty; but I'm not much of a scholar. There are Scriptures in these books that are ages older than Ozias, and some of them I never did learn how to read in the original. In the Book of Beginnings, some of the fascicles are older than Obann itself and written in languages that no man has spoken since the world was young."

A thrill touched Ryons at some place deep inside his being. He had no words to express it. But he was sure that someday he would.

CHAPTER 40

Tidings of the King

It was amazing, Jack thought, how much ground Wytt could cover in a day. They were hard-pressed to keep up with him, and in just three days he led them to the fringe of Lintum Forest. They would have arrived even sooner, had the human beings not had to forage for food along the way.

"Remember the first time we came here?" Ellayne said. "We saw the knuckle-bears." Those were big, horsey-looking animals with bodies like bears and long front legs armed with mighty claws. "They gave us a scare!"

Martis silently recalled his own first visit to the forest. A giant bird killed and ate his horse. The encounter had almost unmanned him, but he was over it now.

Soon they were on a path leading into the forest, and then inside the forest itself, with blackberry bushes all around them and the trees growing higher and thicker with every step they took. Orange flame-butterflies escorted them, and jays scolded from the treetops. They completely lost sight of Wytt. The children plucked sweet berries as they walked. Behind them, Martis led Dulayl.

"It's so sunny and peaceful," Ellayne said. "No wonder Obst liked it so much."

Half a mile ahead, Wytt would not have agreed with her observation. There were disturbances in this region of the forest, and the birds were all complaining. Here and there he caught the scent of unwashed humans still clinging to the ferns and bushes. He didn't like their scent.

He hadn't picked up any trace of Ryons and Cavall. The Forest Omah would know where Ryons was, but there didn't seem to be many of them in this neighborhood. It was in Wytt's mind that there were only a few of them living around here and that they were in hiding. They might know he was in the area, but they weren't letting him find them.

Mardar Wusu had painted the bottom of his face black and the top half red, with a wide white band across his eyes and nose. It was a bad sign, and Goryk Gillow didn't know what to do about it.

"I will leave you the Wallekki and the Griffs—that's half the army," the mardar said. "I'm going to take the Zamzu and most of the Hosa with me and bring our master's wrath to Lintum Forest."

"That's been tried before," said Goryk. "Half the army! Have you received a command from our lord King Thunder?"

Wusu grinned, a fearful sight. "Of course!"

There was no arguing with that. Goryk, of course, knew the secret of the Thunder King—the same secret Gallgoid discovered just before the last Thunder King was buried in the avalanche. The mardars claimed to do all they did under the instructions of their master, conveyed to them magically over great distances; and such was their skill at pretending, that all the subject peoples believed it and looked on the mardars as little less than gods, or devils. But it was all a lie.

Mardars simply did as they thought best and ascribed their actions to the commandments of the Thunder King. Goryk himself did the same.

"It's late in the season to start a campaign," he couldn't help saying. "And meanwhile, what becomes of my campaign to make peace with Obann and quietly draw them into servitude?"

They were alone in Goryk's house. Outside, the work of rebuilding Silvertown went on, with a few recalcitrant slaves dangling from a gallows as a warning to the others. Goryk did not like the idea of having only half the army left in Silvertown to enforce his will.

"Call it what it is," said Wusu, "an expedition to punish bandits who are no good to Obann or to us. Besides, I'll return before the leaves begin to fall."

"But surely it would be better to wait—"

"I've run out of patience," Wusu said. "I want to see Helki's head rotting on a spear. But even more than that, we have need of swift action. We have a chance that might not come again."

"A chance? What chance?"

Wusu paused a moment, obviously pleased with himself and building up to something. Goryk knew him well enough to wait.

Finally Wusu said, "Some of my Wallekki rode in last night. They brought a man to see me, one of Helki's enemies. They picked him up just as he was fleeing out of the forest, and he asked them to take him to Silvertown without delay. They rode hard.

"I spoke with that man last night, and he brought me news." He paused again, then smiled. "The king of Obann," he said slowly, "is now in Lintum Forest. And I am going to capture him."

The fugitive captured by Wusu's scouts was Hwyddo, the outlaw. In his flight through Lintum Forest, he met and spoke to other outlaws and learned that the boy who'd traveled with the giant bird, and claimed to be a friend of Helki's, was none other than King Ryons himself. A man who'd deserted from Helki recognized the king from Hwyddo's description of him.

In hope of earning a reward, Hwyddo made all the haste he could to the east end of the forest, on his way to Silvertown. Maelghin, his companion, snapped his ankle on a twisted root and had to be left behind.

Now Hwyddo was to ride back to Lintum Forest as a guide. "If I take the king alive and kill Helki," the mardar said, "I'll make you Prince of Lintum Forest." Too late, Hwyddo wondered what would happen to him if the mardar didn't take the king and Helki.

With many qualms, Goryk watched the troops march out of Silvertown the next day. He didn't like the half of the army that Wusu had left with him. The people feared the Zamzu, who were cannibals, and now he'd have to do without them. Why couldn't the mardar have waited for Obann to fall into their hands without a fight? As for the boy king being in Lintum Forest at all, Goryk had his doubts about that. As far as his own spies knew, the king was still in Obann City where he belonged.

So Goryk composed another letter to the new oligarchs in the city, to be delivered as fast as his relay-riders could gallop.

The First Prester to Lord Merffin Mord, High Oligarch: Greetings.

Be advised that the army of my master King Thunder has sent a punitive expedition to Lintum Forest to destroy bands of lawless men who break the peace and commit every kind of crime & violence. No threat to Obann is intended. In truth, these outlaws are your enemies as well as ours. Our mission is one of pacification only.

We have not asked you to send troops, as our own are able to quell the outlaws without assistance, & we understand that your first concern is to restore good order in your city & elsewhere.

Meanwhile, my lord the Thunder King has confidence that your desire for peace is equal to his own & awaits your acknowledgement of his New Temple as the means of a lasting & honorable peace between our two countries.

Goryk sighed. Kara Karram was a very long way from Silvertown, and like the mardars themselves, in this matter he was acting on his own. The Thunder King had indeed named him First Prester for the New Temple, and someday Goryk would go there. But if his plans miscarried in the meantime, he knew the Thunder King would have him put to death in some remarkably unpleasant way. A mutiny among the troops left in Silvertown would surely be his undoing.

"I have dared much," Goryk said to himself, "but there's no backing out of it now."

Or so he thought.

CHAPTER 41

The Baron Has Visitors

One thing continued to trouble Martis as they advanced deeper into the forest. He didn't want to talk about it with the children, but he couldn't stop thinking about it.

Lord Reesh had nothing in his whole collection like the little item Martis now carried in his saddlebag. Indeed, Reesh might have traded everything he had for it. And yet the Thunder King had entrusted this rarity to a single agent working in a sparsely populated region of Obann, to overawe the folk of towns and villages.

"He has more," Martis brooded. "He must have more. And he must have things that are greater than this." For the Commentaries spoke of weapons of the ancients that could turn a whole city into rubble in the blink of an eye. Reesh had often wondered about what kinds of ancient relics might be found in other parts of the world, where perhaps the Day of Fire hadn't burned so hot as it had in Obann.

Ah—but if he had them, Martis argued with himself, why hadn't he used them?

Maybe it took time to learn, he thought.

"Hey, look at that!" Jack said, pointing to the ground.

In a muddy patch surrounding a little pool of stagnant water, Martis saw a footprint. "It's still got water in it, and the edges are soft," he said. "Someone passed this way just an hour or two ago. But if he were close by, I think Wytt would have warned us. No telling whether it was a hunter, an outlaw, or one of Helki's scouts."

"I thought Helki cleaned all the outlaws out of this forest," said Ellayne.

"I don't think even Helki could put down all the outlaws in Lintum Forest," Martis said.

Roshay Bault and Vannett had guests for luncheon—Hlah and his wife and child, and a strange sort of man called Sunfish. They'd come down the river, swiftly, by canoe. Had he known Hlah was coming, Roshay would have waited one more day before sending the prisoner, Lodevar, down to Obann.

May had never before been inside a house as grand as the baron's, and marveled at everything she saw. Beside her at the dinner table, Sunfish poked at his food while his eyes darted nervously back and forth. Roshay noticed the dexterity and grace with which Sunfish handled his utensils, and his flawless table manners; and yet he looked like the wildest kind of hermit. Surely there was a mystery about him.

"I'm told there are quite a few of these so-called presters wandering about the country, making mischief," Roshay said. "Do you think they've all come from Silvertown?"

"I'm sure of it," said Hlah. "Silvertown's a very busy place these days. Everybody who does Goryk Gillow's bidding is rewarded. Those who resist him are forced into slavery, or hanged. So there are many who do his bidding."

"So your reports have told me."

"I wish we could drive that Heathen army out of Silvertown," Vannett said. "Our men haven't been properly trained yet, so we can't. But the waiting, waiting for the war to break out again and not knowing when it will—I hate it!"

"The Thunder King is raising new armies in the East," Hlah said, "but that takes time. He lost so many in Obann! And now he'll have to reconquer the Abnaks. My people are in open revolt against him. To save their lives, they'll have to fight him when he comes. If only Obann could send an army across the mountains to help them!"

"No army of Obann has crossed the mountains for a thousand years," the baron said. "It would make quite a few of my ancestors sit up in their graves, if we finally crossed as allies of the Abnaks."

"Quite a few of mine, too!" Hlah said; and everybody laughed but Sunfish.

Sunfish hardly ever laughed, these days. He was at peace only when he held Hlah's baby in his arms.

In his dreams he kept seeing great buildings and crowds of people, and something—he didn't know what—made him certain that all of this had to do with the city of Obann. He'd never been there in his life, and yet in the dreams he seemed to know his way around. All the people in the dreams seemed to know him: or rather, they behaved as if they thought he was someone they knew and to whom they showed great respect. "Who do they think I am?" Sunfish wondered. He spoke with these people, but when he woke, he could remember nothing of the conversation. Trying and trying to remember and to make some sense of it, and failing every time he tried, occupied most of his waking moments. He lived now only to reach Obann and consult a prophet. Nothing else mattered.

"It's going to be pretty busy in Obann by the time you get there," Roshay said. "They're holding a conclave, and the city will be full of presters and their families, their servants, and people looking for favors."

"What's a conclave?" Hlah asked. But Sunfish knew what a conclave was and listened intently.

"Well, as you know, the Temple lies in ruins and we have no First Prester. So the clergy will assemble and elect one. But what they'll decide to do about rebuilding the Temple, who can say?"

"If they rebuild it at all," Vannett added. "Our prester here in Ninneburky says things are going to change, and maybe there won't be a Temple anymore. He has gone to the conclave to find out; he left yesterday."

"How could they not rebuild the Temple?" May wondered. News from Obann reached the hill country very slowly, if it got there at all.

Sunfish felt a mounting urge to scream, and didn't know why. He could only grind his teeth and fight it.

CHAPTER 42

The Invasion of Lintum Forest

Mardar Wusu marched his army down from Silvertown to Lintum Forest, as fast as it could go. He sent agents on ahead to rally his allies among the outlaws, to make them ready for their best chance to rid themselves of Helki. He also sent word that whoever delivered King Ryons into his hands, alive, would be rewarded beyond his wildest dreams.

In all of this he acted wisely. With better than two thousand warriors of his own, and hundreds of outlaws at his beck and call who knew the forest well, he looked forward to a swift and successful campaign. He wouldn't be caught in an ambush like the last mardar to invade the forest—not with all the scouts he meant to employ.

But in other things he'd acted most unwisely.

The Zamzu were big men, feared as cannibals, favorites of the Thunder King and his most loyal subjects. They were equally at home under the trees or out in the open, on horseback or on foot. They were anxious to slaughter any enemies they found.

The other half of Wusu's force was Hosa—black men

from the distant South, plainsmen who knew nothing of forests, peace-loving herders of cattle, who had been terrorized into serving the Thunder King. They were strong fighters because they had rapacious neighbors who preyed upon their herds. But they loathed the Zamzu, and hated and feared the Thunder King. And the Zamzu despised them.

Their chief, Xhama, came to Wusu every day with complaints about the Zamzu. Because he couldn't pronounce the man's name, Wusu paid no attention to his complaints. Xhama's warriors, longing for their far-off homes and families, were already on the edge of mutiny.

To all of this, Wusu was blind.

"Back to Silvertown before the leaves fall!" he promised himself. With Helki's head, and the king of Obann as his prisoner, his master would reward him well. "Wusu the Great, mardar of mardars!"

He marched his army nearly to exhaustion.

News spreads quickly throughout Lintum Forest, in spite of its vast extent. Before Wusu's army came in sight of the trees, Helki knew it was coming, and knew that his enemies among the outlaws were working together to destroy him.

"The whole forest's in an uproar," he told his Griffs. This much and more, they'd learned from men they'd captured. "I reckon we'd better get back to Carbonek before someone else does."

The last thing he wanted to do was stand at Carbonek and wait for his enemies to attack him there. Alone, he could melt into the forest and they'd never find him. But he was not alone. By now a hundred families had settled at Carbonek. How could he move them? They'd built homes, and their crops were almost ready for the harvest. And what of all the wives and children? He turned it over and over in his mind as he and his rangers hurried back to the settlement.

"We can't stand and fight, and we can't run away," he said. Last time, he led a thousand men to the eastern half of the forest and ambushed and defeated ten thousand. But he didn't have a thousand men anymore, and he couldn't leave Carbonek undefended.

"We should have wiped out all those outlaws during the winter," said Tiliqua, the chief of the little band of Griffs. "So what shall we do, your honor?"

"Fried if I know!"

When they came to Carbonek, the king was there.

"It never rains but it pours!" Helki thought, as the boy king flung his arms around him. They didn't quite encircle his waist.

"Helki, Helki!" Ryons cried. "Oh, I've missed you! Are you surprised to see me?"

"Downright flabbergasted," Helki said. "Why aren't you in Obann City, where it's safe?"

"God called me here."

The great hound, Cavall, stood up and slobbered Helki's face. The hawk, Angel, flew to his shoulder and perched there. All around him, the settlers rejoiced. "As if I could save them!" Helki thought. "Folks are going to be mighty disappointed in me, before all this is over."

Nothing would do but to hold a feast that very evening. Ryons told the story of his trek from Obann; Perkin introduced Helki to Baby in his corral; and everybody reveled.

Helki let them enjoy themselves. Tomorrow morning would be time enough to tell them the bad news.

———

There was another army, King Ryons' own, on its way to Lintum Forest. But knowing nothing of the urgency of the situation, the king's army came on slowly. They liked to make camp early so that Obst could teach them in the evening. Attakotts on foot and Wallekki on horseback scouted ahead of them, but so far had neither seen nor heard of anything to provoke haste. If they could have known their king was in the forest, they would have rushed to join him.

"I know in my heart he's there," Chagadai said to Obst. "Isn't that what Gurun's message meant—the one about setting the throne in Lintum Forest? We Ghols would go on ahead and look for him. But then we'd only get lost in the forest, and you'd have to rescue us."

"Who knows where King Ryons is?" said Obst. "God has hidden him."

They would have hurried, too, if they'd known Jack and Ellayne were in the forest, instead of being safe at home in Ninneburky. And they would have worried, if they knew what Wytt knew.

Four men were hunting Martis and the children, and the Forest Omah were nowhere to be found. One man went on ahead, purposely leaving tracks that Martis followed. With a hundred of the Forest Omah to help him, Wytt could have driven off the hunters. But the Omah had left that part of the forest, and Wytt was alone.

These men, he could tell, lived in Lintum Forest and knew it well—but not as well as even the dullest Omah.

Without having to put it into words, Wytt perceived that they were enemies. If they had good intentions, Martis would have said, "They'd have come out to meet us by now." The hunters followed the travelers stealthily, and Wytt had not yet warned the children. He had another plan.

When he judged his opportunity had come, and having diligently prepared for it, he stole up on the three who were behind the travelers and jabbed one with his sharpened stick—right in the calf, as hard as he could—and shrieked.

The man shrieked, too, and yelled a curse as he grabbed his punctured leg. Wytt paused to brandish his stick and chatter at them, making sure they saw him.

"Sons of bats! Eaters of filth! Worms that walk!" would be a close approximation of what he said. Then he turned and fled down a side path.

"Cusset little rat!" cried the man who'd been stuck.

"A Skrayling!" said another. "After him, lads!" And the three men, enraged and distracted from their business, chased after their tiny enemy.

Wytt had already scrambled up a tree he'd climbed earlier, and ventured out onto a branch that overhung the trail. When the men appeared a moment later, he screeched to attract their attention.

"Botflies! Here I am, up here! Come and get me!"

They heard him and stopped to look up, trying to see him through the foliage.

Before they could pinpoint his location, he thrust with his stick and pried free a hanging hornets' nest. It fell straight down and landed at the hunters' feet. A cloud of maddened hornets flew out of it, looking for something to sting.

The men ran off in three different directions, each

pursued by a mob of furious hornets that stung and stung again. The victims' screams and curses echoed through the forest long after the men themselves were out of sight; and Wytt was satisfied.

CHAPTER 43

When You Tread Among Fools

Helki told everyone the bad news first thing in the morning, and then conferred with Perkin, Ryons, and the headmen among the rangers and the settlers.

"We can't stay, and we can't run away," he said. "All I can think of doing is to take just a few of our sneakiest rascals with me, and go out and raise the biggest ruckus we can. Everybody else will have to stay here and do the best they can in case there's an attack."

"How many is 'a few'?" asked one of the settlers.

"Half a dozen, tops."

The other man laughed out loud. "Against an army? That's crazy even for you, Helki!"

"Ain't much of a plan, that's certain," Helki said. "If anybody has anything better, I'm listening."

"Take me with you," Perkin said, "and Baby. I think Baby might be able to start a panic or two."

"Take me, too!" Ryons said. "And Cavall and Angel. I don't want to be left behind."

Helki shook his head. "You're not a woodsman, Perkin. You'll step on sticks and make noise, and spoil everything.

And as you're the only one who can handle that bird, I reckon he'd better stay here, too. He'll come in handy if there's fighting. But the hound and the hawk might do as much as a dozen good men, so I'll take them."

"But what about me?" Ryons cried. "Cavall's my dog, and Angel's my hawk—and everybody tells me that Obann's my kingdom. So maybe this time I ought to fight for it."

Some of the settlers smiled and shook their heads; but Helki didn't.

"That's just the kind of loopy thinking that appeals to me, Your Majesty," he said. "Carbonek might be a safer place for everybody else, without you and me in it. And I was there when Jandra told us you were the king chosen by God. I haven't forgotten that! But if you do come with me, you'll have to stick close and do everything I say. And I do mean everything."

"I will. I promise."

There were protests against this, but the more Helki heard against it, the better he liked the idea. The discussion went on into the afternoon before he reached a final decision.

"Here it is," he said. "Bandy will stay here, in command. Everybody must obey him. He's an Abnak, and he knows this kind of fighting."

"I take many scalps," Bandy said. "We make them afraid to come to Carbonek."

"I'll go out with Andrus"—this was a young man, the very best of Helki's woodsmen, whom he'd trained himself—"and the other five I've mentioned, and with King Ryons, his hawk, and his hound. We'll leave right after we have a bite to eat: I want to be far from this place when the Heathen army enters the forest. Along the way we'll kill as many outlaws as we can. And when we get a look at the army, we'll see what we can do.

"But you be careful, Bandy! Ysbott the Snake and Gorm Blacktooth are never far away. Between them they must have forty or fifty manslayers."

Bandy nodded. "I know it," he said. "But soon they won't have so many. Maybe we feed some to the big bird."

"I surely do hope so," Helki said. It's a cuss't fool plan, he thought, and everybody knows it. But what else can we do?

In the city of Obann, where Helki thought Ryons would have been safe, presters and reciters and their servants were gathering from every corner of the country. They came to Obann for the conclave, to select a new First Prester and discuss the rebuilding of the Temple. There were even a few of the old oligarchs in town, looking to get their seats back.

Gurun went to bed, uneasy in her mind because things seemed to be happening so fast. She was homesick for her simple life on Fogo Island. Had a storm not blown her down to Obann, she mused, "by now I'd be married a year to Lokk," her father's friend. Lokk was almost as old as her father, but what of it? If she'd hated the marriage, she had the right to declare it ended and go back home.

"Home!" she sighed. What she wouldn't give for one glimpse of ice-islands floating in the cold, blue waters of Fogo Sound!

Her maid was dismissed, her chamber door was locked; and she was just about to climb into bed and blow out her lamp when the door of her wardrobe creaked open and a man stepped out.

Her blood froze. This was the end; this was an assassin sent by Merffin Mord—

But it was Gallgoid, and he held a finger to his lips for silence.

"How did you get in here?" she whispered.

"I have a key. I have all the keys," he said. "Sit down. I have things to tell you."

Gurun sat on the bed. She had no fear of Gallgoid. He remained standing. He carried no weapon that she could see.

"The king's councilors are exchanging letters with the enemy's supposed First Prester in Silvertown," he said. "That man is a traitor named Goryk Gillow. Merffin and the others have decided to join him in his treason."

They were going to make peace with the Thunder King, he said. The Thunder King had a New Temple that would be Obann's Temple, too. "They've convinced themselves it's for the good of Obann. And they think they're all going to get rich."

"How do you know this?"

"Better I don't tell you. But I know. And there's more," Gallgoid said. "During the conclave, amid all the excitement, certain persons are to disappear. The Abnak chief, Uduqu, is to be discreetly murdered. They'll say he went off to join the army. Your prophet—the little girl, Jandra—and her nurse are also to be disposed of."

"They would murder a child?" With a great effort, Gurun didn't raise her voice.

"It might be awkward for them if the prophet were to

reappear," Gallgoid said. "They don't want any prophets in Obann."

Gurun shook her head. Knowing the Scriptures as she did, she knew there was no end to human wickedness. But to encounter so much of it in real life was a shock.

"There's more, isn't there?" she said.

He nodded. "You, too, my lady, are to disappear. They'll say you returned to your own country, over the sea. But they mean to murder you."

Somehow that was less appalling than the idea of murdering a child. "Anyone else?" said Gurun.

"Preceptor Constan. And a few more, but no one you know."

"What about the king?"

"He'll be allowed to live a little longer," Gallgoid said. "The Thunder King wants him. For the time being, they'll keep him here in Obann. The poor boy is a simpleton, and they think they can make good use of him. But once their position is secure, they'll send him East.

"Meanwhile, they're not sure how to manage the conclave. They would prefer to have the First Prester that the Thunder King has provided, this Goryk Gillow. The conclave would prefer to elect a new one. So far, Merffin has not decided what to do."

Several moments passed before Gurun spoke again.

"What shall we do?" she said.

"I think the wisest course would be to get you all out of the city before the conclave opens. Send you to Lintum Forest and place you under Helki's protection."

"Can you do it?

"Yes. It won't be easy, but I can."

Gurun thought hard. "Then there is something I must tell you now—something you don't know," she said. She took a deep breath. "The king who is here in the palace, the simpleton, is not a fool. He is only pretending. But he is not King Ryons, either. That, too, is a pretense. He is here because the real King Ryons went away, and we don't know where."

The spy grinned as he listened to the tale of the lost king and his substitute. When Gurun finished telling it, he bowed.

"I salute you, lady!" he said. "I suspected you were keeping a secret from me, but I never dreamed it was such a thing as this. You've outdone me in deception—very well done indeed!"

"I want you to save Fnaa, too," she said.

"I will. But thinking he was truly King Ryons, my plans called for him to stay here longer than the rest of you."

"He must not!" said Gurun. "With Uduqu and Jandra and me all gone to Lintum Forest, who would protect him?"

"I will," Gallgoid said. "With my life."

"And Preceptor Constan?"

Gallgoid shrugged. "He would never consent to leave Obann. He wouldn't miss the conclave, and there's no prying him loose from his work. I'll do whatever I can, but I think God will have to protect him."

"And what if something happens to you?" Gurun asked.

"Oh, I'm safe," Gallgoid said. "I'm only a minor clerk in the palace, whose work is so obscure as to be beneath anyone's notice."

Among the first to arrive in the city for the conclave, and among the most important, was Prester Jod from Durmurot, Obann's westernmost city. Lord Reesh had once accepted Jod's resignation, but after the destruction of the Temple and the disappearance of Lord Reesh, the western clergy had restored Jod to his post. It wasn't strictly by the rules, but they wouldn't hear of choosing anyone else.

"You'll be elected First Prester," Constan told him, "if you allow someone to nominate you."

Jod had come to the seminary that day to see the work being done on the scrolls. He walked with the preceptor from desk to desk as the copyists labored on what would someday become new books of Scripture for all the people of Obann.

"I won't deny I've been thinking about a nomination," Jod said. He was a big, handsome man, well-known for his integrity. He would be an ideal First Prester. "I've been praying about it, too."

"With you as First Prester, our work here will be secure from meddling," Constan said.

"That's one of the few reasons I would have for wanting to be First Prester—to make sure God's word goes out to all the people: even to the Heathen."

Constan nodded. He and Jod agreed.

"The trouble, of course, is that many will want a return to the old ways. They will insist on it."

"The old ways are over and done with," Jod said. "They were not God's ways. I'll try to make the conclave see that."

Constan had heard rumors of the Thunder King's New Temple in the East. So had Jod, but decided not to speak of it: not until he had a better sense of what the conclave thought of it. The whole idea was monstrous, he thought; but he had already found a few presters who seemed receptive to it. But many of them wanted there to be two Temples: one in Obann, the other in the East, and both Temples under their control.

"Tread carefully," Jod reminded himself, "when you tread among fools."

CHAPTER 44

How to Pack a Chamber House

Although the river was carrying them along at a good clip, Hlah paddled the canoe steadily. May sat in the prow with the baby in her arms, facing her husband. Between them, with an arm flailing over the side, lay Sunfish. Every few minutes, he groaned. Occasionally he sputtered broken bits of Scripture.

"Is he going to die on us?" May said. "What's wrong with him?"

"Who knows?" Hlah frowned and kept on paddling. "He was almost this bad when I first found him lost in the marshes, starving and babbling and shivering. He came out of it, by and by. Maybe he'll come out of this."

"He needs a doctor. Maybe we shouldn't press on all the way to Obann."

"My people would say he was in a shamanistic trance, communing with some god. But when a shaman comes out of his trance, he remembers everything. Anyhow, he needs a prophet, not a doctor. Besides, the best doctors must be in Obann City."

Suddenly Sunfish gave a great cry and sat up, rocking

the canoe. He opened his eyes wide and looked around, confused.

"Easy, Sunfish! You almost tipped the canoe!"

"I'm sorry, Hlah."

"How do you feel?" May asked.

"Tired," Sunfish said. "Oh, so very tired!"

"You looked like you were having a bad dream."

"That's just what it feels like," he said. "Only when I wake up, I can't remember anything about the dream. Just crowds and faces and lots of people talking all at once. I wish it would stop."

For no reason at all, the baby giggled. That brought a weary smile to Sunfish's face.

"Another two or three days on the river," Hlah said, "and we'll be in Obann. We'll be in time for that conclave."

"Conclave," muttered Sunfish; and by the look on his face, you'd think he'd been invited to the conclave, and dreaded it. You'd think he knew all about it.

But that was impossible, Hlah thought.

As the king's army approached Lintum Forest from the north, Looth, the Attakott, was troubled.

"We've been right up to the edge of the forest," he told the other chieftains, "and we haven't met any of Helki's scouts. He should have men on the plain, watching the approaches to the forest. That's what we used to do, when we were with him. But he has no one there."

"My riders haven't seen any of his people, either," Shaffur said.

"Nor mine," said Chagadai.

The chiefs decided to march the army faster. Helki was too good a general, they knew, to neglect to post scouts outside the forest.

"He's come to a bad end, finally," Shaffur said. "I always thought he would."

"He may be having trouble," Chief Buzzard said, "with no men left to spare for scouting duties. But we'll know better when we get there."

So they picked up their pace, and Obst prayed hard for Helki's safety. He'd known Helki for a long time. There was always someone trying to kill Helki: "And they haven't done it yet," Obst thought. But now Helki had people depending on him, and he couldn't just vanish into the trees as he used to. He would have to defend those people, somehow.

Goryk Gillow waited for news of the conclave.

If the king's councilors in Obann had their way, if they could get the clergy to agree with them, he would rise high in the favor of the Thunder King. The New Temple would be the only Temple. If the conclave rejected him and elected another First Prester, it hardly mattered. They would never find their way out of the trap he'd laid for them.

He sent messages to Kara Karram to keep his master informed: first by specially trained birds—a secret shared by all the mardars—and then by relay riders. But the success or failure of the plan was his responsibility.

And that fatzing fool, Wusu, was putting it all in jeopardy! Goryk had to wait for news from that quarter, too. If Wusu came to grief in Lintum Forest, it might inspire a mutiny among the troops left at Silvertown. Goryk had asked his master for reinforcements, but they would be a long time getting there. Meanwhile his collection of Wallekki and Griffs and Dahai—not to mention scores of Obannese who'd joined him—went about their duties grumbling, and even deserted in little dribs and drabs. In the absence of Wusu and the Zamzu, they weren't easy to control. They were Heathen and didn't care a jot for Goryk's new chamber house or his pretensions as First Prester.

He kept the people working on the city's defenses, embellishing the chamber house, and growing crops to feed the army. Silvertown was a mining center, and not much for agriculture. There was never enough food to go around, and the people resented having to feed a Heathen army while they themselves went hungry. Carts came every day with provisions from the east side of the mountains, but only just enough to stave off famine.

He had but one man to confide in, a former Obannese sergeant named Iolo, who'd been drummed out of the service for drunkenness just before the city fell. Goryk made him a captain, and his aide. Since then, oddly, Iolo had given up drinking. It didn't do much for his temper, and most people in Silvertown took pains to avoid him.

"You shouldn't worry so much, First Prester," Iolo said. They were watching the work on the main gate, which was almost finished. For some reason Iolo's face reminded Goryk of a gnarled tree stump. "Everything's coming along just fine."

"Ever since I made assemblies compulsory at the chamber house, more and more people have been sneaking off and not coming back," Goryk said. Anyone who didn't attend assembly was whipped. "But in case they send someone from Obann to negotiate, I want them to see a packed chamber house full of people enthusiastically reciting prayers. I'm sure they'll send someone, sooner or later."

"Don't you ever get a bit uneasy, leading those prayers? And you not even ordained?"

Goryk laughed. "If God were going to strike me down for blasphemy, Iolo, He would have done it by now!"

Wytt still hadn't found the Forest Omah. He needed their help, so he went farther afield to seek them. It never came into his head to explain what he was going to do. One morning he didn't come when Ellayne called him, and that was that. But they knew he wanted to find the other Omah.

"I guess he's out looking for them," Jack said.

"I do wish he wouldn't just go off without a word," Ellayne fumed. "I know it's his way and all, but I'll never get used to it."

"Never mind," Martis said. He was already saddling and bridling Dulayl. "The thing for us to do is to get to Helki's castle. I don't like the three of us wandering around by ourselves. It's dangerous."

A funny thing for an assassin to say, Jack thought.

Trusting that Wytt would always be able to follow their trail, they resumed their search for Carbonek. They'd been there before, but they were now approaching it from the west and didn't know the way. Martis hoped to find settlers or hunters who would show them, but so far they hadn't seen another human being—only footprints here and there. That the makers of the prints never showed themselves put

Martis on his guard for enemies.

They hiked all day and made camp, with nothing left for supper except some berries they'd gathered along the way. That was another reason they missed Wytt. He usually found food for them.

They were just getting their fire going when Dulayl, hobbled and tethered to a fallen tree, snorted and whinnied. Out came Martis' short sword, ready in his hand. He drew it so smoothly, you couldn't hear a whisper from the sheath.

"Who's there?" he called. "Show yourselves!"

"That we will, traveler," someone answered from amid the trees. "But unless you want to get stuck full of arrows before you're three seconds older, you'd better drop that sword."

Martis complied; he had no choice. And out of the forest stepped half a dozen men in rags of brown and green, with bows in their hands and arrows ready to let fly. They were obviously outlaws, Jack thought. Helki must not have been able to rid the forest of them all. Or, worse, they'd been able to come back.

"Do you see what I see, Totta?" said one of the bowmen. "A boy with dark hair—looks like we've found that lost king everybody's looking for! The big boss will be pleased."

"This is not King Ryons!" Martis said. "He's just my grandson, and his name is Jack."

But none of the outlaws believed him.

CHAPTER 45

How Jack Became a King, Almost

As soon as they entered the forest, Mardar Wusu began to have trouble between the Zamzu and the Hosa. And the Obannese outlaws who guided them had trouble with both.

Everyone feared and loathed the Zamzu, eaters of men. The Zamzu knew it, and in their arrogance, taunted the Hosa.

"We are warriors—not old women to be mocked!" Xhama complained to the mardar. "The Zamzu say that when we are deep inside the forest and the food runs out, they will eat us one by one: but they will not eat our hearts because they think we're cowards. But they will find that our spears are very sharp!"

Wusu despised the thick accent with which the Hosa chieftain spoke Tribe-talk. He despised him for complaining. Wusu was not a fool, but now he behaved like one.

"Can't you stand a little teasing?" he answered.

"We don't like being in the forest. You can't see even a single spear-cast ahead in any direction because of all the trees. It is not a good place to make war."

"Stop your whining," Wusu said, "or I'll feed you to the Zamzu with my own hands."

He was fool enough to take Xhama's sullen silence for submission. But Xhama was wise enough to realize that from now on the Hosa would have to take care of themselves because their general didn't know how to keep good order in an army. "We shall keep good order among ourselves," he told his men, "and be ready for whatever happens next."

Traveling swiftly, Helki and his few rangers found the army when it was only two days' slow march into the forest; and its scouts had not found him. Keeping a safe distance, Helki led his men around the army, to its rear.

"Let's start a little fire behind them and give them a scare," he said. "The wind is just right, so they'll have to hurry to stay ahead of the flames. And it's going to rain this evening, so we won't have to worry about burning the whole place down around us." And to Ryons, "You stick close to me, Your Highness! We don't want you stumbling into the fire."

Ryons watched in fascination as the men started a fire and skillfully steered it in the right direction. He'd seen a grass fire once, from which his Wallekki tribe had to flee in much disorder. He'd almost been left behind. But Helki made this forest fire his servant, and by mid-afternoon it was roaring after the Heathen and chasing them deeper into the woods. Angel flew overhead, and by her cries and movements, Helki always knew just where Wusu's army was.

"How do you do it?" Ryons wondered.

"I know the ways of hawks," Helki said, "and she was my hawk before I gave her to you. She and I work well together."

Helki's little band kept clear of Wusu's scouts, except for one unlucky outlaw whom Andrus dropped with a well-placed arrow. A little before nightfall it began to rain as Helki had predicted: but the army had toiled hard under the hot sun, and now they would have a late start making camp in the rain.

Helki waited for the rain to stop. In the middle of the night, alone, he crept as close as he dared to the Heathen camp. He moved through the woods like a spirit, unseen, unheard—until he raised his voice and bellowed.

"I'm Helki, the flail of the Lord! And the only men of you who remain in this forest will be dead men. Not I, but the living God, will slay you!"

He fled from his place silently, no man pursuing him, and didn't stay to observe the commotion that he'd caused in the camp.

Had he stayed, he would have seen Wusu's outlaw allies swarm into the woods in every direction, cursing and roaring and trying to find him in the dark. He would have seen the Hosa leap to their feet and, by the weak light of their dying campfires, form themselves into a defensive square, spear and shield in every hand. And he would have seen the chiefs among the Zamzu ignore Wusu's orders and shake their fists and weapons in the faces of the outlaw chiefs.

"This is your fault! Where were your scouts today? Where are they tonight, and what have they been doing? You worse than useless bunch of dung beetles!" That was what the Zamzu said. The outlaws didn't speak their language, but they knew they were being insulted.

"I will sacrifice the next man who speaks!" Wusu cried. He shoved to the ground the nearest outlaw captain, and the Zamzu laughed. It took him the better part of an hour to restore peace in the camp; and as the scouts came trickling back with nothing to show for their efforts, they received many a poisonous glare from their allies.

A good night's work, Helki would have said.

The outlaws had food, and they sat around Martis' fire to enjoy it, after tying Martis' wrists and ankles. They didn't share the food with their captives.

"Nice work, us catching the king!"

"I'm not the king!" Jack said, over and over again.

"Tell us another one, Your Highness."

"You should've stayed in Obann, King. Did you like it in your palace?"

No, they didn't believe Jack for a moment. Ignorant louts, Ellayne thought: all they could think of was the fabulous rewards they were sure to get. They belonged to some outlaw chief named Ysbott, who'd sent his whole following out on a king-hunt.

"I wonder why Helki let the king wander away from Carbonek," said one of the men. "Maybe he thought we'd be sure to bag him there. But the boss outguessed him this time!" And they all guffawed.

Night fell, the outlaws passed around a skin of wine; and Ellayne remembered something that her father had once read to her. It gave her an idea.

She spoke up unexpectedly. "It's no use, Grandfather," she said to Martis. "We'll have to let them see the treasure. Then maybe they'll take it and let us go."

Martis had no idea what she was talking about, but he

instantly decided to pretend he did. "They'll just take it from us, Layne," he said.

"Here, now—what treasure?" someone growled. "Nobody said anything about a treasure."

"Let's see your treasure, boy! Maybe it's a king's ransom."

Oh, they thought they were being sly. They think we're idiots, Ellayne thought. But she said, "I'll show it to you. And you can have it, too, if you'll only let us go."

"First let's see it!"

She got up and went to Martis' saddlebag, groped around in it for a moment. Just then Jack realized what she was going to do, and almost cried out to her to stop. But something made him bite it back.

Ellayne brought out the ancient object that they'd stolen from Noma. The six outlaws stood up for a better look. The dark forest seemed to close in all around them.

"Behold!" said Ellayne.

She pressed the knob, as she'd seen Jack and Martis do, and there was light. The darkness made it seem very bright indeed. The outlaws all quailed back a step.

"Behold the mystic power of the witch, Ellindalay! Five hundred years ago she died, but her evil spirit lives on—in here! So you'd have to say she never really died. Behold!"

She intended to show them the woman's face with the huge eyes, the face that resided somewhere within the talisman. Jack made it appear by fiddling around with the rim. But Ellayne must have done something different, probably twisted it the wrong way, because instead of a face, it brought forth music—a tinny little stream of notes that seemed loud in the surrounding silence. Ant-music, as it were. She almost dropped the cusset thing! But she kept her wits about her.

"Down, dogs—down on your knees before the power of Ellindalay the Witch! You've seen the light of her evil spirit, and now you've heard the music of her imps. Her curse is upon you! I have only to say the word, and you're all dead men."

"M-m-mercy, good sir!" The man's teeth chattered. He could hardly talk.

"Jack, take their weapons. Cut Grandpa loose," Ellayne said. The music kept on playing. The men were nearly scared to death, she thought. Jack plucked their knives out of their sheaths and freed Martis, who lost no time in recovering his sword and cutting the bandits' bowstrings.

"If you want to live," Ellayne said to the kneeling men, "you'll do everything I say. You'll lead us straight to Carbonek, and there surrender to Helki. If not, I'll say the magic word and the witch's spirit will leap out and destroy you. A miserable death! You'll die with this horrible music in your ears. Yield, you dogs!"

"W-we surrender!"

Martis tied them up securely. Only then did Ellayne squeeze the knob again, and both the light and the music ceased. Jack threw some more wood onto the fire.

The travelers ate what was left of the outlaws' provisions. A while later the children lay down to sleep—if they could—with Martis on guard, his short sword in his hand. "I won't kill you," he told the prisoners, "because that would be a kindness. But at the first sign of rebellion, I'll turn you over to the mercies of the witch." The men didn't look rebellious now, not in the least.

Just before he finally fell asleep beside Ellayne, Jack whispered, "Whatever made you think of it?"

She smiled to herself; Jack couldn't see her smile.

"It's all in Abombalbap," she said. "You know—those stories you think are so silly and aren't good for anything. Abombalbap killed a witch and took her magic wand. And when the Red Knight's henchmen came for him, he waved the wand and threatened to put a curse on them. He couldn't really use the wand, but they didn't know that."

"Don't even whisper that again until we're safe at Carbonek!" Jack said. And freed from the onus of being taken for a king, he fell into a dreamless sleep.

CHAPTER 46

How Fnaa Remained a King, for Now

By the time they reached Obann, Sunfish was in a stupor almost all the time, and Hlah could barely maneuver him out of the canoe. People were coming to the city from all over Obann, and the guards at the Water Gate hardly noticed Hlah, May, the baby, and the big, bearded man who babbled incoherently and couldn't walk. With traveling money given to them by Baron Roshay, Hlah hired a cart and one of the few places to stay that was still available—a little shed behind a stable.

"You're lucky to get this," said the owner. "Everybody's here for the conclave, and all the rooms are taken. What's the matter with your friend?"

"He needs a doctor," Hlah said, "although if you could ask him, he would say he needs to see a prophet."

"Will a seminary student do?"

"I think so," said Hlah, who had no idea of what a seminary was.

"When my nephew comes home this evening, I'll ask him to pop in and see you after supper. If he can't help, he'll probably know where to find a doctor. As for prophets, there haven't been any in this neighborhood since the great siege. They hanged the last prophet I know of."

May wanted to see sights, but she went no farther than the front of the building to which the stable was attached. There she stood marveling at the unending parade of people and carts up and down the street, and the tall buildings that made the street a canyon. She'd never seen so many people in one place in all her life, let alone a cobblestone street or buildings faced with stone. Compared to Obann, Ninneburky was not much more impressive than their own little settlement of cabins in the hills.

"Did they really hang the prophets?" she said. "What would ever make them do such a wicked thing?"

"Who can say?" Hlah answered. This was his first visit to Obann, and he thought the place looked sinister. Abnaks do not live in cities—in which my people are wiser than these, he thought. "We shouldn't leave Sunfish alone for too long."

"No, of course not," May agreed, and they went back to the shed.

The seminary student bent over Sunfish, who lay on his back on an improvised cot. Sunfish's lips were moving, but his eyes stayed closed.

"Do you know what this man's saying?" the student asked Hlah.

"He usually recites Scripture."

The student stood up. "Yes—and he's word-perfect! There aren't many scholars who can recite like this—and in the original, ancient language, too. Who is he?"

"I don't rightly know," Hlah said. "I found him wandering alone, half-starved and out of his mind. He doesn't remember who he is, so we named him Sunfish. They say he knows all the Scriptures, every bit of it, by heart. But he falls into these spells and has dreams that scare him, but which he can't remember when he wakes. He wanted to come to Obann to consult a prophet. He's a good man, and many people love him."

"Isn't there anything you can do to help him?" May said.

The student shrugged. "I don't know. I work now under Preceptor Constan, copying the Scriptures. The preceptor's the wisest man I know, and I think he might be interested in this fellow. He's too busy to come here, but if somehow we could bring your friend to the seminary tomorrow, the preceptor would probably make some time to see him. Maybe he'll know what to do."

"Thank you! Yes, we could have him brought to the seminary, if we can hire a cart," Hlah said. "Will you go with us?"

"Certainly," the student said. "We'll go right after breakfast."

Getting the Thunder King's mardar into the city, secretly, to talk to Reesh, had been hard, Gallgoid reflected. But getting this group out of the city, secretly, might be even trickier. Nevertheless, it was to be done soon.

He gathered them in Gurun's bedchamber, the queen, Uduqu, and Fnaa. Some of Gallgoid's people patrolled the halls to see that no one came too close. His agents were also servants in the palace. No one would notice them going about on various errands.

"The time has come for the three of you to leave this city," he said. "Jandra and Abgayle, too, must leave, although I couldn't find a way to bring them here tonight. But you will all leave unobserved, during the conclave. As the Lady Gurun knows, Merffin Mord and his council plan to murder you and surrender Ryons to the Thunder King. They don't know this boy is not King Ryons."

There were underground passages leading out of the city, he explained, including a long-unused one he'd found inside the palace wine cellar. Once outside and in disguise, they would make their way to Lintum Forest, where Helki would protect them. Gallgoid would remain in Obann to do whatever he could to impede any investigation of their disappearance. He intended, also, quietly to poison Merffin and his colleagues; but he saw no need to mention it now.

"I don't know that I'm up to hiking all the way back to Lintum Forest," Uduqu said, "and I'm not used to fleeing from my enemies."

"They don't intend to kill you in a fair fight, Chieftain," Gallgoid said. Uduqu nodded: anyone could be assassinated, somehow.

But Fnaa ruined everything.

"I won't go!" he said. "I came here to hold King Ryons' place for him, and that's what I'll do till he comes back again. But maybe the rest of you should go. Jandra says God will protect me, and she's a prophet. So I'll stay."

"Chief Uduqu can carry you out of here whether you want to go or not," Gallgoid said.

"But maybe Fnaa is right," said Gurun. "If Obann is left

without a king, who knows what will happen? If he stays, I will stay with him. God brought me to this city all the way from Fogo Island, in a storm. I will stay where He has put me."

"You ought to send Jandra back to Lintum Forest, though," Uduqu said. "That's where she belongs. But if this boy and Gurun stay here, then I will, too. You'll have to make another plan to keep them safe."

"If you stay here in the palace," said Gallgoid, "you will be killed. Sooner or later they will find a way to do it."

"Then we must move out of the palace to a safer place in Obann," Gurun said. "I have eighteen Blays who will come with me and guard us with their lives."

"From poison in your food? From a dagger in the dark?"

"We must put our trust in God," said Gurun.

Gallgoid sighed. "So be it!" he said. "I have in my time been a traitor to God and to my city; and yet God has used me in His service. I don't know why! But I will get Jandra and her nurse out of the city tomorrow, and see about moving the rest of you to a safer place. Everyone will think it strange that you wish to move out of the palace. It will put Merffin on his guard."

"That can't be helped," Gurun said.

With the Temple in ruins, the conclave assembled in the Great Hall at the palace. More delegates were expected to arrive during the next few days, but the deliberations would begin this morning.

Constan remained at the seminary, supervising the

work on the books. Whatever the conclave decided in the end, this was more important. So he was there when Hlah and May came in a cart with Sunfish, and the student found him at his desk in the scriptorium.

"Preceptor, there's someone you should see. I've had him brought here so you won't have to leave the building."

"Whom ought I to see, Clemen?"

The student explained as best he could, which was enough. "Bring him into my office," Constan said. "I'll join you there."

Constan took all the time he needed to see that the morning's work was well under way. Only then did he proceed to his study. There he found Sunfish slumped in a chair, with Clemen, Hlah, and May assembled around him. The sight of the babe in May's arms provoked one of the preceptor's rare smiles.

"We don't often see a baby in the seminary," he said.

"Your pardon, sir! I couldn't leave him; and as this poor man is dear to us, I couldn't stay behind, either," May said.

Clemen introduced them. Constan studied their faces. Urged by Clemen, Hlah told as much of Sunfish's story as he knew. Constan listened silently and stood as motionless as a great stone.

He stood so still because he was using his eyes and ears, and thinking about what they told him. This man called Sunfish was a big, powerful-looking man, unkempt, with a wild mane of hair and a beard that badly needed barbering. Hair and beard were black, shot through with grey. Constan didn't speak because he was sure he'd seen this man before, and trying to remember where.

"Aren't you going to ask us any questions, sir?" Hlah

said. Constan only held up a finger, compelling silence. Clemen gave Hlah a look that said, "He means it."

Constan listened to Sunfish whisper sacred verses: word-perfect, just as Clemen said. But his eyes gave the more important witness.

He knew this man. Slowly, carefully, his imagination cleaned the dirt off him, dressed him in fine clothes, cut his hair and trimmed his beard, and made allowances for the effects of hardship and suffering. There were not many who could have done this, but the preceptor had the most orderly mind in all of Obann City. Still, he would not rush to a conclusion.

Minutes marched by. Just when Hlah was beginning to fear this stolid man had fallen asleep on his feet with his eyes open, Constan spoke.

"Clemen, bring this man to my house on Temple Street. You know where it is. Tell my servants to bathe him, wash his hair, and put him to bed. My bed. But first send Anastys to me."

Clemen went back to the scriptorium and returned with another student. Meanwhile, Constan sat at his desk and wrote a note, which he folded shut and sealed with wax. He handed it to the second student.

"Go to the Great Hall now and deliver this, in person, to Prester Jod—and no one else," he said. "Make sure he reads it right away, no matter what he happens to be doing at the moment."

"Yes, Preceptor."

"Clemen, take these good people to my house with you and wait for me there." He turned to Hlah and May. "Thank you for bringing this man for me to see." And to May, "And thank you for bringing your baby. You have reminded me that we work for the future of God's people. All of them."

CHAPTER 47

How Gorm Blacktooth Was Routed

You would think that men who lived in Lintum Forest all their lives would be expert woodsmen; but in spite of the trust that Wusu put in them, this was not true of Lintum Forest's outlaws. Those men were predators who hunted easy prey—peaceful settlers and if all else failed, each other. Each band knew its way around its own particular territory, but no bandit could hope to match Helki in woodcraft.

In the days following the fire, Helki often came close to the army. They never once caught sight of him, nor found his tracks. Many times Wusu's scouts came within arm's length of him without knowing he was there. When scouts who did that came alone, they never came back.

Helki plagued the Heathen. He raised alarms at odd hours of the night, fraying the warriors' nerves. He brought Andrus along one night, and Andrus brought down a fine-looking Hosa warrior with a single arrow. That caused a stir. The scouts ransacked the neighborhood, but Andrus had slipped away before his arrow reached its mark.

Helki's rangers felled trees across paths that the army was likely to use, necessitating the hard labor of clearing them out of the way. An army used to forest campaigns might have shrugged these off as pinpricks, but this was not that kind of army. The Hosa especially hated their predicament.

"This is an accursed venture," Xhama said, "and no good can come of it." But Wusu wouldn't listen to him.

Sometimes Helki brought Cavall with him. He didn't know the Zamzu had a superstitious fear of dogs, but he soon learned it. When Cavall howled in the middle of the night, it upset the Zamzu terribly. Then it was the Hosa's turn to dole out mockery.

"If we could only bag that mardar," Helki said to his six men, "the rest of them might just give up and go home. It'd be risky, though. He keeps himself in the middle of the crowd, and there wouldn't be time to get off a second shot at him. We mustn't let them catch even one of us alive—too big a risk to the king."

But of course they wanted to try it. "We're all good shots," Andrus said. "If we shoot six arrows at him all at once, one of them is bound to hit him. And that might well be the end of our troubles."

Or the beginning of new ones! Helki thought. "If all six of us go," he said, "then where do we put the king? I won't bring him within a mile of that army."

"But if you could make them leave the forest without a battle?" Ryons said. "Couldn't you leave me in a safe place, Helki, while you try to get the mardar? I promise I'll stay put!"

Helki's men pressed him hard, and he listened to them for a long time before he finally gave in.

"All right," he said, "I reckon it's a chance we have to

take. I'll choose King Ryons' hiding place myself, and none of you will know where it is: safer, that way. The hawk and the hound will watch over him while we're gone.

"Remember—one shot each, and only one, all at the same instant: and then we skedaddle out of there. No one is to be taken alive. You'd be fools to let that happen, anyhow. What the Zamzu don't do to you, the mardar will."

"We know it," Andrus said.

The same day, Martis and the children came to Carbonek with six prisoners. Bandy quickly put them under guard.

"Yes—King Ryons, he was here," he answered their questions, "but he not here now. He go with Helki, go to other end of forest so they can fight Heathen. Maybe they come back soon, I hope."

The defenders of the castle had not been idle, meanwhile. Gorm Blacktooth and his men had come too close, so Bandy found one of their camps and let Baby loose on it. One of the outlaws was killed, and four fled screaming into the forest. Bandy himself, and his tomahawk, accounted for two others. But they didn't know where the rest of Gorm's men were.

"How you catch six Ysbott men?" the Abnak wondered.

Ellayne was about to blurt out, "I did it!" but Martis didn't let her.

"I think that's something better kept a secret for the time being," Martis said. "I'll tell you about it later." It wasn't until after they were settled in the camp and given supper and getting ready to sleep that Ellayne had the chance to ask Martis why it had to be a secret.

"You can't go around telling people you're a witch or the servant of a witch," he said. "If we encourage people to believe these ancient objects have magical powers, we'll be doing the Thunder King's work for him."

"We'd be taking Noma's place," said Jack, who quickly saw what Martis was getting at.

"You didn't complain when I made those men surrender," Ellayne said. "You went right along with it."

"Maybe I shouldn't have!" Martis said. "Those devices, you know, were made by people who perished in the Day of Fire. Lord Reesh practically worshipped those people and the works of their hands. It just seems to me that we shouldn't be too eager to make use of those works."

"The prisoners will talk about it," Jack said. "You know they will."

"Then we'll have to be careful about what we say, when people ask us to explain what we did."

Ellayne didn't argue, but it took her a long time to get to sleep. Thinking it over, she remembered a time, early in their journeys, when she and Jack explored a kind of tunnel made by the people of the Empire times—a tunnel that ended in a massive blockage made of dead men's bones. That, too, was something left over from the old days.

Now she wished she'd never touched the cusset thing; but it was much too late for that.

Wytt finally found the Forest Omah. They'd moved out of the area to avoid the gangs of outlaws tramping all around the woods. Very few of the human beings in Lintum Forest ever see the Omah, who make it their business not to be seen. But most of those humans believed all kinds of stories about the Little People—who could give a hunter good or bad luck as they chose, put a fatal curse on a woodcutter, or keep a person under an enchantment for a hundred years, to turn instantly to dust the moment they lifted the enchantment.

Wytt showed the Omah the lock of Ellayne's golden hair that he wore around his neck. That was all they had to see, to be convinced to follow him and help him. These Omah didn't know how to sharpen sticks as weapons, but they learned quickly.

"We take things from big men, stick them with points when they sleep: scare them and make them go away." That was Wytt's plan, as best it can be rendered into human speech. These Omah had never thought of doing such a thing; but they would do it now, as a service to the Girl with Sunshine Hair. No human being, not even Ellayne or Jack, could explain why. It is something that is between the Omah and the God who made them.

Several dozen of them followed Wytt back to the outlaws' stamping grounds. They found the campsite where the children and Martis had been captured. When that trail led to Carbonek, Wytt realized that his friends were safe and he could carry out his plan.

Gorm Blacktooth had a camp some ten miles from the castle. He moved it every two or three days, sometimes closer, sometimes farther away, and Bandy hadn't found it yet. He had twenty men with him, more or less, with a few out scouting.

This camp was in a clearing by a little pool of fresh water. A huge black tree towered over it. Fires burned at night to discourage bears. Around the biggest fire sat Gorm and a dozen of his men, dining on roasted possum and stolen corn. Gorm was a small, stocky man with a hideous black tooth, much esteemed by other outlaws for his cleverness.

"When Ysbott and his lads join us tomorrow," he was saying, "and we all sweep down on that castle at once—now that we know Helki's not there!—it'll be easy pickings. We'll be living high on the hog for a long time after that, my boys!"

While he boasted, Wytt and a few of the Omah scrambled up the tree, unseen, and settled down to wait. The others hid among the underbrush, careful to avoid three men on sentry duty. The night wore on, the fires burned low, and eventually the men lay down to sleep. With their chief asleep, the sentries sat down and nodded.

Wytt imitated the call of a whip-poor-will, and the Omah came out of hiding. By twos and threes, and silently, they picked things up and carried them into the forest, whatever they could manage—weapons, boots, food, a cooking pot, and one man's fur cap that lay beside him. When they were done, Wytt signaled for the Omah in the tree to go down and take up their positions. He clicked once: and half a dozen Omah jabbed their sharp sticks into a sleeping sentry. They shrieked as they stabbed him, a noise to wake the dead. Certainly it woke the camp. The stricken man sprang to his feet, bleeding from half a dozen little wounds, and howling with pain and alarm. But except for Wytt, concealed in the tree, all the Omah had already run away.

"I've been stabbed!" cried the sentry. "Somebody

stabbed me!" The whole camp was in an uproar, and Gorm had to knock a few heads together before he could get the fires lit again. Only then did they discover that many of their possessions had been stolen.

"But who could have done it?" someone said. "If it was Helki and his men, they would have killed us while we slept."

"Well, I got stabbed!"

"Go on—let me see!" By firelight Gorm examined the man's wounds. "These are flea-bites, you big baby! You didn't get a proper stabbing with a knife."

"I didn't see who did it, Gorm."

"Because you were asleep, burn you for a lazy crock!"

"But who could have come into the camp and taken all our stuff?" another man wondered. "Why, even our cooking pot is gone!"

"And my otter-skin cap, too!"

They were still trying to sort it all out when the black of night gave way to the grey of early morning. And then Wytt climbed out on a low-hanging branch and shrilled at them.

"Look at me, rodents! We are mighty, we are sly! You stink! Eaters of dust!"

He danced on the branch, threatening them with his little stick, and made so much noise that they all looked up and saw him clearly. But before any man could think what to do about it, with the ease and swiftness of a squirrel he ran out to the end of the branch and launched himself into another tree, and so vanished from their sight.

"The Little People!" someone cried. "I saw it! Did you see him, Gorm? It was the Little People who attacked us."

"And put a curse on us, too!"

"It was a squirrel," answered Gorm, "nothing but a chattering squirrel."

"It was no squirrel that did this!" said the sentry, brandishing his punctured hand.

"Nor stole our cooking pot!"

"Nor took my hat!"

Before the morning was an hour older, the campsite was deserted. Gorm Blacktooth couldn't rally his men. He could only follow after them, berating them, as they retreated as far from that place as they could go.

As for Wytt, he was already halfway back to Carbonek.

CHAPTER 48

In Forest and in City

Prester Jod bent over the man on Constan's bed. Sunfish had been bathed, his hair and beard cleaned and combed and trimmed. Constan stood at the foot of the bed, and Hlah and May toward the back of the room. They'd answered the prester's questions as best they could.

Jod stood up straight. "Preceptor," he said, "I think you know who this is as well as I do."

"I wouldn't have thought it were possible," said Constan, "but there can be no doubt of it. You've recognized him, too."

"Your pardon!" Hlah interrupted. "But who is he?"

"He's one of us," Jod said. "Indeed, it was widely expected that he would be the next First Prester, Lord Reesh's choice. But then we all believed he perished in the fire that brought down the Temple. His name is Orth, Prester Orth."

"But I found him wandering in the swamplands by the Chariot River!" Hlah said. "How did he get there? It's a mighty long way from Obann. And he's never been able to tell me anything about it. He couldn't even remember his own name."

"He is one of our greatest scholars," Jod said. He shook his head.

"His house is at the other end of Temple Street," Constan said. "I wonder if any of his servants are still in the city. They will know him when they see him."

"His house has not been sold?"

"It's boarded up."

"Let me think!" Jod said. He sat on the foot of the bed, studying Sunfish. No one spoke. Finally he said, "What do you think would happen, Constan, if we returned him to his own house? We would have to open it and air it out first, and bring back as many of his servants as we can, to clean it up. But what if he woke up one day in his old, familiar surroundings? I wonder if that might revive his memory."

"It might," said Constan, "if accompanied by earnest prayer."

"He shall have that. I'll pray for him myself."

"And us, too," Hlah said.

Jod smiled at him. "You are his truest friends," he said. "Yes, I think your prayers will do him good."

That same morning, Helki left Ryons in a thicket with some food and water. Cavall lay down beside him, and Angel perched in a nearby tree.

Only Helki knew the location of the thicket. He'd had to make a path to it, which he would unmake as he left.

"Whatever you do, Your Majesty, don't leave this thicket," he said. "I reckon I'm the only one can find you here, so you stay put till I come back. Don't wander! There's liable to be a lot of excitement in these woods before this day is done. But I ought to be back by sunset."

"I'll stay," Ryons said, "but I'd rather go with you." He had a bad feeling that after today he might never see Helki again.

"So the Heathen can catch you and take our king away from us?" Helki said. "Don't even think of it."

"Be careful," Ryons said.

"I'm always careful. That's why I'm alive."

Helki ruffled the boy's hair, patted Cavall, and backed out of the thicket. For a few minutes Ryons could hear him covering his tracks, putting everything back the way it was; and then, except for his hawk and his hound, he was alone.

It would have cheered him to know that his own army, full of friends, had reached the northern fringe of the forest and was preparing to march to Carbonek. The Abnaks were sure they could find the castle. The Attakotts and some of the Wallekki would remain behind to keep watch on the plain. The Ghols, eager to find the boy whom they called "Father," had to be restrained from plunging into the forest ahead of everyone else and getting lost.

But the only army anyone in Lintum Forest knew about was Wusu's army. And Helki was on his way to ambush it with six good archers, hoping to deprive it of its commander.

Helki himself had little hope for the plan, but his men wouldn't be satisfied until they tried it. At the very least, he thought, the attempt would slow the army and put a strain on its provisions. "As long as none of us gets caught, it might be worth it," he thought.

"We can't all miss!" Andrus said, as they hurried to get ahead of the army and prepare the ambush.

"You can, and you probably will," Helki said. "But no one ever robbed a nest without first climbing up a tree."

Wytt waited until Jack and Ellayne were alone, coming back from gawking at Baby in his log corral. When he leaped into Ellayne's arms, she almost fell backward in surprise.

"Where the mischief have you been!" she cried, and kissed the top of his head.

In chirps and chitters he told how he'd found the Omah and dispersed the outlaw band. He was just finishing when Martis joined them, and Ellayne had to repeat the story.

"The curse of the Little People!" Martis said, smiling at the thought. "They're probably still running, those men." He paused abruptly as an idea came into his head. He told Jack to find Bandy and bring him back, alone.

The Abnak's eyes went wide when he saw Wytt perched on Ellayne's shoulder. He let out a long whistle of astonishment.

"You make friends with him?" he marveled. "Men say there were plenty of Little People around here once, when they first come to this place. But then the Little People went away. Now they come back?"

"No—he's been with us for a long time," Jack said. Abnaks seldom saw Omah, and believed they were harmless as long as women were careful to put out a pot of gruel for them. Otherwise they would steal Abnak babies.

"I'm thinking," Martis said, "that we might let our prisoners get a look at our little friend, and then let them go. If they spread the word that this place is under the protection of the Little People, most outlaws will leave it alone."

Bandy nodded. "I was going to kill them," he said, "but your good idea much better."

He went on ahead to dismiss the guard who watched

over the hole in the castle floor where the prisoners were kept. Ellayne explained to Wytt, "Look fierce, and give those men a good scare."

"They've already had one," Jack said. "One more ought to do it."

The Abnaks' well-known fondness for scalp dances had already made the prisoners fearful of their future; and they hadn't come anywhere near to forgetting their exposure to witchcraft. But when they saw Wytt, they froze. He glared at them from Ellayne's shoulder, enjoying himself.

"You know what happens to those who anger the Little People," Martis said. "From now on, Carbonek is under their protection. We're going to let you go so you can find your friends and tell them to stay out of this part of the forest. It'll go hard with you, if we ever see any of you again."

"But the witch—?" one of them dared to ask.

"You've seen what you've seen and heard what you've heard," said Martis, "and unless you're complete fools, that will be enough for you. Now come up, and I'll cut your bonds."

Herded off by Bandy, the outlaws lost no time disappearing into the forest.

"Now if only Helki and King Ryons were here," Jack said, "everything would be fine."

Martis shook his head. "You're forgetting there's still a whole Heathen army to be dealt with," he said. "Helki can do amazing things, but it's hard to imagine he can stop an army."

General Hennen lent Gallgoid two of his trustiest

men to escort Jandra and her nurse to Lintum Forest. As for getting them out of the city in the first place, the easiest way seemed safest: right out through the East Gate in the middle of the day, when the streets were crowded with people intent on errands of their own. Gurun explained it all to Abgayle, and at the appointed time and place, they were ready. Hennen's soldiers met them as soon as they came out of the palace—a woman and a little girl, with a frightfully ugly bird hopping along behind them.

Gallgoid indulged himself to the point of accompanying the soldiers, pretending to be a mere acquaintance who'd stopped to talk to them. He was curious about the toddler who was hailed as a prophet. He'd had occasional glimpses of her, but had never heard her speak. Hopefully by the time Merffin Mord found out she'd left the city, she'd be too far away for his servants to catch up to her.

As pedestrians and carts and overloaded donkeys passed up and down the street, Abgayle, leading Jandra by the hand, fell in with the two soldiers and they began to walk together to the gate. Gallgoid brought up the rear, wishing Jandra's bird could have been left behind. With its dirty purple feathers and beak full of sharp teeth, someone was bound to remember seeing it.

But then Jandra stopped, turned around, and held out her hands to the bird, which jumped into her embrace so she could carry it. The ugly thing looked too big for her to manage, but evidently she was used to it. Abgayle and the soldiers waited for her.

As she turned to walk on with them, she looked back over her shoulder, right up into Gallgoid's eyes.

"Sin no more, Gallgoid," she said in a deep, womanly

voice, "for the Lord is with you." And then, instead of falling asleep as she usually did after making a pronouncement, she toddled away with Abgayle's hand on her shoulder to guide her.

Gallgoid stood rooted to the spot, amazed. How could the girl have known his name?

"The Lord is with me?" he marveled. Surely the Lord knew what he was, and what he'd done—"Lord Reesh's favorite poisoner and a traitor to the Temple: that's who I am!" And how was he supposed to sin no more? Well, he could start by not assassinating Merffin and the others—always presuming that would be a sin.

And while he stood and wondered, Prester Jod's servants were already taking the boards down from Orth's doors and windows, opening the windows to let in the air, and asking neighbors where they might find Orth's own servants. The neighbors always asked, "What? Has the prester come back?" To which the answer always was, "Not yet, but we think he's going to."

Jod himself had to return to the Great Hall, where the conclave had begun to debate whether to rebuild the Temple or to resort to the New Temple of the Thunder King. Those who spoke in favor of the New Temple had been coached secretly by Merffin Mord, who didn't wish his own name to enter into the discussion.

"Surely all Obann wants peace," orated Prester Peredyr from the chamber house of Trywath, "and now we have a chance to get it. And have we not already heard of the seminary's heroic labor to make the Old Books available to every chamber house? What could better serve that purpose than if there were, someday, a great chain of chamber houses stretching all the way out to the Great Lakes in the East? How better could we bring God's word to all those Heathen peoples?"

It was a good argument, and many were the heads that nodded to it, but not all. A few of the presters from Obann City scowled openly.

"The Thunder King has proclaimed himself a god," one of them spoke up. "Any Temple that he builds is a monument to blasphemy. Besides, the Temple of the Lord belongs here in Obann, where it's always been."

"How now, my learned friend," Peredyr answered. "Have you not heard there is a different Thunder King? The old Thunder King, the one who made war against us unprovoked—he died in the winter. That's what I've heard, from people who should know. And besides, don't you know the old Thunder King conquered all those Heathen by first conquering their gods and taking those false gods away from them? In that he did us a service. Why, he's done half our work for us already!" And for this the speaker received a light applause.

But Prester Jod had done some coaching, too; and now one of his own allies, Reciter Kyne from Obann City, spoke.

"My lords and brethren," he said, "surely this matter of the Temple is not the business that ought to be concluded first. Whether we rebuild our own Temple, or accept our enemy's New Temple, the first thing we must do is to choose a new First Prester."

"There's already a new First Prester in Silvertown!" someone interrupted.

"Yes—an interim First Prester," Kyne said. "The only

way a First Prester has ever been chosen is by election, in a proper conclave. As for this man in Silvertown, who knows if he was ever ordained? If he wanted to be First Prester, he should have attended this conclave. Have any of you seen him?"

Jod smiled. There was no counter to that argument. Before the day was out, the conclave voted to table all other questions until it could elect a new First Prester. And that, thought Jod, would take some time—several days, at least.

Three archers on the left flank of the army, three more on the right: that was how Helki had arranged it.

They had to climb up trees to get the best angle for a shot at the mardar. Helki had chosen a place where the army would either have to hew a path of its own or string itself out along a narrow path. Half the army would pass by the archers, he reckoned, before they saw the mardar. A few of Wusu's scouts had to be quietly disposed of, too, before the bowmen could take their stations. But already most of Wusu's scouts were deserting him, going out on patrol and not coming back. The army groped its way through the forest like a blind man in a strange room full of furniture. "They never learn," Helki said to himself. "Lintum Forest is no place for an army."

So the Heathen host toiled along, and when Mardar Wusu came in sight, obligingly perched atop a white horse, Helki blew on a leaf between his thumbs and made a noise like the biggest, boldest blue jay ever hatched.

Six arrows flew.

Two of the mardar's Zamzu, marching along beside

him, fell down dead. One arrow buried itself in the haunches of the mardar's horse. One glanced off a helmet, and one stuck into the shaft of a spear.

But one pierced the mardar in the fat part of his upper arm. With a roar of pain, he toppled off his horse—wounded, but very far from being killed.

By then Helki's men had already dropped out of the trees and escaped, to rendezvous later at a predetermined place. So none of them saw Xhama, the chief of the Hosa, lift up his spear and shield or heard him cry, "Enough! Hosa, my brothers, we have had enough!"

Instead of rushing into the woods after the archers, the Hosa turned and charged back the way they came. Instantly the Zamzu perceived that the Hosa were deserting, and they tried to stop them, hacking with swords, flailing with clubs. The fierce fighting was better than anything Helki would have dared to hope for.

The Hosa wielded short spears, good for throwing or for stabbing. Just now they had need of both. The Zamzu were ferocious, but the Hosa's action took them completely by surprise. The cowhide shields weren't much protection, but they were enough. Rallying behind their chiefs, with good discipline, the Hosa fought their way clear of the army and rushed in good order to the east. Their plan was to march until they were out of the forest; and they knew they could travel faster than the Zamzu. The Thunder King's favorites gave chase for half a mile, but then trooped back.

They found Wusu on his feet again. Someone had had to push the arrow all the way through his arm and break off the head and fletching before the shaft could be removed. New he waited for someone else to bandage him.

"Mardar, the Hosa cowards have deserted us," said one of the Zamzu chiefs. "What shall we do?"

Wusu showed his teeth at him. "Do?" he cried. "I'll tell you what to do, you dog! We go on!"

So they went on, with half an army and no scouts worthy of the name, into the heart of Lintum Forest.

CHAPTER 49

How the King Was Captured

All day long Ryons sat in the thicket, waiting for Helki to come back for him. The day grew hot and flies tormented him, but he kept his promise and didn't venture out. Beside him, Cavall curled up and slept. He couldn't see Angel, but he knew she was somewhere overhead.

"This is even harder than being a slave!" he thought. He would have loved to take a nap, but it was soon too hot to sleep. He wished he knew how, like Obst, to burrow so deeply into prayer that he lost touch with his surroundings. He did pray for Helki's safety, and for the friends he'd left behind in Obann, and wondered if someday he would hear God answer him. But all he heard now were the cicadas endlessly droning in the treetops. Time crawled by so slowly that he began to lose his awareness of it.

He was jolted to his senses when Cavall suddenly sprang to his feet and growled under his breath, with his hackles rising all the way down his back. Angel screeched—just once. Ryons' pulse began to race, although he neither saw nor heard anything to be afraid of.

"What is it?" he whispered, as if Cavall could answer

him. He laid a hand on the dog's neck and felt its whole body tense.

Then, at last, he heard something—men's voices, and heavy bodies thrashing in the underbrush. Helki's rangers wouldn't make such noise! And whoever it was, they were coming closer and closer to the thicket.

Could it be the enemy, chasing Helki? But Helki wouldn't lead pursuers anywhere near this place. He'd lead them into a swamp, or someplace even worse.

Ryons felt sick. The Thunder King had vowed to put out his eyes. Where was the man of God when you really needed him—the man who'd led him out of the palace, past all the guards? "God," he prayed silently, "haven't You promised to protect me?" And he remembered Obst saying, "God never lies, my boy. He always keeps His promises."

Louder and louder: they were all around him now, practically on top of him. Cavall knew better than to bark or growl, but he was ready for a fight. He showed his teeth.

And then, as if called up by magic, a big black man suddenly appeared in front of him and peered straight into the thicket, right at him, and started calling out in a jumble of incomprehensible language. Men called back to him. All Ryons could do was to stand up and take a firm hold of the loose skin on the back of Cavall's neck. Other men were coming quickly, and if Cavall attacked them, they would kill him.

By ones and twos they came, pointing at him, jabbering. Ryons had a few men like these in his army, but just now he couldn't remember where they came from. He wondered if these men had killed Helki. He felt like he was falling, feetfirst, into empty space.

But then, for no reason he could think of, Ryon's fear slid off him like a discarded cloak. He stood and waited for whatever was going to happen next, as calm as if the man of God stood right behind him.

Finally came a man who had a headdress of white plumes. The others made way for him until he stood right in front of Ryons.

"Who are you?" he said in Tribe-talk. His accent was very strange, but Ryons understood him.

As a slave among the Wallekki he'd learned to lie as naturally as he would draw a breath. It saved him many a beating. But this time—he couldn't have told you why—something made him tell the truth.

"I am the king of Obann, chosen by God," he said. "My name is Ryons, and this forest is part of my kingdom. Who are you men, and why are you here?"

The big man stared at him, amazed. It was a moment before he could answer.

"I am Xhama, son of Qoqa, chief of the Red Regiment among the Hosa people, and these are my warriors. We came to this accursed forest to hunt the king of Obann and to kill a man named Helki. But now we have fought against our mardar and his Zamzu and separated ourselves from his army." He paused, thinking. Ryons didn't interrupt him.

"We have fought against the Thunder King today," Xhama said, "and for that we shall all be killed. Our home is very far from here, and the enemies along the way are more than the sands of the desert. And yet we have captured the king of Obann, where the mardar failed!"

So these men were Hosa, Ryons thought, like his friend Hawk, and Hawk's brothers.

"Chieftain," he said, "if you're wise, you will let me capture you. My army serves the living God. That's why your armies are destroyed whenever they come into Lintum Forest. But you can serve God, too, and live."

Xhama started to laugh, but stopped short.

"You are truly the king of Obann?" he said. "And yet you tell us this, your enemies?"

"Swear an oath to me," said Ryons, "and be my friends."

Xhama's men began to mutter. He turned and made a speech to them in a language that was full of pops and clicks. Whatever he said, it provoked them into a babel of discussion that went on for several minutes. Finally Xhama quieted them.

"What about this man, this Helki, who attacks us like a devil and gives us no rest?" he demanded of Ryons.

"Helki is my general and the servant of God. He's the master of this forest. If you make friends with me, he'll be your friend, too."

Xhama thought, hard. Death was the only reward for any rebellion against the Thunder King, and he and his men had earned it. If he surrendered the king to Wusu, the mardar would take the credit for having captured him and someday soon the Hosa would be massacred—probably as soon as the army got back to Silvertown, if it returned at all.

"It seems we must choose between death at the hands of the mardar, or death in this forest," he said to his warriors. "Or else we must surrender to this boy, this king of Obann, and become his men. Perhaps then we can finish off the Zamzu and be revenged on them."

The warriors all looked at each other, puzzled and surprised.

"Who is this child," someone asked, "who dares to say such things to warriors?"

"He's brave," said another man. "Look and see how he doesn't tremble."

"Boy king," Xhama said, "we cannot decide such a great thing in a single day. For the time being, you must be our prisoner. Tonight, when we have made and fortified a camp, we'll talk of this again."

"I'll go with you," Ryons said: not that he had a choice. "Just don't harm my dog."

"We don't make war against beasts," said Xhama.

Ryons whistled sharply, and extended his arm, and Angel flew down to him. The Hosa raised their eyebrows.

"This hawk obeys you!" Xhama said. "As if you were truly a great chief!"

"Helki gave her to me," Ryons said. Then, as Helki and Chagadai had taught him, he made a "tsk-tsk" noise with his tongue against his teeth, and Angel flew away.

"Why have you released your hawk?"

"To find Helki; and Helki will find you," Ryons said. Xhama didn't like that, but it was too late for him to do anything about it.

"Come!" he barked at his warriors. "We must go much farther before we camp, lest the Zamzu come and find us sleeping."

Just before sundown Helki returned to the thicket. Ryons wasn't there. Helki hadn't expected to find him there:

the signs left all over the neighborhood—broken twigs and trampled vines, with here and there a footprint—had already told him what to expect. The Hosa had stampeded, and they wound up here. But he was surprised when Angel shrieked and landed on his shoulder. The hawk nuzzled his ear, and he stroked her feathered breast.

"So the black men took our king, little sister!" he said. "It doesn't look like they've done him any harm, and it seems Cavall went along without a fight. I don't think they could've gotten too far ahead of us."

These Hosa had no woodcraft at all, he thought. They kept blundering off the path—that was how they'd found the thicket—and a baker from the city could follow the track they made.

The rangers had all escaped from the enraged Zamzu who'd charged into the forest after them, and they were now making camp. Helki's news dismayed them.

"What good have we done at all," Andrus cried, "if the Heathen have taken the king?"

"They won't be able to keep him," Helki said.

"They'll use him against us as a hostage."

"That's just what I'm afraid of. That's why I'm going to go on ahead a ways and see what I can see. You boys rest for now, and follow me at first light."

"We're ready to follow you now!" Andrus said.

"No—you're all young men, and you need your sleep," Helki said. "Don't pout! I reckon there'll be plenty for all of you to do tomorrow."

"And if they've killed our king?"

"Then none of them will get out of this forest alive," said Helki.

CHAPTER 50

How Orth Regained His Memory

Gurun suddenly sat up in bed in the middle of the night, with words of prophecy ringing in her mind: "I shall set Ozias' throne in Lintum Forest."

Jandra spoke those words. Gurun heard them from Abgayle, weeks ago. Not knowing what it could mean, she sent messengers to pass it on to Obst, who'd left the city with the army. Since then she hadn't given it a thought.

But now she knew the meaning of the prophecy.

"Oh, you fool, Gurun!" she scolded herself. "You should have listened to Gallgoid."

Because she wasn't truly a queen, but a freeman's daughter from Fogo Island, it never occurred to her to ring for a servant and have someone haled out of bed so she could talk to him. But in the morning she would have to speak to Uduqu, and especially to Fnaa: because the prophecy changed everything. If only they could have understood it sooner!

When Sunfish woke in the morning, he found himself in a luxurious bed, looking up at a plastered ceiling nicely painted along its borders with curling vines in green and gilded arabesques. He was alone. A polished hardwood door shut off the room from the rest of the house. Beyond it he could hear muffled noises—footsteps up and down stairs, and back and forth, a persistent tapping as of a gently applied hammer, and furniture being moved about. Although finely woven curtains were drawn across the windows, the light of day was already strong enough to penetrate. He knew it couldn't be earlier than mid-morning.

Beside his bed hung a soft bell-rope. Without pausing to wonder how he knew what it was for, he tugged it twice.

A minute later his door swung open and in came a lean, white-haired man in black livery.

"Good morning, my lord Prester—and may I say what a pleasure it is to see you here again. I thought it best to let you sleep."

"Fergon. Yes, Fergon," Sunfish said. Only now he knew his name wasn't Sunfish. He was Orth, Prester Orth. He lay in his own bed, in his own house; and this was his butler, Fergon.

"How did I come to be here?" he asked.

"Preceptor Constan's servants brought you here last night, my lord, after some of Prester Jod's people made your room ready and fetched me. Some of your own servants have returned; and the house is full of workmen who are restoring it to its rightful condition. I dare say they'll be finished by the end of this day. Meanwhile, you can have your breakfast if you want it. Enid is back in the kitchen, overjoyed by your return to us."

Orth shook his head. "Not just yet, Fergon. I want to be alone for a while longer. I need to think! Open the curtains for me before you go."

And so he stayed in bed, alone in the sunshine, as memories washed over him. He remembered being Sunfish, he remembered Hlah and May and the little village in the hills. But he also remembered being Orth; and those memories were not as pleasant.

Constan and Jod must have recognized him. That was why they'd brought him here. But they couldn't have known, no one knew, how he'd come to leave Obann in the first place: he and Lord Reesh.

What had happened to Lord Reesh? Where was he? Orth didn't know. He'd deserted Reesh's party before it came anywhere near the mountains. He wondered if anyone knew what he and Reesh had done together. They didn't know, he thought. Otherwise, they would not have returned him to his house.

Meanwhile, all he had to do was to look out the window to see that the city of Obann still stood, still prospered. He remembered Hlah saying the Thunder King's vast army was destroyed and the city miraculously saved. So our treason, he thought, had been for nothing.

And yet God had spared him. Here he was.

Why?

Early in the afternoon, he rang again for Fergon.

"Bring me something to eat," he said, "and send for Prester Jod and Preceptor Constan. There is something I must tell them."

"And so you see," said Gurun, "the king must rule Obann from Lintum Forest. That is the clear meaning of

Jandra's prophecy. That is why King Ryons himself departed secretly. There is no reason for us to stay here in this city."

Fnaa, Uduqu, and Dakl listened intently. They sat in Gurun's bedchamber with the door shut. Outside, Shingis the Blay and two of his warriors kept the hallway clear of eavesdroppers.

"Well," Uduqu said, "do we leave the city now? And how do we do it?"

"I can't go," Fnaa said. "I have to hold King Ryons' place for him."

"But this city is not his place anymore," said Gurun.

"Will Gallgoid help us again?" Uduqu said. "He went to a lot of trouble for us last time, and we let him down."

"I have not yet been able to speak to him."

"He'll be mad at us," Fnaa said. "Why don't I just tell fat Merffin and his friends that they can't come to the palace anymore?"

"They don't need to come anymore," Gurun said. "The palace is full of their spies. Sooner or later they will murder us."

Dakl said nothing, just glanced back and forth from one face to another. Dread was in her eyes.

"This will take some thought," Uduqu said, "and not the kind of thought I'm good at. We need Gallgoid."

"It seems to me," Gurun said, "that the sooner we leave the palace, the better. I would like to leave today."

But none of them knew where they ought to go.

Sitting beside Orth's bed, listening to him, questioning him, Jod and Constan missed their suppers. They didn't notice, and evening gave way to night by the time Orth fell back to sleep and they left him.

The workmen were gone. The interior of the house looked like a prester's home again. Having both been there before, Jod and Constan retired to Orth's parlor and ordered the butler to ensure their privacy. They knew Fergon would strictly see to it. They settled in comfortable chairs, close to one another, and spoke in muted voices.

"Well?" Jod said. "Do you believe it?"

"I do."

Jod shook his head. "I wish I didn't! But the question is, what are we to do about it?"

"Accede to his wish," said Constan. "Let him do what he says he has to do."

The prester sighed. Anyone who didn't know Constan would think he didn't care; but Jod respected Constan's judgment. The preceptor always said exactly what he meant, and said it simply.

"It's dangerous," Jod said. "It might start riots in the city. It might even bring about the end of religion in Obann, as we know it."

"Maybe, as we know it, the time has come for it to end," Constan said.

The prester smiled at him, warmly. "Preceptor," he said, "I have never in my life been more afraid of anything than I am of this business!"

"Quite a feeling, isn't it?" Constan said.

Exhilarated, the prester made his way home to his Obann townhouse. There he was surprised to find swarthy little men, armed, standing guard before his door. His aide stood on the steps, helplessly spreading his palms.

"Who are these people?" Jod asked. "Why are they here?"

"Queen Gurun's bodyguard, my lord. There are more of them in the house and a few more in the stables. And the queen awaits you in your drawing room. The king is with her."

He would have said more, but Jod pushed past him and hurried to the drawing room.

Gurun and the boy king were there, along with a scar-faced barbarian and a single handmaid. A sword of colossal size leaned against Jod's favorite couch.

"Your Majesty! My lady! To what do I owe this honor to my house?" Jod cried.

"Your pardon, my lord Prester," Gurun said, "but we beg leave to stay with you until the conclusion of the conclave." She turned to the big man with the scalp lock and the shaven head. "This is Chief Uduqu, who guards the king, and my maid, Dakl. I have also brought my bodyguard of eighteen men." She paused, then added, "I am afraid it's necessary. We have come here because, of all the men in Obann at this time, you have the greatest reputation for honor and integrity. I could not think of anywhere else for us to go."

Jod's head spun. Nevertheless, he bowed to Gurun and the king.

"All that I have is at Your Majesties' disposal," he said. "Please sit down! We'll have something to eat, and while we eat, you can tell me all about it—whatever it is that brings you here."

CHAPTER 51

A Great and Terrible Light

The Hosa marched until they found a clearing big enough for them to stay the night. They made a proper camp, gathering brush to make a palisade around it—nothing would get through that without making a lot of noise—and posting plenty of guards.

Xhama estimated he now had some five hundred men left out of the thousand he'd led out of Silvertown. Some had been lost as stragglers, and more had been killed in the fight with the Zamzu.

They offered Ryons neither violence nor disrespect as they made him march with them. Cavall seemed to like their company; "A good sign," Ryons thought.

His own fear never came back to him. Maybe the man of God was with him, after all, and you just couldn't see him. Ryons had the feeling that if he could only turn his head suddenly and look in just the right place, he'd get a glimpse of him. But it would have been bad manners, so he didn't try. Meanwhile, Xhama spoke of his faraway homeland, of his herds of cattle and his crops of corn and melons, and his two wives.

"But then came the Thunder King's mardars," he said, "and they cast spells that made our cattle die and our corn wither. They said they would dry up our women if we did not obey them. We must either serve the Thunder King or see our whole people starve to death."

There was little enough to eat that night. The Hosa carried rations, but they had to make them last. And after their meager supper, Xhama gathered his chiefs in the middle of the camp to discuss what to do. Ryons sat on a log behind him, with Cavall at his feet, understanding nothing of what was being said in all that long debate.

"We should press on to Silvertown," said one of the chiefs, "and get out of this horrible forest! Maybe, if we give the boy to Goryk Gillow, the Thunder King will let us go in peace."

But not many of the chiefs thought that this was likely. A few laughed scornfully.

"I have been thinking about this, all the time we marched," Xhama said. "Listen to me, my children.

"We have rebelled against the Thunder King, and we are all dead men. But this boy says his God can give us life again! Our own gods could not protect us from the Thunder King. They are, instead, his prisoners. What good did they do us?

"But now there are many who have rebelled against the Thunder King, and they are still alive. They serve in this boy's army, and the God of Obann honors them. It is my thought that we should do the same! If the king will have us for his friends, I myself would serve him willingly. And we shall wash our spears in the blood of those who would enslave us."

A few of the chiefs whooped, then a few more. They sprang to their feet and briefly danced. Cavall barked, and Ryons held him tightly, lest he should attack. But Xhama turned to him with a brilliant smile upon his face.

"It's settled!" he said in Tribe-talk. "My warriors are now your warriors, and we will swear an oath to you of our own free will. No one will ever say that you compelled us."

Ryons stood up. The chiefs fell silent.

"Tell them," he said, "that I'll be true to them, and as good a lord to them as I can be. But tell them this, too: that if they wish to follow me and be my men, then they must learn to believe in the true God, and no God but Him. Tell them that God will protect them and make them strong against their enemies—just as He has protected me. And God will destroy the Thunder King."

Xhama turned back to his men and translated, making a long speech of it.

And the Hosa that night danced in Ryons' honor and swore to serve the living God.

There was rejoicing, too, at Carbonek. Late that afternoon, an Abnak scout who understood Tribe-talk emerged from the woods with the news that King Ryons' own army was on its way and would join them in another day or two.

"So we're saved!" Jack said, as the settlers bustled about, preparing a celebratory feast. "If only King Ryons and Helki were back with us, everything would be just fine."

"But what about that Heathen army that's on its way here from the East?" Ellayne said.

"Oh, I guess King Ryons' army can take care of that!"

Ellayne looked up at Martis. "What's the matter, Martis?" she said. "You should be happy, but you look worried."

"I always worry when things are going well, Ellayne. That's the best time for them to go wrong." He forced a smile to his face, but it didn't stay long.

He was thinking about what other potent objects the Thunder King might have acquired, left over from ancient times. If he could afford to give them to his agents who traveled throughout Obann, he must have found a trove of them. What powers might they have?

"We're saved for now, I suppose," he said. "I'll feel better about it when the king and Helki return. They went out with six archers to fight against an army, and no one's heard from them since."

"No one's heard anything," Jack said.

While the Hosa danced, and the settlers at Carbonek feasted, Goryk Gillow received a messenger who'd come all the way from Kara Karram.

It was a mardar named Zo, a little, bow-legged man whose people inhabited the Lake of Islands. You would not have guessed he was a mardar, to look at him; he didn't advertise it. But he spoke excellent Tribe-talk, and Goryk welcomed him into his house.

"Your pardon, comrade!" Zo said, as he reached for Goryk's ceiling and bent his body this way and that, stretching himself. "I'm full of kinks from riding horseback—I'll never get used to it. A reed boat on the water, that's the only way to travel."

"You've come a long way, Mardar," Goryk said. Zo had brought a bulky leather box with him, stitched shut with leather thongs. This box now lay on the floor. Goryk was curious about it.

"I've come because our master King Thunder understands your problems and wishes to help you," Zo said.

"I am glad he has received my messages and taken thought for me," Goryk said. "Are you the help he has sent? Or is it the contents of that box?"

"The one will do you no good without the other!"

"Let me first give you some refreshment, Mardar. I wish my chairs were more comfortable; but as you can see, they've been cobbled together by men who are something less than skilled artisans."

He gave Zo some fresh-baked bread stuffed with shredded chicken, and a cup of mead. The mardar had never tasted mead before—it is made with fermented honey—and pronounced it excellent. After they had exchanged a few more civilities, Zo got up again, drew a knife, and cut the cords that bound the box.

"You'll have to be careful with this," he said. "Also, try to keep it a secret for as long as you can."

The box was stuffed full of a kind of dried moss, which Zo pulled out by the handful and tossed aside. When it lay in heaps on the floor, he reached into the box and took out a much smaller one, which he placed gingerly on Goryk's tea table.

What was it? A dull black cube about the size of a militiaman's helmet, one face of it sported what looked like the flared mouth of a trumpet. "Examine it closely," Zo said, "but don't touch it yet."

On another face of the cube Goryk saw a tiny arm protruding from a vertical slot, and two round, white lumps nestled in black rings.

"What is it?"

"Our master has explored the mighty secrets of the ancients. This is one of them," the mardar said. "Inside this box is imprisoned a devil, in such a way that it cannot get out. This little arm and these two buttons, here, compel the devil to do your bidding, and to cease. It has great powers, but it is the slave of whoever holds this box."

Goryk had never heard of such a thing. Had he been a real prester, and studied at a seminary and read the Commentaries, he would have known something of the power of the ancients: power that led them to destruction in the Day of Fire. As it was, he didn't believe in devils. But he realized that Mardar Zo, and their lord the Thunder King, knew infinitely more than he did about such things, so he kept an open mind.

"What can it do?" he asked.

"At your command," said Zo, "the devil will wail at your enemies so loudly and so horribly that they will be afraid to advance against you. But if they do, then at your command, the devil will shoot forth a great and terrible light—a light so fierce, that it will strike blind anyone who looks at it. With this power, you, standing alone, can put a small army to flight."

"Have you seen it do these things?"

Zo nodded. "I myself have commanded the devil in this box. With it I put down a rebellion on one of the islands in the Lake of Islands. Rebels dove from their boats and drowned, rather than stand against the devil's power. Now all the islands are quiet and obedient.

"Now you may pick up the box. But be careful not to touch the arm or the buttons."

Goryk was careful indeed. To his amazement the box weighed next to nothing. Its smooth casing felt like no kind of metal he had ever touched before.

"Do not ever try to open the box!" Zo said. "No one can do it. But if you were to handle this thing carelessly or to abuse it, the result would be disastrous to you."

"I'll never do that," Goryk said.

"The little arm commands the devil to wail. If you push the arm up, you will hear a kind of click, and then the noise. The farther up you push the arm, the louder the devil will wail—loud enough to drive a strong man mad. Push it back down, until it clicks again, and he will be silent.

"If you press the top button, blinding light will instantly flash out of the horn, which you will have pointed at your enemies. Don't point it at your friends! Press the lower button, and the light will be cut off instantly."

Goryk set the box back on the table. Not for a moment did he think Zo might be lying or exaggerating.

"Use it only in great need, comrade," Zo said. "Our master says that sometimes these objects, because they are so unthinkably old, may cease to function. The power inside them finds a means to escape."

"I'll be very cautious with it; I promise you."

"Come next spring, our master will send you fresh troops from the East. He knows you need them, and they'll be yours to command. In the meantime, whatever else may happen, you will have this devil to protect you."

Awe crept into Goryk's mind. Whatever doubts he had about his wisdom in siding with the Thunder King, those fled away. But one question remained.

"Why didn't our master send some of these with the

army that besieged Obann last summer?" he asked. "A few of these would have been better than a thousand catapults."

Zo gently touched the top of the box. "There are not many of these things surviving from the ancient days," he said. "They're hard to find, and the power has already escaped from most of them that are found. And then it takes time to discover how to command the power.

"Last year, nothing like this was available. But as time goes on, there will be more—maybe even many more. So our master has assured me."

"With this power in our hands," said Goryk, "there will be no defense against us."

CHAPTER 52

A Confession to the Conclave

Jah and May and the baby had accepted Preceptor Constan's invitation to stay at his house. Early in the morning, he called for them.

"Your friend Sunfish wants to see you," he said. "We are going to the conclave today, but he wants to see you first."

"Is he well?" asked May. To her it sounded like their friend wished to speak to them before he died.

"He has remembered who he is," Constan said.

They couldn't get much more out of him as they rode to Orth's house in a coach that Prester Jod had sent for them. Jod was already there, waiting for them in the morning room with Sunfish.

Sunfish wore today the ragged homespun clothes in which he'd traveled from the hills, but his hair and beard were washed and trimmed. He was really quite a handsome man, May thought: very distinguished-looking, even in the worn-out clothes. She wondered why she'd never noticed it before.

Sunfish embraced them. Tears glinted in his eyes.

"My friends!" he said. "I can never repay you for all you've done for me. The days I lived with you were the happiest days of all my life; and because of them, I find myself at peace with God. No man can receive a greater gift than that! I wanted to be sure I told you that, in case we never meet again."

"Why should we never meet again?" Hlah said.

"There's no time to discuss it," Prester Jod said quietly. "The three of us must be off to the conclave now. My coach will take you back to Constan's house."

May wanted to protest; but Hlah sensed there was something brewing which he and May were not supposed to know about, so he quieted her with a squeeze of her elbow. They said their good-byes. May kissed Sunfish's cheek, and Sunfish kissed the baby.

"I'll never be able to think of you as Prester Orth," she said, "but always just as Sunfish. Our Sunfish."

"I hope you'll never call me by any name but that," Orth said. "You know, as Prester Orth, I thought I had all that any man could want. But I didn't have true friends. I was a much richer man as Sunfish than I ever was as Orth."

"We must be going," Jod said.

———

In Lintum Forest the sun rose to find most of the Hosa sleeping the sleep of weary men. But their sentries were awake and watchful, exhausted though they were.

Ryons slept, too, with a rolled-up sack for a pillow, but woke when Cavall barked sharply. Cavall kept on barking, waking many of the Hosa, who were not very happy about it. But Ryons noticed that he wagged his tail and grinned, so there was nothing to be afraid of. Besides, he was surrounded by brave men who'd sworn their oaths to him.

Angel called from up in a tree, then flew down to perch on his arm.

And Helki stepped out of the woods.

The sentries cocked their spears. Ryons cried, "Stop!" And Xhama, now on his feet, commanded the guards to stand at ease.

"I come in peace!" Helki called, grinning.

"That's my friend—that's Helki!" Ryons said.

"We receive you in peace, O Helki!" Xhama answered in Tribe-talk. "We who were your enemies are now your friends, and Ryons is our king."

"It's true, Helki!" Ryons added.

Past the amazed sentries strode Helki, with his rod.

"I know it's true, Your Majesty," he said. "Angel led me straight to this camp, and we got here in time to watch the celebration. But I thought I'd better wait till morning to show myself."

He walked up to Ryons, knelt, and kissed his hand. The Hosa who saw it clapped their approval. Word spread throughout the camp that their enemy had come—but as a friend.

"Well, Your Majesty!" Helki said. "It looks like I won't have to rescue you after all. Looks like you've rescued yourself! King Ozias himself couldn't have done any better."

That was saying too much, Ryons thought. "It was all with God's help," he said.

"You have given us a miserable time in this forest, Helki the Rod," Xhama said.

"I had to," Helki said. "But that's over now, and I'm here to make amends. I reckon I can best do that by finding your men some food."

"We are hungry," Xhama said, "but not yet starving."

"No one starves in the forest, if he knows its ways. My boys will bag some venison for you. Meanwhile, there's a nice stand of wild blackberries not a quarter-mile from here and bean-bushes that have just come into season. You'll be all right."

Soon there were foragers at work, and Helki sat down with Ryons and Xhama to discuss what to do next.

"There are still the Zamzu to be dealt with," Xhama said.

"We'll deal with them, all right," said Helki. "They're slow, though. You'll have time for more rest and a good feed, and then we'll catch up to them. After that, we'll all go back to Carbonek where the king's throne is."

The Hosa would do well at Carbonek, Ryons thought, being farmers as well as fighting men. They could clear more land and plant more crops.

"I don't know much about these things," Helki said, "but as I see it, Your Majesty, you really are a king—our king, of God's own choosing. You didn't stay in the thicket like I told you, but I'm proud of you."

Ryons didn't know what to say to that. It made him blush. But Xhama said, "Our king, too, Helki—and his God shall be our God."

Presters, reciters, preceptors, scribes, scholars, and servants packed the Great Hall. Many of them recognized Orth when he came in, and babbled questions and comments at each other. It broke up the debate they'd started over who should be the next First Prester.

Jod pushed his way to the dais and spoke to the conclave's president. After repeatedly pounding his gavel and calling for silence, the president finally made himself heard.

"Your attention, brethren! Prester Jod begs leave to speak to you on a matter of great importance."

Jod ascended to the podium. "I only wish to introduce a man who is already well-known to you," he said. "What he has to say to you, he speaks of his own free will—and against my own advice, I add. All I ask is that you hear him out. Prester Orth, the podium is yours."

It shocked them into silence, to see Orth up there in rags. Most of them had seen him and heard him speak many times before, and he'd never appeared in any but the costliest and most fashionable attire. They knew him as a great man, the likely successor to Lord Reesh—as a man whose favor some of them had worked hard to cultivate. What was he doing, dressed as a beggar?

"My lords and brethren," he said, "I come before you only to make my confession. After you've heard it, do what seems best to you.

"My lords, I am a traitor—to you, to my country, to our Temple, and to God. I have sinned a great sin, and God punished me for it by taking away my senses for a year. Now He has restored them, so that you can punish me."

Jod stole a glance at Constan. The preceptor's face was serene, revealing nothing of his thoughts. Jod admired him for that.

"Because I desired to succeed Lord Reesh as First Prester," Orth said, "I created counterfeit Scripture and arranged for it to be 'discovered' by an unsuspecting scholar. I saw to it that my own false verses were authenticated. It was Lord Reesh's intent that those spurious verses of Batha the Seer were to counteract the dire warnings of various prophets in Obann.

"Working with Lord Reesh, I betrayed our city to the Heathen. We let their warriors into the Temple through a secret passage, while we escaped via the same. We made a covenant with the Thunder King, your enemy. In return for the destruction of Obann, the Temple was to survive, with Lord Reesh continuing as First Prester and myself as his successor. That our plan failed was due to divine intervention, God Himself having chosen to show mercy to this city, and no thanks to us."

Except for the sound of Orth's voice, stark silence reigned in the Great Hall. It was the silence of incredulity, Jod thought. The delegates didn't want to accept what Orth was telling them. They were waiting for it to turn out to be something quite different from what it seemed.

"Deluded by our vanity and sinful pride," Orth said, "we convinced ourselves that we were the Temple of the Lord and the future of Obann. Let the city and the Temple fall. The Thunder King promised to give us a New Temple. We would rule it: Lord Reesh first, then I.

"Such was my orgulity! My folly! As if I were anything without the Temple! As if the Temple were anything without God! But in my delusion, the Temple was God—and I was the Temple. So the sinful man makes himself God in his own mind."

Jod studied the faces in the crowd. They hated Orth's words; they hated him; and yet he held them spellbound.

But what will happen, Jod asked himself, when this pent-up hate breaks forth in all its fury?

At Prester Jod's townhouse, he'd left his servants under orders to obey Gurun in all things, and to be ready to transport her and the king and their people out of the city the moment she requested it—"or even before she asks," he said, "if you see any sign of a disturbance breaking out in the city." The king and queen were to be carried all the way to Jod's estate at Durmurot, and there protected against all who might harm them.

Shingis came into the morning room to report that his Blays were all on guard around the house, but that so far all seemed peaceful.

"What do you think, my lady, is going to happen?" he said. Unable to manage Tribe-talk except in a kind of pidgin, he spoke in his own language. God had given Gurun the gift of understanding foreign languages, and being understood.

"I think we are going to leave this city very soon—maybe even today," she said. "Prester Jod fears there will be trouble. But he is a great man, and we should be safe under his protection."

Shingis bowed his head. "Wherever you go, we'll go with you," he said. The Blays were so far from their homeland, they'd given up all hope of ever seeing it again. Gurun thanked him, and he left the room.

General Hennen was the only one in the palace who'd been told the king and queen had gone to Jod's house. Gurun hadn't been able to contact Gallgoid, but she knew he would find out all about it sooner or later—if he hadn't already. Meanwhile, she'd advised Hennen to pull his own troops out of the city and try to rejoin the rest of King Ryons' army as soon as he could.

"We must be guided by the prophecy, General," she

said. "The throne of King Ozias is to be established not in this city, but in Lintum Forest. The Lord has spoken it."

"Then that's where I'll go," Hennen said, "and five hundred good spearmen with me."

For the time being, there was nothing to do but wait in Prester Jod's drawing room. Fnaa found it irksome.

"If we're going to go, I wish we could go now!" he said. "As long as I'm not going to be king anymore and live in the palace, we might as well be going."

Uduqu laughed. "You liked being king, did you?" he said.

"Well, it was better than being a slave in Vallach Vair's house. Gurun, why can't we go now? That prester said we could, if we wanted to."

"You may get your wish sooner than you think," Gurun said. In truth, she had a longing to go to Durmurot. It was the city in Obann that was closest to the sea, and over the sea lay Fogo Island, her home.

"I think the boy's right," Uduqu said. "There's nothing left for us to do in this city. Why don't we make tracks for Durmurot? If need be, we can always come back."

Maybe it was wiser, Gurun thought, to start such a journey before there was trouble in the city, and not after it began. Maybe it wouldn't be so easy to get out during a disturbance.

She rang for Jod's butler.

"Make ready the carriage," she told him, "and tell the prester when he comes—and no one else!—that we've gone to Durmurot." She smiled at Uduqu. "As you say," she added, "we can always come back."

Around noon that day a party of Abnak pathfinders, with the fifty Ghols on horseback following, and Obst mounted on a donkey in their midst, arrived at Carbonek. At the sight of their old friend, Jack and Ellayne ran to greet him. Martis followed slowly.

"Obst, Obst—you're back in the forest, where you belong!" Jack cried.

"I belong wherever God puts me," Obst said, as he hugged the children. Wytt chattered at him and ran up onto his shoulder. Behind him, Ghols dismounted. "But where are Helki and the king?"

"No one knows," Martis said. Briefly, he explained the circumstances.

"If only we'd come sooner!" Chagadai said. "Well, we must ride out and look for him."

"You ought to rest first," Martis said, "and wait for the rest of the army to get here. King Ryons is with Helki—which means he's as safe as he can ever be, all things considered."

Grumbling, the Ghols began to hobble their horses. Settlers thronged around to greet Obst, whom they knew. It wasn't until much later that Martis and the children were able to speak to him alone.

"We're back to stay. At least I think we are," Obst said. "Jandra has prophesied: it's God's will for the throne to be set in Lintum Forest, not Obann City. When Ryons returns, he'll have to have a proper anointing, as described in Scripture. And a coronation!"

"But there will have to be some wise plans made, too," Martis said. "Come—I want to show you something."

Inside the ruins of the castle, in the shadows, Martis

showed Obst the ancient object that the children stole from Noma. Obst trembled as Martis demonstrated its uses, and let out a relieved sigh when Martis returned it to his saddlebag.

"Except for its power to terrorize the ignorant, the thing is harmless, as far as I can tell," Martis said. "But I fear the Thunder King has obtained a great number of such things. He's sure to use them against us. And some of them, I think, will not be harmless."

Obst nodded. "Yes, we'll have to plan for that," he said, with a sigh. "No end to it!" he thought. He looked at Jack and Ellayne. "And we'll have to do something about getting you two back home to your family."

"Not yet!" Ellayne said. "Yes, all right, it's time we went home. But we want to see King Ryons first."

"We've gone to an awful lot of trouble for him," Jack said.

"You can stay until God brings him back to us," said Obst.

"And then it's back to Ninneburky!" Martis said. "And if your father the baron locks your bedrooms from the outside from now on, I, for one, won't blame him."

CHAPTER 53

How Orth Was Judged and Punished

Orth had always been well-known for giving long and eloquent speeches. Today he outdid himself, carrying his confession into the early afternoon.

He told the conclave everything, all the details of the treason he'd enacted with Lord Reesh. "But my guilt," he said, "is my own. All that I did, I did willingly. Lord Reesh tempted me, but I yielded eagerly to that temptation. He never forced me or deceived me. My sin is all my own."

He revealed how they'd carried out their treason: their negotations with the mardar, their eagerness to take up residence in the Thunder King's New Temple, and their journey east, in which Orth lost his nerve and later his reason and deserted.

"For many months I lived with simple people in the hills, teaching them the Scriptures. They named me Sunfish, because I could not remember my own name, nor my former station. That was a happy time.

"But when I slept, horror crept into my soul. I could not understand it, or remember anything of what I dreamed, when I awoke. Friends brought me here to Obann, and yesterday morning I awoke in my own bed, in my own room, in my own house. And I remembered everything."

The delegates sat still and silent, held captive by his words, made speechless by the revelation of so much wickedness. They might tear Orth to pieces on the spot before this day was over, Jod thought. There had always been rumors in the city that certain persons had let in the Heathen, but these had by now nearly died for lack of nourishment. Now Jod wondered what would happen when Orth's confession got out of the Great Hall and into the streets and taverns of Obann. Was there anything that he, Jod, could say or do to forestall a disaster?

"I have come to the end of my confession," Orth said. "I have sinned. I have been guilty of great folly. But even as all things end, other things begin.

"I have been told that certain Scriptures have been found in Old Obann, written in Ozias' own hand, and that in our seminary a great work has been undertaken to render the Old Books into modern language and make God's word known to all the people."

An inspiration burst into Jod's mind. Whether it would be for good or evil, he had no time to consider. Quietly he rose from his seat and made his way to the podium—where he had not long to wait.

"I am glad that I have lived to see this day," Orth said. "In this new work, God has found the means to undo the evil that I've done and to make good come of it."

At that moment he noticed Jod standing there, and Jod caught his eye.

"Prester Jod? Yes?"

"Your indulgence, Prester!" Jod joined him on the

speakers' platform. The delegates stared at them, too surprised to make an outcry yet.

"Brethren," Jod said, "we have heard things today that we never thought to hear, and learned things that we never thought to learn. In all this, God has shown us the way we ought to go.

"When the bell on Bell Mountain rang, many of us believed it was to ring in the destruction of the world. When God stayed His hand, and the world continued, we dismissed the bell from our minds. War came upon us—such war as no man living ever saw. Had the Lord not performed a miracle of deliverance, this whole city would have been destroyed, and we would not be assembled here today.

"We need a new Temple and a new First Prester. The Thunder King has built a Temple, but how can we be enticed to go there? His Temple was to be the reward of treason. It is a snare to us.

"Our own Temple lies in ruins. Where shall we find the money to rebuild it? But I say, let God's word itself be our Temple! Let Heaven itself be the roof of our new Temple, and the four corners of the world its walls."

He spoke the words as fast as they came into his mind, not stopping to analyze them. They came, and he spoke them.

"As for a new First Prester," he said, "I know that many of you would choose me. In this you honor me. But I realize now that there is a man more fit, more deserving, than I—a new man, shaped by suffering, broken down and then remolded by God's hands."

He laid a hand on Orth's shoulder.

"Brethren, I give you the only man I can think of as

First Prester. Approve him now, this very moment, by your acclamation.

"I give you First Prester Orth!"

The hall erupted in applause. Later, Jod could only ascribe it to the spirit of God moving among the delegates, in which Preceptor Constan concurred. As one mighty voice they roared their acclamation. "Orth, Orth, Orth!" they cried. They rose from their seats and waved their arms. They stomped their feet until the building shook. Jod let it go on and on, not wanting it to end. But eventually it did come to an end, and the president gaveled the conclave into silence. Willingly the delegates gave him their peace. They wanted to hear Orth again.

"My lords!" he sputtered. "How can I accept this honor? I am a sinner, a traitor, and a fool. I came here to be punished, not exalted!"

"But this is your punishment, First Prester," said Jod. "Your punishment, and our reward."

That evening Constan came home and gave the news to Hlah and May.

"Sunfish is First Prester?" May cried. "Our Sunfish?"

Hlah shook his head. "How could it be?" he marveled.

"And him dressed in all those dirty old clothes!" May added.

Constan indulged in one of his rare smiles.

"I'll try to explain it to you over supper," he said. He sighed. "God shakes the world, so that the things that cannot be shaken will endure. He is not done shaking yet! Where we shall all be a year from now is in His hands. I am content."

Follow the Entire Adventure with the First Four Books in this Exciting Series!

You won't want to miss a single moment of this thrilling adventure, so be sure to get *Bell Mountain*, *The Cellar Beneath the Cellar*, and *The Thunder King* to complete your collection. These engaging stories are a great way to discover powerful insights about the Kingdom of God through page-turning fantasy fiction.

Ordering is Easy!
Just visit
www.ChalcedonStore.com

CPSIA information can be obtained
at www.ICGtesting.com
Printed in the USA
FSOW01n0456010715
8397FS